CITY OF SORCERY

BOOK FIVE OF THE HUNDRED HALLS

A HUNDRED HALLS NOVEL

THOMAS K. CARPENTER

City of Sorcery

Book Five of The Hundred Halls
A Hundred Halls Novel

Hardcover Version

by Thomas K. Carpenter

Published by Black Moon Books

Cover design by Ravven
www.ravven.com

Discover other titles by this author on:
www.thomaskcarpenter.com

ISBN-13: 978-1-958498-04-0

The Hundred Halls Universe

SEASON ONE

THE HUNDRED HALLS
Trials of Magic
Web of Lies
Alchemy of Souls
Gathering of Shadows
City of Sorcery

THE RELUCTANT ASSASSIN
The Reluctant Assassin
The Sorcerous Spy
The Veiled Diplomat
Agent Unraveled
The Webs That Bind

GAMEMAKERS ONLINE
The Warped Forest
Gladiators of Warsong
Citadel of Broken Dreams
Enter the Daemonpits
Plane of Twilight

ANIMALIANS HALL
Wild Magic
Bane of the Hunter
Mark of the Phoenix
Arcane Mutations
Untamed Destiny

STONE SINGERS HALL
Song of Siren and Blood
House of Snake and Tome
Storm of Dragon and Stone
Sonata of Shadow and Thorn
Well of Demon and Bone

THE ORDER OF MERLIN
The Order of Merlin
Infernal Alliances
Tower of Horn and Blood

CITY OF SORCERY

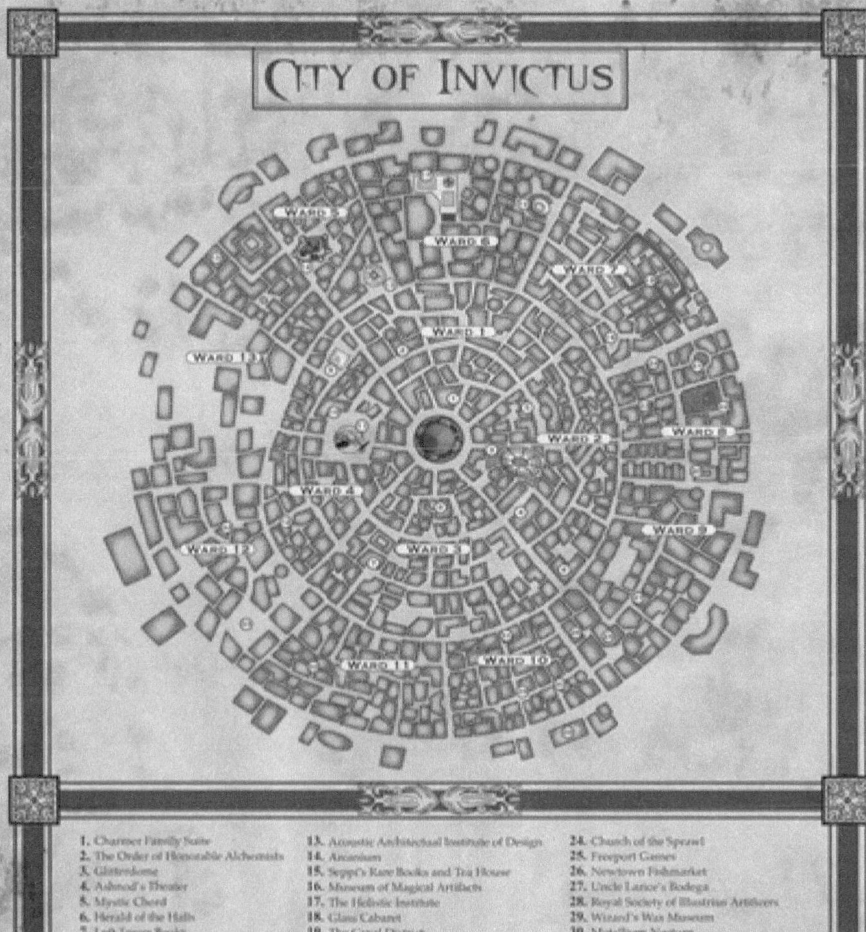
City of Invictus
Ward 1
Ward 2
Ward 3
Ward 4
Ward 5
Ward 6
Ward 7
Ward 8
Ward 9
Ward 10
Ward 11
Ward 12
Ward 13
1. Charmer Family Suite
2. The Order of Honorable Alchemists
3. Glitterdome
4. Ashmod's Theater
5. Mystic Chord
6. Herald of the Halls
7. Left Tower Books
8. Protectors
9. Coterie of Mages
10. City Library
11. Statue of Invictus
12. Amber & Smoke
13. Acoustic Architectural Institute of Design
14. Arcanium
15. Seppi's Rare Books and Tea House
16. Museum of Magical Artifacts
18. Glass Cabaret
19. The Canal District
22. Invictus Menagerie and Cryptozoo
23. Goblin's Romp
24. Church of the Sprawl
25. Freeport Games
26. Newtown Fishmarket
28. Royal Society of Illustrious Artificers
29. Wizard's Wax Museum
31. Howling Madwoman's Fortunes and Spells
32. Enochian District
33. Oba's Autumnal Garden
34. Gamemakers Hall

ONE

The choking jungle air stunk of rotting vegetation and fresh blood. Panting and out of breath, Mags desperately wanted to take a break after escaping the two-headed constrictor, but there was no time for fear if she wanted her choice of Halls. It was a top score or nothing for Mags.

Thankfully, the claustrophobic jungle was behind her, and she hadn't yet used any of the items they'd given her for the first phase of the Proving Grounds. Mags pulled her rune-covered arm across her forehead, wiping away the sweat and grime from tumbling down the hill.

After a short jog across a spongy peat bog, she reached a doorway that led to a square room covered in silvery tiles with a single rune on each. Reflexively, she rubbed the rune-tattoos on her arm as she studied the challenge. Certainly, she had to get past the area and reach the doorway on other side, but what was the puzzle?

There were thirty-eight different common runic languages that were suggested studying material for passing the Trials, but at a glance, Mags saw examples of the more obscure pictographs, which indicated there was more to the puzzle than memorization.

Mags checked her palm for the time. She'd put a modified rainbow-skin spell on her hand, which would slowly transform the color of her pale skin over the course of an hour. The center of her palm, up to the calluses, was purple and blue, which meant she'd been in the Proving Grounds for twenty minutes. The top time so far was twenty-three minutes. Dealing with the snake had cost her time, but if she could avoid using her items, she'd get bonuses, which would put her in the lead going into day two. Assuming, of course, she could finish the trial within the next ten minutes.

"Come on, Mags. What's the solution?"

The room was forty feet long and twenty feet wide, with each tile at a square foot. Examples of at least ten of the common runic languages were displayed on the tiles. The tiles were a metallic silver, which put a stone in Mags' gut, for reasons she couldn't quite qualify.

She checked her palm again, annoyed by the way the blue was turning green at the base of her fingers.

"Why these languages and not the others?" she asked as she scanned the board for clues. "There's the first five symbols for the Astral runes, there's the Sumerian ones...wait, they're in order."

Mags tried to find a series that led across the room, but it was hard to see the runes further out due to the angle. She really needed to step onto the board to see, but if she took the wrong path, would she be punished for a misstep?

In the end, Mags picked the Mongolian rune set because it reached the farthest across. As she stepped onto the first rune, Horse-Man, she nearly fell due to the mud caked onto the soles of her sneakers. Mags ripped them off, then her socks, and wiped her feet on her thighs, using the yoga tree pose. Once they were clean, she hopped over three tiles to land on Moon-Harvest, but skidded forward until her toes crossed the threshold onto an Astral rune: Doorway.

A painful shock slammed into her toes, cramping her foot, making her stumble towards the rune behind her. She barely managed to keep her balance.

After teetering for a bit, she spotted the third rune and made the short jump, landing cleanly in the center. She paused, remembering the jar of ointment that they'd given her in the beginning. It had the property of turning into a hard shell when spread on a surface. Her journey across the room would be much easier if she used it, but that felt like a trap to her. The Proving Grounds were meant to reward creativity and knowledge, not blindly accepting what was already there, so she decided not to use the ointment.

Mags was readying to move to the fourth tile when the room started to tilt. She made the jump, but landing was already becoming difficult. With her arms wheeling for balance, she found the fifth, Arrow-Arrow, and made the jump successfully, trying to spot the sixth as she flew through the air. Landing, her feet lost traction for a moment, but she gripped with her toes and managed to hold on.

The next jump wasn't as clear cut, as she spotted two runes that looked similar to the seventh, Spirit-Breath. With no time to waste, she made the leap, realizing she'd chosen the wrong rune as she flew through the air.

The shocking impact knocked her off her feet, and as she slid down the slope towards a chute at the end, she was shocked again and again, until she felt like popcorn on a hot plate. Mags barely registered the slide through the metal chute, but eventually she was deposited on a little island surrounded by a massive chasm.

Every muscle ached. It felt like she'd been hit by a wrench about two dozen times across her body. Some of the shocks had hit hard enough to scorch her arms, creating a lingering burnt-hair smell.

Lying on her side, Mags punched the hard stone. "Fuck!"

At twenty-five minutes, she had no chance to get a top score, and now she risked going into day two with a dangerously low score, and possibly not even finishing the course, which would knock her out of the Trials.

As she checked her surroundings, she realized it was even worse than she thought. The chute had left her near the beginning of the jungle. It was a decent jump across a gap to reach the edge, but doable with the rubber ball, which would give her extra spring if she swallowed it.

Mags doubly cursed herself for not taking extra time at the puzzle. If she'd only found a way to scout the whole floor, she could have made her way across in rapid time, avoiding the extreme floor tilt. Her impatience had cost her.

And now she had to go through the jungle again, a prospect that was less than inviting. She knew there were at least three other two-headed snakes in trees. She'd been lucky that she'd only had to battle one. She wouldn't be lucky a second time.

The chasm behind her was at least one hundred feet across, but it looked like it reached the area near the end of the Proving Grounds. The whole setup was U-shaped. It was possible to get caught back up, if she could make the jump.

Suddenly, the idea of finishing at the top was back on her mind.

"If I can get across, I won't be last."

But when she looked over the edge, the vast emptiness was imposing. She couldn't see a bottom and didn't want to waste time dropping something. The island was only ten feet across, not enough for much of a running start.

Mags eyed the runes on her arms. She knew a way to suppress them, but it would be dangerous, and she didn't know if it would be enough to get her across.

"I've got to finish at the top." She stared at the tantalizing cliff edge across the gap. "Fuck. Why am I even thinking about this?"

The blue-green on her palm was turning yellow. Time was running out.

Mags moved towards the jungle on her little island, backing up until her heels hung over the edge. The spell to suppress the runes wouldn't last long. She wasn't even supposed to know about it, but it was hard for the doctors to hide it from her when she had to go back to the hospital for semiannual checkups.

For a moment, she considered not using the rubber ball, but decided her impatience had cost her at the last obstacle. Better to make sure she crossed the gap than be filled with fatal regrets.

The rubber ball tasted a little like vomit, which made swallowing it difficult, but once it was past her esophagus, it dissolved and she could breathe again.

Mags gave the jungle one last longing look before suppressing her protective runes with a simple spell that was only three words and two gestures. Her body tingled with faez, indicating it'd taken effect, and she felt buoyant, but vulnerable.

"I hate snakes, anyway," she said, before sprinting towards the far cliff, slamming her foot down to leap across at the last moment.

She flew through the air, and realized that she might not make it across. Mags cast the suppression spell a second time, which seemed to lift her higher in the air. She floated like a feather on a breeze. She hit the rocky soil on the other side, tumbling into a messy roll that left her dizzy when she came to a stop. It took a few moments to notice that she'd broken her left arm, a couple of fingers, and at least three ribs. The protective runes had snapped back into place around the time she'd hit, but not fast enough to keep her from injury.

"At least it wasn't my legs," she muttered as she climbed to her feet, grimacing as the broken ribs put a spear into her side.

Mags found a path and followed it down a slope to a darkened archway. Getting past the final challenge was going to be extremely difficult with broken bones, and she didn't know any healing spells. She stepped through the threshold to be startled by a triumphant gong.

She was back in the entry room. Exhausted and injured, but elated, Mags limped into the main area, and as she did, her name went up near the top of the list at #8. Margaret Dubois.

There was brief scattered applause, but it died quickly. Mostly she received glares from those lowest on the board who were further at risk of not making it past the trials due to her score. Mags was going to find a healer when she noticed one of the fifth years working the far side of the room, handing out toiletry packets for the night in the dormitory.

With her broken arm held against her side, Mags made her way over, blurting out as soon as she reached her, "Awesome Aurie!"

Aurelia Silverthorne was standing behind a table in her formal dark robes. Her shoulder-length black hair had been straightened, the bangs cut across the front. She looked different to Mags than she remembered, harder, wiser, as if Aurie had been tempered in hot flame. There was something that suggested danger, the same feeling Mags got when she saw a patron up close, but there was also kindness and warmth in her gaze.

Aurie's mouth worked the air, but no sound came out. She glanced at the board, then back to Mags. "Elegant Emily?"

Mags limped away from the table, feeling something akin to a sunbeam trying to burst out of her chest. Aurie joined her. "I'm not supposed to go by that anymore. Margaret's my middle name, and Dubois is my mother's maiden name, but you can call me Mags."

Being near Aurie was making Mags' face tingle. Her feet felt like she was floating inches off the floor, so she checked to make sure her runes were still intact.

"Wow, you're so tall now, but I guess that happens," said Aurie, laughing. She checked behind her to make sure no one was listening. "So I guess they're being cautious about the name—hey! Congrats. That's a great score!" She gave Mags a hug until she yelped. "Are you okay?"

"Nothing the healers can't fix." Aurie's face wrinkled with confusion, so Mags added, "The item, it fixed the curse, but my bones were too brittle and light by that time. They're like a hummingbird's bones. So I have these runes to keep me safe from injury."

Aurie rummaged through her robes and handed Mags a vial of golden liquid. "Here, they give us these in case the healers are too busy. It'll help you for now, but you'll still need to catch up with them."

The golden liquid tasted like watery honey going down, and a warm glow followed as her bones knitted together. There was an awkward silence, and despite having dreamed about this day for years, Mags didn't know what to say.

"Thank you for saving me," Mags blurted out. *I've been dreaming of this day for four years.*

"I didn't do anything," said Aurie, cheeks flushing. "The lichwood tea was only delaying the inevitable."

Mags leaned close and whispered, "I know it was you. About the item, the *artifact.* It had to be. I know all about your parents. You finished their work. I wasn't supposed to know what it was, but I figured it out later."

"Don't tell anyone," said Aurie quietly.

"I wouldn't dare. You gave me back my life. I owe you everything."

Aurie frowned. "You owe me nothing."

"But I do. That's why I have to get into Arcanium. I want to make you proud, be the Wind Dancer you said that I'd be. It's all I've ever wanted," said Mags, not knowing what to do with her hands. Her broken fingers still ached from the healing potion, so she picked at the hem of her shirt.

"Magic. The Halls. It's all very dangerous," said Aurie with the look of a worried mother. "As they say, there are no B-students in the Halls, only dead ones."

The disapproval wounded Mags. "I know," she said, a little too forcefully, then pulled back. "I've been working hard. I don't do anything but study."

"It's more than studying." Aurie shook her head. "I'm sorry. When I was your age, I wanted nothing more than to be in the Halls. I shouldn't judge you. I guess I get protective of people I care about."

It was Mags' turn to get red-faced. When she'd been stuck in the Children's wing at Golden Willow, Aurie had been the only thing that had given her hope. She wanted to tell Aurie about the dozens of pictures that she'd colored of her, still had pinned to her wall, along with the newspaper articles from when the HARPERS won the second-year contest, the trial of magic, the accident at the Dragon Well, and any other time that she had appeared in the *Herald of the Halls*. But she knew that Aurie didn't have time for a fawning, aspiring first year, what with all the important things she had to do. Aurie hadn't even graduated and she was more famous than alumni that had been out for a decade, or at least she was more famous to Mags.

"What are you going to study for your fifth-year project?" asked Mags.

Aurie took a deep breath and kneaded her hands together. There was a weight on her shoulders, an unresolved tension that was keeping her wound up like a spring. "I haven't totally decided yet. For a while I thought about following in my father's footsteps, you know, Arcanium-style, but I can't help thinking about other *items* out there, things that can help people, like you."

"You could be a great discoverer, like that one guy who had a TV show," said Mags breathlessly.

"I'm not interested in fame. I've had enough of that," said Aurie.

Mags almost blurted out that she'd been following Aurie and her sister's exploits in the *Herald of the Halls* for years, and that she was an inspiration, but the look on her face convinced Mags to change her argument.

"I know you don't want to believe it," said Mags, "but you saved me, and so many other people too. I bet there are things out there more awesome than the Rod—" Mags threw her hand over her mouth. "Oops, than the item."

"And more dangerous," said Aurie.

"Then don't get those."

Aurie gave her the squint-eye, then followed it with a grin. "You sure have appeared at an opportune time, but I don't know. Sometimes having too many options is worse than none at all."

"But you're so much like your mother, the way you rush into danger, fearlessly battling demons, or saving people that no one cares about. It's like when she killed that escaped Red-Eyed Horror with only her scarf and a piece of string and only in her second year! I figured it was a no-brainer that you'd follow in her footsteps."

Aurie looked taken aback. "I didn't even know that about my mom. How did you learn that?"

"I, uhm, I'm sorry. I guess I got a little too...I'm really sorry," said Mags, wanting to crawl under a rock.

Aurie put her hand on her shoulder, chuckling. "It's okay. I'm really glad you told me about that. It might just be that you've tipped the scales with your enthusiasm."

"Really?"

Aurie smiled, nodding.

"Oh my word. That's the best thing ever!" Mags clapped her hands and threw her arms around Aurie. This time, she hugged her back, squeezing.

When they pulled away, Aurie said, "I should get back to work, and you need to get some rest. It only gets harder."

"I'm not worried," said Mags, even though she was. "You'll see, I'll get into Arcanium. I'll make you proud."

Aurie put her hand on Mags' shoulder. "I'm already proud."

She patted it, before gently pushing her towards the healer tent on the other side of the auditorium. "Go get healed. Get some rest. I'll see you when you're finished."

"Thank you again, for everything."

Aurie smiled and waved. When Mags spun around, she almost fell over her bare feet, and a giggle escaped from her lips. She felt like her runes weren't working and she might float away, a soap bubble drifting into the warm heavens. Mags threw her arms around her midsection, giving herself a squeeze.

"There's no way they're going to keep me out of Arcanium now!" she yelled as she neared the healer tent, eliciting stares from the mages and her fellow students, but she didn't care. Even if it were only a little thing, she'd given something back to Aurelia Silverthorne, and that was before she'd gotten into the Halls. Mags couldn't wait until she was a member of Arcanium.

TWO

The salty sea air burned in Pi's nose as seagulls cried overhead. The ocean was choppy with sharp white tips on the waves. She blocked the sun with her forearm as she gazed upon her destination: a haze upon the horizon, a little island beyond the outer banks.

She'd eaten a bowl of clam chowder in Ashbury Park which sat in her stomach like a ball of lead and she was sleepy from the long drive up the coast road. No one answered when she knocked on the yellow door, so she walked down to the beach.

A man was throwing a ball for a brown long-haired dog. When her shoes hit the sand, the dog veered towards her in a loping happy stride. The mutt dropped the ball in the sand and shoved its head into her thigh.

Pi crouched down and dug her fingers into the dog's wet fur, scratching as it panted.

The owner came running up. He had gray hair, a salt-and-pepper beard, and leathery tan skin that suggested a long life outdoors.

"Tasker, really, you can't just expect everyone to pet you," he said upon approach.

With a grin splitting her face, Pi said, "It's okay. He's a sweetie. Are you Malcolm?"

He nodded, and spoke in a New Jersey accent. "You must be Pythia, then."

She reached out and shook his outstretched hand. "Pi is good."

Malcolm snatched up the ball and launched it in a high arc. It splashed into the leading edge of the waves, and Tasker went bounding after it.

Malcolm wrinkled his face. "You sure you want to do this? The people I normally take on are typically more desperate. You look like the opposite of desperate."

A seagull went soaring overhead.

"I need answers," she said, handing over the paperwork that she'd been required to bring.

After reading the papers, he gave a little sigh, as if he'd given this speech a thousand times before, only to see it ignored. "You know, even if you get your answer, you'll never be allowed to leave. You won't want to leave. That's how this works."

"I am aware," said Pi.

"Then I have to give you this disclaimer before I take you to her. At the end, I'll need your arcane mark so everyone knows you asked for this." He took a little in-breath, drew a symbol in his palm, and exhaled over it. "I, Malcolm Rollins, of the Federal Bureau of Supernatural Creatures, will take Pythia Silverthorne to Euphony Island to visit the supernatural creature known as Alcyone. Alcyone is a Class Five SN, which means no rescue attempts will be allowed. If you can't leave of your own volition, you aren't leaving. Do you understand and accept these dangers?"

After a series of hand gestures from Malcolm, a glowing box appeared in the air between them. Pi added her arcane mark, and the glyph disappeared with an audible pop.

When the dog returned, Malcolm threw the ball for him, but it didn't seem like his heart was in it.

"So what now? Where's your boat?" asked Pi.

Malcolm pulled a cell phone from his pocket and tapped on it, before shoving it back in.

"The boat will be here in a few minutes. While we wait, I need to remind you that you cannot have any magical trinkets, enchantments, or technology on you. Alcyone will not see you if she can smell even a whiff of magic or electronics."

Pi nodded. "I left them in my rental."

She hated not having her leather jacket or her cell phone, but if she wanted answers she needed to follow the rules.

"You really have to do this? You seem like a nice young lady with her whole life ahead of her. No one leaves her island, and I mean *no one.* The people I normally take are dying and want to know the answers to something important to them before the end. Is there something wrong with you that I can't see? I'm sorry to pry, but it bothers me to take such a healthy looking person to the island."

"I'm perfectly healthy, and I know what I'm doing," she said.

"And you know what Alcyone is? What she does?"

"If you hear her voice, you'll never want to do anything else. Eat, drink, or leave. Those that hear her eventually die."

The sadness in his eyes warmed her heart, but didn't do anything to diminish the knots in her stomach.

"Your funeral."

While they waited, Malcolm let her throw the ball for Tasker. He kept glancing at her and shaking his head. Eventually, an unmanned boat beached itself below them.

"There's your ride," he said. "Climb in and it'll take you to the island."

"You're coming with me?"

"Oh, hell no. Thank god for technology. I have an app that controls the boat. If by some miracle you survive, stand on the beach and wave, and I'll come get you. I'll keep watch until evening—if you're not free by then, you ain't never leaving, and I'll notify your next of kin."

Pi ran back up the little rise and grabbed the backpack she'd left in the weeds.

"What's in the bag?" he asked.

"Nothing magical. Don't worry," she said, but she was worried.

After giving Tasker a good ear rub, Pi leapt into the small boat. The little motor revved into life, dragging the craft back into the waves, before turning and heading towards Euphony Island.

As the boat hopped through the choppy waves, Pi unzippered her backpack. "Might as well get this over with."

She pulled out a pistol attached to a cup. The gun was a theater prop filled with blanks. Before placing it to her ear, she considered applying a pain blocking spell, but decided against it, in case the creature could detect it.

With her finger resting on the trigger, and the cup attached to the gun against her ear, Pi took a deep breath and squeezed.

The explosion knocked her into the gunwale. It felt like the right side of her head had been hit with a bat. She checked around to make sure she hadn't dropped the pistol into the water. Without the pistol, she'd be a goner. She had a moment of panic, but calmed down when she found the pistol under the seat.

Blood ran from her ear, and she heard nothing but a steady buzzing. It felt like someone was digging a screwdriver into her head. The discharge from the blank had flash burned the side of her cheek.

Before she could lose her nerve, Pi placed the cup on her left ear and pulled the trigger. The pain was worse the second time. When she was finished, she snapped her fingers and yelled to make sure her eardrums were completely ruptured. She didn't hear anything but buzzing.

Pi tossed the gun over the side so Alcyone didn't get the wrong idea. It disappeared into the waves. Then she cleaned the blood from the sides of her head. There was nothing she could do about the migraine pounding the backs of her eyes. She wished she'd brought a pair of sunglasses. The sun hadn't bothered her before, but now that her head was throbbing, each glint of light on the waves was a dagger to her brain.

When the boat hit the rocky beach, Pi threw the backpack over her shoulder and leapt out, soaking her sneakers in the foamy wash. She paused as she made sure she still couldn't hear, and in that moment of reflection, she realized the beach wasn't as rocky as she first thought. Scattered bones covered the gray-black sand.

A few feet away, a silvery-blue fish was trying to wriggle its way up the beach, side heaving as it slowly died. From her vantage, Pi saw other fish, turtles, and sea creatures making their way towards the center of the island. She worried that bursting her eardrums might not be enough to protect against Alcyone's voice.

Pi made her way towards the center, stepping over the many bones. The further she went inland, the harder it was to avoid crunching the sun-bleached carcasses.

"They're just sticks," she mumbled to herself as she wobbled up the slope.

Pi was woozy and sick. The explosions had damaged more than her eardrums.

A copse of beech trees formed a ring at the center of the island. Pi was surprised that the beech trees could survive in sandy soil until she remembered the dead animals providing nutrients.

Further in, a general rotting smell assaulted her nose. She wished it'd been her olfactory senses blown out rather than her hearing. Combined with the motion sickness from damaging her eardrums, Pi felt ill and had to keep swallowing back bile.

An upthrust of rock lay at the center of the beech trees, which contained many dead seagulls in their boughs. Near where she stopped, a half-rotting sea turtle with one flipper chewed off remained. Other bones and carcasses in various states of decay were littered around the area, but none were in the water, which was curious. At least three sets of bones were human shaped. One had a head of hair on the skull.

A darkened cave peered from the stone, and as soon as she saw it, a chill went down her spine. She knew she was being watched.

"Alcyone," shouted Pi, "I bring a gift in trade for your wisdom."

It was strange to speak and not hear oneself. There was a vibration in her head that let her know she was talking out loud, but she had no idea if she was shouting or whispering.

A shape moved from the darkness of the cave. When Pi saw her, she steeled herself from recoiling, lest she offend. Alcyone had long stringy hair that clung to her naked emaciated body. Her breasts were nothing more than bumps on her chest, and her ribs and shoulder blades protruded from her skin. Nails longer than her fingers, caked with dried blood, hung at her side.

Alcyone approached within twenty feet, looking warily at Pi. When the creature spoke, Pi heard nothing, but her eyes followed Alcyone's lips, revealing her words. Weeks ago, Pi had ingested three books about lip-reading.

"You're different than the rest," said Alcyone, leaning on one leg.

"I need an answer," said Pi, shifting the backpack to the front.

Alcyone surged forward, pointed her claws at Pi, and said, "Stop or I'll cut your throat!"

Pi froze. "I brought a gift."

"Your life is my gift," said Alcyone.

"Not today."

Alcyone sniffed, then her face screwed up in anger. "Where is the enchantment that hides your hearing? How are you deceiving me?"

"That doesn't matter," said Pi. "What matters is that I've come to your island without magic or technology, and brought you a gift in exchange for your wisdom."

Alcyone spat on the rocks. "Fuck your gift. Fuck your wisdom. I want your blood. I want your flesh."

Every ounce of Pi wanted to call up faez and do battle with Alcyone, but she knew that's what the creature wanted, for Pi to break the agreement. If she let even a thimbleful of faez into her mind, Alcyone would attack, and Pi wasn't sure about her chances of surviving. A Class Five SN on its turf was about as dangerous as it got. The sphinx she'd tangled with a few years ago was only a Class Three, and she'd had Ashley with her to escape it.

Before the creature could take another step closer, Pi pulled the gift from her backpack and threw it across the distance to land at Alcyone's feet.

Alcyone crouched down and scooped up the glittering headband with both hands. The diamond-encrusted tiara cost around eight thousand dollars, but if it got her the answer she sought, then it was worth it. The creature examined the item, rolling it over in her hands, before staring suspiciously back.

"It's real," said Pi.

"If it's not, I'll hunt you down and make a necklace of your bones."

Pi knew it was a bluff, but nodded anyway.

"May I ask my question?"

Alcyone cradled the tiara as she rocked in her crouch. "Ask. But you only get one. All anyone gets is one."

This was the part Pi was concerned about. She'd been ready to visit the island for weeks, but worried that her question wouldn't be up to the task. When she'd met Invictus, or at least the facsimile of Invictus, in

Semyon's mind last year, he'd left her with a riddle.

Pi was certain it was a clue about how to get into the Spire, but her investigations had come up well short of the goal. Visiting Alcyone was a desperate measure.

"Tell me the answer to this riddle. *When the error of the quarterarch you shall know, then through the thresholds you shall flow.*"

A sneer formed on Alcyone's mottled lips. Even though Pi couldn't hear, the disdain was evident in Alcyone's expression as she spoke. "That's not how this works. You cannot ask that."

"It's a question with an answer," said Pi. "I brought a gift and followed the rules. You owe me an answer."

Alcyone picked at her yellowed teeth with a long fingernail. A crazed smile surfaced, followed by a blackened tongue that licked the edges of her teeth. Alcyone looked ready to discard tradition.

Pi kept her magic on a hair trigger and her gaze focused on the creature's lips.

"Very well," said Alcyone, "I accept your gift and I owe you an answer. You're right, I do know this one, and even why it's so important to you. The best part is that I know you're destined to fail."

"The answer, Alcyone," said Pi, suddenly wanting to get as far away from the island as she could.

With a lazy-eyed wink, Alcyone turned her head so Pi couldn't see her lips anymore, and spoke. The creature's jaw moved, but Pi couldn't tell what was being said. When Alcyone was finished, she faced Pi again and grinned.

"You cheated," said Pi. "You didn't give me your answer."

"I only cheated as much as you did. If you heal your ears, I'll tell you again. I'll even give you permission to use magic. Does that sound like a deal?" asked Alcyone.

Pi grunted in frustration. She'd been planning this visit for over a month. She was sorely tempted to do as Alcyone suggested, and heal the damage to her eardrums, but that would make her susceptible to the voice.

"Fuck," said Pi under her breath.

"It pains you to be thwarted from your goal," said Alcyone.

"Your goal was to drink my blood."

Alcyone gave a half-shrug. "Girl's got to have something to pass the time. Especially looking like this."

"I should take back the tiara."

Alcyone pushed it onto her boney head. The glittering tiara looked odd on the corpse-like body. "Try it."

"Can we trade something else? I need that information," said Pi.

"My terms are clear. It's not my fault you didn't think it through," said Alcyone.

After a moment of consideration, Pi said, "I'll do it."

Alcyone's lazy eye fluttered. "No tricks. The spell can only heal your hearing, nothing else."

"Agreed," said Pi, wondering if she was insane for agreeing.

"I will only tell you the answer if you can hear me. No lip-reading, no recording, nothing but hearing," said Alcyone.

Pi nodded.

"I'll be here when you're ready," said Alcyone, crossing her bony arms.

Pi concentrated her spell on her right ear. It wouldn't matter if she could hear out of both. The spell was straight out of the Golden Willow hospital manual. While eardrum rupture was rare, it occurred enough that the doctors kept the spell at the ready. Thankfully it didn't require material components. The hard part was enunciating the spell without being able to hear, especially with the lexology modifications.

The faez tickled her ear on the way in as it healed the rip in the tiny organ, and then sound rushed in like an ocean. Despite her deafness lasting less than an hour, it felt like she was hearing for the first time in years.

Pi crumpled to her knees.

"Damn that hurts," she said, cringing at the volume. "Okay, I'm ready to hear the answer."

Alcyone licked her lips. "The answer is that it's a light shining your way into the Spire, the path to taking control of the Hundred Halls, to replace the wizard known as Invictus."

"Yes, I know that..." said Pi, and halfway through speaking, the seduction of Alcyone's voice took hold. It was like hearing the greatest pop song of all time on repeat, without getting sick of it.

Pi managed to get one more phrase out before her thoughts were sundered by the enchantment. "You promised an answer—that's not an answer."

"It's the answer you need, and the one you paid for," said Alcyone. "Now sit back and rest because I'm not going to wait for you to die, I'm going to slit your throat right now and taste your hot blood rushing into my mouth."

The words bounced around in Pi's mind, and somewhere deep inside, she knew this was bad, but the rest of her didn't care. It was worth her life to hear Alcyone speak. Pi vibrated with a pleasure that would have slayed a bus full of heroin addicts.

Alcyone approached. Disgusting, hag-like Alcyone, who had the voice of a billion angels. Pi watched in rapture, trembling as if the universe had an orgasm, and she was its conduit. Whatever reasons she'd had for coming to visit Alcyone were lost to the voice.

When Alcyone put a bony hand on Pi's shoulder, the fingernails scratching her shoulder blade, she leaned in for the embrace.

In that moment, as Alcyone leaned down to tear Pi's throat out with her yellowed teeth, the world returned to its previous thump-thump deaf state. The spell that Pi had put on her eardrum wore off, and the rip, carefully knitted with faez, sundered again.

Without Alcyone's voice keeping her enthralled, Pi was horrified by the creature's touch. As Alcyone's teeth brushed her neck, Pi thrust her away.

The surprised Alcyone fell backwards over the rocks. Pi wasted no time. She sprung the other way, sprinting between the beech trees and leaping over broken skeletons with their marrow sucked clean.

Without hearing, she couldn't know if Alcyone was following, or screaming in rage. At every step, Pi felt the promise of sharp nails on her back. When she hit the rocky beach, Pi kept going, wading into the waves.

She spared a glance backwards to see the hag stumbling after her. The waves slammed into Pi, choking her with foamy brine. She threw herself into the ocean, not caring to wait for Malcolm's boat.

When she made it past the crashing waves, Pi saw that Alcyone had stopped on the rocky shore and was pursuing no longer. But now Pi was fighting with an unruly ocean that suddenly seemed as eager as Alcyone to kill her.

Her jeans and sneakers formed an anchor on her legs, making it hard to swim. Just when Pi feared the water would claim her, the remote-controlled boat appeared. Pi pulled herself over the gunwale, collapsing into the bottom to rest after the harrowing escape.

When she caught her breath, Pi dared to peek over the bow to see Alcyone still standing on the beach. At this distance, she looked like a skeleton with hair, except for the glittering of her brow.

To assuage her frustration about Alcyone's trickery with the answer, Pi flipped her off. Then she climbed onto the bench for the ride back to shore. Despite not getting the answer she'd hoped for, Pi counted herself lucky that she was alive. And though she still didn't know the answer to the riddle, she knew for sure that it was a way into the Spire and to take control of the Hundred Halls.

THREE

When Aurie had first received the note from Semyon indicating where they were to meet, she'd been confused because the address was a house in the first ward, not far from where Malden Anterist lived. The massive mansions with their security guards and protective enchantments made her skin tingle as she strolled down the sidewalk. Not a leaf or blade of grass was out of place. The whole neighborhood looked like a picture in an architectural magazine.

Semyon waited for her on a park bench beneath a gazebo in a little common area park. The grass was softer than a mattress, and bounced at each step. Semyon wore a tan corduroy flat cap and was reading from a tablet.

"Not the location you were expecting," said Semyon, resting the tablet on his crossed knee.

"There are stranger places, but no, not what I was expecting," said Aurie, glancing around. "I don't feel like we're allowed here."

"Of course we are," said Semyon. "Despite the Hall politics, and the events of last year, this is a functioning university with rules and expectations of decorum."

Her experiences said otherwise, but she wasn't about to argue with him.

"Do you have any idea why we're here?" he asked.

"At first I thought I might be studying under you for my fifth year, but then I realized if that were the case, we would have met in your office, so no, I have no idea," she said.

"Do you know who Sam Arlington is?" he asked.

"I vaguely remember the name. Didn't he have some TV show where he discovered artifacts, or other ancient magical items?" asked Aurie.

"*Arlington's Artifact Hunters*," said Semyon.

Memories flooded in from her childhood. "I remember him now. He was trading in stolen artifacts, items looted from graves and other protected places. I don't remember much, but I remember the scandal. Mom wouldn't let us watch that show after the trial."

"Your mother worked with him," said Semyon. "Your father too. They came out of the Halls at the same time. They were good friends."

"What? That can't be right. I remember them telling us how wrong it was what he did," said Aurie.

"What parents tell young children can sometimes be at odds with the realities of the world. Their work was complicated, and those are difficult subjects to get across to a ten-year-old."

Her stomach sunk with the realization that he was telling her the truth. If it were coming from anyone else, she wouldn't have believed them, or wouldn't have allowed herself to believe it.

"Is this part of my lessons? Teaching me my parents aren't as awesome as I thought?" said Aurie, crossing her arms.

His eyes sparkled with mirth. "Your parents *were* as awesome as you remember. They were special people and I miss them dearly, but the world requires difficult choices. And now you will have to make one too."

"Are you suggesting that I work with Arlington on my fifth-year studies?" asked Aurie, who almost couldn't believe it.

"If you truly want to study artifacts, there is no other person in the world more qualified than Sam. In addition, he knows a lot about your parents. I believe he has a number of their diaries and notes."

"What? Why didn't Pi and I get those when they died?"

Semyon squeezed his lips together. "That is the unfortunate side of work for hire. When they worked with Sam, they worked under contract, which included, due to the sensitive nature of the work, that they couldn't take their notes with them. Not an uncommon thing in the artifact hunting business. But as far as that industry goes, Sam wasn't too bad. He didn't require a memory wipe or anything severe like that. He trusted them, and they trusted him."

"But isn't he Coterie?"

"Yes, he is Coterie, but that doesn't mean that you can't work with him."

"Really?" asked Aurie, her voice rising. "Isn't there someone in Arcanium?"

"This isn't only about studying, or books. Class time in Arcanium isn't enough for what you want to do. Sam has real-world experience."

Aurie squeezed the bridge of her nose between her fingers. A Coterie alumnus with a criminal history? "I'm so sorry, Patron Gray. I know you're trying to help." She took a deep breath and looked him right in the eyes. "But I am concerned about Mr. Arlington. They charged him with felonies, like federal ones. Is it wise for me to work with him?"

"Possibly not," said Semyon. "Sam has never seen the rules as firm lines, but rather as just suggestions. But your parents were able to work with him, and I mean it when I say that there is no one better than him. Plus, he has all the notes and diaries from your parents' expeditions. If you're truly going to study artifacts, then it's going to have to be Sam."

The idea that she would learn more about her parents was too big of an opportunity to pass up. After long consideration, she said, "I accept."

"Good," said Semyon. "I believe you won't regret it—well, I hope so. Look, you don't have to decide right now. Meet him and then make your choice."

His sudden hedging made her stomach tumble.

"Am I supposed to meet him here?" asked Aurie.

Semyon nodded towards the end of the street. "See that house with the wrought iron fence with the pyramids on it? He's waiting for you there."

"You're not coming?" asked Aurie.

"It's best if I'm not seen entering his house." He tapped his flat cap. "I have some obfuscating enchantments keeping our little conversation private."

"What about me?"

"There's nothing we can do about that," said Semyon, "but given your parents' history, it won't be a surprise if you're seen with him. And remember, after graduation, the various Halls work together more often than you'd think. You've been here during a very difficult time."

He stood up, tipped his cap, and winked before he walked in the other direction. She assumed he'd be taking the Garden Network back to Arcanium.

The wrought iron gate to Arlington's mansion swung open when she approached. By the time she reached the door, her heart was in her chest.

An older gentleman with a bushy beard, dusty blond hair, and crystalline blue eyes greeted her. Before he'd gotten arrested for trafficking stolen artifacts, they'd called him the real Indiana Jones, and his fashion choices hadn't changed much since then. He looked ready to join an archeological dig at a moment's notice.

"Aurelia," he said in a warm tone as he shook her hand. "Come in,

I'm so glad you've agreed to work with me."

He was handsome enough that standing in his gaze put a flutter in her chest.

"Thank you, Mr. Arlington. I appreciate the opportunity, though I haven't agreed yet."

"Fair enough, and please, call me Sam. I was a great admirer of your parents. Their passing was tragic, and it still grieves me. I cannot imagine how difficult it was for you and your sister."

He led her into a great room with a fireplace large enough that one could walk into it without ducking. Scattered around the room were glass cases containing objects she assumed were artifacts. The nearest one had a stone knife with a wicker wrapping around the handle. As she passed it, Aurie had a vision of a wicker altar in the forest with blood splattered across it. She reflexively put a hand to her chest when it felt like the stone knife was getting shoved between her ribs.

"You felt that, didn't you? It's awful, but thankfully it only happens the first time," said Sam excitedly. "That's a prime example of an imbued artifact, one that started out with a minor enchantment, but through extended use, and being continually soaked in faez, became more powerful."

"What does it do?" she asked with revulsion.

"Nothing good," he said. "After centuries of sacrifices, its purpose became to perpetuate its use. An artifact like that was once thought of as sentient, but now we know better."

"Is it dangerous to have around?" she asked, keeping a healthy distance between her and the stone knife.

"The wicker knife, as it's known, was able to continue the ritual sacrifices because of the superstitions of the time. Knowledge shields us from its affects, another reason to collect and protect the artifacts of the world. In the wrong hands, they can be dangerous."

"What if you're the wrong hands?" she asked.

He didn't flinch from her question. Rather, he smiled and held his hands up. "A fair point. I do have a history, but I promise you my crimes had more to do with a failure to fill out the proper paperwork than stabbing people in the heart to harvest their blood."

She was about to make a pithy comment, when she noticed a picture with her parents in it. They were standing in excavated ruins along with two other people. Her mother, Nahid, wore a flowery headscarf, and her father only had on his cargo pants. The sun had brought out the freckles on his shoulders. They were young, and full of life, with grins of absolute joy on their lips. Between them, they held a dusty sword, looking recently rescued from the earth.

She was so enamored with the picture of her parents she didn't realize who the identities of the other two people were until she examined them closer. "That's you and Bannon Creed. What are my parents doing with him?"

Sam appeared by her side. "Bannon financed the expedition."

She traced her fingers across her parents' pictures. "They look so young."

"That was their first big find. Do you know what sword that is? That's the fabled Excalibur," he said, excitement buoying his voice.

"Excalibur is real?"

He flicked the glass over the photograph. "The legend overexaggerates its usefulness. It was magically sharp and shone with light upon command, which in that time was a pretty good trick. Probably scared the shit out of its wielder's enemies."

"And now Bannon Creed owns it," said Aurie.

"Yep. That was the first and last expedition he funded, because he learned the hard truth about most artifacts, that they're crap compared to the magics we can make today."

"But not all," she said, thinking of the Rod of Dominion and the

Engine of Temporal Manipulation.

"Spoken wisely," he said.

"But how did they come to work with Bannon Creed?"

He scratched his beard. "When you're a poor archeologist right out of the Halls, you take the work where you can get it, even if it means you work with a shit stain like Creed."

"You don't like him?" asked Aurie.

"I think he's a human dumpster fire."

"But you'd work with him again on the right project."

He held his hands up again. "You got me there. I would. Is that what's bothering you? Are you worried that I'll ask you to compromise your morals?"

"Something like that," she said.

"Well, I probably will," he said. "But that'll be up to you to decide. I can't make you do anything. That's on you."

"I appreciate...your honesty," she said, almost as a question.

"Look, when I heard that the eldest daughter of Nahid and Kieran was looking to get into artifacts, I was excited. I may operate in gray areas at times, it's hard not to in this business, but I loved working with your parents. They were good people, and it's a damn shame they're not alive anymore. The world was a better place with them in it. To be honest, their friendship meant a lot to me, especially after I had a falling out with my grandfather after failing to meet his expectations. If you want to work with me, I promise I'll give you access to their writings. What I ask in return is for your help with a project I've been stuck on for quite some time. So what do you say?"

He offered his hand, which Aurie didn't take right away. She stared at it as if it were a poisonous snake, but Sam didn't retract it. He seemed ready to let it hang there until she decided.

Her heart desperately wanted her to say yes to the offer. A chance to learn more about her parents was a dream come true. The work on the artifacts was a bonus, and not because she needed it to graduate, but because for the first time, it felt like something she could enjoy doing. Despite the tumultuous first four years of her time in the Halls, the danger had given her purpose. Maybe this was what she was meant to do. And if he asked her to violate her principles, she would decline. It was that simple. She couldn't control him, but she could control herself.

When her palm touched his and they squeezed them together, a massive grin formed on his face.

"This is going to be a great partnership," said Sam, blue eyes twinkling. "You won't regret it."

But as he clapped her on the back to show her the other artifacts he'd collected, regret eased its way into her shoulders and hung in the back of her mind like a stormy cloud.

FOUR

Pi had her nose buried in the text of *Draper's Diagrams*. Hew Draper had lived in the 1500s, and after being accused of sorcery, he'd been thrown into the Tower of London, where he carved elaborate diagrams into the stone wall before his eventual escape. She was thinking about having the carvings from the book blown up so she could study them more easily, when she heard a clearing of the throat.

Her sister was standing in the doorway of their apartment in Arcanium, hair in a high ponytail, wearing jeans and a Garbage Kings T-shirt.

"I live here, too, you know," said Aurie, gesturing towards the piles of books and the papers stuck to the walls. "And I'm *actually* a student in Arcanium. Where am I going to get my project work done?"

Pi had been so deep into research, she hadn't really paid attention to the state of the apartment. Every inch of wall space, even the windows, had papers hanging on it. Piles of books formed hallways through the room.

"In your room?" suggested Pi with an exaggerated smile on her lips. "Sorry, sis. I've been ordering books on the Internet by the truckload, anything I can find that Invictus might have been interested in, and a couple of shipments arrived today."

"That would explain the mess of cardboard boxes in the hallway. Can you do this in your room?" asked Aurie.

"Errr...not really. It's full. Plus the light is better in here."

Aurie raised an eyebrow, pointing to the maps of ancient Sumaria covering the window.

"*Was* better in here?"

Aurie rolled her eyes, made her way to the couch, and plopped down next to Pi, pulling her knees to her chest. "I'll deal. Making progress at least?"

Pi examined her work thus far. The piles of books, sketches on the walls and diagrams combined to make her look like she was trying to find a historical serial killer, or was an inbred lunatic who never left her room.

"Invictus had a fascination with the wizards and witches of history. I wish I could have talked to him more than that one time, but at least the books and things from the cottage were still there. Maybe this means nothing, like a burly construction guy who also collects toy race cars, or maybe it's a clue to how to get into his realm in the Spire."

"You already have that clue," said Aurie.

"*When the error of the quarterarch you shall know, then through the thresholds you shall flow*," said Pi. "But what the fuck is a quarterarch? And why is there more than one threshold? None of these books have given me the slightest idea. An archway is an entrance—I thought it could be the place in the statue, but why do I care about the error? Is it a secret lever you push? It doesn't seem like something that important would rely on randomly jabbing the wall until you hit a button."

"Sucks that salty ocean hag didn't give you anything usable," said Aurie.

"I've come to the conclusion her whole shtick is a lie. Who's going to call her on it? Once they hear her voice, they can't do anything else, and she kills them. She probably started the rumor that she had secret knowledge so she never had to worry about finding food. The food comes straight to her. I wish I'd figured that out before I risked my life trying to ask her a stupid question." Pi bent the page to mark her place and set the closed book on her lap. "What about you? How's Sam Arlington?"

The stony expression that etched itself onto her sister's face was one of quiet despair. "September is nearly over and we haven't done anything yet."

"September? When did it get to be September?" Pi shook her head. "Never mind. Continue."

Aurie gave a double shoulder shrug with a frown on her lips. "I've been over there three times and all he does is talk about himself, his adventures, and the things he's collected. He won't let me see Mom and Dad's diaries yet, and he hasn't told me about his secret project either. My fifth year is a bust so far."

"At least it's not as hectic as, well, like any of the last four years. Enjoy it while it lasts," said Pi.

"Error of the quarterarch," mumbled Aurie. "Think it could be a famous arch? Like the *Arc de Triomphe*, or the one in St. Louis."

"There are dozens of arches around the world. But they're full arches, or half, I'm not sure how that works," said Pi. "I thought about natural arches—there are versions in Utah, or Kazakhstan—but those don't feel right either."

"A rainbow is an arch," said Aurie.

Pi sat up straight. A shiver went down her spine. "It is." Then the reality of what a rainbow was came to her, and she slumped back into the couch. "But how do you navigate it? The riddle says you have to go across the threshold, which means to go through it. You can't ever reach a rainbow, just like you can't find the pot of gold at the end."

"It's just an idea," said Aurie, setting her chin onto her bent knee.

"It's a good one. Better than I've gotten so far. I'll do some research on spells related to rainbows. Maybe there's a wizard from history that likes rainbows."

"Are you sure you're on the right track? Why does it have to be related to the books he was reading?"

"Because why else did I see him that one time and then never again? I think he left that memory in their subconscious before he died, and to keep them from finding it, he hid the clues in the room."

"What about his history?" asked Aurie.

"What history? As far as anyone is concerned, he walked out of the woods one day and started the Halls. No one really knows where he came from. I guess Oba did, but we don't know where he's at either. Trust me, if what's commonly known about him was a clue, the entrance to his realm would already have been found. There's a whole industry built by people who think he left the clue in something he did. I wouldn't be surprised if the Cabal patrons are funding research teams to find it." Pi slapped the book on her lap. "That cottage was important, I know it. I just need to figure out why."

FIVE

Standing before massive double doors covered in runes, Aurie felt knots form in her shoulder blades as she waited for Professor Chopra. He'd asked her to meet him beneath the Tower of Letters at the Eight-Fold Door for her lessons. Sam Arlington was her mentor for the fifth-year project, but that didn't mean she didn't have class work. Aurie wasn't clear on what Professor Chopra was going to teach, but the runes on the door told her that a kill room lay behind, a place designed to protect those outside of it from adverse magical effects escaping. Which meant that whatever she and the professor were going to be doing was highly dangerous.

A rattle of keys announced the professor's arrival. He held an iron ring with one big key.

"Good morning, Miss Aurelia. Are we ready to get started?" he asked as he tried three times to get the key into the lock.

"Born ready," she said.

He gave a nervous laugh. "Morning jitters, I suppose. Haven't had enough coffee."

Or too much, Aurie thought.

When the tumblers clicked into place, Professor Chopra yanked the doors open and stepped inside with his arms wide in a victory stance. The sleeves of his formal robes fell around his arms.

"Ta-da!"

The professor nearly tripped over himself as he spun around. She could see by his expression he'd been planning this moment to be special, but he looked more like an overexuberant teenager on his first date than an experienced professor.

While his entrance wasn't impressive, the room was. Aurie let out a soft whistle of appreciation.

The room had good bones. Rather than steel girders or concrete pillars, real stone arches buttressed the high ceilings, suggesting the room had been constructed in the previous centuries, when the Hall was newer. The floor had scars where acid or other corrosive liquids had been spilled. The holes had been patched, but the marks remained.

The air was musty from being closed up for a long time, even though the professor had been in the room already. There were a couple of plastic folding tables set against the wall with newer instruments sitting atop.

In the back of the room, a glass water tank taller than Aurie sloshed with the implication that something was swimming through it, although there was nothing visible in the water. She wanted to move closer to investigate, but Professor Chopra looked eager to speak.

"Big room for the two of us," she said.

"Plenty of room, plenty of room. I bet this is nice having space to do work. Perks of surviving to fifth year."

"Perks, yeah, that's what those are," she said, rolling her eyes while facing away from him. "So what are we doing in here?"

He clapped his hands together, eyes casting about the room, before he hurried to the plastic folding table to retrieve a thick tome with yellowed paper and worn edges. He hugged the book to his chest.

"We're going to make a magical trinket," he said, eyes wide. "I heard your focus study was on artifacts, so I thought we'd tackle something smaller."

"You're the professor."

He nodded enthusiastically. "I have a text that explains how. It's a little old, but it's hard to get the patent rights on modern trinkets. If those damn corporations didn't use patentgeists to sniff out unauthorized versions, we could make one, purely for educational purposes."

Aurie chewed on her lower lip. She realized his excitement wasn't about her, but about this project.

While she was interested in artifacts, she wasn't really interested in making them, even smaller versions like trinkets. The process was usually extremely dangerous. History was littered with horror stories of city blocks being wiped out or all nearby flesh being reduced to goo when a partially made trinket exploded.

"Isn't this dangerous?"

He turned up his nose. "I wouldn't present this project to you if I wasn't confident we could do it. This won't be an artifact like the Destiny Stone, the Helmsman of the Planes, or Charlemagne's Chalice. We're going to make something more intimate, but meaningful."

She wanted to retort that students didn't make them, because there were laws for safety, and generally, mages didn't have that big of a death wish, especially when spells or technology could usually do the same things, only cheaper.

"Great..."

Professor Chopra clapped his hands against the cover of the book. "Don't you want to know what it is?"

"The thing that's going to get us killed? Sure," she said.

He took her comment with a nervous laugh. "That's the spirit, a little gallows humor to take the edge off." He presented the tome to her, first upside down, then the correct way so she could read it.

"*The Magical Works of Henry Galveston Lipton*," Aurie read out loud.

Professor Chopra peeled the cover back along with a quarter of the book, revealing pages with a dense scrawl across them. Notated diagrams with footnotes filled the bottom half of each page. Aurie read the title of the section out loud.

"The Hearthring of Grace? That's it? That's what we're going to make?"

"Impressive, isn't it?"

Ridiculous was what she thought, but she didn't want to curb his enthusiasm, so she make a non-committal noise in her throat that could have been interpreted as positive.

"What does it do?" she asked.

"It has many uses. Clears bad air, cures joint pain, other afflictions, too numerous to name here."

"Okay...so I should take this back to my room and study it for a few days before we begin?" asked Aurie hopefully.

He yanked the tome out of her arms, cradled it against his chest. "No, no. We're going to start right away. It took me some time to prepare this first activity...we should...start right away."

Before she could say otherwise, he marched towards the glass tank, a look of rapture on his face.

"What's in the tank?" he asked

The surface of the water shifted back and forth with tiny waves, suggesting movement from a source. She stared at it for a few minutes trying to catch what it was that was causing it. It didn't help that she was feeling a little rushed. Normally, professors had them extensively study the material before starting the first lesson, so no mistakes were made.

"Water."

Professor Chopra nodded as if she'd said something profound. "Very good. But what's in the water? Take your time. You may use spells if you wish, but they're not necessary."

Aurie knew a lot of lore about water creatures. The Five Elements formed the basis of all magic, so it was useful to go beyond the spells, and understand why they worked, and what supernatural creatures were related to that element. The most common spirits were called Undines, but they had corporal bodies that could be seen and touched.

When she tapped on the glass, the water shifted away, as if she'd startled a creature.

The creature itself wasn't invisible, since that would have displaced the water, making the outline easy to see. Which meant that the creature was made of water. The tank had no lid, but it wasn't trying to escape.

Aurie cast a revealing spell on the glass tank, to which Professor Chopra made a noise of appreciation, again a little overdone for the result. Ghostly runes formed across the four sides. The protective magics had none of the watery markers that she expected. Some suggested demonology, while she'd seen others on air pollution controls.

"This isn't a water creature," she said.

"Good," he replied. "But what is it?"

Why would the professor put it in water if it wasn't a water elemental? Unless the water itself was a layer of protection. Did it absorb water?

Acting on a hunch, Aurie turned her head so the tank was at the edge of her vision. Then she unfocused her eyes and thought about prime numbers. 2, 3, 5, 7, 11, 13, 17, 19, 23, 29, 31, 37, 41...

Right as she hit 41, the hazy shape of a creature formed. It looked like a psychedelic jellyfish with a bad case of acne. A pustule on the dome of the ghostly creature burst, sending out a dollop of yellow-brown gas into the water that was quickly absorbed.

"Are you crazy? That's an Illiopian Death Cloud!"

He didn't seem dissuaded by her outburst. "Quite remarkable, isn't it?

It took me a week to summon it into the tank."

"It has perfect camouflage, and the gases it exhales can eat through anything—steel, concrete, whatever—and the adults are immune to most magics. The gas is fatal to everything at fractions. If that gets out, it could kill thousands before it's recaptured or destroyed," said Aurie.

"Well then, we'll have to be careful. No one said being a mage was easy, or safe. Are you willing to give up so soon?" he asked.

"No, of course not."

When she'd seen her class schedule included Professor Chopra, she'd thought they'd be working on dry texts or mixing exotic runic inks, not summoning dangerous invisible supernatural creatures.

"So what is it for?" asked Aurie, knowing in her gut she wasn't going to like the answer.

"We need to collect its gaseous fumes."

"And how does one do that?" she asked.

"One of us," he said, nodding towards Aurie, clearly indicating who the "one of us" meant, "will have to enter the tank with the creature and collect it using this syringe, properly warded, of course."

"I didn't bring my suit," said Aurie.

"Not necessary. I prepared a Winston's Wet Ward. You'll feel as dry as a desert in there."

"And how do I go about collecting the gas from the Death Cloud? You know, without it murdering me?" she asked.

"Well, the theory is that the female Death Cloud, while submerged in water, is completely docile."

"Theory? You mean this hasn't been tested?" she asked.

"The initial summoning worked as advertised, and I've seen no attempts by the creature to escape, or even test the protective runes," said Professor Chopra without a hint of concern. "So I believe the next phase will work fine."

"How do you know it's female?"

"The females have the bright colorings, while the males are gun metal gray. Are you afraid of going into the tank?" he asked.

She wanted to blurt out that of course she was afraid. The thought of entering a cage with a dangerous creature gave her the cold sweats. It was thought that the plane the Death Cloud came from had been thoroughly wiped clean by their deadly gases until there was nothing left.

Aurie looked at the tank, the tables of materials, and the eager look on the professor's face. He'd gone through a lot of trouble to set this up. Risked his own life when he summoned the Death Cloud into the tank in the first place.

"Are you sure it's a female?" she asked.

"Positive. A male would be throwing itself against the glass trying to break out. I wouldn't be standing here if it were a male. That's what took so long with the summoning, making sure I got the right half of the species. A male would turn the water into hydrochloric acid within minutes."

"Why do they act so differently in water?"

Professor Chopra shrugged away her comment. "Nobody knows. But we're not here to study Death Cloud behavior, we're here to take samples. Are you good?"

"I'll be good," she said, eyeing the stairs leading into the tank with trepidation. "I need to psyche myself up before going in."

Professor Chopra taught her the spells she would need for the gas extraction. The first would allow her to breath and speak underwater for a few minutes. The next would help her see the Death Cloud, but she couldn't cast it until she was in the water due to the runes on the tank, and the final would stun it so she could plunge the enchanted syringe into a pustule. Then, once she'd climbed out, the gas would be placed into a holding field. Professor Chopra had already constructed one and left it on one of the plastic tables.

Aurie climbed up the stairs and stared into the water.

"Everything okay up there?" asked Professor Chopra.

"Oh, yeah, real good," she said sarcastically.

He beamed a smile and gave her a thumbs-up. "Whenever you're ready."

The moment the water breathing spell took hold, she felt a little dizzy. She could still breathe regular air, but it felt like she was at a high altitude. The body had a difficult time conforming to both.

The water was colder than she expected, like slipping into a mountain stream. She dangled her left leg in the water for a few seconds to make sure the Death Cloud wasn't going to attack. When nothing happened, Aurie slipped a little further into the water, pausing occasionally, until she was ready to submerge her face.

The cold water going over her eyelashes tickled. The water was clear. The hazy form of Professor Chopra standing outside the runed tank was comforting.

She relaxed a little, realizing that the professor's preparations were working. She'd entered a water tank with a female Illiopian Death Cloud and was still alive to talk about it. Maybe he'd gotten a bad rap over the years, and the stories had been exaggerated because he was a bit of a stick-in-the-mud.

"Alright, let's get this over with," she said into the water, partially because she was as nervous as a fly in a glue factory, and partially to test her voice in the water before she started the next spell.

As the faez flowed from her lips and into the water, the outline of the Death Cloud came into view. Her earlier impression of a jellyfish with acne remained, except it pulsed menacingly, like a warning light. Thread-thin tentacles with tiny fibers across their length waved beneath the bulbous body. In its own way, the Death Cloud was beautiful, even when that beauty came with a side of global extinction.

Professor Chopra tapped on the glass to get her moving. She'd been hovering along the back side, getting her nerve up for the final part.

She would have to act quickly once she stunned the Death Cloud. Aurie crossed the distance between the glass wall and the creature. The syringe was stuck into her pocket with a protective lid on the needle.

As she started the spell, the Death Cloud floated away from her as if it knew what she was about to do. When the stunning spell hit the creature, it stopped pulsing. It was as if she'd stopped a beating heart.

Edging near, Aurie readied the syringe. There was a ripe pustule on the shimmering blue-green dome that she wanted to harvest. As she reached out, the Death Cloud shuddered as if it were waking up. Aurie pulled back, until she realized it was an involuntary reaction. The creature wasn't moving, and the hairy thread-like tentacles hung limply beneath.

Careful not to brush against the Death Cloud, Aurie jabbed the needle into the pustule and quickly pulled back the plunger until the barrel filled with a yellow gas. The Death Cloud twitched a few times, but otherwise made no motions towards her.

It wasn't until she was putting the cap back onto the needle that she realized something was wrong. She'd been so focused on the Death Cloud she hadn't noticed the coin-sized droplets falling into the water from beneath the dome.

Before she knew it, there were twenty or thirty of these little balls in the water that she quickly realized were baby Death Clouds. And to her dismay, at least fifty percent of them were gunmetal gray.

As Aurie swam backwards away from the Death Cloud, the little males surged towards her. Professor Chopra banged on the glass, his voice muffled by the water, but she could sense his intent by the sharpness, indicating she needed to get the hell out!

Before she could escape, the tiny males had her trapped in the corner. They looked like tiny bubbles being yanked along by invisible strings. The water around each one was turning yellowish-brown.

Aurie had a terrible realization why the females were docile in the water. It was because they gave birth in the water, and when she'd stunned the mother, it'd released its children. Learning this was little solace to the fact that she was about to die once the baby Death Clouds brushed her skin or when the water finished turning to deadly acid. Already her face tingled, a slow burning that erupted across her exposed eyes and lips.

Trapped in the corner, Aurie sent a few waves at the baby Death Clouds, creating currents to pull them away from her, but she couldn't hit them all, and they kept coming back. Even if she could keep them away, the water was turning poisonous and she didn't have long to live.

Aurie had no idea what Professor Chopra was doing outside the cage, but she did the only thing she could think of to escape certain death—she broke the glass.

The tank exploded, sending a flood of broken glass and polluted water across the concrete floor. She tumbled onto her side, rolling away, hoping she wouldn't impale herself on the glass, trying to get away from the baby Death Clouds.

The mother lay like a technicolor lump on the ground where the tank once stood. She was more of a psychedelic ooze than floating sphere of annihilation, but the gooey skin was twitching with the implication that she was waking.

The babies were slowly rising into the air, a tiny armada of death. Hoping that fire would provide a thorough cleansing of the poisonous gas, Aurie produced a wildfire of flame. The closest babies popped like bubbles.

Some escaped her wrath as they'd been scattered wildly about the room. To her left, she spied the unconscious form of Professor Chopra, lying like a rag doll beneath the plastic tables. A trio of baby Death Clouds hovered near his body. Aurie roasted them out of the air, and though it felt like using a flamethrower on a mosquito, it got the job done.

But not all the babies were coming after them. Some of the females were burrowing upward through the concrete ceiling, using their corrosive gasses to eat away the stone. If even one baby Death Cloud got away, there could be dire consequences.

Like an exterminator going after termites, Aurie cleansed the stone with flame, ignoring the backblow that singed her hair and roasted her exposed skin, deciding that a few third-degree burns were worth not dying from deadly gases.

She blackened the stone, and her fingernails, as she sent geysers in all directions. Around the time she began to think she might have destroyed all the baby Death Clouds, she noticed that the mother had awoken and was floating midway between the high arched ceiling and the floor, little pustules of gas exploding off its glistening skin.

Aurie was well aware that she'd just spent the last few minutes eradicating this Illiopian Death Cloud's brood with extreme prejudice.

"Hi," she said. "You're not mad about that are you?"

When the creature pulsed crimson and surged towards Aurie, she knew she was in trouble. She twisted fire into a mini-tornado to do battle with the Death Cloud, but it shrugged it off.

She could banish it, but she didn't have the time, nor did she know the proper spells to make it happen. Only Professor Chopra knew those, and he was unconscious.

"Chopra! Get up!"

She backed away, using her magic to keep the Death Cloud from reaching her, and to destroy the gases emanating from its bulbous skin, but eventually it would get through.

"Chopra!"

The professor stirred, climbing to his knees as she launched fire spears.

"The Death Cloud! You have to get rid of it!"

He stumbled to his feet, palm pressed against the side of his head. He looked around the room, dumbfounded.

"Where is it?"

"*Merde.*"

He couldn't see it, because he hadn't cast the spell like she had. But there wasn't time. The Death Cloud had her trapped in the corner. As it hovered near a supporting arch, the gases melted the stone, like an eon's worth of water damage in seconds. She sensed the gases floating towards her, and when the first particles reached her lips and went into her lungs, she'd die.

Aurie readied a final spell. If it was going to kill her, at least she could destroy the Death Cloud in the process. She planned on activating the runes on the front door, the ones that would annihilate everything and everyone in the room, rendering it completely sterile as if it'd been dipped into the surface of the sun.

As the trigger words reached her lips, she heard Professor Chopra cry out in a loud voice, "*Mors Horrida Nubes Deducere Ex Regno Tuo*!"

At first, Aurie thought it wasn't going to work, but then the floating jellyfish shimmered like heat on a desert highway and faded away, returning to its realm. Aurie followed it up with a blast of flame to burn away the remaining gases.

Then she continued her search for escaping babies, blackening the stone. Professor Chopra joined her in the cleansing, until her eyes were sore from the heat and the room was filled with smoke.

After an air purifying spell, they met back at the plastic tables, amid the shattered glass and stained concrete.

Professor Chopra cleared his throat and spoke as if nothing had happened.

"Well, now. It didn't go exactly to plan, but you got the gas, right?"

The syringe had fallen out of her pocket. Aurie retrieved it and held it up for inspection. The yellowish gas billowed within the barrel.

"Great!" he said, snatching it out of her hand. "I'll go prepare this in the alchemy lab while you clean up in here. Good job. We're on the right track."

Professor Chopra snatched up the tome and marched out of the room, leaving Aurie to lean against the wall and wipe the sweat from her forehead.

"I'm sure it'll get better after this. I mean, it can't get any worse, right?"

SIX

Big Dave's Town was exactly as Pi remembered it. It'd only been four months, but it felt like a lifetime. After Jade's betrayal, she hadn't felt much like coming back to visit. The neon sign for The Devil's Lipstick oozed artificial light into the cavern.

"I can't believe you lived here," said Aurie.

Her sister wore jeans and a black hoodie, with her hair pulled back into a tight ponytail that yanked her eyebrows upward.

"I spent most of my time at the Misfits' island, or up there," Pi said, nodding towards the apartment door above the bar. She'd been up and down those faded white steps dozens of times in the last year.

"Before we head into the backcountry," said Pi, "I need to do something."

Aurie gave her a quizzical look, but said nothing. Pi jogged to the twin bathroom doors outside the restaurant. The light flickered on when she hit the switch.

"Oops," she said when she noticed the urinals on the wall.

Pi pulled a compass out, flipped it over and set it on the counter, and with a purple paint pen, she sketched a trio of runes on the copper backing. When she breathed faez on the runes, the paint crystallized, and she heard a tiny crack.

Pi held the compass flat, and the needle pointed to the east. Thankfully, the exit from the cavern in that direction did not go past the lake, so she wouldn't be tempted to visit Jade's grave.

Back outside the restroom, Aurie arched an eyebrow questioningly. Pi tapped on the side of her head. "You'd be amazed how many people don't care when you go into the wrong bathroom."

They marched away from Big Dave's Town with magelights floating ahead. Every hundred yards, Pi threw a handful of dust onto the stone behind them.

"Bread crumbs?" asked Aurie.

"Keeps anyone from following us. Or at least messes up any magical tracking."

"Paranoid?" asked Aurie.

"Given the subject we're researching, I think that's prudent."

Her sister gave an exaggerated sigh. "Do you really think this is the way to—"

"Aurie!"

"Sorry, but I think it's a bit of a wild goose chase. Yeah, I know you saw *him*, but he's a pretty important figure in their lives, all our lives, so of course Invictus would have been in his dreams."

"If you don't believe in what I'm doing then why did you come?" she asked.

"The Undercity is not a place to go traipsing around by yourself, especially in the uncharted areas," said Aurie. "And this is safer for me than working with Professor Chopra. My biggest worry with him was that he was going to be boring, or such a stickler for rules that it would annoy even me. I never thought that he'd turn into an excitable trinket nerd with zero common sense."

"Anything from Sam Arlington?" asked Pi.

"He's been away for the past month, but we're supposed to meet again this weekend. He sent me a text earlier today that just said *MOMA Tues 1pm*."

Once the compass led them into the open caverns, they stopped chatting and focused on their surroundings. They were led past bottomless sinkholes and minor forests of luminous fungi. At one point, they heard a bird trilling, but declined to investigate, knowing a predator probably lurked nearby.

After a four-and-a-half-hour hike, they arrived at their destination: an oddly round cave with natural walls and half of a stone arch in the center.

Pi shoved the compass into the inside pocket of her jacket.

"You think this is the quarterarch?" asked Aurie skeptically.

Pi pulled out her faez-sensing goggles and placed them against Aurie's face, who then let out an appraising whistle.

"Damn," said Aurie.

With the goggles back upon against her face, Pi examined the room and the arch, which was awash in faez. The whole place glowed radioactively.

"The error of the quarterarch," said Pi. "I think it means that we have to fix it somehow."

Her sister was craning her neck, looking all around. "How'd you find this place?"

"A mind-numbing amount of reading. There was nothing in any book I'd read about Invictus indicating an archway or portal that wasn't already a part of the Garden Network, so I'd pretty much given up on finding it. I was bored and started reading some books about natural arches and found a diary about a couple of Hall students climbing on this quarterarch. They mentioned the heavy residual faez, and I did some guesswork on its location based on the description. This cavern is roughly near the center of the city, where the Spire is."

"How do we get in?" asked Aurie.

"That's what I'm here to figure out," said Pi. "Can you put some wards near the entrance so we can examine this at our leisure?"

"Anything for you, sister," said Aurie.

While her sister was working, Pi moved up to the stone arch. As far as she could tell, it was made of granite, rather than obsidian, as she'd hoped. Obsidian was the best, though not the only, conduit for portal making.

The quarterarch looked like a thick finger, bent and hanging in midair. The whimsical curve reminded her of a Dr. Seuss book, which seemed to support the idea that it was the true portal to Invictus' realm.

Pi started with the simplest spells, attempting to understand the purpose of the stone before trying to activate a portal. If it were truly broken, utilizing it in an incomplete state would be dangerous, and even if it was working properly, she knew that Invictus wouldn't have left it unguarded. Of the many things she'd learned about the head patron, he was paranoid. Like capital P, Paranoid. But she supposed that was to be expected, growing up in the dark ages of magic, when looking at someone funny got you drowned or burned at the stake.

After the first two hours, she'd exhausted the spells she had planned, and she tried to improvise. Pi checked the area for runic switches—a common mechanism for portals—and other similar devices. An attempt at shaping the stone to complete the arch resulted in a minor earthquake, while probing the stone for hidden levers only brought sarcastic remarks from her sister.

Exhausted from the heavy drain on her faez, Pi slumped against the arch and sipped from a water bottle.

"Is that it? You're giving up?" asked Aurie, who'd been reading a dog-eared copy of *The Unauthorized Biography of Henry Lipton.*

"I thought you came to help."

Aurie set the book on her knees. "I came to make sure you're safe. This is your deal. I don't have the slightest idea how to solve the riddle. Plus, I'm trying to prepare for my next class with Chopra. He won't let me see the spell book, so I'm doing the next best thing, reading about the artificer himself. Did you know he spent time in prison for money laundering? His early years were filled with complaints that his trinkets didn't really work. They called him the Kentucky Quack."

"Sounds like a nut job," said Pi.

"That's not even the half of it. He traveled the country with a circus, hawking his wares. Towards the end of his life, he came here. Tragic ending—his wife was really sick, she died, and no one heard from him again after that."

"I'd never even heard of him before your class with Chopra," said Pi. "Can't you put your book down and try to help me for a little bit? We hiked a long way to get here. I'm not ready to go back yet."

Aurie stretched and yawned, climbing to her feet and rubbing her backside, which was sore from sitting on the uneven stone. "My ass fell asleep anyway, so sure. I'll help. What do you want me to do?"

Pi tugged at the short hair on the left side of her head. "If I knew that, I'd try it myself."

Aurie cracked her knuckles one at a time as she approached the quarterarch. She circled it once, then probed it with her fingertips. When she put her ear to the stone and knocked on it as if it were hollow, Pi said, "Quit screwing around."

"Okay, fine," said Aurie with a self-satisfied grin. She grabbed a handful of salt from the backpack and made a circle around the stone.

She spoke in the language of demon summoning, and while Pi didn't know the spell, there was a certain cadence that made it easy to follow the longer she listened. When Aurie finished, the salt exploded into sparks, sending stings against their faces.

"What was that?" asked Pi, knocking the salt from her hair.

"It's not an archway to Invictus' realm."

"How can you know that? I've been here for hours while you only tried one thing," said Pi.

"Easy. Rather than trying to prove what it is, I proved what it is not. It's definitely not a portal."

Pi looked back to the charred remains of the salt circle. She could tell by her sister's smug look that she expected Pi to figure it out for herself. Why would she purposely fail a demon summoning spell? And why put the quarterarch at the center of the circle?

"Was that a slither summoning?" Aurie nodded. Finally, Pi saw the reason.

"I'm an idiot, sis. I see what you did. Using portals creates a residue of pure gallium, which is a summoning component of a slither demon. No gallium means no portal." Pi squeezed her face in her hands. "And I thought I was so close! I guess I should have realized when I found this place through Instagram that Invictus wouldn't have hidden it in such an obvious place."

"What if he didn't hide it in a specific place at all?" asked Aurie.

"What does that mean?"

Aurie gave a shrug that barely moved her muscles. "Dunno. It just seems like an Invictus kind of thing to do."

"Like if he hid it in a rainbow," said Pi. "But which rainbow? And how do you go through it?"

Aurie lowered her chin and spoke in her deepest voice. "*When the error of the quarterarch you shall know, then through the thresholds you shall flow.*"

As her sister said the word "error," a quiver went through Pi's belly. "Say that again." She sat up, every nerve tingling with anticipation.

"That," said Aurie, winking.

"No. The riddle. Say it again," she said, worried that whatever it was that she'd heard was a mirage.

Aurie spoke again, but without the accent. "When the error of the quarterarch you shall know, then through the thresholds you shall flow."

"No, like the first time. There was something in the way you said it," said Pi, and when her sister repeated it the third time, she knew what it was she heard.

"It's not 'error' but 'heir.' I heard the riddle wrong, or maybe it was intended to be confusing," said Pi, "or maybe that doesn't mean anything at all."

"But how does that help?"

Anxious and feeling like she couldn't sit still, Pi paced across the stone. "When the *heir* of the quarterarch you shall know. The heir, as in the person who inherits, or maybe owns it. Whoever owns the quarterarch. Which means it's not something we have to go through, it's something we have to collect." Pi slapped her forehead. "I've been going after this all wrong."

The words and ideas tumbled through her head, things she'd read that made more sense now. She felt like she was on the cusp of a breakthrough. Alcyone's words trickled back into her head.

"Alcyone told me that answer is a light shining my way into the Spire. What if she wasn't lying to me? A light? What is light, but a rainbow."

By the look on Aurie's face, Pi knew she'd hit close to the mark.

"Fuck yeah, I knew it was a rainbow," said Aurie.

"We don't know for certain. And we're back to the same problem. How do you own a rainbow? And why only a quarter of it?"

"A rainbow is full of colors. What if you only need some of the colors?"

"Merlin's tits. I think I know what it is." Pi checked around the cavern to make sure no one was there but her sister. "In the cottage, there were many items, games, books, all sorts of things. One of them was an azure glass about the size of a bowling ball."

"Yeah, so?"

"I've seen one before, I just didn't realize it until now. You've seen it too."

Aurie frowned suspiciously. "I have?"

"Freeport Games. There's an indigo glass ball inside Hemistad's case, the one by the cash register. It's in there with the dice and other stuff. I always thought it was a prop, like a crystal ball."

"Why would it be sitting in a case in Freeport Games?" asked Aurie.

"Invictus and Hemistad were friends. Maybe he asked him to hold onto it. Or didn't tell him anything. But it fits with what I know about Invictus. He loved games, and he was fascinated with the wizards of literature. There's the Wizard's Rainbow from King, or the Palintir from Tolkien. This has got to be it. I know it."

"There's an easy way to find out," said Aurie. "Though I'm not sure he'd give it to us. I don't think he's ever forgiven us for what happened our third year."

"Let me do some checking around first before we go to Freeport Games. I need to decide if we're going to ask him for it, or if we're going to acquire it another way."

"I hope you don't mean steal it," said Aurie. "We both know he's out of our league. Not sure whose league he's in, maybe Oba's, but not ours."

"Yeah, that's why I want to do some checking first." Pi grabbed her sister by the shoulders and bounced. "But I think we're close. I really do. This feels right, really *really* right."

"I believe you, sis." She glanced around the cave. "Does that mean we're done here? I'm starving. I was thinking we could stop by Wizard Burger on the way back."

They went back the way they came, and the whole time, Pi plotted how she was going to steal the glass ball from Hemistad. She felt *slightly* bad that she wasn't going to involve her sister, but if things didn't go as planned, she didn't want Aurie in trouble with Hemistad too.

SEVEN

The guard at the entrance of the Museum of Magical Artifacts waved Aurie through once she showed her ID. They didn't make her go through the metal detector, or examine her for malicious auras or subversive trinkets. It felt downright odd to waltz into a place that employed Blackstone Security and not have her personal space invaded.

She was so weirded out that she almost forgot to enjoy her first visit to the museum. The front half of the building had been styled after the Pantheon, while the back was more like Versailles with gilded columns, although it did have marble gargoyles at every roof corner. The story about the architects who built the MOMA was famous enough that Aurie knew it. When the design was awarded to the first architect, the second one cursed the first so that he died halfway through the construction, and the job was passed on to the second. But when he tried to finish it, the curse rebounded and killed him too. The curse killed three more architects before they realized it was bound to the building, and after it killed the demolition crew, they had to leave the original construction in place while finishing the building in a completely new style.

Sam Arlington, in khakis and a neatly pressed tan safari shirt, greeted her in the Bronze Age Wing, his handsome and familiar face drawing onlookers, and the occasional flash of a cell phone camera. Unexpectedly, he gave her a hug that made her face flush with embarrassment. He smelled like aftershave.

"I told the security that you're my niece," he whispered in her ear before he grabbed her hand and pulled her towards a velvet rope that blocked a side room labeled "Chalcolithic Era" above the door. A Blackstone Security mage with an earpiece and a sidearm unhooked the velvet rope and let them pass.

Without the bustle of the crowd, Sam's hard-soled boots rang out against the marble floor, echoing off the glass cases. His calloused hand was rough against hers. When he let it go, she wiped the perspiration from her palm onto her jeans.

Before he spoke, he took out a black box about the size of a cigarette case and set it on a glass case containing a colorful ceramic bowl. He whispered a trigger word, and a high-pitched whine made her squint momentarily, then it faded away.

"What is that?" she asked.

"It'll keep our conversation private," he said, and when she made a face towards the camera in the corner, he added, "It's okay. I told them I was going to do that. When you're the largest contributor of artifacts to the museum, they give you perks."

"That must be nice," she said, glancing around the room, trying to guess the reason he'd brought her.

"You look very sharp today," he said, catching her off guard. "You remind me of your mother."

"Thank you, I guess," she said, smoothing the fitted aquamarine coat around her midsection as warmth rose to her cheeks. He was more than twice her age and she wasn't at all interested in him. She'd worn a more professional outfit for the visit to the museum, thinking they'd be meeting with the administration about the artifact that he hadn't yet told her about. She hoped he hadn't gotten the wrong impression.

"I brought you here to show you something," he said, gesturing towards a case set haphazardly in the corner with a sheet over it. The clarification of purpose let the tension release from her shoulders.

Sam yanked the sheet from the case with a flourish, like a magician with his best trick. Inside the glass was a crimson skull made of some unknown material and covered in glossy black stones. Upon closer inspection, the artifact looked cheesy, as if it'd been made to give away at a strip mall carnival. There was no placard.

"What is this? A fake or something? I almost expect it to be made out of macaroni," said Aurie.

He smirked. "It's a placeholder. The Crimson Skull has never been found."

"And you want to find it?"

"Well, of course," he replied.

"Why?"

"It's an artifact and I'm an artifact hunter. Does there need to be any other reason?" he asked, his shoulders lifting in careless shrug. His dismissal seemed so practiced and perfect, she knew it wasn't the full truth.

Aurie steeled her face from frowning, a reaction that Pi had called her on more than once. While Sam Arlington wouldn't know her tells, she needed to practice hiding her reaction when she thought someone was lying.

"What does it do?" she asked, keeping her voice light.

He put his hands on the top of the case, leaned down, and put his face near the glass. "No one knows," he said, drumming his fingers. "That's why I want to find it."

"Then how do you know it's a real artifact?" she asked.

He winked. "Because I know these things." He chuckled as if he didn't believe himself either. "There are rumors, of course, but it's hard to separate the truth from the fiction. While the shape of an artifact is often indicates its use, sometimes it just happens to be the item most convenient to the maker, or the one that was imbued with the magic from repeated enhancement."

"Or from the blood of sacrifices," she added.

"Or that." He turned to her. "So you can imagine the properties associated with a crimson skull." He gave her that shrug. "But I don't think they're true."

"What do *you* think it does?"

"Ahh...see," he said, holding up a single finger as if he were testing the wind direction, "these kinds of things are fun to do, to speculate, to guess, maybe even bet, but it is not productive for the professional artifact hunter. It's a good way to die when it turns out the artifact doesn't do what you think it will do."

Aurie sensed he was telling the truth. It was logical, the way he explained it. Especially given the number of artifacts that might be cursed.

But it could also be a convenient truth, necessary to shield her from what he really thought. She wasn't sure, though.

"This is the project you're stuck on?" He nodded. "What's the catch? This feels like something that's going to be highly illegal."

"Not illegal, per se, not yet anyway," he said.

"Mr. Arlington—"

"Please call me Sam."

"Fine, Sam. If we're going to work together, you need to start being straight with me right away. You keep holding back, and it's making me not trust you."

A devilish smile rose to his lips. "You are so much your mother's daughter. She wouldn't put up with my shit either. I wish she could see you now."

"Don't try to distract me with sentimentality," she said sternly.

"Fair enough," he said, steepling his fingers and pacing across the floor like a professor about to give a lecture. "In the mid part of last century, when the length and breadth of magic was really becoming clearer to the public, there were a lot of laws that were passed regarding magic, and especially artifacts. While many of these laws have been repealed, some are still on the books, only because there's no constituency to convince a politician to champion their elimination."

"So the Crimson Skull is illegal?" she asked.

"Extremely," he said. "So much so that the museum was asked to remove their fake version so people weren't reminded about its existence and try to go after it."

"Exactly what you're trying to do," she said.

He held his hands up. "I knew about the Crimson Skull long before this. It was my Coterie fifth-year project."

"If you didn't find it, then how did you pass?"

He gave her a sly wink. "A story for another time."

"I'm not doing anything illegal."

"I haven't asked you to. What I am asking is for you to help me find it. Once its location is known, then I can work on getting the laws changed so I can retrieve it and bring it back to the museum."

"How is finding it going to help get the law changed?"

"No politician is going to stick their neck out until they know it exists and they know it's not dangerous," he said.

"You believe it's not dangerous."

He drew an "X" over his chest. "Cross my heart and hope to die."

"So we're just finding it. Not retrieving it, or anything like that?" she asked.

"I promise."

It sounded truthful, but Aurie still didn't trust him.

"Ah!" he said, reaching into his back pocket. "I almost forgot. The reward."

In his hand was a tattered leather notebook with dirt streaked yellowed pages, half of which had slipped their bindings. Her hands betrayed her and reached for the diary before she could pull them back.

"You don't have to pull back," he said. "I'm giving this to you as a gift. Mostly for listening to me babble about adventures when you came to my house. I'm a sucker for a charming young lady, and I was afraid you wouldn't think I was impressive enough."

"You used to have your own TV show."

His eyes twinkled with memory and a hint of darkness, and though the wrinkles on his face had been smoothed away by magic or drugs, he carried the weight of his years, and something else of which Aurie only got a glimpse. "It doesn't feel like that was me anymore. But go ahead and take it. It's yours."

"The first one's free," said Aurie, staring at the diary as if it were water and she were dying of thirst.

He shoved it towards her. "Take it. I insist. It was your mother's, but of course, you know that."

Just looking at the worn diary made her heart ache. Reading it would be like hearing her mother's voice again, like feeling the caress of her hand across her hair.

"Nahid would want you to have it," he said.

Reluctantly, she took the diary, then squeezed it against her chest as if she were hugging her mother.

"What are you asking for in return?"

"I have more diaries, more notes, some from Kieran, but mostly from her. All I ask is that you help me find the Crimson Skull. Only that. The rest is up to me."

"If we find it, I get them all?"

"Most of them. There are some—"

"All or nothing," said Aurie, her jaw pulsing with intensity. "I won't be able to take knowing there's more without being able to read them. All or nothing."

He studied her face, thoughts passing across his blue eyes like a flock of birds. Then he gave her a slow nod.

When he opened his mouth to speak, she turned her back on him and slowly peeled open the diary. The crusty bindings shifted, sending yellow-brown dust to the tile floor. In her first year, the notes she'd found in the margins of *The Artifacts of the Kings* had been dry scientific texts dealing with the minutiae of her work. As she read the first paragraph of Nahid's diary, Aurie swooned with emotion, stumbling to a bench along the far wall, collapsing against it as her eyes drank in her mother's words.

—the pride of lions that made their home near the dig site came to investigate last night. The big one with the scar on her right haunch, probably the result of a run-in with a hippo, came within fifty feet of the tents, sniffing and pawing at the dirt where we'd placed the wards. The thrill of seeing the big cat up close was something I'll never forget. I wish I could have the girls here with me, but despite the protections, it's not the safest place for children to play. I'll have to get them a lion stuffy on the way through London. Maybe two. They're both so fierce, my little Aurie and Pythia. I miss them every day. The work would be perfect if I could see them at night, hold them in my arms, smell their sweet hair—

Aurie didn't have the strength to turn the page, she was sniffling, wiping her eyes with the back of her aquamarine sleeve.

"I'm going to get my jacket filthy," she said to herself, sighing and staring the pile of papers in her lap with eager reluctance. She didn't know if she could handle reading about how much her mom had missed her. They'd had those lion plushies for years, the ears ragged from being dragged along the floor, the fur worn thin, only losing track of them between orphanages. Aurie had never had a single doubt about her mother's love, but reading the words reminded her how deep those feelings went.

Aurie skipped ahead to a different section. The pages were brittle, stained at the edges with coffee. She could almost smell the dark roast that her mother loved.

—Kieran sent me an enchantment he's been working on to protect against the curse. It's brilliantly designed, but I don't think it's going to be enough. He hasn't seen the analysis. Sam flew in two experts who said there's no way past the protections. They called it the Witch's Dilemma, and suggested that we give up on the Rod—

Her heart soared as she thought about her parents, who'd figured out a way past a no-win situation. While she and Pi had retrieved it, it wouldn't have been possible without their parents' work.

Aurie peeled away the pages, selecting an entry towards the back. She found a sheet shoved in that, judging by the lighter coloring of the paper, might have been from another diary.

August 18th, 2002

I want to tell him not to go, he's too important to me. I'm torn, really torn. It's hard to learn this, and then know that it's ending. I sho—

The cryptic words had only one meaning for Aurie, and it wasn't good. Checking the date against the other entries confirmed her thinking. Whomever her mother was talking about had not been Kieran, since he was clearly back in Philadelphia during this time.

Her gaze fell upon Sam Arlington, who was studying a bronze knife on the wall with his hands behind his back. He'd been at the dig site during that visit. He was handsome and had his own TV show. Did her mother have an affair with Sam? Or had it been someone else?

A desperate need to read the rest of the diaries, not only to reconnect with her mother, but to find out if her mother had cheated on her father, consumed her. First she'd learned that her parents had worked with Bannon Creed, and now it appeared there were infidelities in the marriage.

Her parents were turning out not to be the people she thought they were. Semyon had warned her this would happen.

Aurie marched over to Sam Arlington, cleared her throat, and when he turned, she gave him a terse demand. "I'll agree to work with you if you give me more of her diaries during the process and not just at the end."

"You already made your demand and I agreed," he said. "You can't change it."

"Mister...Sam," she said, holding her emotions in check. "Reading even those few small sections brought feelings that, well, I can't explain. Look, I know what you did when you gave me that. Reading it was like mainlining heroin. You can't really expect me not to want more? I can't wait until the end. That would be too...distracting. And you want me to be focused."

At first, Sam was tight-lipped, skeptical. But the more she talked, the softer his expression became, until he looked reticent.

"And how do you suppose that I dole out the diaries?" he asked, a frown hanging on the corner of his lips.

"At your discretion."

He raised an eyebrow. "And you won't complain about the pace? More demands after the agreement?"

"Nope. You give me that and you've got yourself an enthusiastic worker," she said.

Aurie thrust her hand towards him. It hung in midair a few seconds before his face broke into a grin and he shook with her.

"Welcome aboard," he said. "We're going to have a lot of fun. Just like your mom and I did back then."

"I'm sure you did," said Aurie, holding the diary tightly against her side, steeling herself from reacting. "I'm sure you did."

EIGHT

The security lamp inside the entrance of Freeport Games buzzed with a low intensity, barely audible above the wind. A nor'easter had come down from New England and was battering the coast, too warm for snow, but cold enough to make the rain sting.

Pi's black leather jacket kept the worst of the elements off her, but the weather wasn't why she was worried. Two years ago, they'd accused Hemistad of being the soul thief, and it'd turned out that they were wrong. The real villain had been Liam. Since then, on the rare occasions they'd had time to visit Freeport Games for a gaming session with Hannah, Hemistad had been aloof, barely acknowledging their existence, and finding reasons to be in the back while she and Aurie were in the store. Pi gathered that he was not a man—if he was a man at all—that was used to forgiving others. Time would have to heal their friendship, which was why Pi had decided to break into Freeport Games rather than talk to him directly. She wasn't willing to take no for an answer, so she didn't think it was fair to ask him. Terrible reasoning for sure, she knew, but it was how she felt.

The security itself was laughable, but Pi knew it was only a pretense to keep foolish thieves from forcing Hemistad's hand. He was the real danger.

With a collection of soul fragments at her mental fingertips, it wasn't hard to find the right spells to get inside. The cybermagic soul gave her the runes that would temporarily disable the door alarm. She wrote them in erasable marker so she could wipe them away when she left if the sleeting rain hadn't taken care of them by then. Before she went in, Pi turned off her cell phone to keep it from spoiling her stealth.

Hearing the door click behind her as she slipped inside was a subtle reminder that if she took the indigo glass ball, she would pass a line with Hemistad she probably couldn't recover from.

Seeing the darkened gaming area, tables wiped clean, board games stacked neatly on the shelves on the wall, and huge cardboard cutouts of the latest characters from the anime *Hellion Halls* reflecting the pink glow from the neon Magic the Gathering sign in back put pause in her plans. It was a reminder that despite the Hunger, and the other dangers about Hemistad, he'd created this space for kids to come and relax and game, and most importantly, be safe. Maybe she would just investigate the glass ball, figure out if it was truly a clue left behind by Invictus, and if it was, talk to Hemistad about its importance.

The lamp on the front counter seemed abnormally bright when she clicked it on. The glass case filled with trays of dice, collectable figurines, and a few rare collectible cards was protected with a secondary lock—a metal bar that slipped between the panes, keeping the sliding door from being opened without the key. The indigo glass ball in the corner of the case almost seemed like an afterthought, and looking at it brought both pangs of regret and shivers of anticipation.

After slipping faez-viewing welder goggles from her jacket, and then over her head, adjusting the strap so it didn't bind her ears, Pi reviewed the area for the presence of magic. As she expected, the indigo glass ball glowed—but only faintly. She crouched beside the case, pressing the goggles against the glass, and examined the faez signature. The amount of magic was light, no more than would be required to protect the ball from accidental breakage.

The longer she studied it, the more her heart sank. If this truly were a clue from Invictus, wouldn't it put off more faez? Or was it all that was necessary, and if she could activate it, she would discover some vital information that would lead her to his hidden realm?

Pi jimmied the lock and opened the case. She stuck her head inside to confirm that the window wasn't modifying her view. Much to her disappointment, the level of faez didn't change.

The reasons she'd broken into his store felt more foolish the longer she stared at the glass ball, followed by a rising miasma of guilt. Pi glanced down the darkened hallway, the one that led to Hemistad's apartment above the store. She thought about leaving, and coming back later and explaining everything she'd done. But she worried about the consequences of that conversation, and that she was being naive.

The one thing she'd learned above everything else about Invictus was that he loved games. That was evident from how the Hundred Halls were structured, from the trials that prospective students had to pass to enter, to the second-year games. There'd been other larger-scale activities in the history of the Hundred Halls, back when he'd been alive: mock battles across the city, magical puzzle competitions, scavenger hunts in the Undercity.

And while the games were intended to teach and reward a combination of cleverness, magical ability, and bravery, they came with considerable danger. Even though the second-year games had technically been danger free, the psychological impact of being killed repeatedly had driven some students out of the Halls.

And what better game than to try and find his realm?

These thoughts left Pi biting her lower lip as she stared at the indigo glass ball. Was it a clue? Or was it a trap? Or was it both?

"It's probably nothing," she muttered under her breath.

The indigo swirls on the glass were ordinary. From twenty inches away, the ball looked like she could break it with a good punch. But from twenty inches away it was hard to see the faez up close. Maybe she could learn something if she could hold it in her hands, press it against the goggles.

"A brief examination," she said. "I'll only look at it for a moment, then I'll put it back."

Before she reached in, Pi swept the area for alarms, magical or technological. She even checked beneath the glass case to make sure there weren't proximity sensors. Nothing.

Crouched down, prepared to slip her hand past the rows of figurines with swords and battleaxes, she noticed that the other items in the case had price stickers. Pi went around front and confirmed that the glass ball did not. It probably wasn't significant, but a tremor in her belly was trying to convince her that it was. Years ago when she worked in the store, she'd never had anyone ask about the glass ball, and as she thought about it, she'd never wondered why it was there in the first place.

This more than anything convinced her that she had to examine it, if only to satisfy her curiosity.

"As they say," she said, reaching into the case to grab the indigo glass ball, "curiosity killed the cat."

The smooth ball came away from the velvet cushion easily. It was light, sturdy. Pi stood up, prepared to examine the surface closer, but she noticed a faint line of faez trailing away from the bottom of the ball. Sparkles of energy passed down the line, heading away from the case, towards the darkened hallway at a slight angle upward to the apartments.

"Oh shit."

The roar that followed turned her insides to liquid. It had an ancient haunting quality, like the sound of men being butchered on a battlefield, or the hard earth being ground beneath massive, churning machines.

When she moved to put the ball back into the case, it glowed more fiercely. The earlier light faez had either been camouflage, or it hadn't been triggered yet. With the ball back on the cushion, she pulled away, only to find it stuck to her fingers.

A second roar, followed by a crash, which sounded like a door frame was being ripped off, reverberated through the empty store.

Realizing that she couldn't hide her thievery, Pi made her stand in the middle of the store, hoping to quiet his rage, to explain what she'd done, before he attacked. But when the ceiling-scraping shape moved out of the hallway, thundering forward like an avalanche made of shadows and claws, the idea that reason would work with Hemistad vanished like smoke, replaced with the grim realization that she would have to defend herself.

The impression Pi had, as Hemistad scattered the tables and chairs, was of a prehistoric bear with claws like knives. Except he wasn't a bear, because bears didn't exhale darkness and smell like fresh slaughter.

She tried to set aside the glass ball so she could protect herself, but it'd adhered to her fingers, interfering with the gestural procedures of the spell. Her admiration for the cunningness of the trap was no match for her horror as she realized there was nothing she could do to stop him.

Hemistad cut through Pi's wards and protections as if they were wet paper. A mottled fist of four-inch claws slammed into her gut, lifting her into the air and slamming her against the ceiling. She couldn't scream. Nothing came out but a few spittles of blood.

He threw her across the room. A shelf of board games collapsed beneath her, cushioning her fall. Her gut was a mess of mangled flesh that stunk like a sewer. If she didn't get a healing spell on it soon, she'd bleed out, or get sepsis from the piercing of her bowels.

As the beast that was Hemistad crushed a table beneath his massive paw, not realizing where he'd thrown her, a wave of energy and pain blockers rose through Pi. After last year's experience, she never went anywhere without first renewing her rejuvenating wards. The most dangerous moment was right after you'd been injured. This was when the killing was done. So she'd spelled herself so that at first wound, the spell would release, hiding the agony and giving her a dose of strength and speed.

But no enchantment would help her battle Hemistad in this form. She could see him on the vast grassy steppes of Asia hunting mammoth, or whole tribes of early men.

Pi threw down a smoke charge that quickly flooded into the room, obscuring sight to a few feet. But her goggles gave her the vision necessary to escape, and since Hemistad was blocking the front entrance, she fled towards the well that went into the Undercity.

Knowing she wouldn't have enough time to use the platform and winch, Pi pulled a feather from an inside pocket. The escape from the glass elevator last year had taught her to be prepared for heights.

She reached the well room, finding the platform raised to the ceiling. But that didn't matter, she was planning on jumping. He wouldn't be able to follow her then, unless he could survive a four-hundred-foot fall.

With her free hand, Pi shoved the feather into her mouth. The barbs tickled the back of her throat as she chomped down on the hollow shaft, snapping it in her teeth. Half the feather was shoved into her mouth when the massive shape burst out of the smoke.

Hemistad shoulder-charged her, knocking Pi backwards through the fence and into the hole that led into the Undercity. The impact caused a Heimlich maneuver, and she spat the feather from her mouth.

The pale gray light of the well room faded quickly as she fell through the hole, the wind rushing up around her, caressing her before she hit the ground.

NINE

The last message Aurie had received from her sister was days ago. She tried not to be worried, but she knew her sister and her propensity to get into trouble. On the other hand, Pi frequently went offline for days at a time while she was doing research into Invictus, mostly due to her paranoia that someone might be tracking her, and she'd leave her cell phone in a train locker while she was off the grid.

"I'm sure it's nothing," she said, though her heart said otherwise.

It wasn't like she had time to spare. Between classes, work with Sam Arlington, and studying, she barely had time to breathe. Checking her phone, she realized she was late for Professor Chopra's next class. At least this time they weren't meeting in the Eight-Fold Room, which meant that the work wasn't going to be inherently dangerous, or at least that's what she hoped.

He was standing at a polishing station in the metallurgical lab, hunched over a spinning disc that smoothed metal samples to an even finish so they could then be examined with a microscope. Aurie had used the equipment before. Imbuing metals with spells required the right substructure to hold them, and that could only be accomplished with traditional metallurgical methods.

"Aurelia," said Professor Chopra, lifting the little blue puck from the polishing station and switching the unit off. "I was testing some samples. It looks like we're ready to go."

He wore a white lab coat over a light blue button-down shirt. She hoped the lack of visible protections meant the day's activity would be less life threatening than normal.

"I have everything set up in the other room," he said.

The room beyond the polishing room had metal cabinets on every wall, granite tables, and chemistry glassware collected on shelves. A large glass cylinder the size of a paint can and set on its side took up the central table. Next to it were various rubber hoses, titration tubes, and a blue plastic bucket. *The Magical Works of Henry Galveston Lipton* tome lay on a separate table away from the work area. Seeing it put an ache into her neck. After reading *The Unauthorized Biography of Henry Lipton* she was skeptical about the potential success of the project.

"Today's task is to reduce iron ore to its proper state, then refine it."

"If we're looking for quality iron or steel, we can order it off the internet."

Chopra's face reddened with heat. "I'm well aware, but this metal must be specially prepared. *Henry*"—he said the inventor's name as if they were old friends—"has specific instructions for construction of the rings. After we reduce the ore, we have to add gold dust and a few other precious metals before sintering it with the proper transmutation spell."

"Gold dust," said Aurie, letting the words trail off her lips. Lipton's unauthorized autobiography had detailed the many scams that he'd pulled off in his time. The addition of gold dust seemed like a good way to enrich ones pockets in that time. But on the other hand, not counting the near-death experience with the pregnant Illiopian Death Cloud, the steps to make the trinket had been successful.

After donning leather aprons and safety goggles, they loaded the ore into the glass cylinder and heated it up with Bunsen burners. A clear rubber tube pulled the waste materials from the cylinder, which included hydrogen sulfur, a noxious yellow paste that stunk like rotten eggs. Two hours later, they broke the raw iron out of the cylinder and placed it in a ceramic bowl.

The next stage involved a lot of measuring and weighing of the gold, silver, titanium, a copper-beryllium alloy, a bunch of magnesium, and a few other trace elements. They had to get the mixture exactly right for the enchantments to be effective, or at least that's what the professor told her. But Aurie had her doubts about Henry Lipton and his Hearthring.

Once the final mixture was ready, Professor Chopra instructed Aurie on the proper spells, opening the tome to the correct pages. While she was practicing the gestures, he received a call, his face lighting up the moment he heard the voice.

"Yes, yes, this is Alain Chopra. So good of you to call me back. Uhm, yes, but excuse me for a moment." With his hand over the bottom of the phone, he said, "I have to step out and take this. Practice as you must, but wait for me before you cast the spell, and whatever you do, do not turn to any other pages. Actually, do not touch the book at all."

"Why not?" she asked.

He grew cross. "Just do as I say. I don't have time for explanations." He elbowed his way through the door and disappeared down the hallway.

The moment he was gone, Aurie eyed the tome, checking to make sure he hadn't returned yet.

"Why doesn't he want me to read ahead?" She marched over to the book, hooked a fingernail under the right-hand page, and went to flip it over, only to receive a painful shock.

"Ow, fuck," she said, sucking on her fingers. After checking through the little window on the door, Aurie examined the tome again. She'd never heard of a book that shocked people, unless it was an abjuration spell that Chopra had put on it to ward away her curiosity.

"Don't want me getting into you, eh?" she asked, cracking her knuckles.

The second attempt ended as soon as her fingertips neared the slope of pages. A shock jumped across the distance, making an audible pop as it stabbed her fingers. Aurie cradled her hand against her chest.

Aurie donned a thick leather glove and carefully touched the book at the center of the page. The shock hit her a good six inches above the tome, going right through the leather glove and knocking her arm back.

She flipped off the book while thinking about a way around the ward. If she had Pi's faez-seeing goggles, she could decipher the enchantment and counter it appropriately. But she didn't. And she wanted to know what was in the tome that was so important to hide.

Searching through the cabinets, she found what she needed beneath the sink. She clipped a long piece of wire from a copper reel on the workbench in back, wrapped it around the ground wire that was connected to the pipes, and then dropped the other end onto the tome.

When the lights flickered Aurie knew that either she'd dissipated the stored energy or added more to the ward. It would not end well if it was the latter. Aurie slapped her hand on the right page before she could lose her nerve, relaxing when it didn't blow her across the room.

With the trap spent, she flipped through the pages to find the spell. After she saw the runes placed carefully at the four corners of each page, she realized the shocks were not Chopra's doing, but Henry Lipton's, which, at the very least, reduced her anxiety about the motives of her professor.

The pages leading up to the spell read more like a diary than an instruction manual. She saw words like deepness and sacrifice, and wanted to read more, but she didn't have time if she wanted to learn the spell, so she turned the page to the correct section. Aurie skimmed the spell to better understand the task. When her gaze fell upon the passage explaining how the spell should interact with the ore mixture, she slapped her forehead.

"If I do that it'll turn into a bomb!"

Magnesium was highly flammable, and would have a thermal reaction when she laid the faez on it. She might have thought Professor Chopra was trying to kill her except it would injure him as well.

She was about to examine the next section, when she heard the polishing room door close. He was headed back. Aurie riffled the pages, looking for the spot the tome was supposed to be opened to, finding it right as the door clicked open. She kicked the copper wire across the floor before he saw it.

"Sorry about that," he said warmly. "Are we ready for the next step?"

"I...I was wondering if we shouldn't confirm the procedure once again. I'm still a little gun-shy after the Illiopian Death Cloud problem," she said.

"Terrible. Terrible, it was, but I learned my lesson and have triple-checked the text for errors. No need for a fourth," he said.

"But a second set of eyes..."

His amiable demeanor turned sour. "I told you it was fine. Please start the procedure. Remember, at the end of the year, it is my word that passes you, no other."

"But I—"

"You have to trust me."

She felt like she was going to throw up. She looked back to the tome and thought about telling him what she'd done, but decided that wouldn't turn out well. Maybe if she faked an injury, tripped over her own feet and smashed her head into the desk, that would get her out of it?

Professor Chopra crossed his arms. "I'm waiting. And know that I will be checking you for the proper gestures. I will not tolerate sloppiness."

Except in your own work, she wanted to say back. But then she thought of a solution, but it would only work if he couldn't see that she'd modified the spell, which would be tricky in the small lab.

Aurie started the spell. The professor moved to the side to watch her gestures, mumbling encouragement as she formed them precisely. As Aurie modified the spell, she stepped to the side, blocking his view with her back, then as he tried to move to observe, she went right back to her previous position.

As the faez poured out of her and into the ore mixture, it sizzled but did not explode. He clapped his hands.

"Well done, though I'll have to take points off for that little do-si-do in the middle. Why did you do that? It seemed entirely unnecessary."

Aurie rubbed the back of her neck. "My underwear was cramping my style?"

He held his hands up. "I see. No need to explain further."

The rest of the afternoon went as expected. When they were finished, she had made a ring of iron-alloy thick enough to wrap her hand around, and wide enough to put her fist through, but not her head. But despite the success, the only thing she could think about was how the tome had been wrong, and that another section might be even more dangerous. It appeared that Henry Galveston Lipton hadn't been a fraud, knowingly, but hadn't been a genius artificer either. If she couldn't get ahold of the book before their next meeting, she was in grave danger.

TEN

The shadows from the headlamp played across the rough stone, the edges refracting until they faded to midnight blue. There were other colors reflected across the glistening stone—from chips of granite, faint purplish moss that glowed in complete darkness, and the tiny red eyes of an insect before it scurried into a hole—but the man-child loved blue best.

Ernie had never been in the Undercity before, had always been told to avoid it—stay away, it's too dangerous—but when the voice had echoed in his head, he'd had no choice. In some ways, he hated the voice, hated that his opa, the man who had once cared for him, had used him like a vessel.

The using wasn't done either. Ernie could no more refuse the summons than not breathe, or defy gravity. He felt like an automaton, a robot of flesh and fears, bereft of his free will. This was worse than when he was Echo, when moments were lost to the pattern, annihilated by the wings of a butterfly, because he was aware of his every move, his every step. His only act of defiance was not to run, not to rush forward headlong, to whatever destination the compulsion was sending him. It wasn't much, but it was something.

When claws scuffed the rock beyond his vision, he felt his insides twist and squeeze. Would the compulsion let him defend himself? Even if it did, could he do it?

He summoned flame in his right hand, a three-inch Calcifer with eyes and little orangish-red arms, and held it high like a lantern. The flame was real enough, would burn him if he ran his hand over it, but he couldn't throw it, or use it against anyone. Ernie hoped the demonstration of magic would be enough to dissuade whatever was stalking him.

"Hello?" he asked, hearing the childishness in his own voice, then trying again, hoping it sounded meaner. "Hello?"

It was worse the second time. Even though he wasn't Echo anymore, they treated him like he was at New Horizons.

"I'm not Echo!" he told the thing that was lurking out of sight.

While he stared into the darkness, his headlamp wavering and the flame in his hand casting shadows across the stalactites, the scrape of claws retreated. Pride welled in his chest at making his voice angry enough to scare away a predator.

"Thanks, Calcifer," he told the flame, then he made it disappear. He couldn't make it talk to him, not that he thought it was real, but he wanted it to be like a ventriloquism puppet. The younger residents loved it when he summoned the flame, but he was always careful to keep his distance in case they tried to touch it. He wasn't supposed to use magic at New Horizons.

Along the way, he found a yellowish-gray moss that rippled when he put his hand near, so he scraped a sample using the runed blade he'd won in the second-year contest. The whole time he was removing it from the rock, the urge to run pushed him in the back and tugged him forward, but he ignored it. He placed the moss in a plastic bag, gently folded it into a bright pink fanny pack wrapped around his midsection, and then let the compulsion pull him forward like a trolley train.

Ernie's lower lip trembled whenever he thought about what was waiting for him ahead. He worried that the patron, The Woman Who Was Everyone, that he'd met that fateful day when he stopped being Echo had figured out a way to bring the wish back. This made him drag his feet wherever he could. At least until he tripped and slammed his knee on the stone floor. Then he gave up trying to hold back.

He knew he shouldn't be worried. The compulsion wasn't the same as when he had the wish in him, but it was similar enough that it worried him. Why Invictus had done this to him, he would never know. It still hurt that he'd been tricked into accepting the wish, and it appeared that hadn't been the only thing he'd been misled about.

When he saw a faint light in the distance, Ernie almost raised his voice and called out, but then remembered the thing that had stalked him earlier. It was better if he was small and quiet. *Then* he remembered his headlamp, which made him so visible anyone in this vast cavern would be able to see him from the other side. He fingered the switch before deciding to leave it on.

As he neared he realized the light was purple, almost like a backlight, and it was lying in a pale cradle. It wasn't until he was almost upon the light that he realized it was a person holding a sphere.

When the headlamp revealed the face of the fallen, he cried out, "Pythia," only to cringe at the echo.

He threw himself down, ignoring the crack of his knees against the stone, and put his cheek down to her lips to feel if she was breathing. He felt nothing.

She looked so pure, so preserved, like a body in a coffin. Except her eyes were blackened. Dried blood hung from her lip like a barnacle. When he touched the front of her black shirt, dust crumbled away, covering his fingertips like rust.

"How did you get here?" he asked, glancing around.

To better examine her, he tried to remove the indigo ball, only to find it stuck to her hands.

Ernie put his fingers against her neck. That's what they did on the TV shows, right? He didn't feel anything there either. So he moved his fingers around. Nothing.

"Pythia," he whispered.

Is this why he was compelled? He paled at the realization that he was going to have to tell Ms. Aurelia what happened. That he hadn't gotten here fast enough. He cursed himself for delaying. He wouldn't have if he would have known. Why couldn't he save Pythia, just like he had her sister?

Tears formed in his eyes and ran down his cheeks. He wiped them off with a flat hand.

"I came too late, didn't I? I didn't know I was supposed to hurry. I'm sorry, Pythia. I'm so sorry."

ELEVEN

The letter was addressed from New York, but with no name. Aurie turned it over a few times before slipping her glossy, chipped fingernail under the leading edge and prying it open. It'd been a long time since she'd received a real letter. Everyone sent email these days.

She hoped it was from Pi, even though she knew that it was unlikely. Pi barely wrote on paper when she was forced to in school, let alone as an act of communication. Even the investigation into Invictus' life was done with pictures, or notes in her phone. The piles of books surrounding her in the apartment had been memorized by her sister to an annoying level of detail.

Aurie glanced to the end of the letter to see who it was from. Hemistad. Her mouth went dry. She crinkled the paper as she squeezed it tight. It only got worse as she read what he'd written:

Aurelia,

I have no words for what I'm about to tell you, but I feel it is my duty. Know above all that I did not want to do it, but Invictus spelled me unknowingly, thus I was at the mercy of his cruel intentions.

Your sister found something in the shop. Maybe you know what it was. I fear to say exactly. He must have tied this item to my curse, and when Pythia picked the item up...I'm sorry, I know this is difficult to read, but I knocked her into the hole that leads to the Undercity. Once the item was out of my shop, I was in control of myself again, but by then it was too late. In grief and horror, I fled by another way. I'm sorry, but I'm certain that your sister is dead by my hand.

— Hemistad

Hand to her mouth, Aurie stumbled to her knees. The world seesawed around her, a contradiction of agony and shock. She read the letter again, hoping against hope that she'd read it wrong.

She punched a nearby pile of books. They crashed over the coffee table, bouncing off the couch. She picked up a book and threw it at the wall, breaking its binding.

Her mouth opened as she tried to scream, "Fuck!" but nothing came out. Air had been rendered to dust.

Numbly, she stood, surrounded by the efforts of her sister. Her *only* sister. The only member of her family she had left.

Aurie's world closed around her, the edges fraying until they were blackened, like the crisp ends of burnt paper. Her heart, her chest, constricted in a last-second attempt to keep her sister's death from being a reality.

She wished it was a trick or a lie, propagated by a member of the Cabal or a Hemistad turned against them, but her mastery of verumancy and mendancy told her every word had been written in absolute truth. She could see the shaky penmanship, the blotch of a teardrop at the corner of the paper, the looping scrawl of the H that began his name. These couldn't be faked, they couldn't be a trick, which meant that only one thing was true.

Pi was dead.

It didn't matter that it was hubris. It didn't matter that the bastard Invictus had left Hemistad as a trap. Nothing mattered, not even the Hundred Halls, because what was the point if she was alone?

When the door opened, she was prepared to tell the intruder to "kindly get the fuck out," but when she saw who it was, she couldn't help but stare.

"Pi?"

Looking like she'd been beaten with a bag of bricks, Pi stumbled into the room, closed the door behind her, and leaned against the wall. She held a trash bag that contained something spherical. Her gaze fell upon the letter in Aurie's hand.

"Fuck me, I didn't get here in time, did I?"

"No," said Aurie, voice cracking. "You idiot. You went and broke into Hemistad's place anyway."

"Is that letter from him? Is he pissed?"

Aurie wiped the tears from her cheeks. "No. He's broken up about what he did to you."

Pi looked away. "I'm sorry. I only went to investigate. It got bad real quick. It was probably a good thing I went in like I did, because I was fully prepared. Had we gone in and had a chat with him, he might have killed us both."

Aurie shook the letter at her. "What happened? He said he knocked you into the Undercity."

"It's a long way down," said Pi, letting the trash bag slip out of her fingers and thunk on the floor. "I swallowed a partial slow-fall spell. Not the whole thing, mind you, but enough to keep me from reaching terminal acceleration. The impact? I'd prepared a trinket for a moment like that. Expensive thing, mostly drained my bank account, but it worked. Converted the impact, well, most of it." She pointed at her blackened eyes.

"Where have you been?" asked Aurie.

"It saved me from the fall, but put me in a protective shell. You won't believe this, well, maybe you will, but Ernie found me. That fucker Invictus put more than the wish in him. He also put the second clue in Ernie."

Aurie's eyes flitted to the trash bag. "So it *is* a way into Invictus' realm?"

Her sister nodded soberly. "Yep."

"Where's Ernie? Why didn't he come back with you?" she asked.

"He left afterwards. I gave him quite a scare when I popped up. He'd thought I was dead. The trinket held me in that stasis until someone came along."

"I wish I could kick Invictus in the nuts for what he's done to that poor kid," said Aurie.

"Me too. Deserves every bit of it."

Aurie saw the dried blood. "Are you still hurt?"

"Not terribly. Not anymore anyway. Hemistad put, like, four-foot claws into my gut, stuck me against the ceiling like a piñata."

"Four foot?"

Pi shook her head. "Exaggeration. Felt like four feet when they went into me."

"What...what is he?"

Pi shivered, then shook it off. Her gaze was etched with shadows. It looked like reliving that moment was painful by the whiteness of her pressed lips.

"I don't know. Something feral, primal. Whatever he was, is, he's tasted blood, lots of it. I can't imagine standing against him, not even with you and the original five patrons at my side."

Without another word, Aurie pulled Pi into her arms, careful not to squeeze too hard, crumpling the letter against her back. She held her younger sister for a long time before pulling away and knocking a strand of hair from her face.

"Dooset daram. You've got to start trusting me, sis."

Wide-eyed, Pi nodded. "You don't have to remind me after that. Whatever game Invictus set up, he's playing for keeps. But I guess I should have expected that. This is for the whole shebang. For control of the Hundred Halls."

Excitement bubbled up in Aurie's chest, making her a little delirious after thinking she'd lost her sister. "Holy balls, Pi. You were right about the clue, which means we're on the path to finding a way into Invictus' realm. And nobody else knows about it. Think about it, the patrons have been trying to trick their way into it for decades, but now we've got the jump on them!"

Pi gave her a feverish smile. "I guess we do."

Buoyed by the idea, Aurie danced around her sister. "And not only that, but you've got the second clue."

"I've got more than the second clue," Pi said cryptically. "I think I know what it is and how to find it."

"What's the clue?"

Before speaking, her sister pulled a miniature phonograph from her leather jacket. The tiny speaker looked like a cornucopia. Pi set it on a nearby stack of books and breathed faez into it.

"There, that should keep anyone from hearing us. I know no one knows, but I'd like to keep it that way," said Pi. "The second clue is..." She cleared her throat and leaned her head back, clearly repeating it from memory.

"When through the looking glass you see
Backwards amid the Giants you'll be
To follow the rainbow and pay the fee
Two makes one and that is key.
Then four more and you'll see

Only through their unity."

Aurie raised an eyebrow. "That shit makes sense to you?"

"The rainbow is the glass balls. I've got the Indigo, and I need one more. That's what the quarterarch means. You have to find two of them. Two makes one and that is the key. That's the fee, the price for getting into his realm."

"But what about the Giants and the looking glass?" asked Aurie. "Or the parts after that."

Pi sighed and scratched the side of her head, where the hair was growing back in. "That's what I'm less sure about. I don't know what the Giants are, but I can guess that the looking glass is some sort of scrying device. Maybe a crystal ball, or a divining stick."

"Seems sort of vague. What's the next step?"

"I'm going to talk to Radoslav. He trades in stuff like that, so he might know where to find one. Plus, I haven't checked in with him in a while, and I'm sure he's not happy with me. He does sort of own me right now."

"Yet you signed up for more time," said Aurie. "He makes the mob look like a bunch of pansies."

"He's not as bad as you think," said Pi.

"I know, you've told me, but I don't trust him. Not that it matters, since you're the one going to see him."

"So you approve of me going to see him?" asked Pi.

"As dangerous as he is, it's nothing compared to waiting around and letting the Cabal figure out how to get into Invictus' realm before we do. You go talk to Radoslav, I've got some things I need to do now anyway, namely a little trip down south."

"You do?"

"Yeah, I found some information on the Crimson Skull for Sam. We think it indicates a place in Peru, not far from Lima. We're going to head down there and check it out."

"Wow," said Pi, "I can't believe you're actually working with him."

"He's not as bad as you think," said Aurie, laughing when Pi raised an eyebrow.

"Sounds familiar."

Before Pi left for the showers, Aurie thought about telling her sister about her suspicion that their mom had an affair with Sam, but decided against it until she had proof. She figured Pi would take it better than she had, but didn't want to burden her while she had more important things on her mind.

TWELVE

A trumpet cried a haunting melody on the speakers at the Glass Cabaret. The place was pretty empty. Pi went in through the front door and chatted with Dagon the bouncer about his latest girlfriend troubles for a few minutes before seeking out Radoslav. For being a thick neck, he was a rather sweet guy, though she'd seen him break a guy's arm when he wouldn't leave the club, so she knew he could turn mean.

Nellie was behind the bar, polishing a highball with a rag. She wore the traditional white shirt and black tie combo with her dirty blonde hair up in a high ponytail. She was as straightforward and efficient as a mechanical pencil, which was why she'd lasted as Radoslav's assistant for so long. Pi noted that the rag was actually wet, and that she was actually cleaning the glass, which meant that her boss was going to be out for an extended period. Nellie, along with everyone else that worked the bar, had not a spark of faez in her.

When Nellie's gaze reached Pi, the corner of her left eye twitched a little, but she turned to hide the loss of control.

"Hey Nells," said Pi, leaning against the bar, "do you know when he's gonna be back?"

Nellie pursed her cobalt blue lips, which made Pi almost ask if she'd ever been confused for a robot, before making the barest minimum of a shoulder shrug. "He didn't say."

"You're the keeper of the calendar, could you check? I wouldn't ask if it wasn't important," said Pi.

"If it'd been in there, I would have told you," said Nellie.

"Gotcha, sorry. I know you're busy and all, I just thought, you know, since we both worked for him, that you'd help me out," said Pi.

She thought about lying and telling Nellie that Radoslav wanted her to know, but decided against that because he'd be pissed if he found out, and despite her rigid exterior, Pi actually liked Nellie.

Nellie glanced around the nearly empty room, then gave the tiniest of exasperated sighs, and a quivering of an eyelash, before saying, "I'll check the computer."

Pi wasn't about to lie, but she wasn't about to trust Nellie either, so she threw a little metallic burr that stuck onto the back of her shirt as she went into the back room. Pi brought out her cell phone and tapped on a little program she'd written. After a few keystrokes, the front of her phone showed the calendar that was on Nellie's computer. Her boss hadn't left a record of where he was going.

"Sorry, Pi," Nellie said when she came back in. "He's out. I don't know when he'll be back." She paused. "Which usually means a couple of weeks, or more."

"Damn. Thanks for checking," she said.

On the way out, with her fists shoved into the pockets of her leather jacket, she told Dagon, "Good luck with your lady friend."

"You okay?" he asked, arching his eyebrow.

"I need to talk to Rads, but he's not around. Sounds like he went somewhere far away."

"Nah. He's in the city," said Dagon.

"Really?"

"If he leaves, he has me feed his cat. He hasn't asked," said Dagon.

"Any idea where he went?"

He shook his head. "Not a clue."

Not wanting to give up so easily, she went and checked on his warehouses in the thirteenth district. She'd learned he had a few near where she'd summoned Pazuzu, so many years ago. It didn't even feel like it had happened anymore.

From Allanon Avenue, she spied her warehouse, with its broken windows and graffiti-laden walls. Partial sunlight reflected against the few panes of glass remaining. The towering oak that had snapped during a storm stood sentinel over the rear of the place. Pi could only see the top of it from the street, but the rest of it was a vivid memory to her.

Further down the cracked pavement, Pi reached Radoslav's warehouse cluster. A line of six black SUVs with the kind of heavily tinted windows that said *don't fuck with me* sat out front. Pi crept along the sidewalk, craning her neck in all directions. Vehicles like that usually came with soldiers in runed armor and mage-killing bullets.

In her gut, she knew Radoslav wasn't going to like her skulking around his business, but she'd come all the way out to the thirteenth ward, and she wanted to make sure that he was there before she wasted her time waiting.

When she heard the whine of an electric charge, Pi tensed and immediately put her hands up. A little red dot formed on the right breast of her leather jacket.

A man with a shaved head and bushy beard stepped out of the shadows, runes glimmering into existence as the enchantment faded. He was ten feet away with a pistol trained on her. He spoke in Russian into a radio on his shoulder.

"Fuck," she muttered under her breath, anticipating the inevitable disappointment from Radoslav.

"Don't move," said the man in a thick Russian accent.

"I wasn't planning on it."

"Are you spy?" asked the man.

"No," she said. "I work for Radoslav. I came to see him. I...I didn't know he had a meeting." She pointed one finger back the way she'd come, careful not to make it look like spell casting. "No harm done. I can come back later."

The soldier shook his head. "Harm. Done." He motioned the barrel of his pistol towards the warehouse. "Come, we see about this. Spy."

He pushed her forward, making her stumble.

"Not necessary, I'm happy to come along," she said.

"Happy," he said derisively. "No spells, or dead wizard."

"I gathered that," she said, mostly to herself.

The warehouse, which had looked pretty beat up on the outside, was the complete opposite on the inside, indicating it was being obfuscated. The hallway had been freshly painted. There were frosted windows on the doors, and Pi heard the riffling of paper on the other side. She'd screwed up more than she'd initially thought. She'd always known that Radoslav dealt in acquiring and trading items of interest, but she hadn't realized his operation was this large.

The inside of the warehouse was full of neat rows of metal shelves with crates labeled with scanning codes and eight-digit numbers. Pi wasn't sure why she was surprised that it looked like a government warehouse, considering the orderliness of the Glass Cabaret, but she'd thought his peculiarity was a function of his personality, not a pathos that extended to a larger operation. She liked thinking he was merely a misunderstood trader, who sometimes specialized in dangerous items, rather than the head of a criminal organization.

Radoslav stood over an open crate that glowed faintly, surrounded by a dozen men with shoulder-holstered automatics. He looked as he always did, thin, milky-pale, edges cut with a razor, like staring into the night sky above a city, knowing infinite stars were there but not being able to see them.

He was talking to a gentleman whose blond frosted hair and untucked island shirt made him look as if he'd recently arrived from the Caribbean. His very presence seemed the antithesis of Radoslav's existence, yet her boss had a faint grin of amusement on his lips as he stared into the crate.

The contents, which Pi could not see, had a transcendent effect on Radoslav. Always, he carried with him the sins of his past, a weight held like armor and a curse at the same time, but for this moment, he was different, almost youthful, without scars or regrets.

This air of gaiety shattered the moment he laid his eyes upon her. Soul-crushing disappointment followed, and as Radoslav turned his attention towards her, she had to fight the urge to throw herself on his mercy, begging at the hem of his crisp black designer pants.

"Who da fuck is this, Raddy?" asked the guy in the island shirt, dispelling the notion that he wasn't as Russian as the guards with his even thicker accent. "You know her, don't you?"

"I'm sorry," she said. "I didn't know you had business. I was only coming to see you."

Without taking his eyes off her, he closed the crate with a resounding thud. Knowing what she did about him, that he'd been created to enact genocide on his people, a fate that he'd mostly avoided by coming to her world, had given her an appreciation for Radoslav. That made it harder to withstand the thin line of disappointment squeezed from his lips.

Before the guy in the island shirt could take one step forward, Radoslav said, "Ivan, no."

Ivan ignored Radoslav, moved near her, close enough she could smell his cologne, and gave her a once-over that evoked shivers. "Nyet? I say nothing."

"I know you. The answer is no."

Suddenly, the congenial atmosphere turned dark. While Pi appreciated her boss' protectiveness, she didn't think the pair of them could survive against a dozen men with mage-killing bullets. Pi was certain the guy with a pistol against her ribs could do the job alone.

"I only want to know her name," said Ivan.

Radoslav gave her a nod.

"Pythia."

"PI-THEE-A," he said, exaggerating each syllable. His smile reached everywhere on his face except his eyes. "Pythia. You are mage, Pythia?"

"Yes."

"A good one?"

"No," she said.

"Ha," said Ivan. "You would not work for Raddy if you weren't the best. Or did you lose a bet with him? Maybe this is trade? Yes? You could do much better than him. I could use someone of your talents. Yes?"

Without breaking eye contact with him, she said, "No."

He reached out and touched the dark blue highlights in her hair, brushed the shoulder of her jacket. "I did not fucking ask you." He turned to Radoslav. "I want her in the deal."

He gave the crate a pained look. Shook his head softly. "No."

The answer was like dropping a glass in a quiet room. The earlier cooperation broken by one word. Pi tensed, trying to find escape routes without looking like she was.

"Maybe we take her."

Like a black crystal growing into existence through a boiling mist, a massive two-handed obsidian sword covered in green runes slowly appeared in Radoslav's hand. The runes seemed to drip with pulsating jade light, hungry and unrelenting. Every eye in the warehouse was on the blade. The taste of acrid fear rose up in her throat.

"Then deal is off," said Ivan without so much as a glance.

Pi had no idea what was in the crate, but there had been joy on Radoslav's face when he was looking at it. The expression had seemed almost alien. She knew there was a greater than zero chance that she was projecting her emotions onto him, but the fact that she'd ruined his deal made her cold with distress.

"I will work for you," said Pi.

Ivan's face lit with victory. Radoslav glared back with betrayal.

"One day, only," she said. "You can use my talents as a *mage*."

When Ivan's lip curled with disappointment, she added, "It's the best you're going to get."

She sensed he was about to take his men and the crate with him, so she concentrated on her vocal cords, thrumming them with faez-vibrations as she said, "Take off your clothes."

Without a moment's hesitation, Ivan reached up and started unbuttoning his island shirt. She'd only directed the use of the Voice at Ivan, but the two guards behind him started tugging off their shirts.

It wasn't until his tanned, hairy chest was exposed that Ivan realized what was happening. The longer he tried to resist the compulsion, the wider his eyes got. Radoslav watched with lazy anticipation.

As Ivan unbuttoned his pants and started to pull them down, Pi husked out a breath that released the spell on them. When she'd used the Voice, it was like chains had been attached to her vocal cords, linking them to the men, and the relief at releasing them was palpable. Except the aftereffects made her feel like she'd been punched in the neck. She swallowed and stared back at Ivan as he stood silently in contemplation, pants loosely undone.

"One day," he said finally. "My choosing. You come when I call, and you perform without hesitation."

"One day," said Pi.

"Come, friends," said Ivan to his men as he buttoned his pants, leaving his shirt open. "It is time to leave. A deal is a deal."

As the men left, the press of a gun removed itself from her spine, letting Pi breathe again.

"Until we meet again," said Ivan as he strolled past as if he were merely walking down a boardwalk avenue.

When only she and Radoslav remained, he said, "You shouldn't have done that."

"I screwed up your deal," she said. "I had to fix it."

"Not with Ivan," he said, then noticed the blade in his hand. He shook his fist and the weapon disappeared into smoke. "It took me a long time to set up this deal in a way that would not endanger my lifestyle. One day will be a lifetime."

The news that being entangled with Ivan had worried Radoslav was not good.

"What if I don't do what he asks?"

She wasn't entirely sure if Radoslav had shaken his head, or if his eyes had indicated that it would be unwise, but his whole demeanor flashed a big black *NO* at her.

"He would kill everyone you know, everyone you cared about. He doesn't care about collateral damage."

Pi had a moment of insight about her boss. He'd wiped out a whole wing of the maetrie society, and could put fear into a queen, so he was not personally in danger from a gangster like Ivan, but if he went to war, then Nellie, Dagon, and his other employees would be brutally murdered.

"Well, I had to see you. It's important."

Radoslav studied her, his black eyes the veils of night. "Your talents grow with each year."

"What doesn't kill you, makes you stronger."

"Or leaves you a cripple," he replied. "Or indebted."

"True."

His gaze softened slightly, if granite could soften. "Speak your mind."

"I'm looking for something, but I can't tell you why, or what it's for. I don't really know exactly what it is either, but you acquire things, so...I need to find a *looking glass.* I assume it's a scrying device of some kind. Something like a crystal ball."

"That's a rather large net," he said, and though he was answering her, his focus was on the wooden crate. That it was the size of a desk suggested that the contents could be almost anything.

"It's in the city, and it's probably protected somehow—no, definitely protected. I'm guessing that it's hiding in plain sight," said Pi.

The last bit caught Radoslav's interest, and he turned his head slightly, eyes narrowing.

"Give me a few days and I should be able to provide a list, suggestions on where to look," said Radoslav, fingertips caressing the crate. "But that's all I can do. I'm leaving for a while on business. I'm afraid I will be unreachable for some time. Will that be acceptable?"

"Yes," said Pi, heart pounding against her chest with anticipation. "That would be awesome. What do I owe you?"

"Nothing."

Pi had been prepared for any request, like more years of service, or a specific task, but not that. She knew that he hated being out of balance with his debts. That all deals had to be for something in trade. Altruism was a foreign concept to him.

"Thank you?"

He nodded, a clear indication that it was time for her to leave. She would never accuse Radoslav of impatience, but this was on the road to it.

Before she left the warehouse, he called out, "I'm leaving you in charge of the Glass Cabaret. Stop by from time to time, and make sure everyone is doing okay. I will, of course, let them know about this arrangement before I leave."

The news that she would be in charge gave her pause. Was this the cost? Or was this a benefit? Either way, it was another thing she had to worry about. She nodded her acceptance, and her last image of him as she stepped through the door was of him leaning against the wooden crate, milky-white fingers splayed and bent, a hunger invading him that left her cold. Pi hoped whatever she'd given up for information was worth what she had wrought.

THIRTEEN

The herd of tourists in their day glow rain jackets and day packs marched down the asphalt road towards the rows of buses. They were smiling, anticipation for visiting the Inca ruins, Machu Picchu, making them talk too loud. It'd been over a day's journey to reach the eastern part of Peru, so Aurie did not share their joy.

Sam had taught her a spell to ward against the altitude sickness, but she hadn't been ready for the scale of the mountains themselves. The eastern coast of the United States had not prepared her for the jagged rocks jutting into the sky, and a horizon that seemed both everywhere at once, and so distant that it was unfathomable.

"Beautiful, isn't it?" said Sam, whose clothes and gear fit him like a second skin. He looked to be in his natural habitat, surrounded by rocks and trees.

She breathed out a *yes*, but it felt insignificant against the backdrop of their surroundings. Sam jogged down the slope to an old Toyota truck the color of old rust, and hopped into the back. Aurie joined him, and before she could get completely situated, Sam tapped on the roof and the driver took off.

During their two-hour drive into the mountains, Sam extolled her to drink water constantly.

"When you're on expedition, you can't rely on magic for everything. Get used to building up your muscles, learning the old ways of archeology," he said. "You don't want to be in the middle of nowhere when your spells fail you, and they will. Invictus is a natural home for magic—I've always thought it works better there, where we understand it. But out in the wild, things happen. You can't expect to fireball your way out of a mess."

Aurie mostly kept her mouth shut. Though the spell had kept her from getting nauseous, she felt exhausted by the higher altitude, and the stark differences between the Peruvian countryside and her city took getting used to. Back in Invictus, it was almost Halloween, and the Weird Circus would be on street corners, practicing their bone-shaping magic. It was also the time that foolish students would often attempt summonings, only to have the demon escape its bonds, kill the student, and rampage through the city until it was banished or killed. It was chaos, but chaos she understood.

The truck left them on the side of a mountain, where they headed up a dirt road. Her backside hurt from the bouncing across gravel roads, and before long, her shoulders ached from the backpack.

Dizzy and sore, Aurie regretted her decision to come on the expedition. *What am I doing out here*? she asked herself. But as difficult as it was, she refused to give up. Maybe it was pride, maybe it was remembering that this was what her mother had experienced, but she pushed through it.

After an hour, a military Jeep loaded with soldiers came flying down the road after them. Sam took one look at them, a frown tugging on his lips, and said, "Let me talk to them."

As the Jeep skidded to a stop, sending up a plume of dust, Sam walked towards them with his hands in a neutral position, speaking to them in

Spanish. Aurie had ingested a couple of books on the language before the trip, but having the knowledge and understanding were two different things. Still, she could tell that they weren't supposed to be on this road, and the soldier in charge was letting Sam know that.

From a distance, it sounded like an argument. The soldiers in back were fingering their guns. Aurie kept her hands on her hips and a spell on her tongue in case things went bad.

Halfway through the discussion, the tone changed, and suddenly the soldiers were laughing. Aurie hadn't seen Sam cast a spell. However, within minutes, they were shaking hands, and the Jeep turned around. The soldiers gave her a wave as they drove off in a cloud of dust.

"How did you do that?" she asked.

"How did I do what?"

She wrinkled her nose. "You charmed them. A spell. I'm sure of it. But I never saw anything."

He had a grin the size of a mountain. "I told you, you can't rely on magic for everything. We chatted and I explained that we were on an expedition. Mostly I empathized with them about the poor pay and long hours they have to work."

It sounded like the truth, even though Aurie didn't want to believe him.

They stopped for lunch after that, refilling water in a mountain stream. Sam repacked her gear, showing her how to organize her things, like putting her sleeping bag on the bottom so it padded her lower back.

By evening, she had blisters on her right foot and could only mumble a tepid response whenever he asked her a question. The whole purpose of the trip, to follow up on a lead about the Crimson Skull, seemed ancillary to the pains in her feet. In her twenty-four years, she couldn't remember ever hiking anywhere, not even once, and especially not in the mountains.

Sam, on the other hand, looked twenty years younger. He had a spring in his step and a song on his lips. He was TV handsome back in Invictus, but he had an honest glow to him in the jungle mountains.

Had he been closer to her age, she could see falling for him. But knowing that her mother might have had an affair with him made the whole idea rather squicky, leaving her with a simple appreciation of his good looks.

That evening, while they were sitting around the fire, he offered to show her how to make a grass rope.

"And why would I need to know how to do that?" she asked.

"You never know," he said. "Your magic could fail you at the worst possible time."

"My magic has never failed me."

He raised an eyebrow at her.

"I get your point," she said. "But I'm exhausted."

"Your mother showed me how to make a grass rope on one of our first expeditions together. I thought it might be something you'd like to learn," he said, giving her a strange look.

The mention of her mother brought a tug of guilt to her midsection.

"I would like to learn," she said, "assuming I get to stay off my feet."

His face broke into a grin. "Once we pick the grass."

They didn't make a long rope, but Aurie worked at it enough to understand the principle. When she was finished, she kept a section of it hanging from her belt, in memory of her mother.

The next morning they ate trail bars and some edible flowers that Sam had picked. Her feet were a mess, so Sam put a preservation spell on them that would help the blisters heal quicker. But that didn't save her muscles from their aches. By lunchtime, her feet felt like they were made of tree roots.

"How are you doing?" he asked as they munched on dried fruit.

Aurie stared at the sticky bar in her fingers, trying to convince herself she needed to eat it. "I feel thin. Like I'm a ghost trapped in eternal agony."

He chuckled. "Such eloquence suggests you're doing better than you think. If it makes you feel any better, during my first expedition with Nahid, we had to stop on a mountain for two days while I threw up and cried. She nursed me through the worst of my sickness, and once I could get food back in my belly, the rest of the trip went great."

Aurie nibbled on a corner of the fruit bar. "What was she like?"

His eyes twinkled with thought. "I think she wore that flowery headscarf so people would think she was soft and underestimate her. But she wasn't. She was hard. In all my years, I never outworked her. She never gave up, never came unprepared. When I graduated from Coterie, I was a cocky mage with too much appreciation for my own talents, especially magic. But when I struggled, she never chastised me, never treated me differently, even though our Halls were rivals. I cared very deeply for your mother."

His eyes grew pained, and he looked away. Aurie sensed that he was embarrassed by his revelation, and he went for a walk, claiming he had to water the trees.

When he returned, they broke camp and headed further into the mountains. By lunch, Aurie felt better, and though her muscles still ached, especially her shoulders and feet, it felt like she'd moved past the worst of it.

Sam slowed to walk beside her. "We're nearing our destination. You're the lead researcher on this, what's the game plan?"

Aurie hesitated. She hadn't expected him to put her in charge of this part of the expedition. She had a plan, of course, her brain wouldn't let her *not* formulate one, but the idea of actually putting it into action seemed to shatter it in her mind.

"The Crimson Skull is associated with sacrifice, which makes it rather hard to find, since there are countless ancient civilization that relied on sacrifice to fuel their superstitions. This is especially true of this region, since there were human sacrifices at Machu Picchu. But the Skull is older than this settlement, which means it's unlikely that it was used here.

"But I did find a reference to a valley that locals avoid. The place is associated with death, and sometimes sacrifice. This, again, is unremarkable, except that there was a report from the 1800s, when explorers got lost and wandered into this valley. They said the place gave them vertigo, like altitude sickness, even though they'd been in the mountains for weeks. They claimed that a bloody demon attacked them, taking two of their members, and when they eventually found them, they'd been killed, and the final note about the event, written in Spanish, was *cráneo carmesí*."

"Crimson Skull, you've told me this before," said Sam, nodding. "What are we going to do?"

"I'm getting there. Sorry, I guess I need to work myself up to it. My theory is that the Skull, if it's real, must take control of someone. It wasn't a demon, it was just a man covered in blood, and he probably scalped them, hence the crimson skull," said Aurie. "But really, I don't expect to find anything. Honestly, when I brought this to you, I didn't expect that we would come here to investigate. I thought you'd tell me to keep looking. What made you believe that it was a good idea?"

He wore a wry smile. "I didn't. It does sound like a story, rather that the truth, but I've been banging my head against this artifact for decades, so I thought it'd be worth giving it a try. Plus, it's probably for the best that our first time out is uneventful, to give you a taste for how real artifact hunting works, which is that it's mostly hiking, reading ancient texts, and filling out paperwork."

Before heading into the valley, they layered themselves with protective enchantments. Sam pulled a holstered pistol from his pack and hooked it to his belt. There was no trail to follow, they had to hack their way into the jungle, which slowed their progress to a crawl.

Up to that point, the cool mountain weather had kept Aurie mostly dry, but swinging a machete left her drenched with sweat. If anything had kept Sam and her mother from getting together, it had to be that they stunk like weasels and were covered in grime during their trips.

Near the bottom of the valley, near a stream that meandered over rocks and under roots, Sam paused.

"Did you hear that?" he asked.

Aurie tilted her head. "No?"

When they resumed, Aurie felt an uneasiness creep into her shoulders. The pack made her feel slow, and she wished they'd been able to leave them at the entrance to the valley. When something flashed through the trees, somewhere to their right, Aurie froze.

"Did you see that?" she asked through gritted teeth.

"Yes," he said softly. "That was too fast."

When they came over a ridge, something crimson came flying up and over them. Aurie fired a force bolt into the trees, sending up a plume of leaves.

A colorful parrot soared over them, noisily accosting them for its fright. Aurie and Sam broke into laughter. He leaned against a tree, wiping his forehead with the back of his hand.

She reached for her water bottle and pressed it hungrily against her lips.

"Nothing like a little mistaken identity for a good—"

His words were lost when the forest rose up around him, enveloping him like a hungry maw.

The thing-made-of-the-jungle had Sam by the midsection. He screamed, a hoarse, raw sound that pierced her ears.

She saw red eyes and a massive collection of leaves, moss, dirt, and vines that whipsawed around them.

Aurie dropped her water bottle and sent a twisted flamespear at the creature.

The jungle-thing rumbled, dropping Sam onto his back, and he tumbled down the slope, his shirt torn, exposing raw flesh.

When it surged towards her, Aurie hesitated. It was like an avalanche of jungle and earth and rocks, except it was moving up the slope, rather than down.

Aurie threw herself to the side. It clipped her feet, sending her rolling after Sam.

The jungle thing smashed into the trees, snapping trunks as wide as her leg like toothpicks, roaring with frustration.

She rose to her feet next to Sam. His side was bloody, flesh raked.

He set his feet and squared his shoulders towards the creature as it crashed towards them.

"Together, flame!"

Shoulder to shoulder, Aurie and Sam blasted the jungle-thing with a whirling vortex of fire, a miniature apocalypse.

The attack slowed the creature, but it punched through the fire, scattering flame and ashes in all directions. Like a massive gorilla made of plant material, it charged after them, red eyes glowing with menace.

"Run!" yelled Sam.

As they escaped through the trees, limbs and leaves whipping their faces and arms, Sam fired his gun at the creature, but it helped even less than the fire, so he tossed the gun away and pulled out a metallic ball the size of his fist.

"Just keep running," he said as he launched the silvery ball behind him.

She kept her legs pumping forward, but when she heard the tearing of earth, the grinding of stone on stone, and the roar of the jungle-thing, she glanced back to see a stone wall rising from the ground.

"It's not going to stop it," he said. "We have to find another way."

They each downed a potion that gave them more strength and speed, but the way the rainforest was exploding behind them told Aurie that they couldn't outrun the creature.

When they broke into a clearing, Aurie thought they had a chance to escape until she saw the massive tree at the center. Its trunk was as wide as two cars, front to back. The canopy created a tent over the wide clearing while massive vines hung like curling ropes to the moss-covered floor.

The vines weren't the only things hanging in the tree. Dangling from the limbs were hundreds of animals, necks strangled by vines, skin from their skulls rotted away until only a crimson mush remained. Aurie saw the boots of a soldier near the back. The soil was littered with old bones, cracked and sucked of marrow.

"A carnifex tree," said Sam.

"I didn't think those were real."

"Neither did I."

The veneer of the experienced traveler was wiped clean from Sam. Aurie was witness to the naked fear in his gaze. He looked shaken by the realization of what was after them.

As the jungle roared and shook, he turned to her. "I'm out of tricks. Drop your pack. You'll move faster. I can distract it for a little while. Long enough for you to escape from the valley. It won't follow you once you're out of its range."

"I'm not leaving you," said Aurie.

"Don't be stupid. At least one of us should survive."

"I'm better off keeping you alive. If I'm alone, I'll probably get lost and die of starvation. We're both getting out of here."

He nodded grimly.

"We don't have to kill it," said Aurie. "Just distract it, or slow it down enough for us to escape."

"Suggestions?" he asked, keeping one eye on the jungle.

"I don't know," she said. "I'm working on that."

"Work faster."

When the jungle-thing came rumbling from the trees, Aurie hurled chunks of rock mixed with force at it. The spell-concoction broke into dust when it hit the creature.

Sam was chanting, his fingers gesticulating through a complex spell. To give him more time, Aurie fired alternating Five Elements spells at it, but it still didn't slow.

When it neared, a vine-limb came whipping out, sending her tumbling across the clearing to land in a pile of bones at the base of the trunk. She looked up in time to see the carnifex engulf Sam before he could finish his spell. His screams pierced the valley.

Aurie was about to fire at the creature again when she remembered that it derived its power from the tree. She couldn't attack it directly, but maybe she could hurt it in its heart.

She put her hands against the gnarled trunk, thought about what would harm it most, and started whispering lies to it that its bark was dry and turning to dust, and that beetles were boring into its weak flesh.

The bark around her hands crumbled, and air hissed out of the decaying wood beneath, but it was far too little against a tree that was the size of a small building. If she had a few days, maybe she could rot a large section, but they'd both be long dead by then.

At the sound of a second scream, Aurie looked up to see Sam break free from the jungle-thing as steam and popping noises erupted from the pile of vegetation. His flesh was bloody, and most of his clothes had been scoured from his body, but he pushed his way free as if it were giving birth to him.

Aurie ran over, grabbed him by the hand, and pulled him free. He crashed to the ground. There was a sizzling sound from inside the mound of living vegetation.

Aurie didn't wait around to see what would happen. They ran up the slope, following the path of destruction. Sam had lost his boots, gear, and most of his clothes, and he looked like he'd been flayed with whips. His skin was bright pink, bubbly in some locations, but he was alive.

"I sucked the water from its body," said Sam as they climbed up the valley. "It turned to steam as it came out, roasting me. But that won't stop it for long."

"How are you still moving?" she asked, eyeing his ruined flesh.

"Just keep moving," he said hoarsely.

The jungle-thing resumed its chase when they were halfway up the valley. The potions they'd ingested were wearing off. Aurie wasn't sure how Sam was still standing with so many injuries, but they'd deal with it if they escaped.

As Sam slowed, she put her shoulder under his arm and took some of his weight, helping him up the mountainside. They'd lost their original path, so they had to force their way through thick vegetation.

When they came to a rocky stream cutting across the slope, Aurie stood on the mossy stones in the middle of the stream and helped Sam cross. She looked up in time to see the jungle rise up, vines whirling around her. One grabbed her ankle and yanked her backwards.

Aurie put her hands around the vine and shouted mendancy at it, and it crumbled to wood dust. She got up and ran, jumping across the stream as Sam blasted it. Landing face-first in the leaves, she thought it would reach her again easily, but then when she got up, she found the jungle to be silent again.

"I think it left us," he said. "We made it past its barrier."

She looked at his broken, bloody skin.

"We're not out of danger yet," she said. "Can you make it to the trail?"

He nodded, but she could see the pain setting in now that they weren't being chased.

By the time they made it to the top, Sam was nearly unconscious. She quickly set up a tent, placed what little healing spells she knew on him, and laid him inside.

His flesh was on fire and she feared it would get infected, so she boiled the remainder of their water and used a rag to clean the dirt and leaves embedded into his bloody flesh. He moaned and cried, but otherwise stayed unconscious.

As she was cleaning around his hip, she found a tattoo that appeared as she touched it. The design was of a swirling shape that made her think of a galaxy.

Late that night, with care and the frequent reapplication of enchantments, his fever broke, and he fell into a deep sleep. Exhausted, Aurie curled up outside the tent and slept until morning.

She woke with insects attacking her lips. After eating a meal of dried nuts and fruit, she refilled their water from the stream on the slope, being careful not to cross to the other side.

When she came back, he was awake, sitting outside of the tent.

"Thank you," he said. "Thank you for not leaving me."

"Of course," she said. "Are you okay?"

"I'm through the worst of it. I look worse than I am. When we get back to Lima, I know a healer who will fix me up right."

"What was that tattoo on your hip? It appeared when I was cleaning your wounds, but disappeared later," she said.

His lips thinned. "Something from when I was younger. Nothing important. Now let's break camp. It feels like I have the worst sunburn ever, and I don't have boots anymore."

The journey back to Lima took three days due his lack of footwear. They caught a ride with the soldiers in the Jeep once they made it back to the main dirt road. They seemed amused by the damage he'd sustained, joking that she'd caused it.

By the time they were on a plane back to Invictus, Aurie realized she'd learned a couple of things. She knew he was lying about the hidden tattoo, though she didn't know why. She also knew that Sam had been in love with her mother. Whether or not those feelings were reciprocated, she didn't yet know. And finally, Aurie knew, without a doubt, that despite their near-death experience, she'd loved every moment and couldn't wait to go on her next expedition.

FOURTEEN

Aurie was waiting for Pi at the Eight-Fold Door beneath Arcanium. Her face was a little wind-burnt from the journey through the Peruvian mountains, but Pi had never seen her sister so alive. She looked like she was bursting at the seams.

"What's the deal?" asked Pi.

"You said you needed a place for a summoning," said Aurie, tapping on the runed door with her knuckles. "I provide."

"I thought only the professors had access to this room," said Pi.

Aurie produced a thick iron key from a pocket and opened the door. "He leaves his office open all hours of the day and night."

"How are classes with him?"

"They're not. I've been too busy working with Sam. I've missed the last three classes."

"Don't you have to have his approval to graduate?" asked Pi.

After the trip to Peru, Aurie was starting to wonder what the point of graduating was if she was going to be an artifact hunter. She *planned* on graduating, but mustering the energy to attend one of Chopra's classes when they were potentially fatal had been difficult.

"I'll figure something out. There are more important things, like Invictus' Spire."

Pi whistled at the massive stone room and meandered around, admiring the scars in the concrete. After hearing her sister describe the battle with the Illiopian Death Cloud, she could almost see it in her head.

"If you've got other things to do," Pi called to her sister as she made her way back to the front, "you can head out, and I'll lock up after I'm done."

To her surprise, Pi found Aurie in the center of the room with a container of Morton's salt in her hands.

"What do you need to summon?"

Pi bit her lower lip. Her sister wasn't a fan of summoning demons. The only reason Pi had asked her sister about a space was that finding a place outside of Arcanium that was safe enough for the summoning *and* protected from scrying was nearly impossible. She didn't want to go through the trouble of talking to a demon if someone could overhear them.

"I need answers. Radoslav was no help. He gave me leads on a couple of scrying devices, but they were well known, and had no similarities to the indigo ball. I'm out of ideas."

"What about the ball itself? Found nothing there?" asked Aurie.

"It has a slight faez signature, like a frequency, but I don't know what it means, or what it's for."

"Let me do the summoning," said Aurie, resolutely.

"Really?" asked Pi. "I mean, Black Bart was one thing, but I need real answers, answers I can't find with a simple hair. Are you sure you want to be in on that?"

Her sister looked almost eager. "I get it. I can be overprotective. But this is important, and I know if there was an easier way, you would have taken it. Let me shoulder some of the burden. You're already in debt with Radoslav, and Black Bart, and who knows who or what else?"

Pi looked away. "Yeah, there is that...and speaking of debts, I've been meaning to tell you about one. An unexpected complication from when I went to see Radoslav."

When Aurie arched an eyebrow, Pi explained, laying out the situation in perfect detail. When she was finished, she waited for the inevitable condemnation from her sister.

There was a moment Pi thought Aurie was going to rebuke her, but her face screwed up, and she switched to a determined stare.

"That sucks, Pi. I'm sorry," said Aurie.

"Thanks, I appreciate that," said Pi, hooking her thumbs in her jeans pockets. "We both know, of course, that Ivan's day will come at the worst possible time."

"Naturally. So where's the spell? Do you have a tome hidden around here?"

Pi grimaced and pulled a crumpled piece of paper from her front pocket. "I have it mostly memorized. I brought this for luck."

After her sister read through the summoning a few times, she said, "I think I've got it. Not that difficult—well, at least the summoning part."

They shared a worried glance. "You still good with doing this? It's a doozy. Not going to be pleasant by any means."

"What's the worst that can happen?" asked Aurie as she poured the salt into a circle, then took out a penknife, pricked her palm, and dripped blood at five points.

Pi hated watching her sister perform the ritual, not because she was worried about her making any mistakes, but because she wasn't the one doing it. The needle-tight attention to detail required, while full of tension, left no mental space to be worried or nervous. Pi was practically chewing her fingers off watching Aurie gesture through the complex finger motions and chant the pseudo-Latin phrases that would call the demon through the thin layer that separated their two realities.

"Sideous. Sideous. Sideous. Hear my call and answer me," said Aurie.

There was no peal of lightning or brimstone-laden smoke erupting from the center of the circle, yet Pi knew the summoning had worked. The smell of faez was thick, like there'd been an electrical fire.

A bulb of white greasepaint emerged from the stone, expanding like a balloon until it was as large as a head. A tuft of bright red hair popped out the top, while ears and a nose grew. The nose was covered in bloody greasepaint. Thick finger-painted arches formed on the eye ridges.

Pi held her breath as she watched the clown-figure expand into the space, growing taller and taller. It was larger than either of them. All Pi could think about was the clown-demon getting loose and dragging her back into the stone.

Aurie, on the other hand, did not look impressed. She had her arms crossed as she stared back at the demon-clown, nostrils flaring.

The clown-demon hissed, showing teeth like yellow-brown razors.

Aurie said nothing.

Before their eyes, the white greasepaint skin bubbled, deforming the clown until it was an unrecognizable blob. This didn't last long. It hardened into a sleek black alien creature with a bony exoskeleton and slaver dripping from its jutting jaw.

Still watching with a resolute stare, Aurie looked almost bored.

The demon changed form again, this time into a hulking man who looked suspiciously like Bannon Creed.

"Nope," said Aurie.

The demon-Creed's skin turned bright red, the head expanding, until it looked like a sports mascot. Pi almost expected it to have a T-shirt cannon, or a basketball under its arm.

The mascot-demon opened its mouth, revealing the yellow-brown razor teeth again, and said, "If I don't get what I want, neither do you. Stop resisting. Let me in."

Aurie closed her eyes for a moment, then uncrossed her arms and let out a big sigh.

"Fine. Do your worst."

The big plastic eyes on the mascot spun, and the demon broke out into laughter, unsettling Pi. The bulky form shrunk, red felt covering changing to freckled skin.

As soon as Pi saw the coppery hair, she exchanged glances with her sister. Aurie's forehead was knotted.

"You killed me, A," said demon-Kieran. "You failed your mother and me."

The demon-Kieran held his arm up, and his skin bubbled bright red with burns. "Blew me up. Told you to watch yerself. Careful with your magic, but you didn't listen. And look what happened."

The shock of seeing Kieran was etched on her sister's face. She didn't look frightened, but sad. Pi considered ending the summoning, until the demon-Kieran shot her a look and curled a finger at her.

"You failed her, too. She was a nice young girl until you started watching her," he said.

"I know," replied Aurie. "But she still turned out pretty damn awesome. Come on, demon. If this is the best you can do, then you probably don't have the answer we're looking for. I think I'll send you back."

"No! No!" hissed demon-Kieran, showing his yellow-brown teeth. "I'm just getting warmed up. You were right to summon Sideous. Your pain for my information. You'll see, you'll see."

Pi wasn't surprised when the figure of their father turned into their mother. Despite knowing that it was a demon in disguise, her heart ached with seeing her in her flowery headscarf. At least until the demon-Nahid opened its mouth.

"You think you can follow in my footsteps? You think you can do what I couldn't do? Who do you think you are, Aurelia? Look what happened at the clinic, heck, look what happened a few weeks ago. You nearly got Sam killed, just like you do everyone else."

Aurie's eyes grew watery, but she did not look away, taking the demon's abuse with her chin held high.

The demon-Nahid marched to the edge of the salt circle, staring at Aurie with a smirk on its lips.

"Yes, yes. I see it. Your fear. It eats at you because you know it's true," said demon-Nahid.

Alarm registered in Aurie's face. "No. Shut up."

The covert glance in Pi's direction made her say, "What's going on?"

The demon-Nahid cackled, completely ignoring that it was damaging the illusion, but whatever it had gleaned from Aurie's head had been injurious enough that it didn't care.

Demon-Nahid curled an arm in midair as if it were hugging someone close to it. Then it did the same with its leg, and started humping the air.

"She knows the truth, that I used to fuck that Sam Arlington. And who wouldn't? How could I keep my hands off him on expedition? I loved to crawl around the campfire—"

"Shut up! Shut the fuck up!"

Aurie surged forward, and for a moment, Pi was afraid she'd cross the salt circle. But she stopped short.

Pi didn't realize she was scowling at her sister until the demon looked back at her and grinned with yellow-brown razor teeth showing.

"She hasn't told you, has she? How delicious."

"It's only a speculation," said Aurie, pleading with her eyes. "I would have told you if I learned it was true."

Pi was annoyed that Aurie hadn't told her. She bit back her anger. "It's fine. I understand."

"No!" screamed the demon. "You should be mad. You should be angry. She's keeping secrets!"

Aurie's expression of concern melted into relief. "We're not a soap opera, stupid demon. We're not going to hate each other just so you can feast on it."

"Then you're not getting any secrets!" said demon-Nahid.

"You owe me, demon," Aurie shouted back. "Tell us what the looking glass is."

It laughed. "You didn't give me enough of the good stuff."

"You got enough to give us an answer," said Aurie.

"Fuck you!" said demon-Nahid as it flipped Aurie off and blew a wet raspberry. When it had finished, it snapped its fingers and disappeared in a puff of smoke.

As soon as it was gone, Aurie put her fingers to the bridge of her nose. "I'm sorry, sis. I was going to tell you."

"Dooset daram. You don't have to apologize. Not for that. Stupid demon."

"I didn't get the answer," said Aurie, throwing up her arms. "We're running out of options. Any other demons would want too much for the answer, and it's not like we can find the answer on the internet."

"Yeah, I wish," said Pi, and as soon as she did, she looked back to her sister, who had the same expression. "Or can we?"

"What if the looking glass is the internet?" asked Aurie, pulling her cell phone out of her pocket. "Maybe it's like Sam was telling me on our expedition, you can't rely on magic to solve every problem. What if he wants us to use the tools we have?"

"I think you're right, sis. Damn. Why didn't I see this before?" asked Pi, pacing around with her hands shoved into her hair. "I know what I need to do. It'll take me a bit to program, but I can do an image search. I bet it's in there somewhere."

Pi ran over and hugged her sister, kissing her on the forehead. "You're the best. It might take me a few days, but be ready. I think we're going after the second ball soon."

FIFTEEN

A ghostly dragon with pink feet as long as a freight train soared over the Glitterdome while colorful fireworks exploded around it. The city was alive, chest-vibrating booms and endless crackers providing an overlapping cacophony. Smoke hung over the buildings as if the streets were a battleground.

The display was visible to Aurie, who was in the tenth ward, standing outside Wizard's Wax Museum as her sister bypassed the security systems. The museum was a chateauesque three-story building with turrets and steep angled roofs. The street was completely empty, so Aurie hadn't bothered hiding, and they had face-obscuring enchantments to protect them from cameras.

"New Year's Eve is a great night for thieves," mused Aurie. "No one is home, everyone is looking at the sky, and they're drunk as a skunk who fell into a wine barrel."

"Are you suggesting we're thieves?" asked Pi, crouching before the locked back door. The coloring of her leather jacket had gone matte black, absorbing the light rather than reflecting it. Aurie admired the usefulness of her sister's trinket, wishing there'd been a pair of them that day. Something shimmered at Pi's hip, but Aurie turned her attention back to the fireworks above the city center.

"Not thieves," said Aurie. "Scavengers, like on a scavenger hunt. Are you going to tell me why we're not out with our friends?"

"There will always be more nights to make fools of ourselves. Think of it this way. I'm saving you from a lifetime of regret after you make out with the bartender for another free shot."

"Sometimes I wonder what it'd be like to have a normal life," said Aurie.

"Not me," said Pi. "No interest."

"I don't want that to be me," said Aurie. "I just wonder what it's like."

The door wheezed open, revealing a dark opening. "That was a little tougher than I thought it was going to be. That mix of technology and magic is a bitch to bypass."

After sweeping the entrance for security enchantments, they went inside. Before Aurie's eyes adjusted, she nearly bumped into a figure standing near the entrance.

"Merde, that's creepy," she said, raising her hand and sending a floating magelight into the museum. It cast moving shadows across the motionless figures, giving them a semblance of motion.

The wax figure before her was a man in a woolen robe with a rough hemp belt and a scraggly mustache and beard. A painted wooden rosary hung from his fist. The plaque at his feet read St. Francis of Assisi.

Aurie whistled softly. "I bet the Pope wasn't happy about this wax figure."

The black with gold letter sign hanging from the ceiling said "Historical Figures Suspected of Being Mages."

"You still haven't told me what we're looking for," said Aurie. "Or have you already found the second glass ball and want to show off?"

Pi stood before a map of the museum that listed the various sections: Famous Modern Mages, Fictional Mages, The Infamous, Wizards of History, Historical Figures Suspected of Being Mages, and Fictional or Real? She flashed a sly grin at Aurie, before jabbing her finger into the map at Fictional or Real?

Aurie caught the intensity in her sister's gaze. "You think you know where it is, but you haven't retrieved it yet."

"I don't want a repeat of last time," said Pi. "And my gut tells me that Invictus' game can't be completed solo. His whole history with the Halls suggests his preference to teamwork and family."

"A dysfunctional family," said Aurie, thinking about her suspicions of her mother's infidelity. She hadn't talked to Sam since the trip to Peru, partially because he'd been away on business, but mostly because they didn't know where to look next.

The magelight floated ahead, revealing the checkerboard wooden floor winding through the museum until they reached wide beige carpeted steps. The place smelled like fresh paint, Aurie guessed from the frequent touch-ups to ensure the wax figures looked real.

The Fictional or Real? section had around twenty dioramas featuring the wax mages. An ancient Chinese man named Wu Yang reclining on a daybed was the first one they passed. He wore voluminous light turquoise robes, and a fan made of crane feathers dangled from his hand.

Before Aurie could read the inscription, Pi dragged her through the maze of pathways until they reached a diorama in the back that resembled a cave resplendent with crystals that glittered as the magelight approached.

"Merlin Ambrosius," said Pi breathlessly.

The depiction of the literary figure was a mixture of myth and history. Aurie was no expert in the fashion of that time, but the heavy woolen robes dyed a faded purple seemed realistic. He had a classic wizard complexion with a wrinkled expression of distaste and a white beard that grew wispy at the ends.

Three different brass displays explained the possible links to historical figures that might have inspired the literary legend.

"You think this is where the second is hidden?" asked Aurie.

Pi nodded, then spoke:

"*When through the looking glass you see*
Backwards amid the Giants you'll be
To follow the rainbow and pay the fee
Two makes one and that is key.
Then four more and you'll see
Only through their unity."

It took a moment, but Aurie got it when she repeated the clue. "Backwards amid the Giants. The giants are the old wizards and backwards indicates Merlin, who the legend says lived backwards through time."

"Exactly," said Pi. "I'm sure this is it. I even found old articles about how Invictus like to visit this museum during off hours. They didn't say which wax figures he stopped at, but I think Merlin was one of them. It fits with what I've read about him. He had a fascination with the mages of history—two of the books in that cottage were the *Maharal of Prague* and *The Diary of Farmer Weathersky*. Both figures are here in the museum."

Aurie examined the crystal cave, touching the stone to find it was painted foam blocks. "Do you think it's a hidden chamber?"

"I don't know," said Pi. "I thought it might trigger from the first ball."

"Well, let's go back and get it," said Aurie, confused.

Her sister reached to her side and lifted something heavy that Aurie couldn't quite look at. Every time she tried to see what her sister was handling, Aurie felt the strong urge to look away.

"What's causing that effect?" asked Aurie, when Pi pulled the indigo ball from what seemed like empty air.

"It wouldn't fit in the jacket, so I had to come up with something better. I gleaned the spell from the enchantment placed on the glass ball when it was in Hemistad's shop. We'd been standing next to it for years and had never thought to ask what it was. It took some work to reverse engineer it, but it works great."

Aurie whistled in appreciation. "We should armor up."

It took a few minutes, but they layered themselves with enchantments. If there was to be a battle, they wanted to be ready.

With the indigo ball in her hands and facing the wax figure of Merlin, Pi said with grim determination, "May the games begin."

She moved forward, one step at a time, stopping for a breath before continuing with the next step. Aurie kept her head on a swivel, expecting an attack to come from everywhere. When Pi gently touched the wax figure with the ball and nothing happened, Aurie deflated.

Pi wore a scowl. "I'm sure it's Merlin. I really am."

"I believe you, sis. It makes sense. Walk around the diorama. It might be something in the cave that triggers it."

After Pi wandered around the diorama, holding the indigo ball out like a divining rod, for ten minutes, covering every inch of the area, she returned to the front with Aurie.

Her sister's shoulders slumped while her jaw pulsed. "I *know* this is it. I know it. What am I doing wrong?"

Aurie rubbed the back of her neck, working at a burr in her thoughts as she repeated the clue:

"When through the looking glass you see
Backwards amid the Giants you'll be
To follow the rainbow and pay the fee
Two makes one and that is key.
Then four more and you'll see
Only through their unity."

"See," said Pi. "It's gotta be Merlin."

"Something you said makes me feel like we're missing something, but I can't pinpoint what it is," said Aurie.

She read the texts on the three historical possibilities of the legend of Merlin. He might have been a madman named Myrddin Wyllt, or a Romano-British warlord named Ambrosius Aurelianus, or an unnamed druid from the sixth century living in southern Scotland.

When she was finished, the burr remained. "It's not this. Not here." Aurie snapped her fingers. "It's the thing you said about family and teamwork. What if you need a second person? That it's gotta be a team of at least two people? *Two makes one and that is key.* Two makes one. Maybe two people make a team, then the one more is a key?"

A sense of revelation took over Pi's face and she handed the ball to Aurie. The glass was cool in her hands, smooth.

Aurie slow-marched to the wax Merlin, her heartbeat doubling at each step, skin crackling with anticipation. The moment her shoe scuffed the edge of the platform, a shimmering shield exploded around her.

"What the—"

She looked all around her to find she was trapped inside a bubble. Pi stood on the outside, her hands hovering near the shield. Her expression was a mix of excitement and concern.

"This is it, I knew it."

"What's going on? What's happening?" asked Aurie, panic rising up in her chest. She forced herself to take a deep breath so she wouldn't hyperventilate.

A scream made Aurie jump. She turned back to find her sister sucking on her fingers. "Don't touch the shield. It shocked me."

When the wax figure of Merlin twitched to life, Aurie set the indigo glass ball on the checkered flooring and prepared for battle.

"Em wollof syas nimos," said Merlin.

"Shit. What is that? Was that a spell?" asked Aurie, glancing back to her sister, but not looking too long for fear of missing something.

"I don't know," said Pi, forehead wrinkled. "Keep watching."

The shimmering electric cage made her feel like a prisoner. Her leg bounced as she waited.

When Merlin lifted his hands and gestured with his fingers, Aurie almost missed it because she'd jumped a little. He made the finger-signature for the Five Elements spell of Fire.

"Maybe he wants me to copy him," said Aurie, and she performed the finger movements.

When she received a tiny shock, it jolted her arms.

"The shield got smaller," said Pi from outside.

"I copied him perfectly. How did I get it wrong?" asked Aurie.

Before she could reply, Merlin made the finger gesture for Fire again.

Aurie repeated it, making absolutely sure that every movement was as crisp as a military salute, but the shock came right away when she finished.

"Damn it," she said. "I did it exactly right."

"Maybe you don't copy him," said Pi.

"What did he say at the beginning again?" she asked.

"I'm woolie, or something," said Pi.

Aurie pulled on her ponytail in frustration. Merlin gave her the Fire gesture a third time.

"Try the counter," said Pi.

The Five Elements spell for Water was the easiest. The motions were smooth, suggesting waviness. When the shock slammed into her, it took her breath away.

"That one hurt, a lot."

"The shield is smaller again. You've lost about thirty percent of your space. You don't have that many wrong answers left."

Aurie checked behind her. The shield had cut the distance behind her in half, and the section above her head was only a foot above. A few more wrong and she'd have to duck.

Fire again from Merlin.

Tightness constricted her chest. It frustrated her that she wasn't getting it. She was good at puzzles. Why hadn't she figured this one out?

Aurie thought back to what Merlin had said at the beginning. "Wait. I got it. Merlin lives backwards in time. I think he said something about Simon Says."

"Yes!" said Pi. "Simon says follow me. That's what it was."

Aurie had never tried to cast a spell backwards, but Five Elements were simple enough that she could envision it. She was about to try when the shock hit her for a fourth time and the bubble shrank again.

"That sucked. I didn't even get to try. I wonder what happens if I don't have room left," said Aurie.

"Focus on the gestures so you don't find out," said Pi grimly.

When the Fire gesture came for the fifth time, Aurie was ready. She made it in reverse, which felt like trying to do break dancing with her fingers, but when she was finished, she received no shock, and the shield didn't move.

Aurie almost jumped for joy, which would have jammed her hands into the shield above her head. She kept them near her shoulders and clapped.

Merlin gave the Earth sign. Aurie worked through it in her head before making it backwards.

Success.

"You got this, sis," said Pi. "Dooset daram."

Aurie stayed focused on Merlin's fingers. She used the time in between to picture the other three in reverse. When he gave Water, she was ready, and she gave it right back.

He went back to Fire.

Check.

Water, then Spirit. Fire twice. Air three times. Back to Earth. Water.

She made each one.

Then Merlin gave her a little bow and Aurie expected the shield to go down, but he waggled his fingers as if he were stretching them, and she realized the real game had begun. The opening sequence was a warm-up to teach her the rules.

He started with Fire, and as soon as she completed the gesture, he moved to the next, rather than pausing between. Water. Earth. Air. Spirit three times. Earth. Earth. Fire.

On the last, Aurie started to do Earth again, and had to switch mid-finger hook, but she got shocked right away. The shield shrunk until it was only an inch from her head.

"Almost," said Pi. "That was great. Now do it again, but longer."

"Easy for you to say," muttered Aurie, but she had no time to think as Merlin launched into the game again.

Fire. Air twice. Earth. Spirit times four. Earth times three. Fire. Water. Air.

Aurie fell into a rhythm. She gave herself a quick mental check before she started each spell, but the longer the game went, the faster Merlin's fingers flew. After a minute, she found it hard to follow his motions. She barely had time to read what spell he'd performed before he was doing the next.

Beads of sweat formed on her forehead and rolled into her eyes, but she couldn't wipe them for fear of missing a reversed spell. Her fingers cramped from making gestures she was unused to, and before long she was mentally screaming for the contest to end.

Water. Fire. Air. Earth times three. Air times two. Fire. Spirit. Earth.

The game kept going, and Aurie found herself struggling through each spell. Her fingers were giving out. Her shoulders were hunched, and her mind was worn to a nub. She knew a mistake was only a matter of time.

Water. Water. Water. Water. Water. Water. Fire.

She almost missed the Fire, falling into the rhythm of Water.

Earth. Spirit times two. Fire. Fire. Spirit.

When Merlin's fingers moved no longer, Aurie didn't even know what to do. She feared to look away in case there was a third stage to the game. His arms hovered before him as if he were balancing a rod across his forearms.

Then at long last, he lowered his arms. Pi squealed from behind her, but she didn't feel like she was out of the woods yet because the shield remained.

Merlin reached towards his robe, which shifted as if it were cloth and not wax. A bright yellow glass ball appeared in his hand, and he handed it to Aurie. The moment she touched it, a quiver of excitement went through her midsection.

Once it was in her grip, Merlin's hands returned to their original position by his side, and the shield disappeared. Pi was hugging her before she could even turn around.

"You did it! You did it! That was so awesome. I can't believe you made it to the end. I was so sure you'd fumble a gesture when it got so fast."

With the glass ball under one arm, Aurie wiped her forehead with the other, trembling with the aftereffects. "I didn't have time to worry."

Pi grabbed her by the shoulders. Her eyes were wild, a little crazed. "Do you realize what this means? We've got two balls already and no one else even knows about this. We're going to do this."

In her gut, Aurie knew that it was only going to get harder. Invictus wouldn't make it easy for them. But she wasn't about to bring that up.

"We are. We totally are. And all because of you. You figured out the first one," said Aurie.

"And you got the second. I wonder what the next clue is?" asked Pi.

When she picked up the yellow ball, a warmth grew on Aurie's wrist. Before her eyes, a tattoo of the yellow ball the size of a quarter appeared right below her palm. Pi held her arm out. She had one as well, though the color of her ball.

"Was that the clue?" asked Aurie.

"I guess we'll have to figure it out."

Aurie gave her sister a side-squeeze since they were carrying the glass balls.

"Let's get out of here before someone finds us," said Aurie.

When they exited the Wizard's Wax Museum, the fireworks had ended, which meant the New Year had begun. Fresh off their victory of finding the second clue, Aurie felt like a new era was dawning in the Hundred Halls.

SIXTEEN

The city was a giant slushy as a warm Atlantic wind melted the January snows. Car tires cut through the muck, sending brownish-gray half-frozen water flying.

Pi didn't bother dodging the spray like the rest of the pedestrians on the sidewalk. The icy mixture avoided her black jeans as if they had a forcefield around them. It wasn't just the trust in her magic that kept her from reacting, but the conundrum about the missing third clue that had her attention elsewhere. It'd been nearly a month since she and Aurie had conquered the Wax Merlin for the second glass ball, and they'd gotten no further.

At first, she'd been content that no one else knew about their existence, but the lack of progress left her frustrated. She was on her way to Freeport Games to see if Hemistad had returned, so she could question him further. The concern that she'd missed something was burning a hole in her gut.

Pi had her hands in her jacket pockets, charging forward, not another soul on the sidewalk daring to get in her way, when someone grabbed her arm. Her first reaction was to pull a length of twine from her pocket, the spell to ensnare her attacker about to fly from her lips, but then she recognized the thick limbs and dusty brown hair of Ernie, whose rarely-seen-the-light-of-day skin flushed blotchy red.

"Merlin's tits, Ernie. I almost tied you in a knot." A spark of hope filled her chest like a balloon. "Please tell me you have another clue."

The look on his face told her the news would be the exact opposite. In fact, he looked like he had to tell her that he'd run over her cat, or some other horrific news, based on the fear in his eyes and the way he was swallowing nervously.

"P-P-Pythia. Pi. I'm sorry. I couldn't help it. I h-had to," he said frantically.

"You had to what?" she asked.

He shook his head feverishly, as if he couldn't get the words out.

"Are you okay? Is this another thing that...you know who did?" she asked.

He grimaced, but nodded feverishly. "I have to. It's in my head. It won't go away."

Pi tousled his hair to let him know that it was going to be fine. She grabbed his sweaty hand and pulled him into the Pie Romancing shop. The logo had a man in robes pulling a fresh pie from an oven with flames all around him. The line for pie was halfway to the door. The smell of fresh baked crusts with custom fillings washed over her, but she ignored her grumbling stomach and tugged him into an open booth, ignoring the leftover napkins and drink cup still on the table.

After casting a no-eavesdropping spell, she asked him, "What happened?"

Ernie's gaze roved around the room before settling on her. He gave her a weak smile. "Pie and Pi."

She patted his hand. "Whenever you're ready."

He seemed to relax until he tried to speak, then his body cinched up as if it had a drawstring. "I didn't want to tell them. I really didn't. I can't help it."

A sense of foreboding washed over her. "The thing you told me in the Undercity?"

He nodded his head, looking partially relieved that she understood.

Pi grabbed his trembling hands. "This is not your fault, Ernie. You didn't do this. *He* did. Don't you feel bad for doing his bidding. You can't help it. He spelled you this way."

When he took a quivering breath, she thought he was going to break into tears. He blubbered out a "thank you" and closed his eyes with relief.

Pi retrieved some fresh napkins and let him blow his nose so he could continue.

"Others have figured out the clues?" He nodded. "How many?"

"Twelve."

She pushed back against the booth. "Twelve." The words were hollow in her mouth. Twelve teams had figured out the first clue. Some of them might be past the second, or more. All their secrecy had been undone, somehow.

It also meant there was more than one set of glass balls. Which wasn't a surprise, but she'd hoped that wasn't the case.

"Did they say anything about how they figured it out?"

He shook his head.

"Do you remember their names?" she asked.

"I...I don't know, maybe? I remember one girl. She made fun of me when Aurie took me to Freeport Games," he said.

"Violet?" asked Pi, but he shook his head, which brought relief. If she'd been at the clues without telling them, she might have thought Violet had gone back to the Cabal.

"One of her friends."

"Former friends," said Pi. "Alchemists Hall. Do you know her name? No. Any others?"

"I think they all in Halls, like you, like Miss Aurelia."

That seemed significant to Pi but she didn't know how. She was about to ask further questions when she saw a familiar face pass Pic Romancing—two familiar faces, in fact. A feeling that she'd been followed hollowed out her gut.

"Wait here," said Pi. "Don't come out no matter what. Even if it gets dangerous. In fact"—she dug a few bills out of her pocket—"get yourself a pie. My treat."

It was the least she could do. Ernie didn't deserve what Invictus had done to him, and if he'd been alive, she would have slapped the ancient bastard for it.

While Ernie joined the line, Pi marched out the door, straight at Alton Lockwood and Sunil Kapoor, who were walking the other way. Alton looked like he was ready to ski down the slopes in Aspen, while Sunil was wearing a jean jacket over a black shirt.

"Hey assholes," she said.

They spun around, hands moving to gesture, a look of fear on their faces.

"Don't think about it," she said without flinching. "I took on the six of you, I'll take the both of you here without lifting a finger."

"Fuck you," said Sunil.

"I always knew you had the vocabulary of a cheese sandwich," she said.

He sneered back, but she wasn't too worried about him. Alton watched her carefully, like a lion scouting a gazelle from the bushes. The selective amnesia she'd forced on him during her first year looked like it'd been worn away, because his stare spoke volumes.

"I remember you," he said, nodding slowly. "I remember it all."

"Good," she said. "Remember what happened to you when you messed with me."

To his credit, he stayed silent, but she didn't feel great about it.

"What do you want?" asked Sunil.

"For you two to stop following me," she said.

"We're not following—"

Alton put his hand on Sunil's chest, silencing him. "She knows."

"I also know why you're following me, though I can't imagine how you two idiots figured it out," she said.

"It helps to have friends in the right places," said Alton.

"Salty friends," said Sunil, smirking at a private joke.

Salty? She didn't quite get it until she noticed Alton almost hit Sunil again. What would be salty and know about the...?

"Alcyone told you," said Pi, feeling the color drain from her skin. "And not just you, but others. That spiteful hag. How'd you listen to her without getting your face eaten off?"

If she'd known how much trouble the hag was going to cause her, Pi might have fought, Class Five designation be damned. Pi assumed she was mad that her meal had gotten away. The only thing keeping it from being worse was that Alcyone could only give a person one answer.

"I was sitting in the hot tub with a few ladies when my cell phone went off," said Alton. "I didn't believe her at first until she told me a few things that nobody knows."

The quality of those secrets looked like they'd unnerved him by his near shivers. She'd always known she wasn't the only one that he'd messed with.

"And now you're following me hoping to learn something new. Do you ever do anything yourself? Or do you spend your life sponging off other people's efforts?"

"If they're stupid enough to let me, then I'll take it," said Alton smugly.

"I'm not worried," said Pi. "There's no way you'll get far."

With a grin that would have made a nun give the sign of the cross, he slowly pulled back his coat sleeve to reveal a tattoo, the same one that marked her arm. When Sunil did the same, her heart sank.

Before she could say anything, Alton grabbed Sunil's arm and tugged him down the street. "Come on. No need to follow her any longer. Now we know we're ahead of her. And when we take control of the Halls, she and her sister will wish they never fucked with me."

SEVENTEEN

Aurie sat in a plush leather high-backed chair with a mahogany armrest in Sam Arlington's mansion, quietly rubbing the yellow tattoo on her wrist. The year and their chance to save the Halls was rapidly disappearing.

After the news that the secret had been leaked by the siren Alcyone, they'd doubled their efforts to figure out the next clue, but to no avail. She'd been skipping her classes with Chopra, and she wasn't sure if it was because she was too busy trying to figure out the next clue, or she was afraid that they were too late, and it wouldn't matter if she finished out the year in Arcanium.

A big book with pages stuffed into it landed on the table, startling her.

"A little tense? You look ready to break in half," said Sam, grinning, in his I'm-only-a-plane-ride-away-from-adventure outfit.

"Classes," she muttered.

"I've never thought of you as someone who gets rattled by classes, especially after you saved my rear in Peru," he said. "Something else troubling you?"

She mustered a smile to keep him from prying. "It's nothing, and I'm here to help you, not the other way around."

"Aurelia. Aurie," he said, and there was a pleading in his eyes. "I was very close with Nahid...and your father. If there's something you need help with, please, please let me know."

The way he said it almost sounded like he was asking for something specifically. Was he suggesting that he and Nahid had been more than just colleagues?

"It would help me a lot if we could focus on the Crimson Skull," said Aurie, pulling the book with the guts spilled out closer to her. As her gaze fell upon the contents, she noticed a picture of her mother standing in a black forest with a strange squat metal jar in her hand and a look of victory on her face.

"Wait, this book isn't about the Skull?" she asked, opening the book while he looked on with a grin on his lips. There were hundreds of pictures, not all involving her mother, but she was in enough of them that she couldn't stop turning the pages to find more.

"I appreciate the gesture, Sam, but I really should be back in Arcanium studying. I thought you needed my help," she said, fingertips caressing the leather edging of the tome.

"I do, and that's why I'm offering my payment ahead of time. We have a trip to make, a shorter one, but I need you," he said. "You can leave the book here—we can stop by later, or I can send it along to Arcanium when we're done."

Aurie picked up the photograph of Nahid with the squat metal jar. As she looked closer, she noticed runes on the item. Her mother's patient handwriting read "Forest Mother's Pestle," then in another location, written at an angle, "I can't wait to see his face."

"Were you on this expedition?" she asked.

He shook his head.

"The pestle? Do you know where it went?" she asked.

"No. Why do you ask?"

She gave a little shrug. "Curious." If he'd had the pestle, then she would have assumed the "his" in the note was Sam, but since he didn't have it, it was probably her father, Kieran. He could be lying, but if so, he was good enough she couldn't detect it.

He drove them to the eighth ward in a black Suburban with tinted windows. The gray skies of winter hadn't quite left, nor had spring returned. Aurie felt in limbo, much like the weather.

When her phone rang unexpectedly, she worried something had happened to Pi, until she saw it was Violet calling her. She excused herself and took the call, crouching into the corner of her seat.

"Hey."

"Sorry to bother you, Aurie. I was hearing some rumors and I thought I should pass them along. Is it safe to talk?"

"Mostly." The tension in her shoulders twisted. "I assume this is not a good rumor."

There was a pause on the phone. "No." Then another. "A month ago, I started hearing rumors about some items being found, that the Halls might be led by a head patron again, and that certain sisters I know were in the hunt."

Aurie glanced over at Sam, who was busy turning onto Fate Avenue, avoiding a taxi that had gone speeding past with a warning honk. "Those rumors are true."

"I also heard that progress is being made," said Violet.

"But not by us."

"I heard that too. In fact, that's why I'm calling you," said Violet.

Aurie shifted in her seat and banged her head against the window. She closed her eyes, settling her forehead against the cool glass.

"They've gotten in, more than one group."

Shit. Aurie made a noncommittal noise. She didn't want Sam to know how important the call was.

"The entrance is in the place we both know about. The last place you saw your uncle." *The statue of Invictus.* "Only it's under construction again, and I don't think anyone is getting in."

It was the worst possible news, well, nearly so. Alton and Sunil had figured out the next clue, and they were blocking the entrance. They'd theorized that there were seven glass balls to be retrieved, which meant there was still time, but Aurie felt like their chances were dwindling.

"Thanks. Anything else?"

"Yeah," said Violet. "It sounds like only seven teams of two can be active at a time, and they have to be from two different Halls."

"That's good to know," said Aurie.

"I'll let you know more if I find out. Not many know about this, but I'm sure the news will get out soon. I'd better go. I have a board meeting in a few minutes."

"Thanks, and good luck on the test," she said, before clicking the phone off.

"Get some primo intel on an upcoming test?" asked Sam with a grin.

"Uhm, yeah," said Aurie numbly.

The fact that Ernie had told them about twelve teams, but only seven could be active meant that some of the students had died, or been knocked out of the contest somehow. She hoped the latter, but didn't expect that to be true. Invictus was a clever bastard, but a bastard nonetheless.

Sam parked the Suburban next to a combination Korean grocery and BBQ. The sweet, slightly burnt tang of meat wafted from the open door along with laughter and the sizzle of multiple grills. The sidewalks were wide, with pressed concrete showcasing rounded Hangeul characters. Flowery camellia trees populated the street, their pinkish blooms too early for the spring. Aurie had never been in this section of the city. It appeared by the number of businesses and the subdued conversations from its denizens that there was a vibrant Korean-American community.

"Be alert, careful," he said softly, appearing to have contained his normal extraverted self.

Sam led them through an arched passage between buildings that ended in a hidden courtyard suggesting a time from centuries past with steep roofs and a gravel floor. An old woman with dark hair, threaded with gray, sat on a park bench facing the other way, throwing feed to pigeons that cooed and pecked amid the rocks, tiny feet scratching.

A light sense of unease fell upon Aurie's shoulders, making her glance around for a hidden source of danger. Something didn't feel right about the scene.

"Ne Yong," said Sam, inclining his head forward in a semblance of a bow.

Ne Yong looked like she was about to attend a business meeting, wearing a gray jacket with a tree pattern and black pants. Despite her wrinkled appearance, she lifted and sipped from a teacup as smoothly as a teenager, eyes containing a smoldering danger.

In her limited time dealing with the supernatural, Aurie had learned they could hide their appearance all they wanted, but the truth always showed in their eyes.

"You have a lot of nerve coming to see me here, Sam Arlington," she said, clucking her tongue at the end with a note of finality.

"My apologies, Ne. I heard you were in town and wanted to pay my respects," he said, trying to appear small and unthreatening, like a mouse hiding in the grass.

The old woman's gaze passed briefly over Aurie. She felt no overt threat, but Sam seemed to be feeling it. The whole courtyard felt off to Aurie, but she couldn't leave his side to investigate, so she kept her head movements small and searched the area with her eyes.

Ne Yong took another sip from her teacup, using the moment to glower at Sam. "You fucked me on that deal. I paid good money for that dig, and you produced nothing but publicity for yourself. You're a preeny, glossy attention hound. Why should I even allow you in my presence?"

"As I said at the beginning of that project, not every search is fruitful. Not every artifact can be found," he said.

"Artifact?" She clucked her tongue. "That was my necklace, not some fancy. I'll never forgive that girl for losing it in the Mi Kiang river."

As Aurie shifted her vision, intentionally blurring it, she caught fuzzy edges that shouldn't be there. There were glamours on the courtyard, a sense of largeness that shouldn't be there.

"Who is she?" asked Ne Yong, jabbing a wrinkled finger, flaring her nostrils. "I know her smell."

Before Sam could speak, Aurie stepped forward. "I'm Aurelia. You can call me Aurie."

"Why should I?"

Aurie blurred her gaze again, catching more hints. "Why are you hiding what you're doing?"

Ne Yong's eyes widened. Sam put a hand on her shoulder, but she shook it off.

"I don't mean your form, whatever it is. The pigeons, the tea, your clothes. Really? It's a lie. You're doing it because you think we care about appearances." Sam shifted slightly. "Drop the illusion. We don't care."

Ne Yong narrowed her gaze. "Millennials. You ruin everything."

The scene shifted. The pigeons disappeared, along with her teacup, and her clothes and appearance shifted, replaced by a young-looking Korean girl in a gray shirt with pink hearts, a black frilly skirt, and impossibly tall heels. She wore red glasses and her hair was a soft, wavy brown.

On her lap was her cell phone, open to a game with bright beads that shifted on the screen. An energy drink replaced the teacup.

"Happy now?" asked Ne Yong.

The new appearance seemed to bother Sam, who didn't know how to process it.

"Either they fear you or want to have sex with you," said Ne Yong, whose voice had shifted higher to match the appearance, though not enough to fool Aurie. "If you live long enough, you either become an unbearable twit, never satisfied, or you don't give a shit, and let it all go."

"And which one are you?" asked Aurie, receiving a raised eyebrow for her question.

"Neither. I'm striking out in new directions." She looked at Sam. "So what do you want?"

"I'm looking for something," he said.

"You're always looking for something." She smiled, a hint of darkness in her gaze. "No need to tell me. I can smell it on you. You're looking for a bit of luck, aren't you?"

Ne Yong chuckled as if it were a private joke. Sam looked like he was going to ask a question, then he reached into his front pocket and pulled out a small delicately wrapped package tied with red string.

When it was in her hands, she shook it, sniffed it. A mien of disappointment cast shadows across the young face.

"You expect answers?"

Sam shook his head. "I expect nothing."

Ne Yong gave Aurie a secret smile. "He lies well, that one. He hasn't told you, has he?"

"Ne Yong," said Sam, insistently.

Aurie turned to him. "What?"

"She's messing with you," he said.

Which was true, but Aurie sensed something else. "Is it about Nahid?"

A spark lit in his face, but before Aurie could question him further, Ne Yong clucked her tongue. "Nahid's daughter. That's why I recognized your scent."

This news made Ne Yong lift her chin and appraise Aurie in new light. It also confused Aurie, because if Ne Yong had just become aware of who her mother was, the information that Sam was withholding couldn't be about her.

"Your roots go deep," said Ne Yong, tapping the glass on her cell phone with long pink fingernails. "Quite a family."

"My family is dead, except for me and my sister."

Ne Yong shifted her crossed leg, smoothing the ruffles on her black skirt.

"Can you help or not?" asked Sam.

"You know better than to pressure me," said Ne Yong.

"I'm beginning to think it's not worth it," he said.

Her lips thinned from anger. "I'm not worth it? I'm not *worth* it?" Then her eyes rounded, before narrowing. "Wait. You're trying that patented Arlington magic on me, aren't you? That was subtle, so subtle I almost missed it. Cocky of you to think you could influence me like that."

Sam's cheeks reddened, but he said nothing.

"Fine," she said, rolling her eyes, "I'll tell you. But only because you have amused me for a brief spell. Not because of your gift, which is entirely outdated." She tossed the box onto the gravel. "What you seek is in the city, and you're not the only one looking for it. That's all I know."

"In the city?" asked Sam incredulously. "But how?"

Aurie was surprised to learn that the Crimson Skull was in the city as well. Sam seemed to be taking the news hard. He was shaking his head as if she'd told him he had five minutes to live.

Ne Yong crossed her slender legs, tapped on the cell phone idly, and shrugged her petite shoulders. "Who knows? I hear things, and as luck would have it, they're often useful."

Sam nodded soberly. "My thanks, Ne Yong. I'm afraid we must

leave."

As Aurie turned to follow, she said, "Good fortune to you."

Ne Yong seemed to find her comment amusing.

As she left, Ne Yong's voice followed her out. "You should get him to tell you his secrets."

At the black Suburban, she asked, "What was that about? What secrets?"

His eyes raced with thought. "I—" he started, but it almost looked like he'd been frozen, as if something was preventing him from speaking. "I...there's a time and place for everything, but not now. I couldn't even if I wanted to. If others are looking for the Crimson Skull, then we have to double our efforts."

"Why?" asked Aurie. "I thought this was a personal project. Something to burnish your artifact-hunting credentials. This sounds like something more."

Sam looked like he wanted to say something. The muscles in his face and jaw were fraught, as if they were rebelling from the act of speaking. Eventually he was able to calm himself and take a deep, cleansing breath. He put the vehicle in drive. Neither of them said another word the whole way back.

EIGHTEEN

The book of photographs was spilled across Aurie's bed, scattered around the indigo and yellow glass balls like water around a pair of islands. The sight of the stupid glass balls gave Pi a low-level migraine every time she looked at them. They'd performed every sort of investigative magic they—or anyone else in Arcanium—could think of, to no avail. The only thing they ever got was a faint faez signature, almost like a frequency. Each ball had a different one, but they couldn't figure out if it was important.

Pi was picking through the pictures to pass the time. In this time of trouble, it was comforting to see her mom and dad.

"Have you talked to him since?" Pi asked.

Aurie was sulking in the corner, knees against her chest, arms wrapped around her knees. "Nope. He won't tell me his secret, or why he lied about the importance of the Crimson Skull. He keeps telling me that he can't, but he won't say why. He can go rot in his mansion for all I care."

There was frustration in her sister's voice. Pi knew it well, she'd been feeling that way since Violet had called them a week ago to tell them Alton and Sunil had figured out the key and had entered the portal in the statue.

Once the secret to the third clue had been uncovered, four other Cabal teams followed.

"I don't understand how they passed us," said Aurie.

"Besides having the resources of the Cabal behind them? Everyone in Arcanium has been helpful, but it's one Hall against many—we don't stand a chance," said Pi. Realizing how she sounded, she added, "I'm not giving up, but I don't know where to look next."

"Agreed, and neither do I," said Aurie, chin resting on her knee. She looked up. "Maybe we'll get lucky and the remaining puzzles will finish Alton and Sunil for us."

"I prefer to do it myself," said Pi. "Just to make sure. They're like a fungus that won't go away, needs to be burned out."

"Ever wonder what it'd be like to have Mom and Dad around?" asked Aurie suddenly.

"All the time," said Pi.

"Yeah, me too. It's weird to miss someone you don't know that well."

Pi frowned. "Of course we know them."

"They're our parents, they only showed us one side of themselves. Not even counting the fact we were little bitty for the majority of our time with them. We don't really know them at all," said Aurie.

"I know how much they loved us. That I know for sure," said Pi resolutely.

"Without a doubt," said Aurie. "But what if they weren't the people we thought they were?"

A knock on the door interrupted them. "It's me, Deshawn."

He had bags under his eyes, and his clothes were rumpled.

"Find anything?" asked Pi hopefully.

"Nope. Another all-nighter in the library, but nothing. We're gonna burn the Biblioscribe out at this pace," said Deshawn.

"Well, thanks for trying. We'll figure it out eventually," said Pi.

Deshawn scratched the back of his neck. “I didn’t come to tell you about my exhaustion. I just heard that they found the fourth clue.”

No one had to say who *they* were.

Pi punched the bed, spilling photographs onto the floor. “I can’t believe we’re losing to those two!”

As Deshawn rescued a photo, he said, “Hey, wow. Is that your mom? She’s beautiful.”

He had a Polaroid in his hands, studying it with his mouth slightly open.

“Wipe your mouth, drool boy, since that’s our mother you’re panting over,” said Pi.

He wiped his lower lip and examined his hand, wincing when he realized she was messing with him. He picked up a few other photos and started looking at them.

“I didn’t know your mom had a tattoo,” said Deshawn.

“What?” said Pi, hearing Aurie say the same thing.

“You must be mistaken,” continued Pi. “She doesn’t have one.”

Deshawn shook a picture at her. “Take a look for yourself.”

Drawn by the intrigue, Aurie joined her as they examined the photo. The scene was at a camp with olive canvas tents. Three men were holding a dead alligator in their arms. The one on the right had a rifle slung over his shoulder. His neon orange shirt suggested the early 1990s.

“She’s not in this picture,” said Aurie from beside her.

Deshawn jabbed the photo with his forefinger, not at the three men with the alligator, but at a woman in the background, facing the other way. She wasn’t wearing her headscarf, and a man had his arm around her waist, absently tugging the shirt high enough to reveal a tattoo.

“That’s Mom,” said Pi. “Who’s the guy?”

In a flat voice, her sister answered, “Sam.”

Pi studied the photo again, noting the familiar way they were touching each other. It looked like more than coworkers.

"Whoa," said Deshawn, holding his hands up. "I didn't do anything, did I? You both suddenly went a little intense."

"Not you," said Aurie. "We're learning some things about our parents that we didn't know before. Processing it, is all."

"Is this what you were talking about earlier?" asked Pi, receiving a nod from her sister.

"Let's focus on the tattoo," said Aurie. "Anyone know a spell that will blow it up? I have a suspicion."

Pi snatched the picture out of Aurie's hands. "Spell? Sometimes, sis, I think you forget we have computers."

She placed the photo on their combination printer and scanner. Soon, the picture was blown up large on her laptop screen. After running the area through some pixel cleaners, the hazy shape of a swirling tattoo was apparent on her hip.

"That's the same tattoo I saw on Sam, same spot and everything."

"Do you think?" asked Pi.

"Possibly." Aurie shook her head. "Probably."

Pi cupped her hand over her mouth. "I can't believe that. I mean I do, but, what about Dad?"

"What are you two being all cryptic about?" asked Deshawn.

"We think our mom cheated on our dad with Sam Arlington," said Aurie.

"The TV show guy? Artifact hunter?" asked Deshawn. "Wow. I mean, sorry. That's messed up."

"Does a tattoo really mean that?" asked Pi.

Aurie became introspective. "It's not only that. I've found other little notes and things in her diary. I don't think Sam knew they were there or he wouldn't have let me see them. Like this picture. It's so rare that she didn't wear her headscarf, that *I* didn't even notice her."

"We don't know for sure she did anything," said Pi. "And even if she did, I'm not judging her."

"I'm not judging her either," said Aurie.

"You certainly look like you are."

Aurie shook her head. "It's hard to process, that's all." She frowned. "The other thing I'm wondering is why the tattoo disappears."

"That's easy," said Deshawn. "If you've got a side chic or dude, and you want to get matching tattoos, there's a way to make them disappear unless certain conditions are met."

"His hand is touching her hip," said Aurie. "Like when I was cleaning his wounds and it appeared. Maybe because I'm her daughter I triggered it."

"Wait a second," said Pi, staring at the indigo ball tattoo on her wrist. "What if there's more to these tattoos than what we see?"

She placed a finger against the center of the indigo ball and let a little faez travel into it. A few sparkles appeared on her wrist, but quickly faded. Her sister performed the same trick, but without sparkles.

After a moment of thought, Pi snapped her fingers. Faez was the energy of magic, and any type of energy had a signature. Faez in particular had similarities to musical frequencies, which was why some Halls used magic or their voice.

"The frequency on the indigo ball," she said, and Aurie's eyes went wide with understanding.

Pi applied faez to her tattoo again, this time adjusting the frequency to match the glass ball's. A list of formulas appeared across the length of her wrist, bringing with it a surge of excitement, like butterflies had taken roost in her chest.

When Aurie matched her trick, revealing similar but different formulas, they cheered.

"What do they mean?" asked Deshawn.

Before anyone could answer, the formulas started to fade, so they did it again, this time taking pictures and printing them out so they could study them. There were many lines of formulas, but many of them were repeats. They identified seven unique formulas.

"I don't get it," said Pi. "None of them make sense. They all equal infinity."

Aurie squinted at them before agreeing. "What's the catch? Are we supposed to derive an infinite frequency? Or is there a clue hidden in them?"

"Let's try eliminating those that are the same. Maybe the leftovers will tell us something," said Pi.

She grabbed a red marker and X'd out the numbers and symbols that were found in other formulas. When they were finished, they'd eliminated them all.

"I guess that's not it. Any ideas from your mathmagic mind?" asked Aurie.

Deshawn, who'd been quietly ruminating, spoke softly and quietly as if afraid he was going to disturb a thought. "What if it's not so complicated? What if infinity is the point?"

"We're looking for more clarity, not less," said Pi.

Deshawn blinked a few times, clearly looking for a way to explain his thought, before reaching out and grabbing both of their wrists. He turned Aurie's arm and placed it next to Pi's.

"Infinity," he said.

"The symbol! The sideways eight," said Pi.

She jammed her arm against Aurie's until the tattoos touched. Nothing happened.

"Apply faez," said Aurie.

When they each added the proper frequency of faez, the tattoo of a ball morphed into a key.

"It worked!" Pi kissed Deshawn on the cheek, making him blush.

Aurie was still staring at the key tattoo on her wrist. "What about the last clue? *To follow the rainbow and pay the fee, two makes one then one more is the key*. I thought we'd need three to get in?"

"I don't know, sis. Maybe we're not understanding it as we should, but the tattoo on our wrists is enough for me. We can go through the statue portal now."

Aurie bit her lower lip. "If we can get in."

"If we can get in."

NINETEEN

The square containing the statue of Invictus looked like a war zone rather than a tourist hotspot. Aurie stood in a luxurious apartment in a nearby high-rise, leaning against the sun-lit glass, watching soldiers with automatic rifles, black runed armor, and Blackstone Security badges roam around the barricaded area.

The official story was that the barrier between this world and the infernal one had thinned, endangering the city with demonic incursions, which technically was true. They'd let a few demons rampage through the area to help with the cover story.

The souvenir shop had been barricaded with cinderblocks. Oblong, portal-like magic detectors were set up outside. Anyone going in was subjected to a lengthy examination to confirm they were who they said they were.

"Impressive, isn't it?" said Violet as she strolled into the room wearing a sleeveless mauve pantsuit. Her hair was a soft, strawberry blonde. "You should be proud they're worried about you and your sister enough to put up such protections."

They shared a warm hug. "I'd prefer they underestimate us."

"It would make it easier," mused Violet.

Her pocket buzzed. She pulled out her phone and stared at it distastefully before silencing it.

"You look tired," said Aurie.

Violet had little red marks at the corner of her eyes where she'd clearly been rubbing them. "Running a company while finishing your classes and helping your friends break into a heavily guarded statue is hell on sleep."

"You're finishing your studies in Arcanium? I kinda thought you'd dropped out once you took over the *Herald*," said Aurie.

"Oh, hell no. The Hall work is probably one of the few things that I really enjoy, and Semyon let me design a curriculum to help keep me safe from those sycophants on the board. But enough about that. What else do you need besides this apartment?" asked Violet.

"Thanks again for this," said Aurie. "We couldn't scout the statue without it."

"It's ultra-exclusive, so as long as everyone uses the private elevator, and only my transport in and out of the garage, you'll be fine," said Violet.

"Speaking of," said Aurie, as the door opened. Pi and three other girls stepped into the apartment. The girl with the loose afro, Sasha, if Aurie remembered correctly, gave a low whistle.

"This is some serious rich shit, here," said Sasha, running her fingers across the polished copper with gilded leaf backing on the couch. A tray covered with a white towel sat in the center of a glass table. The newcomers eyed it, but didn't move to peek under the towel as Aurie expected them to.

"Hey Violet," said Pi. "Thanks for letting us use your digs."

They made introductions. The other girls were Yoko and Bethany, friends of Pi's from when she lived in the Undercity. Yoko had a quiet intensity about her, while Bethany rubbed her arm absently. Her neck turned translucent for a moment, revealing muscle and tissue, and veins pumping purple blood.

"Only three?" asked Aurie. "I thought you said five."

Sasha, who had her thumbs in the loops of her belt, said, "Nobody knows what happened to Sisi. She took off after we left the Undercity. I miss her, but...you know, she was creeptacular. And Stone Arm Nancy, she's working in the city for some dude, but we couldn't get ahold of her. Probably on business, and couldn't get free."

"Is this everyone?" asked Violet.

"Hannah had a test, otherwise she would have been here, and the gang at Arcanium is available for whatever we need," said Pi. "So yeah, this is it."

"There's one more," said Aurie, hating to contradict her sister. "He's late, but we're going to need his help if we're going to get past all that security."

"I thought we weren't going to involve him," said Pi, crossing her arms.

"We need him, his expertise," said Aurie, feeling the heat rise to her cheeks.

The others were looking between Aurie and her sister with confused looks.

"What's going on?" asked Violet. "I thought you two had a plan worked out."

"We do," said Pi.

"But it's not going to work without him," said Aurie.

Pi tilted her head. "Are you sure this is about the statue?"

Anger flared in Aurie's chest. "Do you really think I'd risk everything just for that?"

Her sister bobbed her head a little as if she were considering the argument. "Good point, but—"

"It doesn't matter because I'm already here."

Everyone turned to find a handsome dark-skinned guy with a boyish smile and webbing tattoos across his arms sitting on the white couch with his feet on the glass table. His ice-blue gaze roved around the room confidently, and when Aurie locked eyes with him for a moment, a shiver of good memories went down her spine.

"Everyone, this is Zayn Carter," said Aurie.

Violet stepped forward, throwing her arms up. "How did you get in here? My security is the best."

Zayn breathed on his fingernails and polished them against his skin-tight black shirt. "Obviously not the best. But don't worry, part of your protection is that nobody knows that you're here. Without Aurie telling me how to get here, I would have never known."

Aurie checked her sister, who was frowning. If there'd been any other way, she would have left Zayn out of it, but their plan had holes in it without him.

"Zayn is a graduate from the Subtle Arts Hall," said Pi flatly.

Violet spun around. "You let a Cabal mage in here? What are you thinking?"

The other three women were glaring at Aurie. She caught Sasha glancing towards the door as if she were having second thoughts.

"I promise you that Zayn is on our side," said Aurie, holding her hands up. "He helped us a few years ago, at great risk to himself, and against the wishes of his patron."

Sasha shook her head. "No way. That's the whole point of his Hall. They get all double and triple agent on people. He could be playing you."

Bethany poked Pi in the arm. "Is that true? That he could be a double agent?"

The room was getting away from Aurie. She thought they'd take the help, especially with her and Pi vouching for him.

"Trust me, he's on our side," said Aurie.

"You're only saying that because you were sleeping with him," said Pi.

Every one of them turned and appraised Zayn with this new knowledge. A few noises of appreciation were given.

Zayn put his hands up. "Hey! Am I a piece of meat?"

Violet shook her head as if she were waking up from a good dream. "I think that news makes your judgment suspect. How can we trust him? We're putting ourselves in enough danger as it is."

"Isn't control of the Halls worth it?" asked Aurie.

Sasha shook her head dismissively. "Nope. I will walk away from this shit if we're not going to do it right."

Even the quiet Yoko looked uneasy about Zayn's involvement, chewing on her lower lip.

"I don't know," said Aurie. "What can I do to convince you? We need him. Think about it. Did any of you see him come into the room? He sat two feet away from you, Sasha, and you didn't even notice until he spoke."

Sasha rolled her eyes. "Doesn't prove anything about his loyalties."

Zayn stood up, prompting the others to step away. "What if I put a Faithless Curse on myself?"

This idea seemed to appeal to the others, and they nodded in agreement.

"Zayn, are you sure? Those are notoriously unreliable. Curses like to interpret the triggers in the worst way," said Aurie, her gut twisting.

"Look," he said, "I know how important this is. I know Alton Lockwood better than you all. If he was the one to take over the Halls, he'd turn the school into his personal petting zoo, if you know what I mean."

"I'll let you stay if you take the Faithless Curse," said Violet.

The others added their agreement. Everyone but Pi.

"Pi?" asked Aurie.

She gave an exasperated sigh. "It's not that I don't like you, Zayn. No offense. But you could have other hooks in you."

"A Faithless Curse is pretty rock solid," said Aurie. "Come on, sis. You know it's the only way."

Pi heaved a heavy sigh.

"Fiiiine, I'm in. Like you said, it's worth the risk," said Pi, but the way she looked at Zayn suggested she wasn't going to trust him.

Aurie knew what was bothering her sister. She'd asked Pi about Zayn, and when she'd said no, she'd brought him along anyway. It was another time that she'd tried to be a parent to her sister.

"So what's the plan?" asked Zayn, strolling to the window.

"Curse, first," said Violet.

"Right," he said.

Zayn rubbed his hands together and winked at Pi, who stuck her tongue out semi-playfully. It appeared Pi wasn't going to hold his Hall against him.

A light metallic taste hit the back of Aurie's throat as Zayn summoned faez into his arms, giving them a warm glow.

"If I betray the Silverthorne sisters or their friends while helping them get into the portal inside the statue of Invictus, cross my heart and may I die before I wake again."

He drew a big "X" on his chest with a finger. The glow faded within seconds. His jaw tightened, and he closed his eyes.

When he opened them, he said, "Are we good?"

Pi nodded.

"We're good," said Aurie.

"So what are we facing?" asked Sasha.

"The first line of defense, as you can plainly see, is Creed's personal army, also known as Blackstone Security. There's at least a fifty-foot gap between the outer barrier and the cinderblock wall around the old souvenir shop. Crossing that without being detected will be a doozy. The next line of defense is a magic detector that provides a way for them to confirm there are no doppelgangers or other polymorphed folks trying to sneak in using someone else's identity."

Aurie gave a heavy sigh. "If we get past that, there's the inner portal, which is keyed with a password. This is probably the easiest part since we've been through there. The portal will take us inside the statue. Once there, things get really tricky. There are more guards, a heavily warded two-man door which can only be opened from the inside, and finally, at the inner portal, there's an invisible Gorgonmancer."

"What the hell is a Gorgonmancer, and why is it invisible?" asked Sasha.

"A Class Five supernatural near-invisible entity that can turn you to stone with its gaze, has three-inch claws that can slice through runed iron, and is meaner than a rhino on speed," said Aurie.

"Why would something invisible need to turn things to stone? Wouldn't you need to see it for that to happen?" asked Bethany.

"This isn't a medusa," said Pi. "It only needs to see you, not the other way around."

"That sounds awful," said Bethany.

"It is," said Aurie.

"How'd you get all this information?" asked Zayn.

"Violet has connections, plus magic, of course, and old-fashioned scouting," said Pi.

Bethany tapped on the window. "What's the big deal about the security? Can't we just figure out how to bypass the statue walls? Get right in without having to bother with guards, magic detectors, and invisible guardians?"

"That's the first thing everyone thinks of," said Aurie, "and it makes sense. Except we've been inside the statue, and we know what it's made of. There's no way to teleport in, or even break through the outside. The whole place was designed this way, not by the Cabal, but by Invictus."

"Got it," said Bethany.

"*Now* what's the plan?" asked Sasha, tapping her foot.

"You haven't even told them the best part," said Violet.

"Oh, yeah, I almost forgot," she said, laughing at the joke. "They've got a rotating group from the Order of Telepaths checking anyone in the square for thoughts about breaking into the statue. So there's no way to approach without getting picked out by them. They're housed right inside the souvenir shop on the first floor."

"Aren't telepaths notoriously unreliable?" asked Zayn.

"That's why they have a group of them, to cover for mistakes," said Aurie. "So while we're breaking into the statue, we're going to have to not think about it."

"That's impossible," said Bethany.

"Not impossible," said Pi. "But not easy either. This has been one of the areas that's been tripping us up about getting in. Why it's taken us weeks to get to this point."

"Why is that?" asked Zayn.

With dramatic flair, Aurie ripped the cover from the tray on the glass table, revealing a dozen squat jars filled with a yellowish liquid that pulsed eerily.

"Because everything we're going to tell you," said Aurie, "you need to forget."

TWENTY

Pi couldn't remember why she was standing on the corner of Fifth and Hex in the early morning without her leather jacket and only a cell phone in her hand. It was chilly, and she squeezed her arms around herself, rubbing them for warmth, examining her surroundings for clues to why she was there.

She didn't recognize the exact location in the city, though she guessed it was an outer ward, since the Spire could be seen through some residential buildings to her right. The buildings were mere outlines as muted pinks colored the sky above. A gentle wind gave the air a fresh smell as if it'd been washed clean.

A taxi passed her, slowing to see if she needed a ride, so she waved it on, bumping a hunk of broken glass with her boot. It skittered over the edge of the curb and into the sewer drain. Other chunks of glass lay on the street before her as if she'd dropped them.

"People can be so rude," she said, knocking the dangerous shards into the drain. After she was finished she surveyed her surroundings again.

"Why am I here?" she asked, checking the phone to see if it had an answer. As she turned her wrist to check the screen, she noticed a message in her handwriting on her wrist: "Watch the video."

Her mind, hazy and unclear as if she'd woken up from a decade-long nap, struggled to comprehend the word "video." Eventually, she fought through the fog, opening up phone, and found a video ready to play.

As her fingertip brushed the triangular play button, her face appeared on the screen.

"Hey, it's me, Pi, or really it's you," said Pi from the video.

She hit the square stop button, reeling for a moment at the strangeness of the situation, when a black limousine with tinted windows pulled up. Pi wondered if she was supposed to watch the video longer, when the door opened, revealing only darkness. A whiff of heavy cologne assaulted her nose.

"Get in," came a familiar voice with a thick accent.

When she hesitated, a darkened window lowered until she could see a pale man. Her mind strained to recognize him, but it only gave her a headache.

"It's me, Ivan. Get in, PI-THEE-A," he said, laughing at himself. "It's time to pay the bills."

Even though she couldn't remember him—why was everything in her head so blank?—and she sensed he was extremely dangerous, she didn't sense that he was dangerous at this moment. Or maybe that it'd be more dangerous *not* to get in. He knew who she was, anyway, and hadn't attacked her from the get-go. It seemed safer to get in, and find out who he was, and why he thought she needed to pay bills.

The seats were dark crimson leather that crunched when she sat on them. Ivan wore an island shirt with coconuts and parrots. His cologne was at near gag levels.

"Where is leather jacket? It good look for you," he said.

gave a whimsical one-shoulder shrug.

"What do you want, Ivan?" she asked, his name feeling unfamiliar to her lips. She felt like if she knew him, she didn't know him well.

"It been quite challenging to find you. For week I have my pet mages searching for you. No one can find you. Not anywhere. It like you disappear from city. Then, Orlando wake me up, tell me you showed up. Right here. So I come see you before you disappear again."

Not that she wasn't concerned before, but having a man of his means searching for her with mages that were operating around the clock suggested this was no ordinary encounter.

"That's how you found me, but not what you want," she said flatly.

"You owe me debt, debt I intend to collect," he said.

"I'm busy," she said.

He waved a single finger at her as if it were a wiper blade on a windshield. "That's not how deal works. You promised a day. Anyway, it doesn't matter, I want you to keep doing what you're doing."

"Then what do you want?"

He smoothed the wrinkles in his pant leg. "When you win, when you take control of the Hundred Halls, I want my own Hall."

Part of her screamed to get out of the car. Whatever he was talking about was something she didn't want to hear, but she knew sudden movements would probably get her killed. She'd heard the click of a gun from the window behind her when she first sat down.

"Sure," she said, hoping to make him go away as fast as possible, "whatever you want."

"You think I don't know what you are doing? Everyone in the fucking city knows, everyone who is anyone. I will not be left out," he said, slapping his knee on the last four words like percussive punctuation marks.

The tension had risen until she was suffocating. Without knowing the whole picture, she didn't know what to say, so she kept her lips sealed.

Ivan broke into laughter. "It does not matter what I say, it only matter what I do, or what I can do. That is the way world works."

He pulled out his cell phone, which only reminded Pi of the video waiting to be played on hers. He flashed a picture at her, and this time the face was familiar enough that she recognized it, though it took a few seconds to conjure the name.

"Ernie."

He was tied up and sitting on a pea-green couch. Fear had contorted his face and his eyes were swollen and blotchy from crying. Rage welled up in her chest.

"Very good, PI-THEE-A," he said. "If you cannot deliver for me, then you can kiss your friend goodbye." He snapped his fingers. "Time to get out."

Swallowing her pride, Pi scrambled out of the limo as fast as she could as if it were contagious with the black plague. The vehicle sped away, wheels squelching, as if it were as concerned about maintaining a safe distance

Standing on the sidewalk, on the corner of Fifth and Hex, Pi's mind whirled with confusion and anger. A growing sense of understanding was forming, mirroring the light on the horizon, but she knew, unlike the sunrise, that this was not a good thing, even if she didn't know why.

To quell her curious thoughts, Pi pulled out her phone and hit the play button. It was worse than she thought.

TWENTY ONE

The little blue dot on the map blinked in and out, hopping two streets over before returning to the south side of the canal. Bethany banged on the side of her cell phone, growling at it to behave.

"They're going to kill me if I mess this up," she said, anxiety mounting in her chest.

When Aurie and Pi had laid out the plans to get inside the statue, Bethany had been perturbed that she'd been given a minor role—mostly because her sometimes translucent skin made her conspicuous. Now that she couldn't find the damn place she was supposed to go, she felt like they'd been right all along.

Bethany craned her head back and forth, trying to figure out which way to go. This little section of the seventh ward was dubbed Little Venice because an enterprising businessman had put in canals around a three-square-block section filled with bars and restaurants.

The stone-lined canals were empty of the narrow boat taxis that shuttled people around the area. Old wrappers and cigarette butts floated in the brackish water. She'd been in the area once at night, and it'd been glorious, with magelights casting an enchanting glow on the colorful boats and moss-covered willows as men and women chatted softly and floated along the canal. She'd thought it'd looked like the realms of Fae. But now, in the chilly early morning, the spells that had given the place its appeal had worn off and it was a little depressing.

"Why does this asshole have to live in such a confusing place?" she asked, jogging up the sidewalk and crossing a curved wooden bridge to find the cross street. The white signs with black lettering read "Sprite" and "Holly."

With two fingers, Bethany expanded the map to find where her target lived.

"Gotcha," she said, and as if the dot was done messing with her, it jumped back to the original location.

Time was short, so she sprinted up the street to her destination, only to find herself blocked by a canal with no bridge in sight.

A door shutting alerted her to the man in dark pants, a dark jacket, and a runed Kevlar vest leaving his three-story shotgun-style house. The street across from the canal was a line of trendy buildings; mercenary work seemed to pay well.

"Great," she said, looking for a quick way across. She was supposed to be walking past his house at the moment he left, not staring at him from a hundred feet away.

"Bethany, you're so stupid, this is why they didn't give you a more important job," she muttered. "You can't even get across a stupid canal, thirty feet wide."

She checked her wrist for her swimming charm, only to remember that Pi had lost it last year getting into Arcanium through the moat. The water looked over her head, and even if she could swim well, she'd be soaking wet.

The Blackstone guard had locked his door and was headed the other way. At least he wasn't getting into a car, or she'd be screwed. She had to get to him, or the Silverthorne sisters would never get into the inner chamber of the statue.

When she checked her watch, the skin on her arm went translucent, revealing muscle tissue and pumping veins. She was so used to seeing the inside of her flesh that it normally didn't register, but in that moment, it was a reminder of the curse that Alton had laid upon her, and the fear that had led her to leave Coterie of Mages after a single year. She had regretted that decision, regretted it every day of her life since. Bethany wished she had stayed, even if it'd meant they'd have killed her, rather than leave and be left with that feeling of missing out that plagued her every moment.

The Blackstone guard was turning the corner. Bethany stared at her phone, wishing she could call the others, tell them not to go into the statue. But she couldn't—not that she didn't have their number, but they'd all taken forgetful potions and wouldn't even remember why they were going into the statue. It was the only way to get around the Order of Telepath mages.

A confusing cocktail of rage, frustration, anger, and despair wracked her limbs until she was shaking, shaking her fists. Tears squeezed from the corner of her eyes.

"No," she said, "I'm not screwing this up."

Bethany leapt into the water, forgetting her phone, her fears, and the fact that she couldn't swim for shit. The impact jarred her, sent water up her nose. A dead bug went into her mouth, and when she spat it out, more water went in. She immediately regretted not taking off her shoes and jacket.

The weight of her clothes and the acid of rage in her muscles contributed to dragging her down. She flailed at the water, slapping, going nowhere, making more noise and splashing than progress.

There was a part of her that justified this failure. That she never bothered to learn the simple act of swimming, hadn't been able to hack it in Coterie, and was failing spectacularly at the simple task she'd been given. Maybe it'd be better if she stopped fighting and let herself get dragged to the bottom.

No!

The word was cacophonous in her head. She let loose again in her mind. *No!*

Bethany kept repeating it, like a mantra of defiance, pulling herself to the surface, stroking her arms forward, until her fingers jammed into the stone wall on the other side of the canal. A fingernail tore off. The exposed flesh stung, but she ignored it and pulled herself up the sloped wall.

At the top, she threw herself onto the sidewalk like a drowned rat. She got up and started running down the street, ignoring the horrified stares of the couple in neon running clothing pushing a stroller on the other side of the street.

Bethany pulled the antidote from her pocket and threw it into her mouth, nearly spitting it back out based on the rotten milk taste, but swallowed it down. Now all she had to do was dose him with the suggestion spray that Violet had given her.

When Bethany hit the corner, she saw the guard standing halfway down the block, thumbing through his phone.

Bethany walked-ran towards him, and when he looked up, she waved at him.

"Hello! Can you help me?"

He had a light brown beard and hard eyes. His hand went to the holster on his hip. "Stop."

Bethany froze, holding her hands up. He searched her with his eyes.

"Hey, whoa, I'm sorry," she said, praying that her skin wouldn't turn translucent, making him more suspicious. "I need help."

"I don't help," he said, carefully unclipping the cover on his pistol.

"Look," said Bethany, hoping he was interpreting the quivering in her voice as weakness as she kept walking forward, "I got really drunk last night at the Hunt. I dropped my scarf into the canal and when I tried to lean over the edge and get it with a stick, I fell in. My phone is toast. I just need to call my friend to pick me up."

"Not my problem," he said in a tone of voice that would have normally made her turn and run.

The corners of his eyes narrowed as she kept walking. She was ten feet away, too far away to use the spray.

"Stay right there," he said, pulling his pistol out, but keeping it pointed at the concrete.

"Please," she said, edging forward with little steps. "I'm freezing and I just want to go home and throw up in the privacy of my own bathroom."

He shook his head. "Something ain't right about you, so I suggest you stay right there, or I'll put you down and claim it was self-defense, and I might just be right about that."

At the far end of the street, a black SUV with tinted windows turned the corner.

"Your ride's here," she said, but he didn't look away. "Please, before you go, just a call."

He stared her down. "I ain't looking."

She was only about eight feet away. The SUV was pulling up to the curb. The moment his attention turned, she surged forward, pulling the squeeze mister from her pocket and cupping it in her hand.

Bethany grabbed his arm, and using the motion to hide her other hand, sprayed the mist upward.

"Get the fuck away," he said, pushing her back and leaping away. He pointed the pistol at her. "You make one more step towards me and you'll breathe through your chest."

When the SUV stopped, a window rolled down. "Everything okay?"

"This crazy bitch keeps coming," he said.

"Can you help me? I just need to call my friend," she said, then buried her face in her right hand, careful to keep the one with the squeeze spray in her left and behind her leg.

"We don't have time for this, Jake. Get in. We're already late for our shift," said the voice in the SUV.

After holstering his gun, giving Bethany dirty looks the whole time, Jake got into the SUV and they drove away. Only then did Bethany take a breath, half-collapsing onto the curb, burying her face in her hands because she didn't know if she'd hit the guard with enough suggestion spray.

TWENTY TWO

The video ended, and Yoko hit the pause button, keeping her face on the screen so she could study it. As far as she could tell, that had been her. The Yoko in the video had talked about the time when she was six years old when she lived in Tokyo with her parents, and she'd stolen a kiwi from the fruit vendor, but had felt so guilty about it, she'd hidden it under her bed rather than eat it, until it'd turned mushy, covered with mold, and when she went to throw it away, a beetle the size of her thumb had crawled from the inside.

Yoko was sitting in a cafe near the statue of Invictus. A half-eaten Ruben on a plate with fries was in front of her, along with a glass of tea, and a second glass, empty except for a trace of pulsing yellow liquid in the bottom. The cafe was mostly empty; the soldiers in the square had probably run off their clientele. She pulled the ear bud out, shoved it into her pocket, and scanned the skies.

The Yoko in the video had said to start the illusion when the storm rolled in, but the skies were light blue, and the sun, though behind an apartment building on the east side of the square, was shining.

Yoko knew she was going to do what the video of Yoko had explained, but the question was if she *could* do it. She'd never made an illusion that large, or complex, with that many moving pieces.

The guards in runed Kevlar jackets milled around the square behind the barriers, automatic rifles slung over their shoulders. As she studied the cinderblock walls, the silvery arch of the magic detectors, and the general layout, she realized that she knew the area. Though it was hard to place a conscious thought onto any one thing, the place had an intuitive memory to it, like returning home after years away, and walking to your favorite shops without remembering what their names were.

Yoko knew the storm was coming before she saw it, and not only because video Yoko had told her. The sharp metallic scent of faez hit her nose, only for a moment. The guards glanced around, sensing it as well, but she doubted that they knew the difference. Faez smelled like an incoming storm, when the sky was green and the wind had died.

A gust of wind blew through the square, throwing their hair around, scattering dust into mini-plumes. Her napkin was blown off her table, and she had to squint. The bushes between her and the square rustled. A car alarm went off in the distance.

Part of her knew that other mages, friends from Arcanium, were standing on the buildings surrounding the statue of Invictus, summoning a storm, but she knew she wasn't supposed to think about it.

As the first fat droplets of rain splashed down, thudding into the awning, making the guards glance into the sky with disappointed frowns, Yoko retreated inside the cafe. She stood at the window, as the sheet of glass wouldn't affect her magic, and started picturing the illusions she wanted to form.

When a stab of lightning hit the statue, she could hear the guards shouting at each other. Rain came down in sheets as they debated.

Drawing forth her faez, Yoko highlighted the area she wanted to affect with her mind. The illusion covered the rain-soaked area, right over one of the guards. It was impossible to match the rain or his motions with her illusion, so she replaced the scene en masse, hoping the blurring motion of the rain would hide any mistakes.

She caught a shift of motion at the edge of her illusion. Her gut twisted with the thought of what might have happened, and a little guilt wafted up, but she pushed it away and focused on the next illusion.

Once she was ready, Yoko used her phone to call a number the Yoko on the video gave her. When someone on the other end answered in a semi-familiar voice (was it that good-looking Arcanium student Deshawn?), she said one word: "Now."

A second bolt of lightning drove down into the square, this time hitting the cinderblock building. Sparks went everywhere.

As the guards ran to the entrance to the statue, Yoko concentrated on the guard she'd placed the illusion on, hiding a large suitcase at his side as best as she could. This guard made it into the entrance before the others, slipping through the silvery archway, and then he was out of her range, and there was nothing more that Yoko could do for him. She hoped whatever she'd come here to do had worked, and slipped down the alleyway as the storm petered to a light drizzle. As Yoko walked down the subway stairs, she heard the sounds of sirens.

TWENTY THREE

The antidote to the memory potion tasted like black licorice. One moment Pi couldn't remember why she'd ridden in an extra-dimensional suitcase into an industrial basement, and then the memories came flooding back and vertigo sent her vomiting behind a light green generator with rusted hold-down bolts.

Pi wiped her mouth with her sleeve. Zayn was closing the latches on a suitcase, standing next to a runed archway, which placed them in the basement before the statue of Invictus. Aurie came around a row of shelves, spitting and making yuck faces.

"I shouldn't have eaten scrambled eggs with hot sauce this morning," said Aurie.

"You two back in business?" asked Zayn.

He held himself like a dancer. His eyes never stopped moving. He was simultaneously perfectly still and a bundle of energy.

"Everything go okay up top?" asked Aurie.

Zayn paused. "I think so. The telepaths never detected me."

"You think so?" asked Aurie.

He pulled out a cloth and wiped the water from his face. "It should be fine. No one figured out I'd taken their place."

"How do you do that?"

"Secret of the Hall." He winked.

Her sister's concern sparked a memory for Pi, of climbing in a black limousine and seeing Ernie's face on a cell phone. She didn't know what to do about that, except keep going forward.

"You good?" Aurie asked her.

Pi thought about telling her sister about the encounter with Ivan, but decided it was a complication better left for later.

"Let's get moving, before those telepaths look beneath them and send up the alarm. Once we're in the statue, we're good," said Pi.

Aurie said to Zayn, "You should get out of here. And thanks, we owe you big time."

"You owe me nothing. I'm doing what needs to be done," he said. "And maybe when all this is over, we can go on a real date. Something normal. I know a great Korean BBQ joint."

"Will it ever be over?" asked Aurie, and Pi could see in her sister the conflicting emotions of desire for Zayn, and weight of responsibility.

"Come on, you two, stop mooning over each other."

Aurie stuck her tongue out, while Zayn rolled his eyes. They were nice eyes—her sister had chosen well.

Side by side, they stood before the archway.

"You know, if the password has been changed somehow, we're screwed," said Aurie as she reached out to trigger the correct runes in order.

Before her hand touched the stone, Pi grabbed her sister's arm. "Wait. Let's armor up before we go in."

"But they don't know we're coming," said Aurie. "I thought we were going in blank, in case of magic triggers, or anything like that."

"I...I'm not sure, but I feel like it's our best move," said Pi.

Aurie's forehead wrinkled. "Is this the Oculus soul?"

Pi hissed at her sister.

"Sorry, forgot," she said. "But is it?"

"I don't know."

Aurie searched her face. "Alright, you look a little spooked about something, I'll take your word for it. Armor up."

The enchantments took a minute to apply. Pi worried the whole time she was making a mistake, letting her fears get the best of her.

"Ready?"

Pi nodded.

When the third rune glowed silver, Pi's world rotated around her. The moment of vertigo was lost amid the barking explosions on the other side.

Three soldiers with semiautomatic weapons and runed armor blasted them with bullets. The shield deflected the majority, but some got through at a slower speed, hitting her in the chest and arms with a heavy punch.

Pi was pushed against the stone wall, held there by the repeating fire of three semiautomatics. Eventually her shield would fail and the bullets would rip her apart.

The gestures for a force bolt kept getting interrupted by the impacts. If one bullet, even slow, hit her in the neck or face, she'd be out.

When the soldier on the left had to reload, it gave Pi a tiny window, and she sent a force bolt into the other two. Aurie followed up with a twinned firespear that charred the soldiers into twitching corpses.

"Oh, the smell, that's horrible," said Aurie.

Pi tried not to look at the dead soldiers. Even though they'd been trying to kill them, she felt remorse for their deaths.

"Let's keep going," said Pi. "I guess they know we're coming."

"I hope one of those isn't the guy we need," said Aurie with a frown, nodding towards the corpses.

They jogged up the stairs, finding, as expected, a wall with a door. This door wasn't in the statue the first time they'd come here years ago, and from Violet's reports, they knew they wouldn't get through it easily.

A camera hung above the door, and servos whined as it centered on them.

"Hi," said Pi, waving.

A voice came through a speaker. "Surrender. You can't get through the wall, and reinforcements are coming."

Pi shared a glance with her sister. "I hope this works." Then she faced the speaker, and—she hoped—a microphone.

"Jake Arrends, open the door," said Pi, adding a touch of the Voice, but not too much, or she wouldn't be able to talk afterwards.

There was a pause, then shouts came over the speaker, and fighting, followed by gunshots, which they heard through the wall too.

"I don't know how you turned him, but we killed him," said an out-of-breath voice over the speaker. "You're not getting through."

Aurie turned to her. "Ideas?"

Pi didn't get to answer before they heard footsteps coming up the stairs. They both turned and blasted the soldier running up, nearly vaporizing him with force bolt and firespear. This was followed by shouts from below. The soldiers from outside were gathering.

"Turned him," whispered Pi, realizing that they didn't understand the danger, that it'd been her voice that had gotten to Jake, not blackmail.

Pi faced the door and poured faez into her vocal chords. "The Gorgonmancer is loose. Open the door and we'll save you."

When the door swung open, Pi almost couldn't believe it. Pi went in, incapacitating the two remaining soldiers by sending them to sleep, and Aurie followed her. The third man lay against the wall with a bloody hole in his face.

They closed the door behind them, but couldn't lock it, since that required a password. There was another door on the backside, leading into the chamber with the final archway.

"It won't matter if we lock it, the soldiers fear the Gorgonmancer," said Aurie. "Apply the spells."

"My voice is shot," whispered Pi. "I'll have to go in without."

"But the Gorgonmancer will turn you to stone without them, and I can't cast them for you," said Aurie.

Pi touched her neck and gave a shrug of *what can you do*? She didn't want to speak any longer, and ruin what little voice she had left.

"Okay," said Aurie, "once we get inside, it won't matter. Stay behind me, use me like a shield. If the no-look spell keeps it from looking at me, turning me to stone, then maybe you'll be fine."

Neither of them believed that, but they had to keep going forward. Pi could only imagine what they were doing outside. She had no doubt that at least one of the patrons would be coming to the statue.

When they went through the door, Pi was crouched behind her sister, trying to stay as small as possible. They crept up the hallway towards the main chamber. Since the Gorgonmancer was invisible, they didn't know where it was.

Aurie paused at the corner, craning her head around it. Pi had her hands on her sister's back to let her know where she was. Without looking, Pi knew the archway was on the other side.

Her sister scissored her fingers, like a person walking fast, pointing in the direction of the archway. Pi nodded, again with the why-not shoulder shrug.

Crouching into the starting position, Aurie held her fingers above her shoulder.

One. Two. Three.

Pi took off too soon, and almost became tangled in her sister's feet, but they made it away, sprinting towards the archway. As it loomed larger,

Pi felt victory rise up in her chest. They were going to make it. They were going through the portal.

Then a massive silvery runed door came crashing down, right in front of the archway. The impact reverberated through the statue, alerting the Gorgonmancer to their presence.

Pi hit the door, smashing her fist into it.

"Dammit," croaked Pi.

"We're not getting through that," said Aurie. "Not without a few hours' work."

The words in Pi's throat died at the sound of claws clicking on stone from somewhere behind them.

TWENTY FOUR

"Get behind me, now," whispered Aurie.

The claws of the Gorgonmancer echoed through the interior of the statue. Aurie didn't know where the Gorgonmancer was coming from because the oddly shaped walls confused the origins of the sound. Her sister's grip on the back of her shirt cinched it around her middle.

They were trapped. Aurie wasn't one hundred percent certain, but it sounded like the Gorgonmancer was coming from the hallway. It'd probably taken up residence in the rooms in this half of the statue.

Aurie cursed herself for not preparing a spell that could see invisibility, but they hadn't expected to fight the creature, only avoid it and go through the portal. Only the no-look enchantment was keeping it from turning her to stone, but that kind of spell wouldn't last forever, and if they did something overly obvious, the no-look spell wouldn't be enough, which meant she really couldn't cast any spells that required verbal components.

Turning her head, she tried to locate the Gorgonmancer. Maybe she could hit it with a lucky firespear, killing it before it looked at her. That was probably the only spell she could cast fast enough that wouldn't draw its attention.

There was one other spell she knew that could help which was completely non-verbal. It was a spell that created mist along the floor. Deshawn had used at the Spring Formal last year, to give the place a little ambience, and she thought she remembered how to cast it.

Using stirring motions, as if she were a witch at a cauldron, Aurie channeled faez, then she blew out, opening her arms and pushing. Like in a graveyard at midnight, mist formed along the ground, rising up around their ankles.

Aurie watched for signs of movement, but either the Gorgonmancer had frozen, or it masked its motions within the swirls of the rising mist.

After half a minute, Aurie wondered if it'd left, returned to its lair, thinking that the chamber was empty. But then she heard the soft click of a claw not fifteen feet from their location.

Aurie held her breath, searching the area for signs, ready to strike with a firespear. A door opening in the other part of the statue brought a breeze, disturbing the mist and making it impossible to find the Gorgonmancer.

Then she saw the hint of a shape, the curve of a misshapen leg outlined by the mist, and blasted the firespear in its direction. The elemental spell hit. The Gorgonmancer cried out, a hoarse yell that sent shivers down her spine. Aurie readied a second firespear, but knew she was too late. She hadn't killed it. There was no way it wouldn't see her before she could loose the second spell.

Then it appeared, a grotesque beast with an oversized head like a buffalo with a man-like body and clawed bear feet. The Gorgonmancer was facing perpendicular to her, and the blade of a knife stuck from its back. It fell forward, face-first into the swirling mist.

Zayn stepped around the corner, a second knife in his fist.

"Good thing you brought the mist," he said. "I had no idea where it was."

"What are you doing here? You were supposed to get out," said Aurie.

He winked, giving her a smile that made her heart thrum. "And miss out on a chance to save you? Think about how much you owe me now."

"Sicko," croaked Pi.

The realization of what he'd said reverberated across his face. He held his hands out. "No, wait. That's not what I meant. I wanted to help."

Aurie chuckled, winking back. "It's okay. But let's focus on getting out of here."

"Yeah," said Zayn, "about that. I heard Bannon was on his way, probably here by now. Any chance you can get through that?"

Aurie shook her head. "Not without more time and preparation. I guess they added another layer of protection. We need to get out."

Shouts came from the hallway. The soldiers were massing on the other side. Probably waiting for mage backup.

"Thoughts?" asked Zayn.

Aurie pointed to the tower at the center of the statue. "There's a hole we can slip through up there. It'll take us down to the bottom of the statue, might get us past the soldiers."

Zayn leapt into action, climbing up the wall as if he were a spider. When he reached the top, he sent down a rope.

Boosted by spells, Aurie and her sister made the climb. A large metallic ball connected to a thick braid of wires was at the top.

The three of them slipped through the gap in the wire, into the chamber at the top of the tower. The inner walls had bits of old yellowed foam from when Aurie had come through this place the first time.

When they reached the bottom, they found a door protected like the area above. They wouldn't have been able to come through this way from below, but they could leave easily.

The short sprint down the stairs to the archway was adrenaline filled. They made it back to the basement of the souvenir shop, hearing voices coming down the stairs when they arrived.

The three of them hid behind the generators. Zayn put a spell on them to keep them hidden, which allowed them to safely watch Bannon Creed and half a dozen mages go through the portal.

"How do we get out?" whispered Aurie.

Zayn tapped on the suitcase, which was waiting behind them. "Same way we got in."

"What about the telepaths?"

"I'll put you to sleep," he said. "If you're not thinking, they can't detect you."

Aurie turned to her sister. A heavy sadness was thick in her sister's eyes, as if someone close to her had died.

"You okay?" she asked.

Pi motioned towards the suitcase and croaked out, "We go."

Probably she was frustrated by their failure. If it weren't for the danger and the adrenaline, Aurie would be too, but that would come later, once they'd had a chance to regroup. Then she knew it would hit her, that they'd given it their best shot, their best attempt to get into the portal, but they'd been undone by one little protection they hadn't known about. Aurie had no doubt, if they'd had forewarning, they could have gotten through the door quickly. But they hadn't, and so they had failed.

Aurie climbed into the suitcase, lying on her back. Pi joined her, and they lay, side by side. When Zayn peered over the edge, he looked like a giant with ice-blue eyes.

He waved his hand over them. "Sleep."

TWENTY FIVE

Back in Violet's luxury apartment, Pi tumbled out of the suitcase onto the pristine white carpet. Her head was in a fog, her joints stiff from lying like a board in a box.

Aurie was standing in the kitchen amid designer cast-iron hanging pots, drinking from a steaming mug.

"I made coffee."

Pi staggered into the kitchen and accepted a mug from her sister. The dark aroma tickled her senses awake. The coffee burnt her lips on the way down, but provided her with a boost of energy.

"Where's Zayn?" whispered Pi, throat sore from using the Voice.

"Gone," said Aurie, staring out the window wistfully. "Left a note. Said to contact him if we needed help again. I guess I'm not getting that date anytime soon."

"There's a lot of things we're not getting anytime soon, like into that statue," said Pi, looking down at the mass of guards in the square. Both Bannon Creed and Celesse D'Agastine were below, talking with the mercenaries.

"So close," said Aurie, "so damned close. It took us weeks to prepare that attempt, it'll take months for the next. They'll be in charge of the Halls by then."

"We've got another problem, more pressing than getting into the Spire," said Pi.

She explained her encounter with Ivan, and the picture of Ernie on his phone.

Aurie flew into an unexpected rage, slamming her mug down, spilling coffee over the kitchen counter. "He can't do that to Ernie. Let's go get him, burn that fucking Ivan down."

That rage was there for Pi too, but it smoldered deeper. She felt a calmness about it that unnerved her, and she didn't think it was the side effects of the sleep spell.

"It might come to that," said Pi, "but let me try another approach first."

"What kind of help do you need?" asked Aurie earnestly, gaze fraught with concern.

"Nothing, yet," said Pi. "But you might want to let the rest of Arcanium know about Ivan, the danger he presents."

"Can he really be that dangerous for a Hall full of mages?" asked Aurie.

"Radoslav gave him a healthy respect, and that's enough for me," said Pi, the feeling coming back into her vocal cords.

"How can the Black Butcher be afraid of anyone?" asked Aurie.

"He's not afraid for himself, but for the people that work for him," said Pi.

That news sunk into her sister, who was clearly contemplating everyone that Ivan could hurt.

"We should deal with this together," said Aurie.

"I don't want to involve you, yet," said Pi. "Let me try first, and then if something goes wrong, you can help."

Aurie had a flat expression. "I guess." She set down her mug. "I'm going back to Arcanium to thank everyone for their help. Then, I don't know. Take a bath or something."

They hugged. Afterwards, Pi retrieved her phone, then started carefully calling and texting people about Ivan. She didn't want him to know she was trying to find out where he was keeping Ernie. The connections she'd gained from working for Radoslav would hopefully pay off.

"Hey, Nells," said Pi on her phone.

"What do you want, Pythia?" came Nellie's reply, direct and to the point. Even though Pi couldn't see her, she imagined Nellie at the bar in her pristine white shirt and black tie, rubbing the bar down with a marine's precision.

"I need information," said Pi.

"Then use the Internet."

"Not the kind of info you can find there," said Pi. "I need a number from Radoslav's private list."

"No," said Nellie without a trace of remorse. "Otherwise, it wouldn't be a private list."

Pi paced across the carpet. "He left me in charge."

"Of the bar, not his business," said Nellie.

"This is about the bar," said Pi.

"I seriously doubt it," came the reply.

Pi paused. Nellie was right. Not only was this not about Radoslav's business, but if it got back to Ivan how she'd acquired his number, it would put the Glass Cabaret and its employees at risk.

"Nells, I need the number," she said, squeezing her eyes closed. "That's an order. If Radoslav disagrees when he returns, then it's on my ass."

After a moment of silence, Nellie said, "Fine."

Pi heard the phone being set down. While she waited, she listened to the cascading notes of jazz being played over the speakers and worried that she was making a mistake. But she couldn't leave Ernie with that monster.

When Nellie returned, she had Ivan's number. Pi memorized it rather than leave it in her phone. Even knowing the number felt like owning a piece of radioactive material.

"Thanks, Nells."

The call ended without a reply from the other side.

"At least Dagon likes me," she said to no one in particular.

Wearing her leather jacket, Pi left the apartment, heading a few blocks away to an Internet cafe called Coffee & Cats that had photos of famous cat memes covering the walls. While she was waiting for her iced coffee—a soothing treat for her throat—and logging in to a loaner computer, Pi overheard other customers talking about what happened at the statue of Invictus. They had the story all wrong, that another demon had gotten out and had killed a dozen soldiers in runed armor before being put down, but the fact that *something* had happened was spreading. It was possible that Ivan might still think they'd gotten through the portal, but news that they hadn't would reach him, and that would put Ernie in danger. Eventually, she would be forced to call him and try to make a deal, but that would likely only make things worse. Ivan held all the cards.

After an hour of fruitless searching, an unknown call came over her phone.

"Pi?" came a voice in a hushed whisper.

"Yeah?" responded Pi.

"It's your friend with the stone arm."

Nancy. Sasha had said she was working for someone in the city. "It's been too long. Everything okay?"

There was a long pause. "I work for a guy who likes island shirts."

Ivan. Pi's heartbeat thrummed into gear. "Shit. Do you—"

"Yeah," whispered Nancy. "Your friend is here. I'm not with him, but he's in the complex."

"Is it safe to talk?"

"Don't worry, it's a burner. Just don't use any names."

"Can you tell me where you are?" asked Pi.

"We're in the tenth ward, 112 Brimstone Avenue, third floor," said Nancy. "But you don't have much time, he's been moving him around the city. They could be gone by this evening."

"Thanks," said Pi. "I owe you."

After Nancy hung up, Pi called her sister, but no one answered. She was probably asleep, or still in the bath. Getting to Arcanium, then back over to the tenth ward would take too much time. It was already early afternoon.

She hired a ghost taxi. Driverless cars were all the rage, but she knew they had ways of tracking credit cards and passenger names, and she wanted to travel incognito. A ghost taxi could only be paid with gold coins, of which she kept a couple in her jacket for this reason.

The last thing Pi was expecting was an office building at 112 Brimstone. Nancy had said Ernie was on the third floor. But it wasn't like she could waltz in and ask for Ernie.

Pi headed into the parking garage next to the office building, looking for black SUVs with tinted windows. There were four of them in a row. She scanned them for wards, finding a couple that were easy to disarm.

She broke into the SUV nearest to the elevators and searched the backseat to find hooks in the floor and door for connecting restraints. Three big black duffle bags filled with semiautomatics were in back. Pi removed the guns from one bag and put them in back of the next SUV. She locked the axles up on the other three SUVs by heating them up until they bent. When she was finished, she layered enchantments over herself and climbed into the empty duffle bag, leaving it partly unzipped so she could keep watch.

She didn't have to wait long. Ernie's entourage came out the elevators thirty minutes after she'd finished. There were ten men with semiautomatics, two with nothing in their hands—mages, she assumed—and Ernie, who trudged forward with his head down.

Cocooned within the duffle bag, Pi kept as still as possible. The back of the SUV opened, and for a moment, she feared they would open her bag, but they threw something heavy on top of her.

Once they'd cuffed Ernie to the seat, and the engine started, Pi slowly unzipped the bag. The gangsters were chatting about a football game, completely oblivious to her presence in back. There were three of them: the one in back with Ernie was a mage, and two others were in the front.

The SUV backed out of the parking spot, then started moving forward. As soon as it cleared the other three SUVs, Pi put a spell on the man in back, putting him to sleep. He slumped against the seat.

The other SUVs had yet to back out of their spots. A voice came over a walkie-talkie alerting the first SUV that there was a problem. As soon as the driver stopped the vehicle, Pi put him and the other guard to sleep.

"Pythia," said Ernie, his voice high and reedy as she crawled over the back. "Let me out. Let me out."

He rattled his cuffs, jerking against them.

"I will in a sec, but first we have to get away."

The men in the other SUVs were getting out, looking under their vehicles. Pi climbed into the front seat, unbuckled the driver's seat belt, opened the door, and pushed him out so she could get in his spot. The moment she did, the others were alerted. She slammed the door shut, put the SUV into drive, and sped off. They ran after her shouting, weapons drawn, but none fired, since the SUV was likely bulletproof.

She drove up the block, made sure that no one was on foot, then parked. She quickly dragged the two men out of the vehicle, setting them on the sidewalk. An old woman walking her dog gave Pi the side-eye as she went by, but said nothing.

"It's for a practical joke show," said Pi. "You can see it on '*Hall TV*' next week."

Before she got back into the SUV, she rescued the keys from the mage and unlocked Ernie. Then she got back into the driver's seat to pull away.

Ernie was rubbing his wrists in the backseat. "Are you gonna be in trouble, Pythia?"

"Possibly."

She drove back to Arcanium, calling Deshawn on the way. She sent Ernie inside with him, giving instructions to take him directly to Semyon and to find anyone who wasn't in the Hall and make them come back, pronto.

Then she parked the vehicle a few blocks away and called the number she'd memorized earlier.

"You're not very smart, young woman," said Ivan right away.

Pi took a deep breath. "I didn't call to debate, I called to give instructions."

"You dare give instructions to me?"

Pi focused on keeping her voice calm. It would do no good to show weakness. If she didn't get this right, there would be war with his organization, which was the last thing they needed.

"When I agreed to work for you, it was for one day and one day only," she said.

"Deals change."

"Not this one," said Pi.

"You made a mistake."

"No, you have." She put a spark through the phone, enough to get his attention when it bit his lip. "You might want to do some checking around before you mess with me and my friends. I summoned Pazuzu, the

Demon Lord of Storms, before I joined the Hundred Halls, walked away from Coterie when I was only a first year, saved the Jade Queen from an assassination attempt in my second."

"Congratulations," he said, undaunted, "you are accomplished mage. I would not want to face you. But can you save your friends?"

"When we spoke this morning, you said you didn't want to be left out, that you wanted your own Hall."

"This is true."

"The deal hasn't changed. I still owe you that," she said.

"You do?"

"Yes," she said. "I keep my word."

"A word means nothing without means to fulfill it," he said. "Since you are talking to me, it means you did not get into portal, and now, it is unlikely you will ever get in."

"Don't bet on it."

"I have, and I've backed the losing horse," he said.

"It doesn't cost you anything to keep me in the game. If you come after me, then I won't get in for sure, but if you back off, then you still have a chance at getting what you want."

"You ask a lot," he said. "Maybe I don't care anymore. Maybe I only want to teach an ambitious mage a lesson. My reputation is worth more than what you have to offer."

"That's my only offer. Take it or leave it, it's up to you," said Pi.

The silence was unbearable. She waited with her ear to the phone, wanting to speak, even if it was to ask if he was still there, but she knew as soon as she did, it would diminish her.

After what seemed like five minutes, he said, "Very well. I leave you and your friends alone. For now. But if you lose, then I will have to remedy the situation."

He hung up.

Pi stared at the phone a long time before returning to Arcanium.

TWENTY SIX

It was a gorgeous sun-lit day in the city of sorcery, and Aurie didn't care. Three weeks before, they'd broken into the statue and nearly gotten through the portal, but for nothing.

Aurie sat on her bed, looking through photos of her mother on expedition while she played the messages on the antiquated machine in her room. Three were from Professor Chopra, who reminded her that if she did not finish his project, she would not graduate. Four were from Sam Arlington, asking if she would come over and talk. At least twenty were from reporters trying to verify if she and Pi were the seventh holders of Invictus' clues. The final one was a message from Violet, letting her know that Alton and Sunil had found the fifth glass ball.

Looking at the pictures didn't help her mood, because it only reminded Aurie that her mother had cheated on her father, and that she wasn't the person she'd thought she was. This, in its own way, was worse than everything else combined. It weakened the foundations of who she thought she was.

Aurie held the picture that showed Sam with his arm around Nahid, accidentally revealing the matching tattoo. Next to her leg was the diary.

August 18th, 2002

I want to tell him not to go, he's too important to me. I'm torn, really torn. It's hard to learn this, and then know that it's ending. I sho—

It'd only taken a Wikipedia search to learn that Sam had left his expedition life and started his TV show right after this. This note, and the one that read, "I can't wait to see his face," was clearly about Sam. It wasn't that Sam was a bad person, it was that he wasn't her dad.

Aurie couldn't take it anymore. She left a note for her sister, marched out of Arcanium, and took the train to Sam's neighborhood.

The wrought iron gates with pyramids swung open upon her arrival. When she reached the door, Sam was standing there, a warm smile on his face.

"Aurelia," he said. "I'm so glad you came by. I've been worried."

Aurie knocked his arm out of the way and went right inside. As her heart climbed out of her chest, she wheeled on him. She'd been practicing what she was going to say the whole way over, but as she stood there in his house, staring at him, she blurted it out.

"You're a jerk."

"What?"

"Why didn't you tell me?"

His face went through contortions. She could see the recognition in his gaze, but it was like his mouth wouldn't cooperate. "I...uhm..."

"You and my mom had an affair," she said finally, feeling relief at saying it out loud.

His eyes widened, then narrowed. He crossed his arms and tilted his head like a dog listening.

"Where did you get this idea?" he asked.

"The diaries. The matching tattoos," she said.

At the word "tattoo," his hand flinched towards his back. Aurie took the picture from her back pocket and flung it at him. He rescued it from the floor, examined it. After a few seconds of studying, he handed it back.

"That's an impressive amount of investigative work, but I'm afraid you've got the wrong idea. Your mother and I never had an affair. I can promise you that," he said with such surety that Aurie suddenly doubted herself.

"But why the tattoos? And why hide them? I found entries from my mother talking about missing someone, and she wasn't talking about Kieran."

He leaned against the door jam in a relaxed pose. "I can't say who or what she was talking about in those diary entries, but I assure you that it wasn't about me, at least not romantically. I've read the entries—in other places she called me a pretty boy, or a spoon-fed rich kid whose family connections had opened all doors, which at the time was true."

Aurie had read those entries as well. "That doesn't change the fact that you got matching tattoos."

He straightened. His jaw tensed. "I...I..." He paused, wiping his hands on his jeans. "I'm afraid...I cannot." The distress in his face gave him wrinkles around the eyes. "I can't tell you, that's all," he finished rather forcefully.

"You can't tell me? What the hell is that supposed to mean? You were sleeping with my mother, you should at least have the decency to come clean about it," barked Aurie.

"I...I can't," he said.

"Bullshit," she said. "It's not like you have a Cryptic Curse on you."

The flat look he gave her spoke volumes. He went completely still.

"You *do* have a Cryptic Curse on you?" she asked.

He nodded his head.

Gooseflesh ran up her arms. She had the sudden realization that she'd been missing something important. Mages imposed a Cryptic Curse when they wanted to ensure secrecy amongst a small group. You couldn't talk about it, or share information purposefully. The only way was to take the curse on herself, but she wasn't ready to do that, yet.

"The curse has to do with the tattoo?" she asked.

He stared back blankly.

"Did my mother have one?" she asked.

Again, nothing.

"Does the curse have to do with the Crimson Skull?"

When he tried to shake his head, she couldn't tell in which direction, he convulsed as if the curse was shocking him. After a moment of wrestling with himself, he gave her an apologetic shrug.

"The only way I'm going to learn the truth is if I take the curse myself." She held her hands out. "Don't hurt yourself trying to tell me one way or another. I know you can't. But I need to work this out for myself.

"If you're telling me the truth, that you and my mom were not together, then you got the tattoos for something important. Something you were working on. The Crimson Skull is the obvious choice, but that doesn't seem important enough for a tattoo and curse. It had to be something more, something that required absolute secrecy."

She thought back to the diary entry.

I want to tell him not to go, he's too important to me. I'm torn, really torn. It's hard to learn this, and then know that it's ending. I sho—

That was the year before Sam started his TV show, but it was also the year before Invictus died. For the second time, gooseflesh rippled across her arms, leaving her with a shiver. It was about Invictus. They must have known how he'd died, sworn themselves to secrecy while they figured out the truth, or something like that, she didn't have it worked out.

"Let me take the curse," she said.

He hesitated. "Are you sure? It can be quite limiting. You won't be able to tell Pi."

That would be a problem if she needed to convince her sister to help.

"Go over there," she told him, waving at the massive fireplace in the next room. "I have to do something first."

He seemed concerned, but followed her directions, leaving her alone. She sent her sister a text: "When I get back, take the Cryptic Curse from me, I'll explain everything. Dooset daram." Her finger hovered over send, before she added, "And so you know it's really me: Augustus and the stone beetle, and you talk in your sleep, especially after you've eaten too much moose tracks ice cream."

Hopefully the final part would convince Pi to take it. With that settled, she called Sam back over. Taking the curse was relatively simple. Magic like that was akin to Chinese finger cuffs, or a choking knot. Easy to make and get in, but hell to get out of.

The moment the curse trickled over her skin, like having crushed mint rubbed across her body, Sam heaved a sigh that could only be existential relief. But he didn't speak right away. Instead, he led her into the bar, a room with more mahogany than any one place should have, and found a bottle of whiskey, pouring a drink for himself and one for her.

She left it on the bar, studying Sam for clues. Now that he was free to speak, he seemed reticent, or maybe overwhelmed. He always had a cheery glint to his brown eyes, but now they were sharp, questioning.

"Invictus is alive."

The words were a thunderclap in her head. She almost didn't believe him, except for the deadly serious expression on his face.

"What? I don't understand." She showed him the tattoo on her wrist. "How can this be possible?"

He took a belt of his whiskey. "I don't know for sure. I suspect that he's in a suspended animation, a defensive spell, triggered at a moment of near death. It's the best we can surmise, given the data available."

"We?"

"Well," he said. "It was once a 'we,' now it's just me. It was what Nahid and I determined." He rattled the ice in his glass. "You see, Invictus was convinced that the barrier between this world and the demon-haunted one was breaking down. At the time, only Nahid believed him. I failed to see the truth, mostly because of what it would mean for me. I wasn't ready for such burdens. He tried to deal with the problem on his own—he was a great oracle, and thought he was destined to succeed, but it's clear he was not, as prophecies and visions are often fool's gold."

"You said only my mother believed him, suggesting others," said Aurie.

He grew maudlin, took another sip of whiskey. "The tattoo. The Order of Merlin. Mages that would help him defend the city of sorcery. Your mother met his criteria, but not so much with me. My failures led him to rethink its purpose."

"You're doing what you can now," said Aurie.

"I failed them," he said, tight-lipped and grim.

"Are any others left?"

Sam shook his head, a tightly coiled motion, as if too much movement would summon his regrets. He had survivor's guilt. A feeling Aurie knew all too much about.

"Cursed to secrecy, alone and without a way to find help. That sounds awful," she said.

"So you can see why I was excited to have Nahid's daughter join me in my quest."

"Quest? What does the Crimson Skull have to do with Invictus? Or my mother?" she asked.

"I lied when I told you I didn't know what the Skull did. I know exactly what it does. It has the power to heal almost anything, for a price."

"You wanted to find it, and use it to heal Invictus," she said.

"Exactly," he said. "We knew whatever had taken him down had to be powerful, which meant only the most powerful artifacts would work. But we couldn't find the Skull, or a way into his realm. And it appears we would have never been able to get in, since we know it has to be a current student."

"The Rod of Dominion! That's why my parents were looking for it. Not to heal just anyone, but Invictus," she said.

"The Rod would have worked as well. Pity retrieving it was impossible," he said wistfully, pouring more whiskey into his glass.

"It wasn't impossible," said Aurie. "Not with Pi's help and my parents' notes. But it nearly killed us both."

"What? You found it? When?"

"Four years ago, when we first came to the Halls. It's been at a private hospital since, healing those that need it," she said.

"Oh," he replied, crestfallen. "The Rod would only have worked if it was at full strength. If Invictus is in the state we believe he's in, then only a fresh Rod of Dominion would have worked."

"How can you be so sure? How do you know what state he's in?" she asked, though she suspected he was right about the Rod. Golden Willow used its powers sparingly, because they recharged slowly.

"For two reasons," he said. "The first is that he's the one that put these tattoos on us. If he would have died, then they would have gone away. But on the other hand, the glass balls would never have worked unless he was *dead*."

He said the word "dead" with air quotes around it.

"What was he doing anyway? You said he was saving us from a demon-haunted world?"

"The city of sorcery is built on wells of power. The four wells—dragon, griffon, mermaid, centaur—along with the statue, form the structure of the barrier that keeps that world from crumbling into ours. Its proximity is why this place has always been a magnet for magic and magical beings.

But these barriers are breaking down, and Invictus was going to stop it."

"How?"

Sam gave a noncommittal shrug. "By going to the other side and closing it from there, or something crazy like that. He was never clear. If you'd met him, you'd understand. He's...I don't know—a genius asshole?"

She thought of what he'd done to Ernie, and nodded, understanding.

"What happens if someone else wins the contest?" she asked.

"I assume that once they arrive in his private realm, either he'll die right away without the stasis to preserve him, or they'll be free to kill him at their leisure, and take his place. If anyone can."

"So we need to find the Crimson Skull and reach his realm before the others," she said.

"I'm sorry," he said. "I wish it were easier, that our prospects were more optimistic."

"But they are, don't you see?"

He looked at her incredulously. "You can't be serious? Things have never been worse. Through my sources at Coterie, I heard there's only two balls left, and you and your sister have no way to get into the statue now. My sources tell me at least one of the patrons stays on location at all times, and they constantly change the defenses, so they can't be planned around."

"Yes," said Aurie, "but now we have you on our side. And though you may not agree with why Invictus picked you, the fact *that* he picked you *and* that my mother trusted you is enough for me."

"How can you be so buoyant at a time like this?" he asked.

One part of it was knowing her mother hadn't had an affair, and a second was knowing Invictus was alive. Somehow that fact made their efforts more concrete, more salient. And there was a third thing, a thought that had been percolating in her head since the day they'd met Ne Yong.

"Because I think I know where to find the Crimson Skull."

TWENTY SEVEN

The hallways in the first-year wing seemed small to Pi, even though she knew they were the same size as the ones near her apartment. Or maybe she was feeling confined by the Hall, a place that wasn't really her home.

Beside her, her sister seemed to bounce at each step, as if she'd been filled with champagne bubbles.

"I'm not sure what you're so happy about," said Pi. "We're still not getting into the statue."

"You know as well as I do why I'm happy," said Aurie. "There's a chance we can fix this...all of it."

"It won't bring Mom and Dad back," said Pi, feeling guilty for bringing them up when Aurie flinched.

"No," she said. "But maybe we can finish what they started."

Pi was still trying to wrap her head around the fact that Invictus was alive—or dead, or something in-between like Schrodinger's cat.

"You really think the location of the Crimson Skull is in that nut job's book?" she asked.

"There's only one way to find out."

After a knock, Professor Chopra welcomed them into his office, a room filled with miscellaneous cabinets and walls of towering shelves.

"Aurelia? Pythia? I wasn't expecting to see you," he said, setting down a notebook he'd been scribbling in. "I assumed you'd given up on graduating."

Pi readied her opinion about the importance of graduation when the Halls were at risk of being run by a psychopath, but Aurie stepped forward before she could speak.

"I came to finish the Hearthring," Aurie said.

Professor Chopra was taken aback by the announcement. He wrinkled his face up as if he smelled something rotten.

"Why? Under the present circumstances in the city, I didn't think it would be a priority," he said.

"I...I still want to graduate," said Aurie.

Pi knew the hesitation was because of the Cryptic Curse. Since the *Magical Works of Henry Galveston Lipton* was tied to Invictus through the Crimson Skull, neither of them could explain why they needed it.

"I'm quite busy at the moment," said Professor Chopra, sighing. "But we could schedule something for next week. There's only a few more steps needed to finish the Hearthring."

"That's great," said Aurie. "Could I see the tome, study it in the meantime?"

Professor Chopra grew unexpectantly cross. "No, you may not. I've told you that already. Please stop asking."

The intensity of his response made Pi suspicious. He'd been passive before that, congenial.

Aurie opened her mouth to argue, but Pi stopped her by tugging on her shirt.

"Next week would be great," said Pi, giving her sister a forced smile.

At first Aurie didn't understand, and then she unlocked her jaw. "I'm sorry, Professor Chopra. It's rude of me to ask. Next week would be great."

"Good," he said, picking up his pen to indicate that they should leave. "I'll send you an email to let you know when I'm available."

Down the hall, Aurie turned on Pi. "What was that about?"

"I don't know," said Pi, "but asking him about the tome wasn't going to work. He went from casual to crazy in a millisecond once you asked him. We'll have to get the book when he leaves his office."

Aurie glanced back down the hall. "You're probably right. I wonder why he's protecting it."

"I guess we'll find out."

They waited in the study room in the first-year wing, listening for when Chopra left his office. Once he was gone, they hurried down the hall, and after dispelling the wards, broke into his room.

"Where do you think the tome is?" asked Aurie.

Pi went right to the lower cabinet, beneath the towering shelves. She popped the door open with a screwdriver and pointed to the spine reading *The Magical Works of Henry Galveston Lipton* facing them.

"His eyes gave it away," said Pi.

"Don't touch it," said Aurie.

Together they removed the enchantments that would have shocked them, allowing Pi to pick up the book. They took it back to their apartment, and sat side by side on the couch, spreading the tome open on the common area table.

Pi opened it to the early pages, skimming for the proper section. Almost as soon as she'd started, Aurie yanked the book away angrily. "It's my class and my book."

Unexpected anger rose in Pi's chest. She was ready to snatch the tome out of her sister's hands when she remembered the way Professor Chopra had reacted.

"Wait," said Pi, feeling the anger swirl around in her chest. "There must be another enchantment on it that makes us not want to share. It might explain why Chopra got so pissy when you asked him about it."

Aurie's anger deflated with self-reflection. "I think you're right. And I just thought Professor Chopra was a dick."

A bit of magical sleuthing brought out a clever abjuration woven into the ink designed to make the reader possessive of the tome. Countering it was easy once they knew it was there.

"Why would you enchant your own book like this?" asked Aurie. "The shock alone would have deterred most readers. But then to make them not want to share? Wouldn't that defeat the purpose?"

"Maybe he was afraid of being charmed into giving it up?" Pi suggested.

Starting at the beginning, they paged through the tome, skimming for content and understanding of Henry Lipton. Unlike a typical magical tome, which had a central theme, this one was disjointed: part diary, part sketchbook, part magical fragment collection. In one area, he'd made expert sketches of his wife, Grace, in the nude, lounging on a couch or bed. In others, he wrote poems about how the local bovines were out to kill him. There were snatches of spells, typically ones that had rhyming verse, or runes written with weird inks that neither was willing to guess as to the source of the pigment.

"He's much different than I expected from what I read in the *Unauthorized Biography*," said Aurie.

"He was a madman," said Pi. "He loved his wife, that's for sure, but he was a madman."

Aurie read aloud a section: "...dearest Grace, I swear to you that I will not be deterred, not by man, not by beast, not by the secrets of the magi, in my quest to find a way to cure you. You, an angel on earth, have been my salvation, made me a better man. It is only fair, and right, that I, a magi of uncommon ability, must save you from God's curses."

The words hung in the air, the logic of Henry Lipton drawing threads that led them to dive back into the book, reading voraciously until they came upon a section that discussed the various artifacts that might be capable of healing Grace.

"He doesn't name the Crimson Skull," said Aurie, "but the phrases like the *blood mists* and *death's bargain* were common in my research."

They skipped past the section detailing how to make the Hearthring of Grace, looking for more mentions of the Skull. The further they read, the more Henry's penmanship grew shaky, and his prose wandering. By the end, he stopped writing left to right on a level plane, but scrawled across the pages in whatever direction he meandered at the moment. Pi could sense his derangement, his desperation, as he described Grace's rapidly declining health.

Pi jabbed her finger at a passage. "The trail has led me to the place I feared it might be all along, the city of sorcery. If it is so, then I worry that the price will be greater than I can pay. Time is running out."

"It's here," said Aurie. "As Ne Yong said, it's in the city, but where?"

The last section had account numbers and banking records, including ledger entries and lists of purchases. It appeared he'd started a company.

"Persephone, Inc," said Aurie. "Daughter of Zeus and queen of the underworld. The purchases were for digging equipment, payments to workers. That must be why he was scamming people. He needed money to find the Skull and heal his wife."

"It has to be in the Undercity," said Pi, leaping over to her laptop and bringing up her browser. Her skin tingled. "When I was in that race with Inari, the Voodoo Run, one section went past a quarry with old digging equipment. There didn't seem to be a bottom to the hole, and it bothered me to even be near it."

Pi found entries about Persephone, Inc. The company had few records, mostly from historians trying to determine what it had been founded for, and why its mysterious owner disappeared in 1934. In later decades, other companies took up the mantle of Persephone, Inc., but each met the same fate as the first. Workers would die in tragic accidents, equipment would unexpectedly break down, and eventually no one was willing to continue the digging, especially not knowing what the prize would be.

"They all believed there was something valuable in the hole and kept digging," said Aurie, "but I don't think it's really valuable, not in the way they expected."

"But doesn't it have the power of healing like the Rod of Dominion?" asked Pi.

The look on her sister's face worried her. There was an unsettled stillness like standing in the dark and trying not to be noticed.

"Legends of the Crimson Skull are filled with descriptions of death. Yes, there are claims of extraordinary healing, but those are few, and do not seem to result in happiness. Instead, they describe the artifact as bittersweet."

TWENTY EIGHT

The Goblin's Romp smelled like old beer and stale air. Peanut shells crunched beneath Aurie's boots. She noted the nod of familiarity from the bouncer in Pi's direction as they entered the spiral staircase that led into the Undercity. The bouncer's gaze lingered on Sam Arlington as he passed, a moment of recognition, or at least a sense that a man of his obvious wealth did not belong.

Aurie tightened the straps on her backpack as they marched down the endless stairs. While she had imbued herself with enchantments, the straps bit into her shoulders.

When they crossed through Big Dave's Town, they put up their hoods, as not to draw attention. Aurie saw the way Pi glanced longingly at a faded white door at the top of wooden stairs above the Devil's Lipstick.

Once they were traveling the uneven passageways, a magelight floating ahead casting sharp shadows across the rock, Pi remarked, "I can't believe I used to be afraid of this place. Now, when I'm back in the Undercity, I feel like I've come home."

"Not me," said Aurie. "This place always gives me the creeps. It always feels like death could be right around the corner."

Sam, who was quieter than usual, remarked, "Death *is* around the corner. The legends of the Crimson Skull are filled with the corpses of foolhardy seekers. Let us not become one of them."

Pi, who was walking next to Aurie, gave an expert eye roll.

"What's the deal with the Order of Merlin?" Pi asked after a few minutes of silent travel.

From the lead position, Sam glanced back, forehead furrowed. "As I told your sister, we are tasked to protect the city of sorcery."

He seemed to be carrying an extra weight on his shoulders. Aurie had never seen him so despondent.

"Why not the patrons? Don't they care?" asked Pi.

"I think Invictus was concerned that they'd forgotten the reasons the Halls were formed in the first place— mutual protection, a light in the darkness to cast away superstition."

"Then why wasn't Kieran in the Order of Merlin?" asked Pi.

Sam's stride faltered. He paused, shadows collecting beneath his eyes. "I would guess as to Invictus' reasoning, but that is a path to madness. I can only say that I would have welcomed his fellowship."

After speaking, he strode ahead, creating separation between him and the sisters.

"I hadn't even thought to ask that," whispered Aurie, "I assumed he was a member like Mom."

"He's not being completely honest with us," said Pi.

"What do you mean?" asked Aurie, though she had felt it as well. He had something on his mind that was making him churlish.

"I wish I knew, but should we really trust a Coterie alumnus? He's lied to you before about the Skull, why not now?" asked Pi.

Aurie didn't know how to explain to her sister that she trusted Sam, but she'd also sensed he was not being honest, or that something was bothering him. "Fair point. Keep your guard up."

Voodooland, the Appalachian-esque town near the quarry, was abandoned. One of the shacks had been charred in half, as if a great fiery sword had come down on it. Broken glass reflected magelight across the stone. Windows had been smashed and ground into tiny pieces.

"This is why I never let my guard down here," said Aurie.

Pi kicked at the broken glass, which sounded like sand beneath her boots. "Nothing we can't handle."

Sam stood ahead of them, staring into the darkness. When they caught up, he jumped a little.

Aurie shared a worried glance with her sister, who only gave her the told-you-so face.

She felt the quarry long before they reached it. The air grew colder, the echoes deeper. A rusted bulldozer greeted them at the edge, treads broken and dark orange with rust, the gray-green paint peeling off in crumbling sheets.

To their left, circling the quarry, Sam found the way down. Before they got very far, he conjured a ghostly cage with a pale, translucent bird in it that floated ahead of them.

"For bad air," was the only thing he said.

The crunching of rock and the slow traverse put Aurie into a trance. Her ears popped a couple of times on the way down. They stopped after an hour and ate a meal of dried fruit and nuts, washing it down with cold water.

"This is taking forever," said Pi, glancing over the edge. "Round and round on the world's deepest screw."

"We could go faster," offered Sam, "but I think that might be dangerous." He nodded towards the cage.

After another two hours, they reached the bottom, or *a* bottom, Aurie gathered. The air had grown much warmer. Under the straps of her backpack, her shirt was sweaty and gross.

"It's getting harder to breathe," said Pi.

The floor spread out before them. Sam sent questing magelights ahead, shining light on the walls and floor, revealing additional digging. There were more pits, and shafts that went horizontally. The walls were littered with holes.

"They must have thought it was around here," said Aurie.

Pi, who had her faez-viewing goggles on, whistled appreciatively. Then she handed them over to Aurie, who gasped when she put them on.

"If faez was radioactive, then we'd be dead," said Aurie, handing the goggles to Sam, who shook his head in agreement after putting them on.

"How do we find the Skull?" asked Pi.

"There are two kinds of artifacts," said Sam. "The first are made by powerful mages, who upon their deaths leave deadly traps to keep them out of unwanted hands."

"We know all about that," said Pi.

"The second," continued Sam, undaunted, "are artifacts that are created naturally. These often do not have purposeful protections, but sometimes develop defenses based on the nature of their creation."

"Like the Wicker Blade," said Aurie.

"Exactly," said Sam.

"And which type is the Skull?" asked Pi.

"I'd always thought it was the first, man-made," said Sam, "but now that I am close to it, I suspect it's the second which is more dangerous because its defenses might be more insidious and harder to detect."

"Wonderful," said Pi as she kept watching the exploring magelights reveal more tunnels and shafts. "Do you think Henry Lipton ever found it?"

Aurie considered it. "I suppose it's possible, which gives me an idea." She pulled a an item from her backpack—a plastic arrowhead, which was a cheaply made souvenir—and jammed a nail into it. Then Aurie drew out a knife, pricked her finger, and smeared a droplet of blood on the arrowhead. After chanting, and releasing a puff of faez, she held the arrowhead by the nail at its bottom, and it spun around a few times before pointing to the left, away from the questing magelights.

"What is it looking for?" asked Sam.

"Old bones," said Aurie, "the oldest in fact. After starting his company, Henry Lipton was never heard from again. What if he died down here?"

"They might be in the wrong direction," said Sam.

"Then we'll try something else," said Pi, who, when Sam turned his back, gave him a scowl.

Aurie was expecting her sister to make a comment, but she strode off in the direction of the arrowhead. After a hundred yards, they came to a wall of rock.

"There are bones somewhere beyond that," said Aurie.

Sam ran his hand over the rock. "It appears that it caved in a long time ago. The digging from above filled in the rocks, making it appear to be a wall. I bet there's a passage behind it."

"Are you certain?" asked Aurie.

"I've been on countless digs. I know a real stone wall when I see one, and this isn't it," he said. "And we're a ways from the center."

Pi had her goggles on. "The faez is less dense along the wall. No one probably thought to check here."

Using a series of snap-together rods, Sam formed an archway in front of the rock wall. He sung a spell, quiet and haunting, while he gently pressed the rod into the stone. The metal rods sunk into the wall as if it were made of butter. When he was finished, he pulled out three collapsible mini shovels.

"The stone will come out easily, but try not to hit the rods, or it'll collapse again," he said.

After a half-hour of digging, a tunnel was exposed. Sam sent a mage-light into it, which disappeared around a corner after a short distance.

"This appears to be it," he said, gaze heavy.

Before they set off into the passage, Pi grabbed Sam by the arm. "You loved Nahid, didn't you?"

The surprise question revealed the truth in his expression before he tried to tamp it down, giving up when he saw their faces.

"Yes," he said, "but not in the way that you think."

"I knew it," said Pi, anger on her brow as she glanced at Aurie. "This whole thing is about your guilt. You feel guilty because you loved our mother and wanted her for yourself, so you clued Professor Augustus in about the Rod, hoping he'd take out our father, but it backfired and you got them both killed."

"What? No," he said, his face wracked with anguish.

A vast pit opened inside of Aurie. Was this true? Had it really been Sam Arlington this whole time?

"You and Augustus would have been at Coterie around the same time," said Aurie, seeing connections form like a spidery web.

Pi nodded grimly. "It's been bothering me this whole trip, but I didn't put it together until I saw him make the archway. It reminded me of the portal, the one into the Tomb of Kings."

Sam held his hands up, palms forward. "No, no. You've got it all wrong. I had nothing to do with the Rod. And what's this about Auggie Trebleton?"

Faez worked its way into Aurie's mind. Sensing trouble, she squared off with Sam.

Pi shook her finger at him. "He's lying. He had the motive and opportunity. It's not about Invictus, or saving the Halls. He's an artifact hunter, a glory hound. He cares about nothing but himself. All this Order of Merlin stuff is bullshit."

A battle was brewing. Aurie sensed it in her sister's demeanor, but Sam looked like he wanted no part of it. His face was wrecked, his eyes rounded with sadness.

"I swear to you, I would never do that to Nahid, or Kieran," he said. "Yes, I loved Nahid, but not as Kieran did. I loved her because she was family."

Both sisters exclaimed, "What?"

Pi punched Sam right in the arm, hard enough to make him flinch. "You're a rich white guy who got in Coterie based on his family connections. Your grandfather is a Coterie alumnus. He owned a shipping company. How can we be related?"

"All true," said Sam. "When my grandfather did business in what then was the Ottoman empire, he fell in love with Rosanna, your mother's grandmother. They had a child together, my father, Charles. When the war broke out, Charles was sent to the States. My grandmother, bless her soul, accepted him without question. And then I came along."

"But you don't look like us," said Pi.

"So? We're still family, maybe like third cousins, but I never had brothers and sisters, so learning about Nahid was like finding a sister," said Sam.

Aurie shared a look with her sister. She could see it in Pi's face, the same feeling she had. They both wanted this to be true, even though neither felt they could take his word for it. After "Uncle" Liam, they were both wary.

"You had nothing to do with Augustus Trebleton?" asked Aurie.

His gaze bounced between them. "I only know he disappeared a few years ago."

"We killed him," said Pi, defiantly.

"What?"

"He tried to take the Rod of Dominion," said Aurie, trying to reduce the tension. "He followed us into the Tomb of Kings, nearly killing us both. Then the tomb curse backfired on him. We also think he might have killed our mom and dad."

His hand went to his mouth in horror. Aurie watched his reaction closely. She needed it to be true, wanted it badly, which made deciding whether or not to believe him even harder.

"I liked Auggie," he said, his eyebrows wagging up and down with thought. "How could that be possible? That he would do that?"

"Jealousy," said Pi. "He felt disrespected in Coterie because he didn't have the pedigree that others had."

His shoulders softened, a repentant sigh. "It's a shame too, because the Hall has so much to teach. I'm sorry, I really am. I had no idea. I would have killed him myself if I'd have known what he'd done."

"I believe you," said Aurie, seeing him honestly and clearly.

"You do?" asked Pi with an arched eyebrow.

Aurie checked inside herself, parsing his response through the filter of her truth magic. She gave a sure nod.

"Well," said Pi, "this changes things."

Aurie caught a tightening of Sam's eyes at the comment, which meant there was still something he wasn't telling them, but she sensed they would find out soon enough.

"I know how you feel," said Sam. "I wasn't told about my origins until I was headed to the Halls. My father wanted me to know about Nahid, to look out for her. I'm afraid it never worked out like that, she was always the one looking out for me. I was a poor student, at first."

"We should get moving," said Aurie, "but when all this is over, we want to hear more stories about our mom and dad. The real stuff."

"When this is over," he said heavily.

The tunnel was markedly different from the other shafts. The walls were held up with old timbers and had been carved with shovels and picks, maybe a bit of dynamite and magic, but mostly by human power. The whole thing felt like it could collapse at any moment.

It went about two hundred yards straight out before opening into a cavern about the size of a Wal-Mart. The faez was so thick Aurie's tongue felt coated with metallics. The hairs on her arm were standing straight up.

"The barrier between this world and the demonic one is thin here," said Sam. "Stay alert."

"If we have to use magic here, it'll be like wandering into a room with a gas leak and lighting a match," said Pi.

As the magelights explored the cavern, Aurie caught a glimpse of something bright red in the direction the arrowhead was pointing. A chill went down her spine.

"Over there," she said.

The patch of crimson was larger than a skull. It grew as they got closer, shapes made clearer by proximity: a powerful leg, multiple arms ending in claws the size of sabers, a chest as big as a Mack truck, grotesque horns curling from its enormous head.

"Merlin's tits," said Pi, gaping in awe. "That's a demon lord, turned to stone, or some shit."

The creature, long dead, was half in and half out of the wall in a semi-seated position like a king on a throne. At a close distance, Aurie realized the skin wasn't red, but that a fungus grew across the stone, covering the ancient dead beast.

"Did you know this was the Crimson Skull?" asked Aurie.

Sam's jaw hung open. He was mute with surprise. Eventually, he came to enough to shake his head, then added, "No. God, no. But it makes sense. I'm not up on my demonology, but this is a Necrokon. A lord probably, as you said. They heal themselves in battle by taking life from others."

"I found something," said Pi, from the left side of the demon-protrusion. She held up a metal ring about the size of a soccer ball. "They're bones too. I think it's Henry Lipton."

Aurie gravitated to the ring. "This is the Hearthring of Grace. He created it."

After poking around in the bones and old clothes that had nearly turned to dust, they found a chit of metal with a "HGL" in it.

"Henry Galveston Lipton," said Aurie, turning the ring over in her hands. "But why did he die when he was so close to reaching his goal?"

"He didn't," said Sam. "I suspect he succeeded, but at great cost to himself."

The realization of what he meant hit Aurie. "He healed Grace. Gave her life at the cost of his own. That's what the Crimson Skull does. It doesn't heal. It takes life from one and gives it to another. That's what's been bugging you this whole time. You knew this part. You're planning on giving up your life for Invictus."

His sure and steady gaze told her she'd spoken the truth. "I failed him before, failed Nahid and Kieran, too. But I'm not going to fail this time."

Pi punched him in the arm. "You bastard. You lied to us back there. You said you'd tell us stories about our parents, but you knew this is what you were going to do. This is probably why you never told us we were related in the first place!"

"How does it even work?" asked Aurie. "We can't take that thing into Invictus' realm."

"It's bigger than I thought, but there's a way. This petrified demon is a repository for the faez building up in this cavern. It provides the mechanism. But I think we'll only need a piece of the demon, perhaps just a section of horn. I know the ritual to activate it. Then it'll require my life force, and the horn will be ready to take with you."

"Your life force?" exclaimed Pi. "That means you're going to die. Like right now. How can you do that to us?"

He wore a sober expression, like a guilty man at a sentencing hearing. "It's what needs to be done. And technically I won't be dead until the life force is discharged. Until then, I'll be in a comatose state."

"I can't believe this is happening," said Aurie, her face numb. "We just found out that we have family, and we have to say goodbye already? Screw that. Invictus isn't worth your life. You said it yourself. He's an asshole. We don't have to bring him back. We can take control of the Halls, do it our way."

"It's not about the Halls," said Sam, "though that's important, too. We need Invictus to help us close the barrier. He said if it didn't work, that if he didn't close it, that it would only be a matter of time before the wells failed and the demon realm flooded into this one. Maybe within a few years, decades if we're lucky. Assuming nothing happens to the wells."

"Shit!" said Pi, pacing around with her hands shoved into her hair. "I damaged the wells when I summoned Pazuzu, and again when we took on the Cabal in the statue. We're complicit as much as he is."

"Are you serious, Pi? You want to let him do this?" she asked.

"No, of course not, but I don't think we have any choice. It's not like it's going to be easy on our end. We still have to get into the statue, find the remaining *five* balls, and then get to Invictus' realm. All the while, Alton and his merry band of assholes is trying to stop us. It sounds like we've got the shit end of the stick. All he has to do is lie here," said Pi.

"I'm sorry," said Sam. "I shouldn't have told you that we were related. It's making this harder."

"No, you should have told us sooner," said Aurie angrily. "Family tells you about the bad shit, even if it's fucking inconvenient. Don't you get that?"

He winced. "I'm sorry. I told you I was never good at having family. I failed Nahid. I failed Invictus. That's why I'm trying to make it right now. It's what she would have wanted."

Tears welled up in Aurie's eyes. "You suck for even saying that, even if it's true." She put a fist to her head. Every choice was bad. "Okay, fine. Fuck! I'm only agreeing because of Mom. If she thought it was important then it is. Pi?"

Her sister was scraping a tear from her puffy eyes. "Yeah."

Sam climbed onto the stone demon, broke a half-a-foot section of the horn off, and brought it down. The ritual was brief, only a few words and gestures, which seemed so antithetical to what would happen once it was finally activated.

"I'm sorry I didn't tell you both sooner. I should have said something years ago when you first got to the Halls," said Sam, holding the horn tight against his chest. His dark hair was ruffled from the work, and his expression held grim determination.

"You're damn right you should have," said Aurie. "But even still, it was good to know you, even if it wasn't for long enough."

Aurie stepped forward and gave him a long hug. She thought she heard him sniffle, but he'd composed himself by the time she pulled away. Pi gave him a shorter hug, then punched him in the arm, softer this time.

"Why am I always destined to lose my family?" asked Pi as she stepped away.

With her heart in her throat, Aurie watched Sam activate the trigger for the ritual. One moment he was gazing back at her, the next he fell to the stone as if his strings had been cut. Aurie fought with her tears before attending to his body. Pi helped her situate him into a more comfortable position. Then Aurie took the horn and placed it into her backpack.

"What if something comes in here and tries to eat him?" asked Pi.

"He's already practically dead," said Aurie.

"No, what if they eat him before the spell goes off?" said Pi. "Even a few rats, or some determined insects could do some damage."

"Good point," said Aurie. She'd been planning on taking the

Hearthring with her, but placed it on Sam's chest, wrapping his fingers around the metal hoop. They placed a few protective enchantments over him. Then when they were back outside in the bottom of the quarry, they removed the metal bars, collapsing the tunnel section, sealing Sam's almost-dead body into a tomb.

The weight that Sam had been carrying on his way in seemed to have transferred to Aurie's shoulders.

"What do we do now?" asked Pi. "We have to make his sacrifice worth it. How are we going to get into the statue?"

"We don't have time for subtlety," said Aurie. "And I don't think the Cabal will listen to us when we try to explain the stakes, that the whole city is at risk. I think we're going to have to gather our friends, allies, anyone who will listen, and make an outright assault on the statue."

"Even if we could convince enough people to gather against Bannon and his mercenaries, are you really prepared to risk their lives?" asked Pi. "Once we take to open battle, the Hundred Halls might never be the same."

"There are times when we have to do things the right way, using the systems and structures in place, avoiding danger, protecting others," said Aurie, clenching her fists at her sides. "But when the Halls themselves are broken, and the city and all those that live in it are at risk, we must stand up and fight, even if it means people will get hurt."

Her sister's eyes glittered with excitement. "I've been waiting five years for you to say that. Count me in."

As they climbed from the quarry, deep in the Undercity, Aurie worried that she might break the Hundred Halls.

TWENTY NINE

The meeting place was three blocks from the statue of Invictus, outside a comic book shop called Ink Dreams. The top of the statue peeked above an office building.

Pi heard her sister come up from behind. "I thought your jacket would look like a general's outfit or something."

Pi checked the magical leather jacket to find it in the state that she'd found it. "Maybe it's telling me this is who I am."

"Beautiful day for a battle," said Hannah, coming out of the shop with a thin plastic bag sagging with comics. When the sisters raised eyebrows, she replied, "It's buy one get two free day. How can I pass that up?"

As more of their friends showed up—about thirty mages from Arcanium, the remaining Misfits, and a half-dozen from other smaller Halls—Pi fidgeted with energy. The soul fragments were restless, as if they sensed they would be put into action.

Aurie kept checking her phone for the time. "Where are the others?"

Deshawn had his hands shoved deep into his pockets. "The others should be here. Everyone planned to come, even the bookish students that probably aren't much good in a battle."

"Violet got the word out to the smaller Halls," said Pi, frustrated as she looked around at the empty streets. "I thought we'd get more support, but I guess they don't see this as their fight."

"What about Semyon?" asked Deshawn.

Aurie shook her head. "He said he couldn't get involved. He was afraid what it would look like to the others, and I think he's still recovering from last year."

"Do we have enough?" asked Deshawn.

"Enough is who we have," said Pi.

"We have to do this," said Aurie, staring in the direction of the statue. "Time is running out."

There was a resoluteness in Aurie that made Pi proud. While there was no question that she would assault the statue, even if it were only her and Aurie, the way her sister composed herself gave hope to their friends who were having second thoughts. She knew it wasn't easy for them, as they didn't know what she and Aurie knew about Invictus.

Hannah was holding her phone up. "They've cut off coverage. No bars."

"That means they know we're coming," said Aurie. "Armor up. If you don't know the anti-bullet spell, let me or Pi teach it to you."

Pi pulled her sister away from the others. "We need more support than this. It'll be a bloodbath. That armor spell won't work if they use spell-hardened bullets."

"We have to go for it, even if we die trying. You know the stakes." She glanced away, sighing. "I thought Violet would come through for us. I hope the Cabal didn't get to her."

The look was there, the worry that the old Violet Cardwell had returned. "Maybe something happened. They cut off our cell service, after all."

Aurie frowned. "They can't cut off the whole city, and we talked with her this morning. She's not coming."

The others were restless. The younger mages glanced back the other way.

"We'd better go now," said Pi, though she had a heavy heart.

They marched down the street in a pack. There was no traffic. Bannon probably had the streets around the statue blocked off to minimize collateral damage. A lot of things could happen, but the Halls couldn't be seen in open warfare, or the rest of the world might turn against them.

The soldiers in runed armor were ready for them when they arrived, huddled behind barriers, guns resting against their shoulders.

The towering figure of Bannon Creed in ghostly armor called out orders as they approached, giving permission to fire if offensive magic was used. His force shield hung on his left arm, an impenetrable barrier that he could expand at will. Celesse D'Agastine stood on top of the cinderblock wall, surveying the area. Pi didn't see Priyanka, but knew she couldn't be far away. Only Malden's whereabouts were a mystery, since he usually stayed out of personal interventions. If they were lucky, he was watching from the Obelisk.

Three patrons, dozens of mercenaries with mage-killing bullets, and another fifty mages from the Cabal—all upperclassmen by her reckoning. Standing on balconies around the statue were another hundred Cabal mages ready to attack. At the current odds, they wouldn't place one toe into the square before getting annihilated by metal and magic.

Pi's mouth was dry and her heartbeat was thundering in her ears. When she glanced to her sister, she had the brief hope that Aurie had come to her senses and had decided to back off, but she looked more resolute than ever.

"Have you come to surrender?" came a voice from the archway that led into the statue.

Wearing his signature white suit and white tie, Alton Lockwood strolled into the square, glancing at Bannon as if he were his equal. Sunil joined them, along with the other sets of mages that were vying for Invictus' realm.

Seeing those two put a fire in her belly. "What are you so afraid of? Or is it that you know we're better than you, so you have to keep us from competing."

"This *is* part of the competition, my dear Pythia," said Alton. "You don't hand the advantage to your enemy when you've got them by the balls."

"We're not your enemies," said Aurie. "We should be working together. The Hundred Halls was meant to bind mages with common goals. We need that now more than ever."

"And when we win, we'll bind you to us," said Alton, winking. "Finally, you'll know your proper place. As long as you don't cause any problems, we'll get along fine. But it'll be *my* Halls, and we'll do it *my* way."

Bannon, who'd been mostly quiet thus far, gave Alton a healthy side-eye. Pi suspected the Cabal patrons weren't happy that the position of head patron would go to a student, but they had no choice in the matter. They probably preferred Alton Lockwood as the heir, because of his family's connections, and he'd been Malden's personal assistant before his fall from grace.

"We don't want to do this," said Aurie, "but we have no choice."

Alton smirked. "You have a choice. If you leave now, and forget about getting into his realm, I won't disband Arcanium when I take control. If you defy me, then your Hall and any others that side with you will be the first to go."

From behind, Hannah was heard saying, "He can kiss my ass. I'm staying." It drew cheers from the others.

"We're outnumbered," said Deshawn under his breath. "I'll go if you lead, but this is suicide."

"You can leave if you want," said Aurie, "but I'm marching across that square and into the statue. If they kill me in broad daylight, then the Halls are finished one way or another."

From across the square, Alton called out, "The first mage to take a step—"

Before he could finish his statement, Pi took three long strides forward, lifted her fist, and gave Alton the finger. Another cheer went up.

Staring at rifle muzzles from thirty feet away was making Pi's stomach churn, but there was no way she was letting that bastard intimidate her.

Bannon put his hand on Alton's shoulder. He looked like a giant next to Alton.

"Your courage is admirable," said Bannon, "but you'd be a fool to enter the square. Go back to your Hall, forget about Invictus. We outgun you."

"I expected more than this," said Alton, gesturing towards their small group. "This hasn't been worth my time thus far."

"We're just getting started," yelled Bethany from behind them.

"And so am I," he said, shooting Bannon a nasty look as his grin deepened. "If the cavalry was any later, they'd miss all the fun."

"Sirens," said someone from behind. "They've probably got the whole police HQ on the way."

"I hear choppers," said someone else.

They were already outnumbered. If the police, an organization filled with loyal Protectors, arrived, then they didn't have a chance and would probably end up dead or in jail. The tide of momentum receded, only made worse when a helicopter came into view. She and the Misfits had worked all night on a shield that could withstand mage-killing bullets, but if the Cabal were using police choppers, they could fire from above.

A second and third helicopter were approaching from other directions, the echoes from their blades bouncing off the glass buildings.

Pi placed her hand on Aurie's arm to counsel a retreat, when someone cried out. "Those are Herald copters!"

The crest for the newspaper was painted on the bottom of the gun-metal-gray hulls. Men with shoulder-mounted cameras filmed the square.

"Those cameras will be the first to go if you step a foot in here," said Alton, gesturing upward with one arm.

Before Pi could answer, another voice called out from behind them. "If you do that, I'll sue your ass for everything your crooked family owns."

Wearing a black double-breasted jacket over a long olive skirt, Violet Cardwell joined them.

"Sorry I'm late," she said. "Those bastards have the police blocking everything. No one could get through until we convinced some of the patrons they had to get involved and open up the Garden Network."

"My apologies," said Semyon, who appeared out of shimmering air. "I should have joined you the moment you asked, the 'optics of the situation' be damned."

Before Pi or her sister could speak, mages from the other Halls came pouring into the streets surrounding the square. Not a trickle, or a stream, but a flood. It was like the whole Hundred Halls had come to support them. Pi saw students she knew from Freeport Games, others that the soul fragments recognized. Mags, the first year who'd once been known as Emily, stood to the side, along with the other Arcanium students. There was a tall blonde-haired blue-eyed girl with a bodybuilding physique from the Daring Maids. A pack of lanky, skeletal mages from the Weird Circus leered from their corner of the street, as did Brian Travers, Hannah's friend from Tinkers. Professor Delight, the patron who ran their Merlin trials wearing a yellow-and-black track suit, was there too.

Pi's mind whirled with names and faces from her years in the city of sorcery. Her skin tingled with pride as she saw how many students and patrons had joined them. Even the tiny Halls with fewer than a handful of students had braved the Cabal's threats.

The sirens grew louder as dozens of police sedans and SUVs arrived, skidding to a stop. The men and women of Invictus HQ poured out, hands on their holsters. They surrounded the students, who'd surrounded the square, creating a double ring. They looked to Bannon, who shook his head, indicating not to take action.

"You have to let them through," said Violet. "If you don't, or if you lay even one finger on them, I'll publish the information about what's happening here to the world. The protections the Halls receive will be rescinded. They'll know we're too dangerous."

"A pathetic attempt," said Alton, puffing up his chest. "But you're still not getting in. We hold the statue. It's ours."

During his outburst, Celesse joined Bannon. The two conversed for a couple of minutes, waving Alton away when he tried to join them. He glowered from a distance. When they were finished, Celesse stepped forward.

"The Silverthorne sisters may enter the statue unmolested," she said, glancing up at the helicopters with cameras. "We wish you good luck on your endeavors."

Alton barked at them. "No. We will not let them in. We don't have to bow to public opinion. We *make* public opinion. It's about time the world understands who is in charge."

Celesse wheeled on Alton, and though they were a good hundred feet away, Pi heard every word.

"You dolt, it'll poison our victory if we let this turn into a battle. And besides, you only need the last ball to claim the prize. Why risk it for pride? Let them enter. You've got six of the seven. Hurry up and win the damn thing while they're screwing around. Or are you afraid?"

"You'll regret using that tone with me when I become head patron," said Alton.

"God help us all," said Celesse, throwing her hands up as she turned away.

Pi grabbed her sister's hand. "We should go before they change their minds."

"Wait," said Violet, handing her a scroll small enough to fit in her pocket. "This might help you inside. It's the best I could do."

Pi held the slender scroll as if it were made of gold.

"You're the best, Violet," said Aurie.

Violet's eyes crinkled with thought. "I appreciate that, even if it's not true," she said.

When Pi and Aurie moved towards the barrier, a small group—Sasha, Bethany, Deshawn, Yoko, and Hannah—stepped forward as their designated escort. They climbed over the barrier and marched across the square towards the silvery arch. Alton looked like he was gagging on his tongue in anger, his lips white as his suit.

As they approached, Celesse, who wore a Milan fashion runway's version of war attire, gave them a somber appraisal.

"For what it's worth, good luck, though I don't think it's going to matter."

The conciliatory attitude seemed genuine, and not just a sideswipe at Alton. Celesse watched them go by with one eyebrow raised.

Bannon Creed was his normal impenetrable self. Pi didn't waste her time looking at him, because she knew what went on behind closed doors. She could at least pretend to like Celesse, but Bannon, no matter how sensible he was being, would always be a slime to her.

They were careful to take a wide berth around Alton and the other mages. Pi hurried her walk, tugging on her sister's shirt to get her to move faster. The closer she got to the archway that led into the statue, the more concerned she was that something would go wrong. There were too many mages, soldiers, and patrons in one area. It was like playing with sparklers in a room filled with loose gunpowder. The sooner they were through the portal, the better for everyone.

When she was steps away from the entrance, she knew something was wrong by the way the sharp scent of faez struck her nose. There were foot scuffs, a yell from across the square. Pi turned in time to see Alton pulling a handgun the size of a cannon from a temporal pocket in his white coat.

Time slowed. Concerned shouts filled the air, too far away, too late. Even from thirty feet away, the barrel looked like a train tunnel. She knew in an instant this was a heavily enchanted gun with custom bullets that would rip through her wards and any spells thrown in the way.

The world shifted. Aurie grabbed her arm. Pi tried to move, wanted to fly through the archway, but she could barely turn away.

When the gun fired, a cacophonous blast that seemed to shake the city filled the air and Pi thought she was dead, until she saw someone leaping into the way, skull and neck translucent for a moment before the bullet ripped them apart.

The shot was like a spark in a gas factory, and the square exploded with magic. Aurie dragged her into the cinderblock-reinforced building, through the dusty souvenir aisles, and down the stairs to the ruined archway.

"Pi! We have to keep going. Otherwise her sacrifice will be for nothing," said Aurie.

Pi was numb, but not numb enough to dim the sounds of chaos breaking out above.

"This isn't good."

"No, it isn't," said her sister. "Come on."

Aurie touched the runes in the correct order. They went through. Pi hardly noticed the vertigo. She checked herself for blood on the other side, but found none. It was better that way.

The walls had been taken down. There were no monsters blocking their path. The monster was outside in a white suit. Mostly she regretted ever letting Alton live. She should have killed him when she had the chance.

"The portal," said Aurie. "Let's go, before someone stops us."

Pi seemed to wake from her bad dream. Was Bethany really dead? It wasn't right and it wasn't fair. Especially not by Alton's hand. He'd been the one to curse her in Coterie, changing her life forever. That he'd been the one to take her life was downright cruel. Bethany had only wanted to belong, and now she was dead.

"Yeah, I'm..." She bit her lower lip. "I'll survive. Let's do this. Dooset daram," she said, though her heart wasn't in it.

"Dooset daram."

They went through the portal.

THIRTY

Getting through the portal in the statue should have tasted like victory, but instead it tasted like ash. Aurie put a hand on her sister's arm in comfort. It was hard to imagine what she was going through. Bethany was her second friend in a year to die, a kindred soul who'd survived a year in Coterie as well. Pi was like a taut bowstring.

"*Alice in Wonderland*," said Pi, startling Aurie from her sisterly examination.

"What?"

Aurie had been too busy checking on her sister to notice the little table against the far wall. Two short glasses filled with a thick blue liquid the color of Drano sat at the exact center of the table.

"It's one of the books from Invictus' cottage. It was sitting by his bed, as if he liked to read it before bedtime," said Pi.

"We should drink them," said Aurie, stepping forward, but Pi grabbed her arm.

Pi produced a miniature scroll from a pocket. "Violet gave this to me before we left."

Aurie huddled next to her sister to read the scroll as she unrolled it.

A&P

I learned a few things about the trials that you'll face. I hope these help, but take them with a grain of salt. I'm not 100% sure that they didn't purposely feed me misleading information.

ORANGE - A knowledge of history might help?

VIOLET - The hardest, it took them the longest to figure out using all their resources.

GREEN - Don't use magic.

BLUE - A speed run of your Second Year Contest.

The RED is the last, but nobody knows where it is. Everyone assumes the portal in the Spire is where you go once you have the seventh, but that could be a false lead. Good luck.

Love you both!

—V.

"She didn't mention anything about the potions," said Pi. "Does that mean they're safe?"

"Probably," said Aurie, examining the walls for clues. "This reminds me of the Trials of Magic from our first year. We have to survive the Proving Grounds all over."

"Except this time the whole Hundred Halls are at stake," said Pi. "The whole world if you count the impending demonic invasion. I wish Invictus wouldn't have required that stupid Cryptic Curse. This would be a whole lot easier if we could tell them Invictus is alive."

"They wouldn't have believed us even if we could," said Aurie. "I think they've grown to resent him over the centuries."

"Bottoms up?"

"Armor up first," said Aurie. "We don't know happens afterwards."

When it was time to drink, they clinked glasses and took a sniff.

"Smells like what blueberry paint would smell like," said Pi.

Aurie threw the thick liquid back. The potion tasted like sugar-sweetened glue.

She turned to check on her sister's reaction when the room slipped past her. The walls and ceiling soared upward. She could no longer hold the glass, which tumbled from her grip. She felt empty, as if every meal she'd ever eaten had disappeared from her memory. Aurie thought she was shrinking until she realized she was sinking into the floor, leaving her clothes, the indigo glass ball, and trinkets behind.

Within the span of a few seconds, she'd fallen through the ceiling into a new room, drifting until she hit the floor, finding it solid. The floor was chilly against her legs, and Aurie realized she was naked. So was her sister, who somehow managed to land on her feet and was retrieving a gray robe hanging on the wall.

"That was a neat trick," said Pi.

The room they were in had four doors, each one a different color: orange, green, blue, and violet.

The robe was warm and fit snugly around her.

"We left everything up there," said Aurie. "Our spells are gone too."

"Keeps anyone from having an unfair advantage. My leather jacket's up there. You wouldn't believe what I keep in it," said Pi.

"A duffle bag of extra-large condoms and a sock full of butter," said Aurie.

"I can't take you anywhere," said Pi, allowing a grin to color the corner of her mouth.

Aurie marked that up as a minor victory, getting her sister to halfway smile.

"Which door?" asked Pi.

"I think we should save the violet door for last," said Aurie. "What about the speed run? We know that one since we won it."

"I'm not ready for that one. Not yet, anyway."

"Okay," said Aurie. "The green door says don't use magic. Hopefully it's a puzzle that you can solve because of your Invictus research. We could do the easiest first."

"I doubt it'll be easy. The Cabal took four months to make it through these, and they had six teams trying, more than that since some of them died," said Pi, frowning.

"Thanks for the pep talk," said Aurie.

Her sister sighed. "Sorry. I'm, you know, still trying to wrap my head around what happened to Bethany."

"Beating Alton to the seventh ball would be sweet revenge," said Aurie.

Pi's gaze turned murderous. "Us winning will be the least of his problems."

Wanting to change the subject, Aurie pointed to her left. "Green door?"

"Sure."

Aurie didn't know what to expect, but it certainly wasn't a circular room with the green glass ball sitting on a velvet pillow on the far side. Painted onto the floor was a map of the city of Invictus, detailed down to the streets and buildings.

"The third ball is right there," said Pi. "But I suppose it's not going to be as easy as walking across."

A brass plaque set into the floor read: "STIXS TOGETHER TO GET ACROSS."

"Sticks together to get across," repeated Aurie. "Why did he spell the first word wrong?"

"It's a puzzle obviously. Invictus loved his games, thought they were a better teacher than lecture or study. His cottage was filled with them, every nook and cranny. The misspelled word is a clue to solving it."

"We have to get through the city," said Aurie as she tapped on her lower lip. "Do we walk along the path of the streets, or the train lines?"

"The map is too small for walking along the streets," said Pi. "I could be across in five strides. There's only a step between each ward. There's going to be a trick to it. Something we're not seeing."

They paced back and forth, bringing up ideas and conjecture about Invictus' intent for a half-hour. At the end of it, Aurie said, "We have to try something. Staring at the third clue when it's right over there is driving me nuts. What if Violet's concern that she'd been fed bad information was right? What if we're supposed to use magic?"

Her sister, arms crossed, shook her head softly while saying, "Not so sure about that. This feels like a puzzle you can solve without magic."

"Then how?"

Pi gave a one-shoulder shrug while squinting. "Dunno."

"But Invictus' puzzles normally involve magic. We're mages. Shouldn't we be using what makes us special? Let me try one thing," said Aurie. "I know a levitation spell. I can bring it across that way."

"It's worth a try, but I don't think it's going to work," said Pi, standing back.

Aurie stood at the edge of the map, legs spread. She rubbed her hands together to warm them. The room was chilly, and the robe, while comfortable against her skin, let drafts in around her legs.

The spell was quick and easy. If it worked, she'd pull the green glass ball towards her as if it were on a string. The moment she reached out with a touch of faez, a painful shock slammed into her midsection, knocking her sprawling across the floor.

"Ow, fuck, that hurt," said Aurie, holding her stomach to catch her breath.

"I hope you're okay because we've got a new problem now," said Pi, heavy concern in her tone.

"Do I want to know?" Aurie said, eyes still closed.

"There's a timer on the far wall, and it's counting down. Ten minutes—less now, I guess."

Aurie struggled to her feet. It felt like she'd finished five hundred sit-ups.

"Lesson learned," said Aurie.

Pi was scratching the back of her neck. "What do you think happens if we reach zero?"

"Let's not find out," said Aurie. "We can't afford to fail. If you have an idea, talk it out."

"Okay, so what do we know? One, no magic. Two, the misspelling of sticks is important. Three, something about the city is important. A clue about the wards, or streets, or something."

"What about the wards?" asked Aurie, looking down at the map. The inner ring that separated the middle four wards from the outer nine was the Baba Yaga Ring Road. Extra-wide avenues separated the wards like spokes on a wheel, the middle ones radiating from the Spire. "Do you think we could step through them in order?"

"Too simple," said Pi. "Doesn't explain the sticks together part."

"What if we're supposed to make the journey together, hand in hand, like in the *Wizard of Oz* when they start off on the Yellow Brick Road," said Aurie. "Then again, that sounds pretty stupid."

"I think you've got something," said Pi. "That's not it, but we're close."

The timer was down to seven minutes, and Aurie didn't feel any closer than she had when it started.

"Sticks together," said Pi. "Sticks together. Like glue? Maple syrup?"

"Invictus always designed his games to teach a lesson. Like the second-year contest. He wanted the Halls to work together," said Aurie.

"Keep going," said Pi when she paused.

"I...I don't know. I don't have anything more. Except that the whole purpose of the Halls was to keep us from killing each other," she said. "But we can't use magic, so most of my ideas are out."

"Only five and a half minutes," said Pi, "so keep talking."

Aurie shared a worried glance with her sister, who gave her the motion for "more, more."

"Ahh...I don't know. Uhm, so we're supposed to stick together. But we have a map. A map is the city and the city is the Hundred Halls. We have to use all of them to get across. Maybe not in the numerical order, but in some other way."

As soon as she said it, Pi's eyes widened. "Yes, yes, that's it. But what's the order? Keep going, you're on a roll."

Pi made a sideways stirring action with her forefinger. Aurie paced back and forth, hands shoved into her hair, making the strands dance around her face. The gray robe swung and bumped against her legs.

"Three minutes," said Pi after a while. "Just talk, you were doing great."

"Fine. Uhm, yeah. The wards. We need the wards. But"—Aurie snapped her fingers—"sticks together! That's our clue. It's spelled wrong for a reason."

Before that, Pi had been watching her, but now she was focused on the brass plaque. She clapped her hands together once. "Sticks together! I should have seen it before. The grammar is wrong. I mean, that's not what I saw. But that helped me figure it out. It's a misdirection. 'Stixs together' to get across. Not as an action, but that we have to use the words 'Stixs together.' But how?"

Out of the corner of her eye, Aurie saw the timer slip past the two-minute mark, but kept her focus on the plaque.

"Wait, stixs together is thirteen letters like the wards. The letters are a map," said Aurie.

Pi caught onto her conclusion, her face alit with excitement. "One. Two. Three. Four. Five. Six. Seven. Eight. Nine. Ten. Eleven. Twelve. Thirteen. I think we use the name, but I'm not sure that gets us all the letters."

Aurie drew the letters on her palm. When she was working through a problem, it helped her to make a tactile representation. "No, it's not that. We need different letters. First. Second. Third. Fourth. Etc."

"What's the order?" asked Pi, bouncing on her heels.

Less than a minute. They were running out of time. "We're going to have to solve this on the fly. Take my hand. We have to jump to the seventh ward."

Pi pulled her back. "What about the others that have an S?"

"We need the first and second for other letters and we definitely need the sixth for the X," said Aurie.

Leaping together was challenging, but they landed on the seventh ward and nothing negative happened.

"What now?" asked Pi.

Aurie had worked it out in her head, but she'd had to go so fast, she wasn't sure she'd gotten them right. "Tenth for T." They leapt. "Now ninth for I."

When the timer crossed the thirty-second mark, Aurie stopped explaining and only yelled out the ward they had to jump to. "Sixth. Second. Thirteenth. First. Eighth." She paused, deciding between the fifth and the eleventh for the letter E. Not only did she have to get them in order, but they had to be able to leap across. They could leap two wards, but they couldn't go from twelve to eight, or six to ten.

"Ten seconds!" yelled Pi.

"Fifth. Twelfth. Third. Eleventh. Fourth."

After landing in the final ward, they hurried to the velvet cache and simultaneously touched the green ball as the timer froze on "0:02."

As soon as her fingertips brushed the third clue, a tingling sensation etched across her wrist, where the other tattoos were. There were three little balls: green, indigo, and yellow.

Aurie moved to grab the green ball when a chute opened and it disappeared from view. The original door that they'd come through swung open.

"Three down, four to go," said Aurie. "I'll take a big guess and say that it'll be waiting for us with our stuff when we leave."

Pi gave her a knowing nod. "If we leave."

They walked back into the main room. The green door closed behind them, and faded until only a wall remained.

"Which door? Your choice," said Aurie.

"Orange, a knowledge of history will help," said Pi, motioning towards the door. "You first, age before beauty."

THIRTY ONE

Pi walked through the door right behind her sister, but when the door closed, Aurie was gone. No sound, or visual cue announced her sudden departure. The room was rectangular with white walls, as plain as a vanilla wafer.

"Aurie?" she shouted, spinning around, looking for signs of her sister, or what the challenge might be. "Aurie? Olly olly oxen free!"

The children's saying during games of hide-and-seek fell flat in the blank room, and her heart followed. These trials were meant to be solved together, right? She was about to cast a faez detection spell when a soft rumble of machinery made her freeze. Nine holes opened in the floor like eyes. Rising from their depths, nine mages appeared. She recognized Merlin from the wax museum with his wispy white beard and expression of general disdain. The woman with the dark hair, who looked simultaneously young and ancient, holding a wooden pestle could only be Baba Yaga.

Some of the others were vaguely familiar, and Pi was wasting no time preparing for battle, when a gravelly voice announced, "One is your sister.

Choose wisely and you shall earn your reward, while the others will be destroyed. If you cannot choose after the allotted time, then it will be you who must die."

Questions died in her throat as a timer appeared on the far wall reading "10:00" and started counting down immediately.

"Another puzzle, great," she muttered, eyeing the lifelike simulacrums. "Who are you all? Great wizards of history? But that can't be true, because Baba Yaga is a story. Except Violet's note said a knowledge of history would be useful. But maybe that's the point. I'm supposed to find the one that's not an actual wizard of history? This is going to be impossible. I don't even recognize most of them."

The wizards moved as if they were alive, shifting on their little daises as if they were waiting to be called on. An elderly Japanese man in enveloping robes and a black conical hat waved a peacock fan in his face for air, while another elderly man, this one wearing a tan toga and a scruffy brown beard, was picking at his fingernails with a bored expression on his jowls. Pi moved forward, stopped before Merlin, who was on the far left, and checked for faez, only to find the whole room was overwhelmingly blanketed with the golden stuff.

"Okay, so you're Merlin, and you're Baba Yaga." She stopped before a man in a brown linen jacket, dirty trousers, and an odd puffy three-cornered hat.

"Who are you?" she mused, jumping backwards when he replied, "Farmer Weathersky."

"What the hell. You just about gave me a heart attack," she said with a hand over her breast.

He'd spoken in a Scandinavian accent. "I thought you were a fairy-tale character. I remember your book from Invictus' cottage. *The Diary of Farmer Weathersky*. Is that what I'm supposed to do? Figure out which one of you isn't a real wizard? And that one will be my sister?"

Farmer Weathersky inclined his head. "Are you picking me?"

"No," said Pi, right away. "Can you tell me who my sister is?"

He glanced up and down the line, and responded with a shrug.

Pi stepped to the next, a woman in a turquoise toga holding a crook. "Who are you?"

"Circe," she replied.

Pi went down the line asking each in turn to identify themselves. The nine mages were Merlin Aurelianus, Baba Yaga, Farmer Weathersky, Circe, Abe no Seimei, Edward Kelly, Aristotle, Khalid ibn Yazid, and Prospero.

There were too many questions she wanted to ask. Ten minutes? She needed hours to question them to determine which was her sister. Pi held her hands over her mouth in a prayful position, trying to figure out what questions might unlock the mystery of her missing sister.

"How could Invictus set up a puzzle and yet leave no time to solve it?" She paused, letting the thought ruminate. "Unless there is a way to solve it in ten minutes. A shortcut? A clue? I've read about some of you in his books. Others I know from legends and tales."

She marched up to a middle-aged man wearing a four-cornered hat that seemed like a bishop's miter, though she knew it wasn't. He wore a deep frown and had a crease to his eyes as if he were in constant pain.

"You're Edward Kelly. I don't recognize your name, though I feel like I should. What did you do when you were alive?"

Edward Kelly visibly filled himself with sense of purpose, erasing the sadness—the doom—in his gaze until he had a magnetic presence. The transformation was startling and eerie. "I am Sir Edward Kelly. I lived during the English Renaissance, summoned spirits, practiced alchemy, and sought the Philosopher's Stone itself."

"A charlatan. Or maybe not," said Pi, stepping down the line. "What did you do when you were alive?"

Khalid ibn Yazid bowed his turbaned head, stroked his black beard wisely, and said, "I was a prince, and a chemist. I wrote texts about the elements, studied the stars. Fools like him"—he hooked a thumb in the direction of Kelly—"misunderstood my writings."

"All very interesting," said Pi, glancing at the timer, already at six minutes, "but not doing me any good. This is taking too long. I'll never figure this out in time. Why did Invictus pick you? What's the thread that holds eight of you together?"

Except for their connection to magic, Pi could determine no other commonality between them. Aristotle was a philosopher who also had mentored Alexander the Great. Prospero was a wizard from *The Tempest*, a Shakespearian play.

To her knowledge, at least three of them had been real people: Abe no Seimei, Edward Kelly, and Aristotle. At least three of them had been written into fairy tales: Baba Yaga, Farmer Weathersky, and Circe. She knew about the fuzziness of Merlin's existence, that it could have been based on a real person, or an amalgamation of two. Prospero had been made up completely, or so she thought. It wasn't inconceivable that Shakespeare had based him on a real wizard from his time.

Pi jogged down to Merlin, asked him, "Are you a real person?" and before he could answer, she shifted to Baba Yaga and did the same, going down the line in order while keeping her senses tuned for the answer. All nine answered yes, so she repeated the process with other questions.

Can you do magic? Yes.

Are you still alive? No.

Are you my sister? No answer.

Did you know any of the other mages in real life? No.

What is your connection to the others? No answer.

When she was finished, the timer was at two and a half minutes.

"Which one of you is Aurie?" she asked, hearing the desperation in her own voice. "I guess there's a one in nine chance I pick right? We've faced worse odds."

Her stomach turned over. Pi wanted to vomit. She marched up to Edward Kelly and tried to push him, but he didn't budge. She lowered her shoulder and hit him again, only to bounce off as if he were a trampoline. Then she shot him with a spit of fire from a Five Elements spell. He rubbed his arm where he was burnt, glaring at her with distaste.

"You're a rude child," he said.

Pi went up and down the line, hitting them each with a little burst of flame. She received threats and insults, but none of them acted on them. When she was finished, she knew nothing more than she had when she'd started.

With less than a minute, Pi stood before them, scanning back and forth, looking for some clue that might tell her which one was her sister. The illusions were perfect, and tactile. They were maddeningly obtuse.

Thirty seconds left. Did she take a chance and pick one? If she did, and was wrong, then her sister died and she lived. If Pi didn't pick any of them, then she died.

"There's close to a 90% chance you die if I pick," said Pi, "but you live for sure if I don't. I'd rather give up my life than take yours on a foolish chance."

She watched the final countdown with relief and dread. Relief that she'd made her decision and was happy with it, and dread, for fear that the end would be painful.

Ten.

Nine.

Pi wiped her eyes, wishing she'd gotten to say goodbye to her sister one last time.

Seven.

"Dooset daram, older sister. Thank you for always looking out for me." Five. "I hope you find a way to finish this without me."

Three.

Two.

One.

Her whole body tensed as the countdown hit zeroes. The wizards, who had remained their bored selves, faded away, the illusion revealed at last.

Standing on the other side of the place where the wizards had been only moments before, looking equally confused and distraught, was her sister—Aurie. Neither wasted a moment more, rushing across the space to throw themselves into each other's arms.

"I thought I was dead," said Pi.

"Me too," said Aurie. "I couldn't do it. I couldn't pick."

"Me neither. But I don't understand. We were each given a trial? But the wizards are gone. Is the contest broken?"

Aurie never had a chance to answer, as the sound of grinding machinery rumbled from below, and the floor irised open, revealing a pedestal bearing an orange glass ball rising.

Stunned, they released each other, watched until the pedestal clicked into place, and approached apprehensively.

"We won?" asked Aurie.

And suddenly, the trial made sense to Pi. "It wasn't about history, or the wizards. It was a test. A test to see if you'd sacrifice your partner on the slim chance you might get it right, or give yourself up willingly rather than take that chance."

"I guess so," said Aurie. "How in the world did Alton and Sunil pass this one?"

"They didn't. Not honestly," said Pi. "That's why they kept reloading with new Cabal mages every time some died. They were throwing them at the contest, gaming it through sheer numbers rather than any skill."

"Let's get our prize and get the hell out of here. This places creeps me out," said Aurie.

When Pi touched the orange ball, a new tattoo formed on her wrist. When the pedestal sunk towards the floor, they left, returning to the central chamber to face the remaining two doors.

THIRTY TWO

"Speed run or the hardest?" Aurie asked her sister as they faced the two doors, violet and blue.

"It doesn't matter," said Pi. "We've got to do them both eventually."

The violet door was tempting, but Aurie wanted to get the blue out of the way. She'd been dreading seeing the bugs again, because of what had happened two years ago at her clinic.

"Actually," said her sister, "let's do the blue door. After the last two, I really want to unleash some magic."

A lump formed in Aurie's throat. Her sister raised an eyebrow.

"You thinking about what happened to Annabelle?" asked Pi.

"Yeah," said Aurie feeling tangled up inside.

"You won't have to worry about anyone getting in the way this time," said Pi.

"I don't think we're supposed to battle our way to the end," said Aurie. "A speed run implies avoiding conflict, getting to the end as fast as possible. Especially since there's only two of us."

Pi frowned. "You're probably right. Which is a bummer. I kinda liked squashing bugs. It was therapeutic. You think we might need to get to the queen bug?"

"We might," said Aurie, though something about this challenge bothered her. She couldn't quite put her finger on it, but it felt like something was wrong.

On the other side of the blue door was a small room with an obsidian archway. Two tan expedition outfits hung on pegs. The boots and everything fit snugly as if they'd been custom made.

"Let's kill the ground bugs near the flowers first, then ignore the rest. We can head straight into the jungle without disturbing any more," said Aurie.

They went through the archway after covering themselves in enchantments, landing in the thick grass of the abandoned fort, stifled by a claustrophobic heat. The stone walls surrounded by jungle were exactly the same as Aurie remembered, which wasn't hard because she'd had nightmares about the place for years.

"Yuck," said Pi, shaking out her hands, "I'm already dripping with sweat."

Approaching the location of the first bug left Aurie buzzing with anticipation, like watching a familiar horror movie, knowing that scare would come even if she steeled herself. She hated the way the critters burst from the soft soil, driving towards them with razor-sharp mandibles. Killing the ones coming out of the trees was much easier because she could see them coming.

Aurie edged forward to the spot she thought should trigger them. Pi gave her a raised eyebrow and stomped on the ground. When nothing happened, she took two steps forward, expecting the earth to swallow her at any moment.

In a mini-tribal dance, Pi stomped around the spot that should have contained the bugs.

"I guess this one is different than the original. Let's motor before the others arrive."

"Flowers first," said Aurie, motioning towards the purple-dotted bushes.

Without gloves, the sharp ends of the branches scraped up their hands, but they managed to collect fistfuls of flowers, shoving extras into their pockets, before scurrying through the gap in the west wall. Halfway across the clearing, Pi caught sight of a bug coming out of the jungle, and they sprinted to a hiding spot before they were seen.

"That was close," whispered Aurie, crouched next to her sister in the bushes as flies landed on her head and buzzed in her ears.

"It's only three bugs," replied Pi. "No first wave."

"This is *way* different than last time."

The three bugs ambled by on blade-like legs, angular heads bobbing against their gait. Their dark green carapaces glistened in the naked sun.

Aurie felt her sister pull away, deeper into the jungle. "Wait," she hissed. "I want to see what they're doing."

"Speed run," said Pi, elongating the word speed. "Which suggests actually moving."

The earlier nagging feeling that she was missing something had increased. "I want to see this."

"And I want to get out of this place. I can't count the number of times we got murdered by those damn things in this fort," said Pi, angrily waving at a black-winged fly that was dive-bombing her face.

The three giant bugs meandered around the fort. The tallest bug used a scarred foreleg to dig into the soil like a terrier for a few seconds. A beetle the size of a hubcap burst from the ground, expanding its wings to escape before a bladed leg pierced it through the middle, greenish goo dripping into the grass.

"Are you satisfied? It's making beetle kabobs for the queen," said Pi, tugging on her arm.

"What if it's a misdirection?"

"It looks pretty straightforward to me," said Pi. "Violet's note was clear cut. 'Speed run from Second Year Contest.' We were the winners, so it should be easy for us. None of the other teams even made it to the queen's lair."

"Think about it," said Aurie as she watched the bugs in the fort continue to forage. "Each ball has required a different solution. If this contest was designed to find a successor—"

"Or a pair of successors," said Pi.

"Or a pair of successors," said Aurie, and something about that stuck in her mind—why would there be two?—but she dismissed it and finished what she was saying. "Then each ball has tested a different aspect of the mage's abilities. Think about it. The indigo ball was a test of pure power. Hemistad for you, equally ferocious beings for the others. I heard Alton took down a manticore for his. The yellow was a test of improvised skill, performing the Five Elements backwards. Then green was a puzzle that had no magical element to it, and it was only something someone who lived in the city could solve. Orange was a test of courage, to see if we would sacrifice our partner. Which is why I'm not sure about blue being a speed run. We've already had a test of skill."

"What about the note?"

Aurie gave a tight-lipped shrug. "Violet said it could be false information."

"What are you suggesting?"

She hesitated, only because she wasn't sure what she was suggesting, other than not doing the obvious thing.

"I don't know," said Aurie, biting her lower lip. "But I don't see a countdown anywhere and the bugs are acting differently this time."

"That's true," said Pi, peering from the bushes into the sky as if the countdown would be shown up there.

When she wiped the sweat from her forehead, the aroma of the purple flowers reminded her that she had two fistfuls of them. A thought struck her keenly, making her stand straight up.

Pi dragged her back into the bushes. "Are you really my sister or did a simulacrum replace you in the last room, 'cause you're acting crazy."

"It does sound crazy, but I think I'm right. A bug fight sounds wrong. Why repeat what we've already done? When has Invictus ever repeated a game? Every year, the Merlin trials are new. Every year, the Second Year contest is new. You said it yourself, he loves games. Why would he repeat one?"

Pi squinted at her as if that would reveal the truth. "Maybe he ran out of time. Or maybe it's meant to reward experience. Those who did the best in the contest would have an advantage."

This idea took the wind out of Aurie. "That's a good point, but..."

The jungle on the far side of the fort rustled as alien bugs came into the clearing in two lines like a procession. These had black-and-red carapaces. They marched like soldiers. Other bugs scurried out of the old fort, headed almost right for them, but entered the trees about twenty feet away and disappeared.

When a massive tank-sized bug with a flat triangular head strutted from the trees, Aurie went cold. A glint of blue caught the sunlight from beneath a wing of the tank-bug.

"The glass ball," hissed Pi, clapping her hand over her mouth when it came out too loud.

"I was right," whispered Aurie. "We would have run right into them had we raced to the crevice. They must have fed Violet the wrong information."

"But what do we do? There's too many of them and it's not like we can go up and ask them to give it to us," said Pi.

For the second time in a short while, a thought sparked through her mind, making her quiver with both excitement and dread.

"What if we can?"

"You can't be serious," said Pi. "You're not an animalian, though I don't know if they can shapeshift into insects."

Aurie looked at the purple flowers in her hands. "Let's weave a necklace."

"What good will that do?"

"We'll find out soon enough," said Aurie.

"No," said Pi emphatically.

Aurie glanced back at the giant insects in the old fort. They looked so stately, like imperial guards waiting for an emissary. She turned back to Pi.

"Then what's your idea? We can't take them, not easily," said Aurie.

Her sister shook her head, eyebrows squished together. Then she sighed and pushed Aurie out of the way. "Give me a moment. I know a spell."

Pi worked her magic discreetly, barely a whiff of faez was wasted. She frowned as if she didn't like the result.

"The Seréne soul fragment knew a spell. That Hall is obsessed with manipulating people with their voice, and they know what people are thinking, what their mood is. The spell told me that the bugs are calm, but anticipating something, an arrival perhaps."

"Us," said Aurie, working to control the volume of her voice. "They're anticipating us."

"Possibly," said Pi, screwing up her face, "but I don't know if bug emotions are the same as human ones. The spell could be misreading them."

"Do you think I'm wrong about me going out there to negotiate for the glass ball?" asked Aurie.

Her sister looked like she would have preferred to have bamboo shoots shoved under her fingernails than answer the question, but eventually said, "I guess it might work, but I think we'd be safer with the bug-and-guts plan."

"Let me go out there while you stay in the bushes," said Aurie. "If they attack then we'll kill them."

Pi reluctantly agreed. While they made a necklace out of the flowers, the tank-bug marched into the fort and rested its girth onto the grass. Half the soldier bugs filed back into the jungle and disappeared. The remainder seemed to be waiting, Aurie hoped it was for them.

With a flowery necklace hanging around her neck, and the remainder of their flowers stuffed into her pockets, Aurie gave instructions to her sister.

"Wait here," said Aurie. "If they attack, then you'll get the battle you were itching for. If not, then we can get the hell out of here and work on the violet door."

"Don't count your glass balls before they hatch, or something like that," said Pi, clearly reticent about what Aurie was going to do. "What I mean is don't do anything stupid, more stupid than you're about to do. If they look menacing, then GTFO, and we can rain unholy fire upon them."

"How again do I tell if it's any more menacing than normal?" asked Aurie.

Pi gave her a look. "You'd better get moving, before I ruin your diplomacy with a hailstorm of firespears."

Aurie took a deep breath and stepped from the bushes. The giant bugs took immediate notice of her, moving stiffly, blade-like legs kneading the ground in anticipation. Regret came hard and fast like a punch to the gut. When the tank-bug turned its alien triangular head towards her, she had second thoughts.

"We can still kill them," whispered Pi from the bushes.

Aurie took a couple of steps forward, watching the bugs for a reaction. They didn't look welcoming, but they hadn't rushed forward to murder her either.

A black-and-red soldier bug stood at the edge of the old stone wall. She walked towards it, slowly, every motion a deliberate action. She didn't want them to get the wrong idea of what she was doing, if they could get ideas at all. But she'd seen the queen, and the bugs in the lair. There had been a structure and a hierarchy suggesting an intelligence far greater than the insects of her world.

When she was ten feet from the soldier bug, who had made no motion towards her, she said, "Greetings and salutations. We've come to trade you for that blue bauble you have."

She felt pretty foolish as she spoke, as if she were an actor in a B-movie about invading aliens, "take me to your leader" and all that.

The soldier bug took two ambling steps towards her, closing the gap easily. She tensed when it moved, hating in her gut that she was so near this alien creature which had murdered her over and over in the Second Year Contest. But this was why she thought conversing with them was the right thing to do. Invictus never had students run through the same game twice, so the only reason he would have brought them back to this world was to subvert their expectations.

"Is there something we could trade for the blue ball?" she asked.

The black-and-red bug angled its head like a dog listening. The familiar motion brought a ray of hope to a difficult situation. She let a warm smile break across her lips, wanting so badly to turn her head and shoot a grin at her sister hiding in the bushes.

"You understand?" she asked.

The head on the soldier bug bobbed up and down in the human motion for affirmative. A light burgeoned in her chest.

"The blue ball," she said, extending her arm towards the tank-bug. "Can we have it?"

The bug lifted its blade-like leg, mimicking Aurie as it pointed towards the bug holding the glass ball. Then it spun around, shoving its leg directly into Aurie's chest.

THIRTY THREE

When the bushes had quivered shut and the giant insects turned their alien heads towards her sister, Pi reached inward to her well of faez. She hated that Aurie was risking herself like this, but she didn't have an argument otherwise, and if they could get out of this without a battle, they'd be better rested for the last door, the one they were warned would be the hardest.

"Come on, please work," whispered Pi.

Aurie looked so tall, partly because Pi was crouching in a bush, and partly because Aurie's slender legs were accentuated by the folded bottoms of her expedition shorts. But the red-and-black bug towered over her, each blade-like leg nearly Aurie's length.

It took all of Pi's self-control not to rush out when the bug moved forward, closing the distance between it and Aurie.

"Move back," whispered Pi. "It's too close."

A twig snapped in her fist, but none of the bugs noticed. Pi heard her sister speak, and couldn't help but roll her eyes at her choice of language.

"We're not in a B-movie you dork," said Pi.

When the soldier bug seemed to indicate that a trade was possible, Pi sighed with relief. As much as expending a little faez would feel good, the chance of total annihilation was too great a risk, especially when her sister had figured out an easier way.

Pi was considering whether or not it was safe to come out when the soldier bug spun around, shoving its blade-leg through Aurie's chest. A foot-long section stuck out the back of her tan shirt.

"No!"

The world was momentarily lost in a red rage. The soldier bug discarded Aurie like an empty soda can. Her limp body landed in an awkward heap of arms and legs.

The sphere of flame exiting Pi's fist was so hot it crisped the hairs of her arm and blackened her fingertips. The air shimmered, sizzling as the sphere impacted with the soldier bug. The fire wrapped around it like napalm, crackling, moisture whistling from its long limbs like a lobster thrown into a boiling pot.

Pi reached her sister and palmed energy into the wound, searing it closed. A green pus mixed with the blood. Aurie's eyes were vacant and her mouth hung open. Blood had soaked the rip in her shirt where the insect had speared her.

But Pi had no time to attempt any more healing, as more soldier bugs skittered towards her. The closest exploded when she hit it with a ball of concentrated lava, but the others kept coming.

Standing over her sister, she knew that if the battle was prolonged, Aurie would likely die, if she wasn't dead already. It was doubtful Pi could take on the eight bugs, let alone the massive tank-bug that had extended an ugly dripping proboscis from its belly.

The intensity of her fire spells had matched the immediate rage she'd felt upon seeing her sister go down, but sometimes even the visceral emotion that drove the deepest faez wasn't enough. Even her sister, who had off-the-charts access to the raw stuff of magic, wouldn't be able to annihilate the incoming insects in time.

There was an option that Pi knew existed, even if she'd never really thought about it because it was so horrible that her waking mind refused to consider it. But in this harrowing moment, she knew she would never forgive herself if she let her sister die, even if it meant doing the unthinkable.

There were twelve souls in her. At one time, she'd thought they'd assimilated into hers, but when she reached out to tap into their energy, she found them as separate and fragile as soap bubbles floating on a breeze.

For most of the soul fragments, there was little more than a collection of thoughts and memories, barely a fraction of the person who had existed before the soul thief had gotten to them. When she squeezed a smaller one, it popped, sending what felt like limitless energy into Pi. She was transfixed by the rush, almost immobile in its embrace, as if she'd taken a massive hit of heroin.

With preternatural awareness, Pi flung out her hand, and the wave of, she didn't even know what—fire, force, a breaking of the bonds of atoms?—rolled through the insects, turning them into a charred mess of carapaces and limbs.

And almost as quickly as the soul fragment had hit, it was gone, leaving her empty, bones aching from the transfer of power.

The tank-bug lifted its grotesque proboscis. Green-gray goo dripped from the end, a precursor of what was to come.

A second soul fragment provided another burst of energy, and Pi launched a spear of fire, like the tongue of the sun itself, impaling the massive insect with it. The moisture inside, heated to the temperature of volcanoes, exploded into steam, ripping the creature apart, flinging liquid and shattered carapaces in all directions.

The splattered goo burned when it hit Pi in the arm. Tiny droplets seared across her face and arms, sizzling. Acid!

Ignoring her own pain, Pi crouched over her sister. A glob of acid had stuck to Aurie's neck. Pi scraped it off with her fingers, screaming as the liquid melted her skin.

Without thinking, Pi took more soul material and converted it into healing for Aurie. Real healing required physical bindings to complement the magic, but she had nothing but raw faez, so Pi implored her sister's body to heal itself with the energy provided.

Aurie took a heaving, back-arching breath, as if she'd come up for air after being buried alive. She rolled onto her side, coughing.

With her sister alive, Pi ripped off her shirt, wiped the flecks of acid from her skin, and cleaned it from her finger, which throbbed with pain. Little red marks dotted her body.

"Get the glass ball," wheezed Aurie. "More bugs will be coming."

Pi leapt into action. The tank-bug had split into a mess of guts and carapaces, as if a pus-filled flower had exploded. Her boots started smoking when she got too close, so she laid down a rolling bed of fire to clear away the acid. It took five good blasts before she could reach the blue sphere, nestled between a section of the proboscis and a claw.

Another blast of flame washed the glass ball clean so she could grab it. As she hurried back to her sister, who was struggling to her feet, a new tattoo glistened on her wrist, making five matching spheres.

"More bugs," said Aurie, pointing into the jungle.

"Take this," said Pi, handing the sphere to her sister. As she touched it, the silvery archway appeared.

They fell through the portal, landing back in the small room. Pi collapsed next to her sister.

"I thought I was dead," said Aurie. Dark circles ringed her eyes as if she hadn't slept in months. Her face wrinkled with confusion. "How did you do that? I thought that was it for me, especially when I felt the poison course through my veins. Is there some secret spell you're not telling me about?"

An ocean of guilt welled up in Pi. Her throat seized with emotion, the words barely climbed out. "I had to. What I did...I had to. I'm sorry. I'm no better than they are. I'm sorry, but I couldn't let you die."

Her sister searched her face for a few seconds before her eyes widened with understanding. "You used the souls."

A tight nod was all Pi could muster.

"You did what you needed to do," said Aurie earnestly. "I would have done the same for you. I would do worse."

"I'll never forgive myself."

Aurie reached out and pulled Pi into a hug. Pi nestled into her sister's neck, letting the tears flow.

"You would have never forgiven yourself if you hadn't used them," said Aurie.

Pi pulled away, sniffed, and wiped tears away with her fingers. "But now they're gone. I was their caretaker, keeping them safe. It was bad enough what Liam did to them. I made it worse."

"How many?" asked Aurie, after a moment of hesitation.

"I don't know," said Pi. "Ashley is still there at least, but the others, it's hard to say."

"It's okay. Getting into Invictus' realm before the Cabal is too important. We need the both of us."

"No, it's not," said Pi, making fists of her hands. "This is what happened to the Cabal. They were seduced by the easy power of magic. I snuffed out numerous souls as a means to an end."

"Soul fragments."

"There was no difference to me. I felt them, their memories, their thoughts. They were people to me, inside my head. And now they're gone."

They sat in silence for a few minutes until Aurie said, "I hate to say this but we need to keep going."

"I look like I have the measles," said Pi, looking down at her stomach, then noticing the fabric of her bra. "I hope there's no more acid, this thing is little holey."

"Speaking of holey," said Aurie, examining the lump of red scar tissue where the blade-leg had gone through. A little hole at the bottom leaked blood.

When her sister cried out in pain, Pi feared she'd missed some of the poison or acid, and it was hurting her again.

"What's wrong?"

Aurie had a worried scowl. "When I tried to use faez, it was like my whole body had turned to fire."

"That's not good," said Pi. "We have another puzzle to solve."

Aurie tried again, yelping in response. "No, definitely not. I can't use magic right now."

"I must have done something wrong when I healed you," said Pi. "But I've never heard of faez being blocked."

"Maybe it's the aftereffects of the poison, which means it'll fade in time," said Aurie, putting on a brave smile. "I hope."

"Violet door?" asked Pi.

When they went through they found themselves in knee-high grass, and though initially Pi had the impression of being in a vast area because the sky seemed to go on forever, she quickly realized it was an illusion.

With the door closed behind them, they stood inside a giant dome, the inside surface looking like a summer sky. At the center of the dome was a tower, like a giant golf tee, with a dainty violet glass ball sitting at the top. The section of grassland they stood on only went about one hundred feet forward, until it dropped off. From their vantage, they couldn't see what was beyond that cliff, except that it was another two hundred feet to the tower, but Pi had a good guess. The pit formed a circle around the tower, which was essentially on an island.

The tower and the pit weren't the big concern. Pi already knew a half-dozen ways to traverse those to reach the glass ball. What worried her were the three large creatures flying around the tower.

"Are those dragons?" asked Aurie.

Pi swallowed as she thought about facing one dragon, let alone three. "I think they are."

"Then I think we're fucked."

THIRTY FOUR

Dragons. There were a lot of things Aurie knew about the winged lizards. What wizard didn't? Every little boy and girl who could use faez dreamed about befriending a dragon, or having a tiny dragon as a companion like Semyon Gray. Dragons, for the most part, were private creatures, content to roam desolate lands, or pocket realms loosely connected to this one. Civilization had wisely left them alone.

But that knowledge seemed useless in the face of three adult dragons, who were guarding a prize that they would not allow them to claim.

The scales of the dragons were a mixture of reds and golds and coppers like an autumn forest at sunset, or blood-drenched coins. Their wings made powerful strokes, and Aurie could almost imagine feeling the breeze from them, even at their distance.

"Three dragons," said Aurie. "And I can't use magic."

"Maybe if we wait a while, it'll come back," said Pi.

"We have no food or water, and I'm dizzy, probably from dehydration, so I doubt it's coming back anytime soon. I need rest."

"This is why it took them months," said Pi, staring into the sky at the three dragons. "And I don't think we can talk them into giving us the violet sphere."

"Don't worry," said Aurie. "I'm not making that mistake again."

She gave her sister a good long look. Pi had little red dots all over her skin, a wound on her neck oozed pus, her lower lip was bloody, and her gaze held a deep and abiding pain.

"You know, I hate to say this, but there's only one way we're getting that ball," said Aurie.

Pi glared back at her. "No. Absolutely not."

"Do we have much choice?" asked Aurie.

"I can't believe you're asking me to use the last of the souls," said Pi, anguish in her gaze. "I told you already, I'm never doing that again. Even if it means we don't get the violet ball."

Her lips drew a thin white line. She'd crossed her arms. Her eyes pleaded for Aurie not to ask again.

It was clear her sister had no intention of using them, and if Aurie was somehow able to convince her, it would tear her apart from the inside out.

"I respect your decision. I won't ask again," said Aurie. "But now we have to figure out a way to do this with limited magic, and no time to experiment."

The largest dragon, which had a ruby-colored throat, let out a fearsome roar and continued its circling. The air had a hint of brimstone.

"We can't take them head-on," said Pi. "Maybe if we were at full strength."

"It's probably better that we aren't. That's likely what took the others so long, trying to brute force a solution," said Aurie, crouched in the thick grass. As she stared at the tower, she had an idea. "How tall do you think that is?"

Her sister made musing noises. "Maybe two hundred feet?"

"And the pit?"

"From here, I can't tell, but around two hundred, maybe two fifty. What are you thinking?" asked Pi.

"Maybe we don't have to go the tower, maybe we can make the tower come to us," said Aurie. "Assuming the tower is longer than the pit."

"And how exactly are we going to get the tower to come to us? Dragons are territorial. If we try knocking it over with magic, they're going to notice and come calling."

Aurie pulled a handful of grass from the ground. "We'll do it more subtly. Do you remember when you were nine and you used to braid my hair?"

"Of course, you whined the whole time because it hurt your scalp," said Pi.

"We're going to use those nimble fingers to weave ourselves a rope," said Aurie.

Pi screwed up her face. "When did you learn to weave rope?"

"Sam taught me when we were in Peru. He said it was important not to rely on magic for everything in case it failed." Mention of Sam and his sacrifice brought a heaviness to their mood. "Plus, he said Mom had taught him, and he was returning the favor. That was probably bullshit, but I appreciated the sentiment."

"What length do we need to weave?" asked Pi, glancing back towards the tower and dragons.

"At least four hundred feet, probably a little longer," said Aurie.

"Four hundred feet? Are you crazy? That'll take us forever."

"If you come up with a better idea while we're weaving, then we can try it, but if we work fast, we can probably get that done in twelve hours," said Aurie, shrugging and adding, "My best estimate."

Her sister was a quick learner, so it didn't take long for her to pick up the rope weaving. They worked in tandem. Aurie pulled the grass from the ground, knocked the dirt and roots off, and handed them to her sister, who corded the blades together into a tight rope. Pi was able to enhance her speed with magic, so she had the weaving part of the job.

As they decimated a patch of grass, they moved, for more raw materials, and to keep the dragons from noticing them. The grass was high enough they could sit cross-legged and feel safely hidden.

After the first couple of hours, Aurie started to get stomach cramps from dehydration. Pi was able to sustain herself with a spell, but Aurie had no access to faez, so she was forced to endure.

"If you want to take a break, you can," said Pi, fingers moving in a blur, as if they were on fast-forward.

Aurie put on a brave face. "I'll be fine. The longer we stay here, the worse it's going to get. I'll push through."

But after a few more hours of effort, Aurie curled into a ball, the pain in her stomach was so bad. Her mouth was a desert, and a migraine had formed in the back of her skull. The muscles in her hands were giving out. She could barely get a grip on the grass due to the shaking.

Helping was limited to short stretches, yanking grass for a half-hour, then sitting with her hands in her lap as if they were made of stone. The stretches where she couldn't help got longer.

After what seemed like an eternity, Pi declared the grass rope finished. They took a short rest, then prepared to move the rope into position.

Aurie stared at the winding rope, tufts of grass sticking from the sides at various points along the length. The rope was no wider than two fingers, which seemed ludicrously thin for what they needed it to do.

"If I had access to magic, I could whisper some lies into the rope to make sure it won't break," said Aurie.

Aurie grabbed one end of the rope, and Pi the other. They each headed a different direction around the pit, staying crouched in the grass for safety. When the rope dipped over the edge, the weight of it nearly yanked it out of her quivering hands, so she tied it around her waist, a dangerous proposition if it dragged her into the pit.

When they crossed the largest diameter of the circle, and the rope rested against the base of the tower, Aurie had to crawl on her hands and knees, holding onto the grass to keep it from pulling her in. She felt like gravity had failed and she was holding onto the world.

Reaching her sister, she gave a mute cry of victory. Together they wrapped the two ends, until they made a woven cord. There was about thirty feet of excess rope.

"Now what?" asked Pi.

Aurie was lying on her back, knocking her arms together. Her hands were pink and raw from handling the grass. "Can you pull the tower over?"

With a shrug, Pi moved into position, wrapped the double-rope around her hands, and yanked. The tower didn't budge.

Keeping the rope in her lap, Pi closed her eyes and imbued herself with strength. When she was finished, she gave the rope a massive tug, straining until the cords of her neck were sticking out. After a minute of struggle, and no movement, Pi collapsed.

She gave Aurie a sad shake of her head.

They sat a while in silence, until Pi spoke up. "I could climb over and try to sneak up the tower."

"No way," said Aurie. "One, they would see you, and two, I'm too weak to hold the rope."

Silence resumed.

Aurie cleared her throat softly. "What if you boosted—"

"Absolutely not," said Pi. "The souls are off-limits."

Aurie watched the majestic dragons soar around the tower, wings thrusting through the air. If it weren't for the circumstances and the stakes, it'd be a lovely place to have a picnic. The power of the supernatural creatures gave her an idea.

"I think I know how to pull down the tower," said Aurie. "We get the dragons to do it."

Pi blinked rapidly, clearly not believing what she'd heard. "I'm going to assume you have a plan in that head of yours."

"How good are you at using a lasso?"

"Never done it in my life," said Pi.

"Now is the perfect time to learn," said Aurie. "And don't miss, or the dragon will eat me. Well, it might break the rope and eat me anyway, but this way gives us a shot."

"You're going to play bait while I try to lasso?"

Aurie nodded.

"Let's do this then. I want to get the hell out of here," said Pi.

Once they had made a loop with the end and her sister was in position, Aurie moved to a spot near the edge. She needed the dragon to swoop low enough that Pi could get the rope around its neck.

Aurie popped out of the grass and started waving her arms. "Come and get me! I'm a tasty dragon snack!"

The largest of the three dragons, the one with the ruby throat, peeled away from the tower, heading straight at Aurie as if it were coming down the first slope of a roller coaster. Seeing the beast with its jaws open, ready to snatch her from the grass and rip her in two, turned her legs to liquid.

"Run," whispered Pi, from her hiding spot nearby.

Spurred by her sister's voice, Aurie turned and ran, but she felt like she was moving in slow motion through the grass. She didn't want to look, but turned her head in time to see Pi stand and launch the loop towards the incoming dragon. The rope opened perfectly, flying right into the way, but at the last moment closed, missing the dragon by a few feet.

Aurie had stopped running when she thought the dragon was going to get lassoed. She turned, nearly tripping over the grass in her haste, and sprinted towards the wall.

With no room to turn, the dragon landed heavily on the ground, shaking the whole dome. Aurie made it to the wall, but she had nowhere to run.

Certain that she was trapped, the ruby-throated dragon roared, freezing her in place. It slow-marched forward, claws ripping at the earth, its tail, almost as long as its body, swishing through the grass like an angry cat.

There was no escaping the dragon. As it thundered closer, she could feel its hot, horrid breath, which smelled of rancid meat. Its teeth were as long as knives, with old flesh stuck between.

When it was only thirty feet away, the dragon crouched, readying itself to launch forward and snap her in two. Aurie was transfixed.

The ruby-throated dragon thrust forward, and Aurie closed her eyes, expecting to feel the crush of its jaws. When the dragon roared in frustration, she opened them, to find it stuck where it was. Her sister had tied the end of the rope around the dragon's tail.

The beast roared again, and leapt. The tower groaned, steel bending, cracking. The tip of the tower swayed.

When the dragon yanked again, the base of the tower snapped. Aurie ran directly perpendicular, as the dragon used its newfound freedom to snap after her.

She felt teeth close inches from her back as she sprinted around the circumference of the room.

The tower had fallen, tipped over, creating a bridge to the center. Aurie couldn't see if her sister had captured the violet glass ball, but she had no time, as the dragon lumbered after her, slowed only by the rope and tower on its tail.

On the other side, Pi thrust the ball into the air victoriously, pointing towards the nearby door. Aurie pushed herself, as the dragon kept trying to fly so it could swoop after her, but the tower formed a drag, and it couldn't get off the ground.

Aurie reached the door at the same time as her sister. They reached out, hands touching, and burst through the door to land in an unfamiliar room.

The side wall had an archway that mirrored the one they'd come through to get into the statue. Two piles of stuff sat in the corner, including their clothes and her sister's magical leather jacket.

"Oh, thank Merlin," said Pi, pulling the jacket into her arms in an embrace.

"Where's the violet ball?" asked Aurie, suddenly worried.

Pi frowned, then touched her wrist. "We have the tattoo."

Aurie checked, surprised to find the sixth sphere on her wrist. There was something else, something new. Her wrist felt heavy, as if something were inside it.

"You feel that, too?" asked Pi.

"Yeah," said Aurie, "they're with us now."

"Let's get the hell out of here. I need a cheeseburger and a drink the size of Arcanium's moat."

Going back through the portal into the statue was trivial. Nothing had changed on the other side. They made the short journey to the portal that would bring them back to the basement of the statue.

Aurie touched the runes in order, grabbed her sister's hand, and went through. When they landed on the other side they were greeted by a half-dozen men with semiautomatics slung over their shoulders.

A familiar Russian accented voice came from the darkness behind the men. "Right where we expected them, my little Silverthorne sisters."

THIRTY FIVE

Pi blinked, clearing her vision with a wipe of her fingertips. Six men in runed Kevlar vests, wielding semiautomatics—with mage-killing bullets she assumed—had arrayed themselves in a semicircle, the muzzle of every gun pointed in their direction. It wasn't the greeting she'd been hoping for.

Strolling from the darkness, a single ceiling lamp illuminating his flowery island shirt, Ivan looked like the fox in the henhouse.

After everything she'd been through inside, the puzzles, the danger, and especially the dragons, she was not in the mood for more complications.

"If you touch me or my sister, I swear I'll bring this statue down on all of us," said Pi.

"Pi-THEE-a," said Ivan, opening his arms as if he were approaching for a hug. "How can you say that to your knight in shining armor. I here to rescue you. Or do we not have deal anymore?"

She felt a little unsteady on her legs. "So you're not here to kill us?"

"Kill? Me?" He placed his hand over his heart earnestly. "We made a deal, and when I saw the chaos in the square on TV, I knew I needed to come down and make sure my investment would pay off."

"They broadcasted what happened?" asked Aurie, horrified.

"Only for a moment, then feed cut out. But it was enough. But don't worry. Already news makers are saying it was a game, not real fight," said Ivan. "World thinks crazy mage stuff."

Pi put a hand to her mouth. "Bethany." While she was in the statue, she'd forgotten about what Alton had done to Bethany. "That son of a bitch," she muttered.

"What can you do for us?" asked Aurie.

His forehead hunched. "You have the six glass balls?"

"We do," said Pi, when her sister hesitated.

Aurie gave her a look, asking if they should trust him, but Pi didn't see how that knowledge would hurt them.

"Then I take you to the seventh," said Ivan

"You know where it is?" asked Pi.

He gave a secret smile, the kind that made Pi worry that they were dealing with a sociopath.

"I watch, listen. I hear about the other teams, they go to the Spire, they try to get into the final portal. It is easy to know where to go next," he said.

The location wasn't a surprise to Pi. She and Aurie had speculated that's where it was. The first clue even hinted at it, talking about the *thresholds*, plural.

"Can you get us there?" asked Pi.

He winked and headed towards the stairs, motioning for them to follow.

At the base of the stairs, two men lay dead. They'd been shot up pretty good. They were some of Bannon's mercenaries. While she didn't particularly like Ivan, having him on her side rather than the other way around was quite useful.

Rather than going back into the square through the entrance, Ivan led them to the back of the souvenir shop, where a hole had been blown through the wall. Two black SUVs with tinted windows waited outside.

The light outside was dim and hazy, with no sign of the sun. When Ivan saw their faces, he said, "Early morning."

They climbed inside the SUVs, and Pi let out a soft moan of enjoyment when she sunk into the plush leather seat. "I've changed my mind, I'm never getting out of this vehicle," she told her sister.

Ivan hopped into the driver's seat, put it into gear, and sped away. They passed IPC cruisers with their lights on, surrounding the statue. Cleanup crews were working on the aftermath of the battle. Windows in the surrounding office buildings had been blown out. Chunks of concrete had been ripped from the ground as if a giant had pulled them up. A streetlamp was encased in solid ice, and three firemen were reducing it with a fire hose.

"The streets are empty," said Pi, forehead resting against the window.

Ivan spoke over his shoulder. "Mayor declared emergency, no one allowed near city center."

"Then how are we driving around?"

"Diplomatic immunity," said Ivan, glancing at them through the rearview mirror. "I am important Russian. But enough about that. You both look terrible. Between seats is cooler. I have water, some food. Take. Eat. You need strength."

Pi and her sister descended upon the cooler like locusts. She didn't even remember the first bottle of water, and had to slow herself or it might come right back up. There were candy bars and chips, which Pi stuffed into her mouth by the handful. When they were finished, they sunk back into their seats.

"I really want a nap," said Pi, leaning back into her seat with her hand on her belly.

"Only a little bit longer, sis," said Aurie.

Rest would be good, but Pi feared it as well. When they had time to slow down, if they survived, she'd have to reckon with what happened to Bethany, what would happen to Sam, the fallout from the battle in the square. It was like watching floodwaters build up behind a dam, knowing that it was soon to give way.

Ivan took them the back way to the Spire. He drove them through the parking garages, badging them through a couple of gates with a wink.

Pi was too tired to question how he'd gotten those badges, knowing that the answer with men like him was always money and power, two things he had ample amounts of. She hadn't slept in two days, so wasting energy on questions she knew the answers to was not worth the effort.

Stuffed into an elevator with Ivan, his six gun-toting bodyguards, and her sister was the strangest way she'd ever entered the Spire. Ivan was his smug self, whistling softly while they waited for the *ding* and the door to open.

When they entered a large room with wide windows looking out into the city, Aurie said, "I've been here before."

Pi knew the reference, it was when her sister was training mendancy with Semyon.

A set of stairs in the back led to a waiting room. The area was large enough to seat thirty people comfortably on chairs and couches while they waited to meet Invictus. But now the TVs were blank, and there were no magazines on the tables. Pi imagined it was what a doctor's office looked like, though she had no memories of ever visiting one, despite knowing she must have when her parents were alive.

The portal on the far wall was familiar, though Pi had never seen it in person, only on videos about Invictus. The door was made of obsidian. Surrounding it were seven runes, three on each side, and one above the door. The runes were a language that no one had heard of, and Invictus had never given hints to their origin. Pi had a strong feeling the runes and the glass balls were related.

Ivan hopped onto a couch, placing his hands behind his head. "Now let us see magic happen."

Pi glanced at her sister. She was thinking it too.

"No. No way," said Aurie. "You can't be here."

"Of course I can. You are my investment."

"You'll interfere with our process," said Pi. "Think about it. We're solving puzzles set up by the greatest mind of magic. This is like playing basketball against Jordan while trying to paint a Michelangelo. We need to concentrate."

"We don't even know if this room is safe," added Aurie. "You wouldn't believe what we fought inside the statue. If something like that, a demon, or something worse, comes through here, we can't protect you."

Ivan scowled, but climbed to his feet, looking like a child who was told he wasn't getting dessert.

"Fine," he said. "I will take my men and go below, keep you safe from intrusion."

When Pi's stomach grumbled, she asked, "Could we get some pizza sent up? And more bottled water? I'm still hungry."

Ivan threw his hands over his head. "What am I, your waiter?"

"No," said Aurie, "you're our partner. You can't help us with the magic, but you can make sure we're in tip-top form."

"It is okay, I will send someone for food," he said in a languishing drawl before he disappeared down the stairs.

Pi checked to make sure he'd gone all the way down. She put an alarm on the fifth step that would let her know if anyone was trying to sneak up.

They stood shoulder to shoulder before the obsidian door to Invictus' realm, worn down, injured, magical abilities reduced exponentially from where they were only a few days before. But they'd made it to the final clue.

THIRTY SIX

Aurie stared the obsidian door while her sister paced around the room. The seven runes had marks and circles, but suggested nothing familiar to her.

"What if we can't get in?" asked Pi, hands clasped on top of her head.

"Can or will?" asked Aurie.

"Can," said Pi. "I don't know. My brain is fuzzy and fried. I feel like I'm thinking through a straw."

"I feel that too," said Aurie, hand on her chin. "It's like when you cram for finals so hard that you can't actually think during the test because you're too tired."

Her sister froze, snapping her head towards the corner of the room. "Did you hear that?"

Aurie listened. "Nothing. Occasionally I hear Ivan's men laughing, or distant car noises against the windows. What did you hear?"

"I'm probably going mad from a lack of sleep," said Pi, rubbing her eyes. "I swept the room for magic, but this whole place is glowing like the inside of a reactor."

"What do you think it is?"

Pi bit her lower lip. "Like we're being watched. I don't know. So close to the end, it's probably paranoia. And having to deal with Ivan. I don't trust him."

"Neither do I, but we know he's sketchy, so as long as we keep our guard up..."

Pi crouched on her heels. "I need someone to take my brain out, hose it down with a fire hose, and put it back in. Maybe then I could think again. I'm sick to death of puzzles and mysteries."

"You started this," said Aurie with a smirk.

Pi glanced wistfully out the window. "It was fun at the beginning. Exciting and dangerous, even. With Bethany dead, and who knows how many others hurt, the souls, I don't know, it takes a lot out of you."

"I get it, sis, but we've got to push on, we're almost to the end," said Aurie.

"What do we do now? I'm out of ideas."

Aurie rubbed the tattoos on her wrist. "Let's summon the glass balls. Maybe having them here will trigger something, or give us an idea."

Without really knowing how they knew to do so, they placed their wrists together, matching the tattoos with each other. Then they turned their arms ninety degrees, as if they were unlocking a door, and the six glass balls appeared on the beige carpet like colorful Easter eggs.

"Orange, yellow, green, blue, indigo, violet," said Pi.

"We just need red," said Aurie.

They took turns picking them up, rotating them in their hands, and setting them back down.

Aurie snapped her fingers.

"*When through the looking glass you see*

Backwards amid the Giants you'll be

To follow the rainbow and pay the fee

Two makes one and that is key.

Then four more and you'll see

Only through their unity."

As she said the last part, Pi's eyes widened. "I'd forgotten about that. It makes more sense after the statue. We got the four more, but what does the last part mean? Only through their unity?"

"Maybe it's like the key to get into the statue. We need the seventh to unlock the door," said Aurie.

"Yeah, we know that, but we *need* the seventh," said Pi emphatically.

"No," said Aurie. "Then four more and you'll see. Two plus the four is six. We have six. Somehow having six means we can see the seventh, or something like that. Riddles are so frustrating."

"They're frustrating because they're full of misdirections. Only through their unity. Is there another way to say that?" asked Pi.

"Unity. Unite. Together. Grouping," said Aurie, then continued to list off other synonyms. After a few minutes, she ran out of steam.

They were quietly introspective, until Pi stomped her foot and spun around.

"I swear I heard something," she said, marching to one side of the room. "I'm either going mad or something is in here."

"What did you hear?"

"Music," said Pi, staring at the area with a kid's table.

"Music," repeated Aurie. "Unity. Harmony!"

Pi spun around. "Merlin's tits, I'm dense. The glass balls. They each have a frequency signature." She ran over, dropping to her knees and casting a spell. Then she pulled out her cell phone, typed furiously into the browser. "Yes. Yes. That's it. They're a harmony, which tell us what the frequency of the seventh ball, the red one, is."

"Harmony," said Aurie, feeling a lightness in her chest, "that would make sense. It's the final lesson of the contest. We cannot progress without harmony."

Pi rearranged the six glass balls. They'd been in the order of their colors, but afterwards went blue, yellow, violet, orange, indigo, green.

Then her sister pulled a metal rod from her leather jacket and struck each glass ball in their new order, the resulting harmonies resonating through the room. The symbols around the doorway lit up as she hit the notes, climbing from left to right towards the final rune.

As the six notes hung in the air, Pi typed into her browser and held her phone up, and when she hit the button, a seventh note joined the others, rising until there was an almost unbearable vibration that shook the whole Spire.

A seventh ball, the red one, appeared next to the others. Pi reached out and struck it, and the final rune glowed. Within seconds the obsidian door went translucent.

A warmth, an overwhelming emotion of pride welled up. Aurie shared the biggest smile with her sister. They'd done it. They'd solved the final puzzle. The way to Invictus' realm was open.

A slow, sarcastic hand clap from the stairway startled them both. Alton in his blinding white suit had a gun placed against Mags' temple while Sunil stood next to them both. Any questions about how they'd gotten past Ivan were silenced by the fact that the Russian mobster was standing behind them with his arms crossed. His six bodyguards had spread out, making any attempts at magic foolish.

"Congrats-a'fucking-lations," said Alton, pressing the gun firmly against Mags' head, making her grimace. "You win the grand prize."

THIRTY SEVEN

"I thought we had a deal," said Pi.

Ivan stared back murderously. "We did, until better one came along. Of course, I suggested this better deal, because you disrespect me, but who will quibble this point."

She'd known not to trust an asshole like him, but hadn't thought it would come back to bite her so quickly, so she turned her ire to Alton.

"You know you're the herpes of mages, Alton—you keep coming back, and nobody wants you."

Alton pressed the gun harder against Mags' temple. "What passes as wit is going to get your friend killed."

"Go ahead and kill her, whoever she is," said Aurie flippantly.

The lie was skillfully delivered, so much that Pi almost believed it. But Alton was having none of it.

"You seem to forget that I spent a lot of time in Golden Willow. I got to know the other patients quite well, including a young patient with a hero crush on a certain mage of Arcanium. Once I had my memory back, it didn't take long to figure out that you'd worked in the children's ward. I always knew this knowledge would come in handy."

"What do you want?" Pi growled, hoping to preserve some semblance of their pride.

"For you to step out of the way, and let your betters take control of the Halls," said Alton. "If you're thinking about rushing through the portal, then know that your little friend here will die a very slow and painful death. And that it won't stop us anyway, because you showed us how to get through the portal."

This was a deathblow to her ego. She couldn't believe they were going to lose to this asshole and his sidekick, because as tough as she thought she was, she knew there was no way she'd let them kill the girl, even if it meant saving the Halls. It would have been better if they'd lost to the dragon, then she wouldn't have had to endure this moment.

She thought giving up was a foregone conclusion until she glanced at her sister. The tightness of her sister's lips, the way she had frozen, worried Pi. Saving the Halls was of the utmost importance, but would she sacrifice Mags to achieve that?

"Aurie?" asked Pi.

After a long pause, her sister spoke. "Mags...Emily, what do you want me to do?"

She didn't hesitate. "Let them kill me. Better than this creep taking control."

This brought a new level of tension to the room, as everyone expected them to bolt to the portal. The only problem was the mercenaries with guns. If they unloaded a full clip, Pi and her sister would never make it two steps.

"No," said Aurie suddenly, surprising Pi, who was frozen, watching her sister move towards the row of couches near the kids' area. "I can't let you sacrifice yourself like that. I saved you once, I won't watch you die now. We'll step out of the way. You win, Alton."

A dreadful cold filled Pi. She wanted to deny it, to fight. Faez rose in her, right there on the surface, until her skin tingled. Her hands turned to fists.

"Pi," said Aurie insistently. "Don't."

She shook her head, wrinkling her nose as if she were trying to impart information.

"That's right," said Sunil, "listen to your sister. She's not a dumb bitch like you are."

There was a time in her past that getting called a dumb bitch would have turned her into a rage-filled murder machine, but she saw the bait in his words and refused to take it.

"There's only one position at the top," said Pi as she joined her sister, "and you know it's not going to be filled with you."

"Tie those two up, and then let's finish the seventh clue, just in case the portal only works for them," said Alton. "Gag them, too. Their voices are just as dangerous."

The gags went in first, a couple of body-odor-smelling handkerchiefs from Ivan's pockets. Then he did the rope work, wrapping it around her wrists until her fingers were blue. When he was finished, Ivan took position behind them, hands on their shoulders, humming a tune.

Pi couldn't quite figure out what angle her sister was playing, or if there was an angle at all. The whole time, Aurie watched Alton, who still had the gun to Mags' head. Once, when Sunil asked him a question, he started to pull it away, which made Aurie tense up, but then he put it right back.

"You," he said to one of Ivan's men, "take her over there." He nodded to the windowed side of the room. "Keep your gun to her head. If she tries anything, or if these two do anything, kill her. Got it?"

When her sister's shoulders slumped with defeat, Pi knew that whatever she'd been planning had been foiled. Mags was on the far side of the room with a semiautomatic placed against the back of her head. There was no way anyone could reach the guard before she died.

Alton and Sunil summoned their six glass balls, then struck them in the correct order. To Pi's surprise, Alton sang out the final note, finishing the harmony to get the seventh ball. Then they struck it, lighting up the final rune on the portal.

While they were finishing the final clue, Aurie made subtle faces, arching her eyebrows towards the corner, where Pi had heard noises. She didn't understand what was going on until she saw a shimmer along the wall.

There was no time to figure out who or what it was, because Alton approached, cupped her chin, and stared her right in the eyes.

"When this is done, I'm going to finish what I was going to do so many years ago before your stupid sister interfered." He pulled his pistol out. "In fact, why wait. I'd hate for it to happen a second time."

Before he could place the gun against Aurie's head, he froze, gagged, and then his eyes widened until a blade came sliding out through his throat.

From behind her, Ivan said, "Nyet. Not possible."

Pi threw herself into Ivan, knocking him over before he could pull his gun.

Mags screamed, followed by the sounds of gunshots and windows breaking.

Ivan had fallen over a small table. With her hands behind her back, Pi kicked the gun out of his hand, following it up with a second kick to the side of his head. His eyes rolled back in his head.

A spray of gunfire went right over her head. The sharp smell of faez filled the room. Flame shadows bounced across the wall. Someone knocked her onto the couch as bullets ripped past.

She tried to knee her attacker in the crotch, barely missing the target as she realized it was Deshawn.

"What the hell?"

He tugged the gag from her mouth and cut the bonds from her wrists.

She looked up in time to see Bethany with a bloody blade in one hand and a whip of flame in the other, taking on the men with guns. Each time they fired, she jumped to a new spot, seeming to teleport out of the way. Pi didn't know how she was doing it so quickly until she noticed Yoko standing near the kid's table, weaving illusions into the room.

Aurie was wrestling with Sunil near the portal, trying to keep him from entering, but she had no magic, and he was enhanced by his. Pi was about to join her sister, when she saw Ivan grab Mags.

Before Pi could move one finger, make one gesture of spell casting, Mags grabbed Ivan back, and leapt through the open window, taking the Russian mobster with her. The move was so unexpected that he wasn't able to stop her. Pi thought the diminutive girl was dead too, until Mags floated back into the window moments later.

This freed Pi up to join her sister, but she hadn't even gone two steps before Sunil put a force bolt into her chest, pinwheeling her into the back of the nearest couch. He went through the portal before anyone could stop him.

THIRTY EIGHT

The force bolt to the ribs had felt like getting kicked by a mule. Aurie was sure something was broken, but she didn't have time to deal with it. Sunil had escaped into the portal.

Pi was second through the translucent door, which brought relief to Aurie that they would still be able to enter. Then Deshawn tried, but he was left with a bloody nose when he ran into the wall.

"Get Semyon here," she said to him as blood ran down his chin. "Hell, not just him, but all five of the original patrons."

"Are you serious?"

"Trust me and do it," she said as she headed towards the portal.

Traveling to Invictus' realm was instantaneous, and minus the vertigo that she normally experienced when using a portal. She stumbled to the other side, where the scent of faez was so strong it was like getting stabbed in the nose with an icicle. She hesitated, as the scene she beheld was both marvelous and strange. She had no idea which way the others had gone.

The room, larger than Grand Central Station, was a cross between a library and a laboratory. A ball of energy contained within a glass sphere floated near the ceiling, providing illumination and, Aurie guessed, power.

There was far too much to look at and not enough time to take it in. She needed to find Sunil and her sister, and eventually Invictus, if he were still truly alive as Sam had said.

To her left, past what looked like a stuffed alien bug, a book shelf shattered, throwing paper and wood chips into the air.

She heard her sister scream, "Sunil, don't!"

Aurie took off in the direction of the shout, grimacing from the grinding pain of her broken ribs.

When she caught up to her sister, she found a scene that left her cold with worry.

On the wall was a large portal, currently open, shimmering with a sea of golden faez. Dark shapes, highlighted by the glimmering, were moving against the light, clearly demonic, but unable to come through the portal.

Frozen in mid-stride outside of the portal were two figures: a strangely arched Invictus, looking like the figure they'd seen in the holovideo their second year, and a massive demon covered in a thousand blades. The bearded and lunging forward Invictus had a broken vial around his neck, which seemed to have triggered the stasis. His gray robes were stained with fresh blood.

Sunil stood by a pedestal that was covered with gears and knobs and had a giant lever next to it. A pulsing red light was counting upward at the base of the lever. The number on the screen indicated the time elapsed since the stasis had been enacted, an invitation to pull it, if she'd ever seen one. Aurie knew it was the fabled Helmsman of the Planes, because she'd read about it, not completely believing it was real. The stasis field was a fail-safe in case reentry went wrong.

Sunil's hand was resting on the lever. He looked back at them, uncertainty on his face.

"Don't," said Pi. "You'll kill us if you stop the stasis."

"I don't understand," he said, frowning. "I went through the portal first. I was the winner. I should be the head patron. I thought Invictus was dead?"

"He's not dead, but he will be if you stop the stasis. We can fix him, bring him back, but you can't hit the lever," said Aurie.

"But I won't win if he's still alive," said Sunil.

"Get that idea out of your head. This isn't a contest. If he dies, then the Halls are finished. There is no contest and there never was one," said Aurie. "What matters is us sticking together. There are bigger problems, as you can see. Invictus got hurt trying to prevent a demonic invasion, but it didn't work. The barriers in the city are going to fail soon. Look, I won't hold what happened outside against you if you back away from the lever. We'll even let you be the hero, the first one through the portal."

"You lie," he said, shaking as if he were having a minor seizure. "I know about your lying magic. You're trying to trick me. You Arcanium mages are always playing games with words, thinking you're better than the rest of us. I can't trust you. I won't trust you."

He looked ready to pull the lever. But he hadn't yet, giving Aurie hope.

"Sunil, look what you're about to do. You're about to end the stasis, and when you do, those demons, including that big one with the blades, are going to come through," she said.

"But I don't get to be head patron while he's still alive. Look at him, he's practically dead. There are blades sticking out of his back," he said.

Aurie shifted to the side, getting a glimpse of the long gray shafts sticking backwards like porcupine needles. The strange arching of his back became clear.

"Yeah, so? Are you going to kill the demon yourself?" asked Pi.

"I don't have to. I'll flick the lever long enough for him to die, then turn it right back on," said Sunil, sounding like he was convincing himself it was a completely rational course of action. "And then I'll be head patron."

The words, "You're a fucking idiot," never had the chance to leave her mouth, because he slammed the lever downward. The demon was free.

THIRTY NINE

The whole room shuddered as if great gears, long dormant, had shifted forward, starting the machine again.

The stasis ended, and Invictus hit the ground, a host of blades sticking from his back.

Sunil, still holding onto the lever, shouted at Invictus, "Hurry up and die!"

When the bladed demon whipped its head towards Sunil, he lost his nerve and tried to lift the lever into its previous position, but it wouldn't budge.

Sunil ran away, screaming, "But I won, I won," as the bladed demon chased him.

Pi ran over to the fallen Invictus, who was still alive, barely. He was groaning and kneading his hands against the stone dais near the portal, shuddering and coughing, bloody phlegm splattering on the ground.

Had the reopening occurred not long after the stasis had been activated, there might have been larger numbers of demons waiting to pour in, but after twenty years, only a pair of bored or curious demons, no larger than rhesus monkeys, came galloping into the room on all fours, screeching.

Pi turned them into char with a pair of firespears, and before more monkey demons could scurry through, she threw a force shield over the portal.

"That won't stop anything larger, but it'll do for now," said Pi.

"Give me the horn from the Crimson Skull," said Aurie, kneeling with her hand out. "He can close the portal when we heal him."

Pi pulled the chunk of bone from her leather jacket and started to hand it to her sister.

"Are you sure about this? We'll be killing Sam," she said.

Aurie's face was wracked with anguish. "Of course not. I don't want to kill him either, but it's the only way. Unless you think you can heal him."

"The aura healer soul is gone. I don't even think if I used the last soul I could fix him," she said, eyeing the long shafts of metal sticking out of his back.

Aurie shook her hand insistently. "Then hand me the horn. Let's finish this."

No matter how much she wanted to, Pi couldn't hand it over. Even though she didn't know Sam as well as Aurie did, he was their last link to their parents. He'd promised stories about them that they'd never get to hear.

"I have a stupid idea, sis. But I need that demon not to kill Sunil."

Aurie followed her train of thought right away. There was really only one way they could save Invictus without killing Sam Arlington, and that would involve Sunil.

She stood up. "I think I can manage that. It's going to hurt like hell, but if it works, it'll be worth it."

Before Pi could say anything else, Aurie went limping off in the direction of the demon. The vast room had given Sunil enough room to stay ahead of the creature, but he wouldn't be able to keep that up forever.

Aurie went to the head of the rows and cupped her hands over her mouth. "Sunil! This way!"

Pi kept an eye on Invictus, to make sure he was still alive. This wasn't going to work if he died. While she was waiting, she slipped on her faez-viewing goggles and carefully unhooked the thread of Sam's life force from the horn. As soon as she did, it snapped away from her, disappearing, like letting go of a taut rubber band. Whatever happened now, even if they died, Sam would live.

Sunil came stumbling back into the area, running right past Aurie, who steeled herself for the clash with the bladed demon.

Pi waved Sunil over to her around the time the demon roared into view, knocking over a tall bookshelf with a shoulder charge. Aurie shouted, "STOP!" and the demon froze into place. The reverberation of truth magic rang through the room. Then her sister collapsed to one knee, holding up two fingers to show that they only had a short window.

"What's that? What are we doing? You can save us, right?" Sunil asked.

"Only Invictus can save us now. We don't know how to close the portal." At that moment, what looked like a minor tribe of the demonic monkeys started banging on the force shield. Behind that, larger figures approached. "But if we heal him with this, then he can close it, and we'll be heroes."

"But I don't get to be head patron," he said, like a little kid who didn't get a second scoop of ice cream. A couple of the monkey-demons screeched, making him flinch.

"You get to be alive," she said, shoving the horn into his hands. "Press this against him, think about how much you want him to be healed, and fill it with your magic."

"Wha—why can't you do it?"

"I'm holding them back with my shield," said Pi. "I can't do both."

The bladed demon was starting to break free from Aurie's truth magic, and she didn't look capable of stopping it again. Sunil took one look at the bladed demon and nodded his head enthusiastically. Pi almost felt sorry for him as he pressed the horn from the Crimson Skull against the motionless body of Invictus. Almost. Before she could blink, Sunil collapsed, his upper body catapulting over the edge of the dais to crash face-first into the pedestal.

Her heart was in her throat as she waited for something to happen, but Invictus stayed motionless. Pools of blood had collected next to his torso. The blades remained in his back. He was as dead as he'd been ten seconds ago.

"Oh no," she said. "It didn't work. Maybe it was too much, or he died before Sunil used it."

Aurie came stumbling over, holding her side and looking like she'd had an all-night bender. Her worried gaze searched Invictus' body for signs of life.

"I don't think it worked. I might have screwed it up when I released Sam's life force," said Pi.

A host of screeching came from the portal. The demon monkeys had their hands around the edges of the force shield. The barrier was collapsing. Behind them, three more bladed demons approached.

If the demons took control of Invictus' realm, they could use the Helmsman of the Planes to travel to the Hundred Halls and destroy it for good, without even bothering with the wells and the barrier.

As the bladed demon climbed to its feet, Pi grabbed her sister's hand, readying herself for their final stand.

FORTY

Aurie squeezed her sister's hand and pulled her in close, cupping her arm against her own. The barrier behind them was cracking, the demons' wailing growing louder by the second, but she didn't want to turn and see the horde of them rushing in.

"Did you ever think it would end like this?" asked Pi.

"Murdered by demons in Invictus' realm? It wasn't even on the bingo card." She smiled at Pi. "But at least I get to die with you."

The big demon stumbled towards them, still reeling from the effects of her truth magic. She'd paid a heavy price for it; the back of her head felt like it'd been cracked open and stuck with needles.

When it was halfway across the room, they gave each other another hand squeeze.

"Dooset daram."

"Dooset daram," replied Aurie. "I'll see you on the other side."

She closed her eyes right as the demon rose up above them, blades swinging like a pendulum. The barrier shattered at that moment, releasing a bone-chilling chorus of howling.

"*Exarta adlium recendious*!"

Aurie cracked her eyes open just enough to see as hurricane winds ripped through the room. The books, papers, and broken shelves all rattled, but stayed in place, while the massive demon rolled towards the portal like a tumbleweed.

The whistling winds drowned out the screaming demon monkeys, who along with every other demon, were thrown out of the room. As the last demon passed through, Invictus, who was standing behind them, slammed his hand down on the Helmsman of the Planes, and the shimmering golden entrance to the demonic realm turned to stone.

They stood face-to-face with Invictus, the head patron. He was not as tall as she expected, but somehow larger than she'd ever thought. His eyes were clear and fresh, yet ancient. The touch of the Crimson Skull had rejuvenated him, as his wavy shoulder-length hair had been grayed, but now was a healthy dark color. Even his skin, which had been bleached white and burnt black in different locations, had regained its Mediterranean glow.

Invictus glowered at them, the threat of magic simmering beneath his skin like a volcano about to erupt. His gaze flickered briefly to the fallen body of Sunil, then back to them, tightening around the corners with the judgment of a god.

"Who the hell are you and why are you in my realm?"

The sharp rebuke made Aurie recoil in surprise. Pi recovered faster, taking a small step forward.

"We saved your life, you ungrateful bastard, and that includes solving your damn puzzles. Haven't you ever thought of leaving a key with someone?"

He toed the body of Sunil, distaste hovering on his lips.

"And what of this fool? What did he do?"

Though Aurie hated Sunil with the white-hot passion of a star, that Invictus could be so crude as to disrespect the dead when it'd been his life—albeit unknowingly tricked—that had been given to save his lit a fire in her. As anger flared, she knew it was not for Sunil that her anger had been awoken, but for Ernie, whose life he'd ruined when he'd put the wish spell inside of him.

Without considering the repercussions of her actions, Aurie slapped him across the cheek. The impact was thunderous.

"That was for Ernie," she said, taking her place with Pi before he mistook her intent. Her hands were shaking so hard that she put them behind her back. Pi was staring at her with wide oh-my-god-I-can't-believe-you-did-that eyes, but there was also a measure of pride.

Invictus, to her surprise, did not retaliate, and spent a quiet moment in introspection, as if he were remembering the things he'd done before he nearly got himself killed.

He gave them a long look, wrinkled lips pursed with thought the whole time.

When he spoke again, he was more subdued, his words chosen with care. "How did you get in here?"

It was Aurie's turn to be confused. "The game. The seven glass balls. We solved them. My sister was the one to figure it out, and then there was this big thing in the Halls about them. Sunil was from another team. How can you not know?"

"The Wizard's Rainbow," he said, laughing, his voice booming through the room. "It wasn't meant for this purpose, but I guess it did the trick."

"Wasn't meant for this?" asked Pi. "Then what was it meant for? That you're a twisted bastard?"

He straightened, seeming to grow a whole head taller, looked down upon them. "What they're for is none of your business. But don't worry, you will be rewarded for your efforts. I must speak to the others and find out why they've allowed this to happen."

"None of our business? We risked our lives to save you," said Aurie, heat rising to her face. "And the others? There are no others. Not even the patrons helped find you, they quibbled amongst themselves, fighting for control of the Halls."

Pi turned to Aurie, a spark of realization on her face. "He's talking about the Order of Merlin. That's who the *others* are."

He grew cross, his voice rising until he was almost shouting. "How do you know about this? Who told you?"

His dark eyes searched the room as if he expected to find the betrayer lurking amongst the shattered books.

Aurie was about to shout back, yell at him for being an ungrateful ass with the sense of a brick, but then she remembered that he'd been frozen in time for over seventeen years. When last he was alive, so was her mother, and the Halls were functioning. He'd been gone, and everything had fallen apart without him.

Pi looked ready to unleash a hailstorm of insults, so Aurie grabbed her arm and waved her off.

"Invictus, sir, Head Patron, I'm not sure how I'm supposed to address you." Aurie shook her head and started over. "It's 2021. Seventeen years since you were frozen in stasis. There's no one left in the Order of Merlin except Sam Arlington. We're Nahid and Kieran's kids. I'm Aurelia, and this is Pythia."

The moment she said there was no one left but Sam Arlington, his towering form deflated. Sadness rounded his eyes, muting his anger. He leaned against the pedestal as if it were the only thing holding him up. "Nahid's dead? And the others?"

"Everyone but Sam. And he tried to give his life for you to return," said Pi.

"Seventeen years," he said, his shoulders sagging with age. "My hubris has undone me." He paused, looking like a doddering old man for a few breaths before he collected himself, spearing them with his gaze. "I'm sorry about your mother, and your father. They were special people, and so it seems are you two. You really figured out the Wizard's Rainbow on your own?"

Aurie had so many questions waiting to get out, so she wasn't sure why she choose the one she asked. "Each ball was a test, a different skill set that you were looking for, wasn't it? Green for cleverness, yellow for wizarding talent, indigo for power, and so on."

He was amused by her question. "It was never meant to be played without understanding it, but yes, you've got the gist of it. It was a test."

"A test for what?" asked Aurie.

"The Order of Merlin," said Pi, even before Invictus could speak. He chuckled lightly.

"She's got it. The Order. I'd come to the realization that I had to find a new way to pick its members. If you know Sam, then you know that he can be a disappointment. Most of the others were as well, except for your mother. If I would have had two of her, then maybe things would have been different." His lips took on a wistful cast. "I remember you two. We met once, when you were toddlers. I'll admit you both rather annoyed me, not because you were children, but because you were taking Nahid away from me. Her time in the Order was stretched thin between her work with Kieran and her children."

"Another way?" asked Aurie. "You said the Wizard's Rainbow was another way to find members for the Order of Merlin. If not by skill, how did you pick our mother and Sam?"

Even before he said a word, the answer hit her like a gut punch. Pi got it too, as a soft, "Merlin's tits," exhaled from her lips. The thought of it made her dizzy, as if she'd taken too much oxygen and had to lie down.

"Yes, I think you're figuring it out. Which means you know that you're related to Sam Arlington, and that you're also related to..."

He let the empty space hang open for them both to say at the same time.

"You."

Invictus gave them a wink. "Yes. For a long time I filled the Order in the oldest way, nepotism. But the needs of the Hundred Halls, and the world for that matter, have outstripped the ability of my family to handle it. So it is with much amusement that I learn Nahid's daughters have earned their way into the Order while I was away."

Aurie and Pi shared a long look. She felt like a balloon about to float way.

Invictus strode between them, his torn robes hanging on his tall frame. "Enough about that for now. We can speak at length later. But I think, if you say that the Halls have been at each other's throats while I was away, then I must speak to the originals as soon as possible."

"One thing," said Pi, holding up a single finger. "When you were in stasis, did you dream or think or anything?"

"Is this important?"

She tugged on the hem of her leather jacket. "To me."

After a moment of thought he said, "I believe I did, though it's hazy now. But I recall visiting my old cottage, the one I had before the city took root." He arched a bushy black eyebrow at her wide-eyed reaction. "I assume that this will be a good story at a later date."

They stopped at the portal that led back into the Spire.

"What should we do about Sunil's body?" asked Aurie.

"I'll take care of it. We can give him a proper burial after the dust has settled."

They held hands and touched the portal.

FORTY ONE

Holding onto Aurie's hand as she went through the portal made landing on the other side more stable. She didn't even get her normal vertigo. Or maybe it was that Invictus' magic was better than that of the other portals she'd used.

Pi barely had time to let go of her sister's hand before she realized she was staring into the face of Bannon Creed, and he wasn't the only patron in the room. Priyanka Sai was sitting on a couch with her legs crossed, checking messages on her phone. Semyon Gray was speaking quietly with Deshawn, Yoko, Bethany, and Mags near the kid's table, while Celesse D'Agastine stared out the open window, still jagged with glass, at the city beyond. The only one missing was her former patron: Malden Anterist.

While she was prepared for a lot of possibilities in that moment—another battle, a coarse word, an argument—she wasn't ready for what Bannon Creed did: he started to kneel.

"Oh shit," said Aurie, under her breath, "he thinks..."

He'd barely half-genuflected when Invictus came through the portal and the room erupted in gasps.

Bannon quickly stood up straight, but he glowered at Pi as if it'd been her fault that he'd mistaken the situation.

She grabbed her sister's hand and quickly got out of the way. The original patrons drew towards him like misbehaving children reporting to their father for a session with the belt.

From behind them, Bethany whispered, "Is that really him?"

"But he's alive," said Mags.

"Clearly," said Deshawn. "Though it could be another one of Yoko's illusions. It's so good."

Yoko cupped her hand over her mouth, blushing.

Invictus gave them the side-eye, quieting the questions on their friends' lips.

"Where is the fifth?" asked Invictus, in his booming voice.

None of them would meet his gaze. Eventually, Celesse dared to glance up and said, "He's traveling, or he would have been here. We're sorry. We didn't know you were still alive. When the...we thought the worst."

"I thought I taught you better than this. Have we learned nothing over these long centuries?" He sighed, contempt displayed openly. "As for your missing member, I will deal with him alone. It is probably for the best this way. Come, now is no time for reticence, I'm back now. It seems I must reintroduce myself to the world, and you shall help."

He made his way towards the stairs before remembering that the students were still in the room.

"Go ahead, I must have a word."

The patrons did as instructed, heading down the stairs like school children headed to detention.

Invictus stopped before them. "I assume that all of you helped in this matter."

Deshawn croaked out, "Yes."

Invictus inclined his head. "For that, I thank you." He paused, staring at them, and when they didn't move he said, "And now I must speak to the Silverthorne sisters in private."

The others scurried down the stairs after the patrons, leaving Aurie and Pi alone with Invictus.

"The next few weeks and months, years probably, will be hectic. If I've truly been gone for seventeen years, I suspect my return will set the city on fire. I assume this will cause some burden on the two of you. Would you prefer your moment in the sun or would you like to quietly fade into the background until you are needed again?"

"Background," they said in unison.

His eyes glittered with mirth. "A wise assessment. But when the initial excitement is over, do you wish to continue what you started?"

"The Order?" asked Aurie.

"Yes, the Order."

"We would," said Pi, pride welling in her chest.

"Good," he said, putting a hand on her shoulder. "We're going to need the both of you. More than the both of you, really, but let's worry about that later. Do you have somewhere to lie low for the summer?"

"Sam's place," said Aurie, "once we get him from the Undercity. We sort of trapped him in a cave with a giant stone demon."

His bushy eyebrows wrinkled as he headed out of the room, and before he left, he added, "Very well. I will send for you when I'm ready. Again, thank you, not only for saving me, but for reminding me of what I hoped was possible with the Hundred Halls."

FORTY TWO

Freeport Games on a Friday night was its normal rowdy self. Though Aurie and Pi were hiding out in the back gaming room, they shared smiles at the chatter that permeated the other room.

The sisters had come in through the back door, and hid their faces to make their way to the room without being seen. The Internet had exploded with the return of Invictus, and as well with speculation on the battle at the statue. True to his word, Invictus had left their names out of it, though enough people knew about the Wizard's Rainbow that the truth was slowly permeating through the Hundred Halls.

They'd been surprised to find Hemistad behind the counter, looking his normal crotchety old man self. He gave them a nod when they went past, and continued ringing up the two adolescents buying packs of game cards, as if nothing had ever happened, though Aurie could see the scars on the walls and ceiling where the drywall had been patched after his battle with Pi.

A soft knock on the door announced the arrival of the Misfits: Sasha, Bethany, Yoko, and Nancy. The four of them looked fresh, wearing designer clothes that they hadn't been able to previously afford. When Nancy took out her ear buds, Aurie heard some K-pop before she switched it off. After a round of hugs, and laughter, they crowded around the table.

"I love your hair," said Sasha to Pi, who had shaved her whole head down to bristle.

Pi ran her hand along the top. "I'm still getting used to it."

"She's doing her best Tank Girl impression," said Aurie.

Bethany leaned her forearms on the table. A ripple of translucence traveled up her arm like a scan. "Why have you two been hiding out? I thought you'd want to take credit for saving Invictus. You'd be, like, the most famous people in the world."

Aurie shared a secret smile with her sister. They'd talked about it more than once since the initial meeting with Invictus, and neither of their opinions had changed. Between the trials in the statue and the battle inside his realm with Sunil and the demons, they both knew they needed time to recover. The fame wasn't worth the loss of their privacy.

"That's not us," said Aurie finally. "Plus, after those other students died in the battle outside the statue, it would make us feel like we were profiting from their deaths."

The only one they'd lost from Arcanium had been Isabella Gonzalez. Only, as if she hadn't been the whole world to her parents and her friends. It was hard to reconcile the idea that it could have been worse, that so many more could have died, except that the patrons who'd been there had actually done their best to stop the battle and protect the students. Most of the damage had been done by trigger-happy Alton Lockwood and scared mages flinging Five Elements in random directions. Isabella had died when a car had been thrown across the square and trapped her against a concrete barrier.

"I thought we'd lost you that day," said Pi.

Bethany smiled sheepishly, touching her shoulder. "The bullet went in here. He probably only missed because of Yoko's quick thinking. He shot the illusion and not me."

"Not good enough," said Yoko, fiercely determined. "If I'd been quicker, then maybe you don't get hit."

"It's okay," said Bethany, rubbing the edge of the table hard as if she were reliving the moment. "Those healers patched me up quick, and getting shot helps me not feel bad for putting a knife through Alton's neck. Sort of."

"He deserved it," said Sasha, putting her hand on Bethany's back. "For the curse, for shooting you. You should never feel bad about that. Never. Him, Sunil, that maniac Ivan. They got what they deserved."

"Speaking of Ivan," said Pi, who shifted from a slouched position to sitting up straight. "That's one of the reasons we wanted to talk. Do you think there's any chance of retribution from his men?"

"No," said Nancy. "After he died everyone grabbed what they could of value and took off. Some rivals took over his warehouses and operations, but for the most part, his little empire dissolved without him to run it. I guess his men weren't as loyal as he thought."

"What about you?" asked Aurie.

"I'm good. I was only on loan to Ivan," she said, glancing to the other Misfits.

Aurie was going to ask who their patrons were when she realized by their secret glances that the four of them were pledged to the same one, not that their newfound wealth wasn't a clue. It also seemed unlikely they would tell her, since she was, after all, part of the establishment that made non-Hall patronage illegal, especially if she started working for Invictus directly. Better that she not know.

But there were topics safer to discuss. "Do you think you'll be around the city for the foreseeable future?"

Sasha spoke for them. "As far as we know. Why? Something in mind?

I figured you two would want a break for a while before getting involved with anything new."

"I'd like to sleep for a few weeks on a beach somewhere with a good book," said Aurie. "But no, we're not getting into anything right away. Graduating was enough, especially after having to do makeup work with Professor Chopra. But you know, considering, I figure things will eventually get interesting again, and it's always good to have friends to count on."

"We'd still be in the undercity eating ramen and stealing fruit from the fungifolk if it weren't for you two. And now that we've proven our worth to our patron, our luck is starting to change," said Sasha, smoothing her silky pearl blouse.

The other three Misfits chuckled at Sasha as if she'd made a joke.

When it came time to leave, everyone hugged and promised to stay in touch, a promise Aurie knew would be tested in their lives after the Halls.

FORTY THREE

The main room in the Glass Cabaret was crowded with people, which was confusing to Pi until she remembered how busy the city had gotten with Invictus' return. The Glitterdome was sold out with major acts booked for the next year and even the hotels in nearby Philadelphia were overflowing. She elbowed her way through the men in suits and the women in designer dresses drinking martinis and fine wines, to find a spot at the edge of the bar as she waited for Radoslav to notice she was there.

Nellie was working the customers, sliding between the rows of expensive liquor bottles and the bar, serving drinks with quiet efficiency, while Radoslav was quietly talking with a hefty gentleman in a duster with a scarred face who was holding onto a claw-ended staff.

The place smelled different with so many people. Normally, there was a faint scent of smoke, pleasant like incense, but now it smelled like freshly purchased clothes right off the rack, like hope.

Pi got Nellie's attention. The bartender wrinkled her nose and after sighing quietly, came over to Pi's spot along the bar. Nellie gave Pi's new hairstyle a raised eyebrow, but made no mention of it.

"He's busy," said Nellie as she straightened glasses and wiped the counter.

"I have eyes," said Pi, and recognizing her tone, softened. "Thank you for the help before, with the number. You saved a friend."

Nellie didn't seem to know what to do with the gratitude. She looked down the bar as if she hoped a customer would need a drink.

"Not like I had a choice," said Nellie.

"Well, either way, thank you," said Pi.

The pained look in Nellie's gaze told Pi that she had acknowledged it, and before she could move away, Pi asked, "Could I get a whiskey? Now that I'm twenty-one I wanted to have one for real."

Nellie's mouth opened. "Wait? You're not even twenty-one? He put *you* in charge?"

She left Pi's end of the bar without getting her the drink, which for a strange reason, made Pi feel better. Everything that had happened in the last year had been crazy-making, the fate of the Hundred Halls resting on solving Invictus' puzzles. It was nice to get back to normal, even if normal meant Nellie was mad at her.

When Radoslav finally made it to her end of the bar, she was surprised how subdued his aura was. Normally, she had to focus or the desire to obey his every command overwhelmed her.

"If I didn't know any better, I would say you seem content," said Pi.

The corner of his lips twitched, once, his version of a smile. "Things are...less unsure."

"Does this have to—"

Halfway through her sentence, his gaze, which had been directed at the bar, came up hard, and in that moment, she had no doubt that the normal Radoslav was still there because she nearly went running from the bar.

"Okay, okay. Point taken. I'm just glad, you know, that you're doing better."

"I like your new hairstyle," he said, a rare compliment that seemed almost out of character coming from him.

"It's my version of a disguise," she said.

Quiet rose up between them. Radoslav stayed perfectly still, watching her with interest. After a time he asked, "Did you need something?"

"Me? Nothing," said Pi. "I was stopping in. Seeing if you had a job that you needed me to do. I'm still in your debt after all. What do I have? Two more years, or something?"

"Your debts with me are cleared," he said.

"What? I don't understand."

A confusing cocktail of emotions coursed through her. Relief should have been what she was feeling, but instead she was filled with shock and disbelief.

The corners of Radoslav's eyes wrinkled uncharacteristically. "I thought this would have pleased you."

"I mean, getting out of debt always feels good," she said as a hollowness pervaded her. "I guess I didn't expect it. Thank you."

The last part came out as a question. To her surprise, he reached across the bar and placed his hand over hers. There was a tiny shock. His hand was cold. At first she thought it was a romantic gesture, but his face said otherwise.

"There would have been complications going forward, considering the changes to the city," he said.

It didn't take a sleuth to figure out he was talking about Invictus.

"I see," said Pi, bewildered. "Well, I guess I should get going. You... have a busy place now."

He removed his hand and she was struck with a sense of loss. Before she left he bowed his head, and though he spoke no words, she sensed this was a thank you from the deepest part of his soul.

As she turned to go, he said, "Pythia."

"Yeah?"

"Please come back and see us sometime. There will always be a spot at the bar for you."

She nodded and marched out.

After the doors closed, and the tinkling notes of jazz and the chattering of so many people was muted, she wasn't sure if she wanted to cry or laugh.

"Miss Pythia," said Dagon the bouncer, as he was checking someone's ID at the velvet rope. "Are you okay?"

"Of course," she said, mustering a smile for him. "I'll see you around."

As she strode down the sidewalk, past the tourists with their wide-eyed stares as they took in the city of sorcery, she felt this strange uncoiling in her chest. It wasn't until she was about five blocks away that she realized what it was. No longer a member of Coterie, or Arcanium, she would never have a real graduation. In his own way, Radoslav had provided that for her.

Instead of summoning a taxi, or heading to the subway lines, Pi kept walking, experiencing the city as if she were seeing it for the first time, not as a student filled with worries about classes and professors and passing grueling magical tests, but as a woman with infinite possibilities before her.

FORTY FOUR

The flame danced on Aurie's palm, the trickle of faez required making her grimace as if she had a full-body hangover. She shifted, making the paper beneath her crinkle noisily.

Dr. Fairlight shifted the penlight from Aurie's left eye to her right. Aurie tried to stay still, but the light was almost as bad as using faez.

"You can stop now," said Dr. Fairlight.

Aurie's insides felt like a bound spring. She let the flame drop. "So what's the prognosis?"

"Your eyes are dilating naturally and your aura has recovered," said Dr. Fairlight. "How is your sense of smell?"

A tentative sniff proved that the smell of Dr. Fairlight's light perfume was outdone by the sterileness of the hospital. "Mostly normal."

Dr. Fairlight nodded knowingly, and Aurie's mind whirled into gear trying to interpret the motion as either good or bad news.

"By all indications, you should be able to use magic without pain within a few weeks, two months at the longest," said Dr. Fairlight.

"No long-term effects?" asked Aurie.

The hesitation from Dr. Fairlight put a stab of worry in Aurie's gut.

"No, I don't think so. These kinds of things are usually temporary, and I see no sign that your condition should be any different," said Dr. Fairlight, patting her leg.

The release of tension in Aurie's shoulders made her lean back and sigh. "Thank you, Dr. Fairlight."

The woman smiled. "I didn't do anything. It's your body doing its thing."

"Either way, it's a relief to know," said Aurie.

"I really would love to stay and chat, but I'm already behind on my rounds. You should stop by sometime when things aren't so busy," said Dr. Fairlight as she grabbed her clipboard and left.

Aurie was collecting her things when Pi came in with a strange look on her face. The reason for her expression was made clear when Invictus came in behind her and closed the door. She almost didn't recognize him because he'd trimmed his beard and was wearing a tailored suit. He had a fancy wooden cane that he clearly didn't need. Except for the long hair, he looked like a businessman on his way to a meeting.

"I was in the area when I saw your sister," he said. "I was meaning to visit with the both of you, and this will do."

"Is something wrong?" Aurie blurted out.

The wrinkles around his mouth softened. "Not at this moment. But as you know, there is a problem we cannot avoid beneath our feet."

He was referring to the weakening of the barrier between their world and the demonic one. She nodded but said nothing.

"How is your condition?" he asked.

"Getting better. I should be back to normal in a few months."

"Good," he said. "Once the affairs of the city are in order, there is much to do."

"We're ready to get started whenever you need us," said Aurie, and Pi nodded.

"There is time enough later. Enjoy your summer, you deserve it. I didn't come here to put you to work, I came because there is something I need you to do, well, to get someone else to do," he said.

He straightened his neck as if the suit was uncomfortable. Aurie didn't know how to interpret it.

When she didn't answer right away, he cleared his throat.

"Oh yeah," she said. "Of course. What do

"Ernie," said Invictus. "He needs a home. I cannot, should not, be the one to provide that for him. Sam would be a better guardian than I was. Am."

"Who is he to you? How did the most famous mage in the world come to have a child living with him?" asked Aurie.

"Come now," he said, "that should be obvious."

"He's your son!" said Pi.

"No," he said, "but we are related. Much as I am to you."

"And we are to Sam, which means Ernie's our cousin," said Aurie.

"What happened to his parents?" asked Pi.

He looked them each in the eye. When he looked at Aurie, she felt the weight of his experience, like a mountain range from up close.

"The world is a dangerous place," he said.

"Is this what you do? Collect people, family, or whomever you can, and use them until they're dead or a husk of themselves?" asked Aurie.

"I do. I will," he said firmly, accepting her challenge and throwing it back. "If you choose to work for me, I will stretch you to your limits and beyond, possibly breaking you. I did it to Ernie, a young boy, so don't think I won't do it to you."

She locked gazes with him, and though it was like staring off the edge of a cliff, she didn't look away.

"That still doesn't make you any less of an asshole," she said.

He gripped the end of his cane so tightly, she thought either his neck muscles would explode, or the cane would break. Then he broke into laughter, a melodious sound that made her join in.

"Nahid's daughters," he said, chuckling. "I may regret inviting you into the Order."

"You can count on that," said Pi, smirking.

"But can I count on you to talk to Sam about Ernie?" he asked.

"Of course," she said.

"Good," he replied, tapping his cane on the floor. "Then I must depart. There is still so much to do."

Before he could turn to the door, Pi reached out and tugged on his sleeve. "Before you go. I have one question."

"Quickly."

"The wizards from the contest. Merlin. Circe. Baba Yaga. Aristotle. And so on. Are we related to them too?" asked Pi.

The flicker of surprise was unmistakable, even as he tried to hide it.

"How did—never mind. But yes, these are wizards that I, and you as well, share some lineage with," he said, studying Pi as if she were an alien creature.

She tried to follow up with a second question, but he said, "Good day," and swept out of the door, leaving them alone.

Pi had her arms wrapped around her chest as if she were hugging herself, not out of sadness, as she had a contented smile on her face.

"You okay over there?" asked Aurie.

"A month ago, it was just you and me," said Pi. "Now we've got Sam and Ernie, and however crotchety he is, Invictus too. We have a family again."

A warmth of understanding passed over Aurie. Family. She'd come to the Hundred Halls to learn magic, but really, it'd been to find a new family, something she had in spades now, with Arcanium, her other friends, and now actual blood relations.

"This makes me miss Mom and Dad even more," said Aurie, her heart swelling up with emotion.

Pi had a big grin on her face. She sniffed and wiped a tear from the corner of her eyes. "They would be damn proud of us."

"I'm damn proud of us, and I'm proud of you too," said Aurie. "If you'd asked me where we'd be at the end of our five years, I would have never guessed that we'd have won the Second Year Contest, or solved the Wizard's Rainbow and rescued Invictus. None of those things were on my radar in any way. But the one thing I would have been absolutely sure of was that you and I would be together."

"I love you, Aurie. You're the best sister a girl could have," said Pi.

"I love you too. You're the second best sister a girl could have."

Pi pulled away, laughing. "Hey! Why am I second best?"

"You said I was the best, and there can only be one at the top," said Aurie, smirking.

Pi wrinkled her nose in faux indignation. "Which makes me wonder. Had Invictus not been alive, the position of head patron would have been up for grabs. Which one of us should have taken it?"

Aurie grabbed her sister's hand and dragged her towards the door. "Thankfully, that's a question that never needs to be answered, since he is alive."

"Good point," said Pi as they walked out of the room.

"Anyway, we both know I would have been the one to take it."

Pi punched her in the arm, knuckles first.

"Worth it," said Aurie as she squeezed her sister to her side, rubbed the stubble on her head, and kissed her temple.

FORTY FIVE

The mansions in the neighborhood were so opulent that Mags expected a black SUV to pull beside her to whisk her away, but the follow-me sprite bobbed through the air down the manicured sidewalk, a sign she was in the right place. She was checking her jeans and her long-sleeve Garbage Kings T-shirt which hid her runic tattoos, deciding if she had enough time to hurry home and change into something more formal, when a voice startled her.

"Mags!"

Deshawn came running up and draped an arm over her shoulders, making her blush.

"Hey," she said, clearing her throat and trying again when it came out froggy. "Hey, I mean."

He removed his arm from her shoulders and slipped into stride with her. "Ever been in this part of the city?"

"No," she said quietly.

She almost added that her parents were wealthy, but not this kind of wealthy, but didn't want him to think she was bragging.

When they reached the iron wrought gate, Mags paused and turned to Deshawn.

"Did I really get invited to their graduation party?" she asked. "I'm just a first year."

"Relax," he said. "You're a part of this. I mean, you did drop that gangster guy out the window, which might be the craziest thing I've ever seen, and from what I hear, you know them from way back, before the Halls. Plus, you're Arcanium. Let's get inside, I can't wait to see this crazy house. I heard it has a floating pool in back."

Despite Deshawn's assurances, Mags felt like an imposter as she rang the doorbell. She was thankful for Deshawn coming along when he did, because she would have run off otherwise.

A tall girl with rainbow hair opened the door, and as soon as she saw them, she did a little twirl on her block skates. The move drew attention to the shockingly pink dress she somehow managed to pull off.

"Deshawn!" she said, hugging him.

"Hey Hannah."

Hannah faced Mags next, rocking back and forth on her skates. "You must be the famous Mags. Jumping out that window was insane."

Warmth spread across Mags' face. It didn't feel insane at the time, just a desperate attempt at self-preservation.

"Uhm, thanks," said Mags, looking at her sneakers.

Hannah handed them each a copper ball with lines on it, suggesting that it could expand into something different.

"Party gifts," said Hannah, leading her deeper into the mansion while Deshawn wandered the spiral staircase. Mags had a hard time paying attention as they were passing swords and other artifacts displayed beneath glass cases, but this didn't seem to bother Hannah, who spoke at Mach one.

"They only last a week and then they start falling apart, but they're fun while they last. I'm working on a newer version with upgraded enchantments. The problem is the gears aren't ratioed correctly, but I don't have enough room in the elbow joints to use the proper size, but I found a company that can print the size gears that I—by the way, I'm a tinkerer, if you couldn't tell."

Mags held the copper ball on her flat palm. "What is this?"

Hannah lit up like a parade. "Oh, I forgot to explain. Put it up to your mouth, breathe on it, and wait for it to transform."

The sounds of the party grew louder as they reached a huge room with vaulted ceilings. There were twenty or so students from Arcanium, nearly all of them soon-to-be fifth years and graduates. A couple of the professors were in attendance. Professor Mali was holding court with the graduates, telling them tales about her time in Arcanium. Tiny golden sprites were flitting around the room, or sitting on shoulders. Mags checked the copper ball in her fist, making sure it hadn't transformed yet.

There were others she recognized, like the girls from the Spire, the ones she'd overheard being called the Misfits. She had no idea how they fit into things, but Aurie and Pi seem to trust them completely, so Mags found herself thinking of them like another Hall.

Some she didn't recognize, like a chunky guy in a multi-hued blue shirt wearing a boyish expression who was talking with Sam Arlington and the shockingly short-haired Pi in the secondary kitchen. A family of rat-people were chatting with Aurie near a table of drinks. They looked like they felt out of place, glancing around the room, expecting a predator at any moment. She was surprised to see them in such a fancy place, as she knew their communities usually stayed in the Undercity.

A touch on her shoulder and the smell of lavender got her to turn around, coming face-to-face with an elegant blonde-haired woman in an auburn business suit. The woman held out her hand, which Mags reluctantly shook.

"I'm Violet Cardwell, and you must be Emily, or Mags, I mean. I was looking forward to meeting you," said Violet.

"You were?"

"Yes," said Violet. "I wanted to apologize for my behavior many years ago. Though you probably didn't know about it, I was the reason Aurie got kicked out of Golden Willow. She tackled me when I nearly walked by your room with perfume on."

Mags had never heard this story. "I...I didn't know that."

Violet sighed heavily and rolled her eyes, clearly at herself. "We were both much different people back then. Well, I was anyway."

"Everything turned out alright, didn't it?" asked Mags.

A cloud passed across Violet's eyes, something painful, but it disappeared quickly. These fifth years had led complicated lives during their time in the Hundred Halls. Mags wondered if she'd feel the same way in four more years.

"I have to get back to work, the board never ceases to be a pain in my ass, but I wanted to meet you before I left," said Violet. "If you ever need anything, please contact me. You can get my info from Aurie or Pi."

Stunned by the offer, Mags forgot to say goodbye as Violet walked down the hallway, her heels clicking against the hardwood floor.

Mags lost herself staring at an ancient Roman shield on the wall until she heard her name. Aurie gave her a hug almost as soon as she turned around.

"Congratulations on your graduation," said Mags.

"Thanks," said Aurie, wearing a familiar smile on her lips, the same one she used to get when they'd sit on her hospital bed and talk about the latest anime or what she was going to do when she got into the Halls. It had always felt like a gateway to Mags, like her illness didn't exist and she was heading places, even though she knew deep down she wouldn't survive.

A little starstruck and giddy, Mags blurted out, "I owe you my life."

Aurie responded without missing a beat. "And I owe you as well, for dropping Ivan out the window."

Mags blushed. Everyone kept congratulating her about it, and though she'd do it again in a heartbeat to save her own skin, she had nightmares about the guy's sweaty palms grasping at her she spun away from him.

Mags fumbled for an item in her pocket, and Aurie held out her hands. "I said no gifts."

It was Aurie's turn to blush when Mags produced the painted figurine.

"Back when I was in that hospital, when I had no hope of survival, you gave me hope, gave me a reason to live, and then you made it happen, when *you know*, the thing. You told me the day that you gave me this that I would become a Wind dancer, and from anyone else that would have been one of those things people say to sick kids, but you meant it. You really cared. And when things got tough, even after I was healed, with all the tattoos and the struggles, I always reminded myself that I was a Wind dancer, and that being one was hard, and dangerous, and that I was going to be the best Wind dancer ever, to make you proud."

She was going to say more, but Aurie looked like she was holding back tears. Aurie enveloped her in the warmest, best hug ever, and Mags didn't even say anything when she squeezed so hard it hurt.

Eyes full of emotion, Aurie held Mags by the shoulders and said, "I'm glad you're here."

Their little reunion was broken up by a demand for cake from the other fifth years. Everyone crowded into the secondary kitchen, and Sam made a toast to the graduates, and though he didn't single out Aurie and Pi, Mags could tell he was talking about them.

When it was finished, the cake—made into the shape of Arcanium—was cut and handed out. Mags got the conical top of the Tower of Letters with a crystalline sugary tentacle of the Watcher.

The party spilled out into the other rooms and the backyard, and feeling out of place, Mags went up to the second level and stuck her feet through the iron balcony. While she was sitting there, rolling the copper sprite ball around in her hands, she caught a glimpse of Aurie and Pi. They had their arms linked, laughing and talking quietly. There was something about the way they communicated, the easy bumps of the shoulder at a knowing word, the glints in the eyes, that made Mags...not jealous, exactly. She admired the bond between the two sisters. She imagined it'd served them well in their five years at the Hundred Halls.

After a while the sisters left, leaving Mags to quietly enjoy the sounds of the party rising up between her swinging feet. She was content on her perch. That she'd been invited at all was enough for her.

When she remembered the copper ball in her hands, she lifted it to her mouth and breathed warm air across it. The ball stirred across her palm, jumping and shivering like a chick in an egg. The lines cracked open, and a coppery sprite appeared, uncurling and stretching. When at last it was fully extended, a good three inches tall, it faced Mags, gave her a deep and flourishing—if a little halting—bow, and spoke in a tinny voice:

"Welcome to the Hundred Halls."

§ § §

Hundred Halls Background Information

A Short History of the Hundred Halls

The magical university that eventually became known as the Hundred Halls started off as a small school called Invictus School of Magic in 1836. The building was an old tavern and inn called the Brownwater, named after the town it was located. Invictus purchased it because the property was attached to a large parcel of land where they could safely practice sorcery without exciting the local populous. As well, the inn had rooms for the first cadre of students, and a place they could all eat together and develop comradery.

In an interview given in the early 1980s, Invictus recounted those early years of the school. He'd recruited students from all over the country, promising them a chance to develop their powers without the threat of madness which plagued early practitioners. Even so, of the fifteen students only nine remained after the first year. Invictus has said little about the loss of his student body, insinuating they left for other professions, but rumors persisted that those students perished due to magical accidents or taking their own lives due to the faez madness they'd already developed before they'd arrived at the school. At this time, Invictus accepted all ages of students and the patron system hadn't been perfected. These early failures are said to be the reason that the cut off age for the Hundred Halls remains at twenty years old.

The town of Brownwater, which existed on the northwestern side of Pennsylvania, became a hot bed of rumors and claims of witchcraft. But Invictus had cultivated the local politicians, either through gifts of sorcery, or outright bribery, keeping the threats coming from outside the boundaries of Brownwater. During the years 1840 to 1858, there were three recorded major attacks on the school. The first claimed the life of Robert Madison when he was caught riding his horse in the countryside, charming birds to land on his hand. A musket shot took him in the head when the ambush surprised him. Four more students perished in the first attack, but all the men that invaded the school were never seen again. Requests to return their bodies were denied by Headmaster Invictus. By the time the second and third attacks occurred, the school had established safety procedures and no more lives of the students were lost. The same cannot be said of the attackers.

When the Civil War broke out in 1861, there were requests from both sides to join the fight. At first, Invictus resisted the requests, not wanting to spotlight the fledgling school and get noticed by the greater powers of the country, but his hand was forced as the war's toll created a rift in the student body which had come from all over the nation. A group of Southern students, led by Conroy Rutherford, left the school and joined the Confederacy. Invictus kicked them out of the school, then allowed those that wished to join the fight on the Union side to leave without concern for their position within the academy. Notable of this time was Evelyn Grace, a blue-eyed beauty that single handedly turned the Battle of Hoke's Run by defeating Conroy Rutherford in a duel of sorcery before routing the southern troops.

By the time the war was over, the Invictus School of Magic had few students and its reputation either tarnished or venerated based on which side it was being viewed from. During the year of 1866, little happened at the Brownwater Inn, and the students that stayed were said to have rarely seen Invictus.

On October 22nd, 1867, the charter for a new school called the Hundred Halls, which incorporated the new and improved Patron structure, was signed. The original signers included Invictus, Semyon Gray, Bannon Creed, Celesse D'Agastine, Priyanka Sai, and Malden Anterist. The history of some of these mages can be traced through the history of the country, while others arrived in the New World seemingly out of the blue. The first five Halls of the original charter were Arcanium, Protectors, Alchemists, Assassins, and Coterie of Mages.

With Invictus removed from direct interaction with the students, the new academy flourished. The Head Patron was able to focus on recruiting new students and growing the school, while the new Patrons taught their specific specialties. Additionally, double Patron system seemed to reduce the problems with faez madness that had plagued the early years.

The first Hall to open after the original charter was the Holistic Institute, also known as Aura Healers, in 1875, followed by the Royal Society of Illustrious Artificers in 1891. Three other Halls started in the years before the turn of the century—Tenebris Hall, The Equus Society, and The Gunpowder Club—but disappeared before the first world war. This became a common occurrence during the century and three-quarters existence of the university, either because of the changing needs of society, the death of the patron, or other Halls incorporating their teachings and making them obsolete.

The two world wars brought the existence of magic into focus for the entire world. Invictus threw the weight of the school behind the Allies, which helped tipped the final result to victory. While the Central Powers, and then Axis, both had mages in their regiments, they were prone to faez madness and there were numerous examples of destructive sorceries impacting their own troops unexpectedly.

It was the success of magic in the World Wars that led to the passing of laws that codified the Hundred Halls supremacy and forbid the opening of rival schools in other parts of the world. To facilitate these laws, Invictus promised to open up the school to the entire world and the American government, keen to keep the school on their territory, agreed. This paved the way for the Sorcerous Education Act of 1951 which allowed the school to make major land grabs in the region north of Philadelphia and west of New York, creating the structure that would become the city of Invictus.

In the years after the second World War, the Hundred Halls flourished. Before then, there'd only been about thirty different halls at the university, but they swelled to a number over eighty (no one knows for sure). Researchers have suggested that the number has been oscillating between sixty and seventy-five since, though others have argued that the true number is north of a hundred because Invictus does not publish the list of Halls and some form without ever taking a student. These "Ghost Halls" are sometimes created by ambitious mages that wish to use the association with the school for research, or other purposes.

Wards in the City of Sorcery

First – The ward is considered to be the financial home of sorcery related businesses worldwide and many of the wealthiest mages live in its boundaries.

The Order of Honorable Alchemists [Hall] – This school is the premiere place in the world to learn the arts of alchemy. Celesse D'Agastine, its patron, uses it as a place to recruit its future products.

Second – Known as the other entertainment capital of the world, this ward receives the majority of tourists.

The Academy of the Subtle Arts [Hall] – No one knows exactly where the hall is located, but in official literature of the school, its home is noted as the second.

Glitterdome – A massive stadium dedicated to music, big events, and the occasional sporting match.

Ashnod's Theater – The premiere theater for students of the Dramatics Hall.

Herald of the Halls – The newspaper wholly devoted to reporting on the Hundred Halls, the city of Invictus, and related subjects.

Third – Adjacent to the second, this ward receives its fair share of visitors intent on leaving the city of sorcery with a bit of magic to make their personal lives a little bit better—or more interesting.

Protectors [Hall] – A functional looking building where mages are taught to become future law enforcement members, or the military. The most advanced members have often been recruited to other realms as mercenaries.

Left Tower Books – A mainstay of the literary circuit. Authors of books about magic must always make a stop at this wonderful depository of literature.

<u>Fourth</u> – This ward has no singular identity but given its location in the inner ring of the city, it has similar functions to the first three wards.

Coterie of Mages [Hall] – Along with the Statue of Invictus, the Spire, and the Stone Flower of Stone Singers, the Obelisk is one of the most recognizable architectural wonders of the city. A towering structure of pure obsidian, the school provides its home to the most elite of mages.

Statue of Invictus – An enormous statue of the founder of the city. It was gifted by an unknown benefactor. Invictus is said to hate the replication.

City Library – The massive library is a place of scholarship for mundane and sorcerous topics.

<u>Fifth</u> – Many businesses make their home on the eastern half of the

ward while the western section that borders the thirteenth is mostly residential.

Arcanium [Hall] – The academy focused on the study of truth and knowledge, this medieval castle supposedly contains more books than all the libraries and bookstores of the city combined.

Acoustic Architectural Institute of Design [Hall] – Commonly known as Stone Singers, the giant stone flower that makes up the building opens and closes daily with the shining of the sun.

Sixth – Has the highest concentration of banks in the city, but also maintains a large residential area.

Holistic Institute [Hall] – This school contains a teaching hospital that is frequently used by the poor and non-humans of the city.

Museum of Magical Artifacts – A world famous museum dedicated to the display of historically significant artifacts.

Seventh – A mix of residential, restaurants, and bars make this a great place for the recently graduated to enjoy their time.

Canal District – A series of canals, modeled after Venice, snake through this area filled with restaurants and bars.

Eighth – A mix of residential and businesses.

Society for the Understanding of Animals [Hall] – This hall has the largest campus in the city and is tightly interwoven with the zoo, which it helps maintain.

Oestomancium [Hall] – Known as the Weird Circus to most, this halls dedication to exploring the possibilities of transhumanity makes it unique at the school. Their yearly Carnival held each Halloween is a delight and horror to those that attend.

Invictus Menagerie and Cryptozoo – The second largest cryptozoo in the country holds a wide variety of supernatural creatures, but unlike the larger zoo in Portland, this one specializes in the less dangerous kinds.

<u>Ninth</u> – A mix of residential and businesses.

Freeport Games – A quaint gaming shop that has existed in the city since the 1970s.

<u>Tenth</u> – A mix of residential and businesses.

Metallum Nocturne [Hall] – Steam and the stench of burning metal rises frequently from this hall as they are the arcane metallurgists of the wizard world.

Wizard's Wax Museum – A wax museum dedicated to showcasing the history of wizards and mages. True historians find this place rather sketchy on details.

Eleventh – A mostly residential area that has seen better days.

Enochian District – One of the earliest settlements of the city, this district has been forgotten in recent times. It's one of the few places that non-humans dare to live in the light.

Twelfth – This area has the few industries left in the city, though most have left due to the laws passed restricting their operation. Tends towards cracked concrete and rusted out buildings.

Thirteenth – This ward has been partially reclaimed by nature. Few visit this part of the city, despite its border with the prosperous fifth.

The Spire – The tallest building and/or structure in the world. Serves as the administrative home of the Hundred Halls. The top section is the home of Invictus. The enormous tower serves many functions including the Merlin Trials, and the Second Year Games.

Undercity – The region beneath the city stretches as wide as the confines of the outer wards, but moving around is fraught with supernatural danger. A vast majority of this area is unmapped due to the heavy influence of faez, the paranoia of its residence, and the dangers posed to explorers. There are a few known settlements within the Undercity that tend to be the home of non-humans that are unwelcome on the surface.

Big Dave's Town – The largest and most well-known settlement in the Undercity, this kidney-shaped cavern has a population in the thousands. The Devil's Lipstick or the open air market are the most frequently visited. Undercity gangs keep the peace.

Voodoo Land – A village deep in the Undercity populated by a people infected by a sentient fungus.

Wells of Power – Known or seen by few, the four wells are places that faez leaks through the barrier between realms. Each one is protected by a guardian that was placed there by the Patrons.

Other Realms

The Hundred Halls is not just a magical school. The magic of portals creates a network of realms where mages with access can move about freely. Realms do not exist at fixed positions to each other, but move in relation to each other for unknown reasons, creating unusual and sometimes unexpected connections. The Academy of the Subtle Arts is the Hall most connected to the multi-realms, but others such as Coterie of Mages for the Infernal realm are known experts.

<u>The Eternal City</u> – The home of the maetrie, sometimes called city elves, is a place of high magic and high danger that doesn't follow all the rules of more stable realms. In the Eternal City, locations don't always remain in the same place, and even those are ruled by the various courts: Jade, Diamond, and Ruby. Only the most brave (or foolish) mages visit this realm, and of those that do, most never return.

Ruby Court

Queen: Lady Amethyte

Diamond Court

Queen: Lady Zaire

Jade Court

Queen: Lady Kikala

The Infernal Realm – An early precursor realm that was one of the first to stabilize out of the fledgling universe. The understanding of this brutal place is limited and most scholars think, probably wrong. It is awash in demonic creatures that defy human knowledge.

The Veil – This realm exists at the barrier between life and death. Ghosts, apparitions, and otherworldly creatures sometimes pass through into other realms, causing problems and sometimes opportunities. It is rumored that the mages of the Academy of the Subtle Arts can briefly step into this realm to pass out of sight.

Harmony – A stable realm of harsh beauty, Harmony is known to few. The fearsome and explosively fast mystdrakons come from this place and its jungles hide other dangerous creatures that frighten even the most hardened explorers.

Fae – The realm most commonly portrayed in folktales and legends is the place of the seelie and unseelie. Access to this realm has become more difficult in the last century, making its influence less known than the past.

Ice Hold – A cold and inhospitable place that has become a vacation spot for the ultra-wealthy mages that wish to experience winter sports in an entirely different realm than their own. Most only visit the lodges in the mountains, though some adventurous explorers travel further than the known regions.

Montanhas – A mountainous region that was settled by Portuguese colonists a half-century ago and then again by the company Lifestone. The enormous Montas live in this realm alongside the settlers. Surprisingly little is known about the native race.

Caer Corsydd – A backwater fae realm of swamps and bogs. Its dangers are only matched by its beauty. As the home of the Gwyllion, the outcasts of Fae, it is a mix of fairy and unsettled country. The rules that apply to most fae realms do not here, because it was not their homeland.

Danir – The home to a pastural race that is quite civilized. Their extensive farmlands are surrounded by jungle. Early explorers learned about the existence of *mágrithral* which is commonly called magesteel, a material that can easily hold enchantments. The value of magesteel is astronomical, though the Danir no longer produce it, citing environmental issues as the cause.

Black Council – The existence of this realm has not been confirmed. Researchers claim that it's a den of malicious thievery. Serious researchers avoid this realm as a topic of scholarship due to the string of unfortunate accidents that befell their compatriots that sought to unearth the truth.

Brodaria – Home to the Brodarians, a battle-hungry people that spent their days in constant conquest. Mercenaries and fortune-hunters have been known to visit this realm to ply their dangerous trade.

Major Figures of the Hundred Halls

Invictus – The most famous mage in the world, considered to be the oldest living being. Speculation has him to be at least five hundred years old, though many consider him to be much older.

Malden Anterist – The head of Coterie of Mages keeps himself hidden from scrying and other methods of sight through the use of obfuscation enchantments. The reason for this unusual setup is the subject of much speculation.

Celesse D'Agastine – The third most famous person (after Invictus and Frank Orpheum), the head of D'Agastine Industries runs one of the largest multinational corporations in the world. Celesse is known as a fierce business woman who has destroyed those that have attempted to stand in her way.

Semyon Gray – The least vocal of the Original Five, Semyon is known for working quietly behind the scenes to guide the politics of the Hundred Halls in a more humane direction.

Priyanka Sai – The head of the Assassin's Hall is infamous across the realms.

Bannon Creed – As head of the Protectors, as well as the Blackstone Security, Bannon's mages are involved with law enforcement, and the military across the realms. It is rumored that he often plays both sides of conflicts to maximize his financial interests and accusations about drugs or other unsavory acts have often been met with unusual deaths. Journalists steer clear of any topics related to the mage, which only burgeons his untouchable reputation.

Frank Orpheum – A legendary entertainer and head of the Dramatics Hall, after Invictus, he's considered the most famous in the world. His magic tricks have defied explanation, even by those who understand his methods.

Radoslav – The reclusive owner of the Glass Cabaret is an ex-pat maetrie with ties to organized crime across the city. His jazz bar attracts tourists curious about the city fae, and those who wish a favor from him—but at a price. He is the son of the Ruby and Jade Queens, and is known as the Black Butcher for his role in the destruction of the Ebony Court.

Hemistad – The owner of Freeport Games is a curious figure that not much is known about. Mages that have visited his gaming store suggest that he is not who he appears to be, but the extent of his powers are unknown. He makes frequent trips into the Undercity for his own purposes.

The Societies

The societies were originally created to help the city protect itself from the dangers posed by the infernal realm. Their members are pulled from the top halls with the intention of providing a cross-section of skills. Each has its own location in the Undercity where it meets and initiates new members, but the four societies gather together on a yearly basis for meetings, and then again, every four years for a ceremony called the Convergence, which is meant to help gauge the threat of the infernal realm. All four societies have a role in the Convergence.

There are many other smaller societies that were created for other purposes, but these original four are what most think of when "secret societies" are brought up in the city.

Well and Stone – Dedicated to the understanding of faez and the role of the wells of power.

Snake and Tome – Dedicated to developing charisma and the cunning to change the world.

Chroma and Key – Besides Coterie of Mages, this society is a repository of demonology.

Silence – This society focused on predicting the future through the use of augury.

Timeline of Season One

2003: Invictus disappears / Nadia's Triumph

2013: The Reluctant Assassin

2014: The Sorcerous Spy / Wild Magic

2015: The Veiled Diplomat / Bane of the Hunter / The Warped Forest / Song of Siren and Blood

2016: Agent Unraveled / Mark of the Phoenix / Gladiators of Warsong / House of Snake and Tome / Trials of Magic

2017: The Webs That Bind / Arcane Mutations / Citadel of Broken Dreams / Storm of Dragon and Stone / Web of Lies

2018: Enter the Daemonpits / Untamed Destiny / Sonata of Shadow and Thorn / Alchemy of Souls

2019: Plane of Twilight / Well of Demon and Bone / Gathering of Shadows

2020: City of Sorcery

2022: The Order of Merlin / Infernal Alliances / Tower of Horn and Blood

Hundred Halls – Professors / Instructors

Arcanium – Semyon Gray (Patron)

Joanne Mali

Sebastian Longakers

Gill

Moonie

Alain Chopra

Coterie of Mages – Malden Anterist (Patron)

Augustus Trebleton

Phillip Sinclair

Isla Kingsley

Protectors – Bannon Creed (Patron)

Avani Blue

Alchemists – Celesse D'Agastine (Patron)

Alysson Cho

Assassins – Priyanka Sai (Patron)

Carron Allgood

Marilyn Pennywhistle

Maggie O'Keefe

Alliette Noyade

Percival

Matt Konig

Dionysus Minoan

<u>Stone Singers</u> – Ester Starwood (Patron)

Marin Zeng

Asa Lacuerda

Sven Larsen

Art Williams

Robin Leech

<u>Animalians</u> – Adele Montgomery (Patron)

Didi Applebrook

Kako

Cassius King

Vladmir Constantine

Ansel Park

Ernest Valentine

Dramatics – Frank Orpheum (Patron)

Lilly Hathhammer

Glossary Terms

Merlin Trials - The entrance exams to the Hundred Halls that can only be taken during the ages seventeen through nineteen. There are three stages to the trials.

Faez - The raw stuff of magic. Faez is the energy that when shaped by spell or other means creates magical effects. Faez is dangerous to humans, but a tolerance can be built up over time if somehow protected. The patronage system of the Hundred Halls is the most common method.

Patron - The founder of a hall within the Hundred Halls. The patron extends their magical protection to students, keeping them safe from faez madness, and teaching them a specific skill set within the magical world.

Faez Madness - Prolonged use of faez without protection results in irreversible damage to the user's ability to understand and interact with reality.

Second Year Contest - These games require cross-Hall teams to compete against each other for a grand prize utilizing special facilities that keep the participants from physical harm.

Maetrie – Commonly called city elves, though they have no relation to the Fae. Their home is the Eternal City, a realm closer to Invictus than any other.

Major Halls

Arcanium

Nickname: Arcanium

Patron: Semyon Gray

Est: 1867

Motto: Knowledge is Power

Description: Arcanium believes in the value of gaining knowledge, not only about the world around us, but of ourselves. Before we can master magic, we must hone the tool the magic originates from, because a poorly trained mage will not only be a danger to themselves, but society at large. Once a student is capable, they may learn the art of changing spells on the fly using lexology, or how ancient runic languages are the key to solving the world's most difficult problems. Join Arcanium and be a part of the solution.

Coterie of Mages

Nickname: Coterie

Patron: Malden Anterist

Est: 1867

Motto: Limitless

Description: Anything is possible. Here in the Coterie of Mages, we don't believe in limits. If you can imagine it, you can do it. We push the boundaries of what magic is capable of. If this frightens you, then Coterie is not the Hall for you, but if this elicits a sense of excitement and wonder, then apply to the Coterie of Mages. We are the elite.

Academy of the Subtle Arts

Nickname: Assassins

Patron: Priyanka Sai

Est: 1867

Motto: Anyone can be persuaded

Description: Human connections make the world go round. We at the Academy of the Subtle Arts strive to bring people, companies, and countries together. Our mages are the world's most effective diplomats and heads of state. If you seek to join the interconnected world of politics, then the Academy is the right Hall for you.

The Order of Honorable Alchemists

Nickname: Alchemists

Patron: Celesse D'Agastine

Est: 1867

Motto: Perfection is Achievable

Description: The human vessel is a sacred thing. We believe in maximizing our potential through better alchemy. Our potentials cannot be met if we rely on the ordinariness of humanity.

Protectors

Nickname: Protectors

Patron: Bannon Creed

Est: 1867

Motto: To Protect and Control

Description: Order requires commitment. Protectors are committed to the value of human life. To being the shield against those that would tear down society, and create chaos. The Protector Hall teaches the ultimate defense, not only for yourself, but for the world at large. If being on the front lines of the world's conflicts appeals to you, then Protectors is your Hall

Acoustic Architectural Institute of Design

Nickname: Stone Singers

Patron: Ester Starwood

Est: 1891

Motto: Building through song

Description: A song is made up of many notes, just like a bridge is made of many stones. Society cannot function without the infrastructure to hold it together. The Acoustic Architectural institute of Design teaches how to shape the world with only a song.

Society for the Understanding of Animals

Nickname: Animalians

Patron: Adele Montgomery

Est: 1945

Motto: We Are Not Alone

Description: All life is sacred. From the industrious dung beetle to the majestic horned dragon. We at the Society believe that Earth must be shared with all her children and when we do we will truly unlock her endless possibilities.

Holistic Institute

Nickname: Aura Healers

Patron: Sir William Jenner III

Est: 1875

Motto: Health Starts in the Soul

Description: When someone gets hurt, are you the first to run to their side to tend their wounds? If so, then the Holistic Institute is for you. We'll teach you how to mend even the most grievous wounds.

Minor Halls

Gamemakers

Nickname: Gamemakers

Patron: Aldophus Dimple

Est: 1961

Motto: Life is a Game

Description: Life is a game to be perfected. We at the Gamemaker's Hall know the importance of games as the training grounds for life.

Metallum Nocturne

Nickname: Night Metal

Patron: Edward Canterbury

Est: 1908

Motto: Strike. Spark. Surpass.

Description: When the hammer hits the forge, great energies are released. Metallum Nocturn is that hammer against the forge of your soul. Join us, and find out what possibilities we can make.

The Daring Maids

Nickname: Palimaidens

Patron: Alice Hayword

Est: 1908

Motto: Stand

Description: The world is filled with unspeakable cruelty. We seek justice for those who cannot protect themselves, no matter the place. Join us in our fight against oppression.

Hundred Halls – Season One Series

Season One

THE HUNDRED HALLS

Trials of Magic

Web of Lies

Alchemy of Souls

Gathering of Shadows

City of Sorcery

THE RELUCTANT ASSASSIN

The Reluctant Assassin

The Sorcerous Spy

The Veiled Diplomat

Agent Unraveled

The Webs That Bind

GAMEMAKERS ONLINE

The Warped Forest

Gladiators of Warsong

Citadel of Broken Dreams

Enter the Daemon Pits

Plane of Twilight

ANIMALIANS HALL

Wild Magic

Bane of the Hunter

Mark of the Phoenix

Arcane Mutations

Untamed Destiny

STONE SINGERS HALL

Song of Siren and Blood

House of Snake and Tome

Storm of Dragon and Stone

Sonata of Shadow and Thorn

Well of Demon and Bone

THE ORDER OF MERLIN

The Order of Merlin

Infernal Alliances

Tower of Horn and Blood

HUNDRED HALLS SHORTS

Nadia’s Triumph

The Ghostly Light of Hallow’s Eve

The Ascendant Cup

The Whistling Man

Summer Spies

Fear is Forever

Balancing the Ledgers

A Slip of the Tongue

Shades of the Past

Start the first book of the next Hundred Halls series
The Reluctant Assassin

THE RELUCTANT ASSASSIN

The Hundred Halls Universe

SEASON ONE

THE HUNDRED HALLS
Trials of Magic
Web of Lies
Alchemy of Souls
Gathering of Shadows
City of Sorcery

THE RELUCTANT ASSASSIN
The Reluctant Assassin
The Sorcerous Spy
The Veiled Diplomat
Agent Unraveled
The Webs That Bind

GAMEMAKERS ONLINE
The Warped Forest
Gladiators of Warsong
Citadel of Broken Dreams
Enter the Daemonpits
Plane of Twilight

ANIMALIANS HALL
Wild Magic
Bane of the Hunter
Mark of the Phoenix
Arcane Mutations
Untamed Destiny

STONE SINGERS HALL
Song of Siren and Blood
House of Snake and Tome
Storm of Dragon and Stone
Sonata of Shadow and Thorn
Well of Demon and Bone

THE ORDER OF MERLIN
The Order of Merlin
Infernal Alliances
Tower of Horn and Blood

ABOUT THE AUTHOR

Thomas K. Carpenter resides in Colorado with his wife Rachel. When he's not busy writing his next book, he's hiking, skiing, and getting beat by his wife at cards. He keeps a regular blog at www.thomaskcarpenter.com and you can follow him on twitter @thomaskcarpente. If you want to learn when his next novel will be hitting the shelves and get free stories and occasional other goodies, please sign up for his mailing list by going to: http://tinyurl.com/thomaskcarpenter. Your email address will never be shared and you can unsubscribe at any time.